Marc Hammond is the pseudonym of a well-known writer of best selling thrillers. This is his second Futura Spectacular.

Other Futura Spectaculars:

Marc Hammond

The Theseus Code

Futura Publications Limited

A Futura Book

First published in Great Britain by
Futura Publications Limited in 1979

ISBN 0 7088 1551 0

Printed in Great Britain by
Hazell Watson & Viney Ltd
Aylesbury, Bucks

Futura Publications Limited
110 Warner Road
Camberwell, London SE5

Glossary of Cretan Terms

kafeneion – coffee-shop where men gather to drink coffee, water, and lemonade; to play cards and *tavli* (the Greek form of backgammon); and to talk politics.

tsikoudia – raki, the fiery spirits distilled from grape-skins and pips after the pith has been pressed out for wine-making.

krassi – local wine, usually sold from the barrel in any kind of bottle.

Lefka Ori – the White Mountains, which occupy the western end of the island of Crete and contain Sfakia, the home of the Sfakians, wild mountain men who historically have always fought invasion. The vendettas and blood feuds among the Sfakians grew so intense (one family feud cost the lives of a hundred people over several decades) that many were exiled to the eastern end of the island.

nome – Crete contains four administrative districts, or *nomes* – Xanion, Rethymnon, Heraklion, Lasithi.

nomakis – the administrative head of a *nome*, appointed by the government in Athens.

ipastinomos – police superintendent.

enomotarxis – police sergeant.

horofilakas – lit., 'man who looks round the district' – the equivalent of the 'copper on the beat'.

Political Parties – There are many political groupings on Crete. Here are the principal five:

    Neo-democratia: the party of Karamanlis, the right wing.

    Enossis-Kendrion, EDIK.

    ADA.

    Passok: Socialist.

    KKE: the left wing, Communist.

Music and Dancing – The Cretan loses no opportunity to play or listen to the lyre, the bouzouki and the mandolin, and to dance. The dances are mostly performed, without any self-consciousness, by lines of men who cross arms in a semi-circle. The exception to this male dominance is the ritual dance of the bride at the reception after her wedding. By quaint tradition none of the men who dances with her must touch her hand – a handkerchief is held between them as a symbol of purity.

Koumbaros, koumbara – at a wedding, the 'best man' and the 'matron of honour', who play a most important role in the future lives of the married couple and of any children of the union – usually becoming god-father and god-mother.

Bill left his berth around five thirty, unable any longer to stand the oppressive heat of the minuscule cabin, the snoring of the man in the bunk above him and the stink of the feet of the man on the bottom bunk opposite. He pulled on his cotton shirt and summer-weight cord trousers, flicked the comb through his hair and left the cabin.

The area outside the end of the corridor was like a refugee camp, with bodies sprawled on chairs or slumped in the corners, still clutching battered suitcases or cloth bags holding belongings, and carrying straw baskets of bread, vegetables and fruit. No one stirred as he stepped warily across sleep-twisted limbs and opened the door that gave access to one of the decks.

The bright morning light struck him an almost physical blow, and for a few moments he stood there, his eyes unable to focus after the gloom within. Gradually his sight came back and he saw the crystal clarity of the water foaming beside the boat and the startling quality of the view along .the foothills of the mountain range they were passing.

The *Kydon* was turning, prior to entering a long, narrow bay he judged to be Souda, the landfall on Crete, after the overnight passage from Piraeus. He'd arrived at the port late and had only been able to book the cheapest accommodation in a multiple cabin. He'd been in such a hurry to finish his journey from London he would have accepted anything to get him to Crete, even sleeping on the deck as so many people were, some bundled into sleeping bags taken from the ubiquitous back-packs, others wrapping themselves as best they could in the ill-fitting tweed suits that have become the uniform of peasants the world over.

As he climbed to the top deck, Bill was suddenly aware of .the strong smell of herbs that floated from the land

7

alongside which they were travelling. He could identify thyme, mint, even rosemary as separate entities. He smiled to himself; now that he was no longer drinking, he could even detect odours again: herbs from a hillside, already touched by the morning sun, or the all-night stink of feet – take your pick!

'*Schoen, nicht wahr?*' the man standing next to him said.

Bill was startled. He'd been so preoccupied by staring at the land, sniffing its welcoming pungency, that he hadn't noticed the man's approach. But now he could detect him, and his nose wrinkled.

The man was carrying a bottle of beer and had obviously been drinking from it. He held a second bottle, already opened, in his other hand. When he lifted the first bottle and took a long deep draught from it, Bill could almost feel the all too familiar tickle at the back of his own throat. Nothing went down like a cool beer!

The man saw the flicker of Bill's eyes and recognized the lust.

'*Wollen Sie einen Schluck?*' he asked, offering the second bottle.

The waft of beer, of alcohol, obliterated the scent of herbs from the land and the fresh tang of the sea in the morning air. Bill saw with familiar horror his hand involuntarily extended and trembling in anticipation, his fingers twitching with unconcealed desire. He grasped the bottle and felt the shock of its coolness on his palm as his hand clasped it tight.

He forced himself to hold it still and to turn from the man already guzzling a second *Schluck*. He looked across the slopes of the land, bending his mind to remember his purpose in coming here – his two-fold purpose.

'Crete,' he said out loud, though talking to his inner self.

'*Ja. Schoen, nicht?*'

Bill fixed his attention on the land, seeing the snow lying on the peaks of the high mountains, the tree- and scrub-studded slopes, the scar of a road running along a hill. Smoke rose slowly from houses concealed by the lush green growths, and flecks of colour were splashed everywhere. He bent his head to look down into the stunningly green water which, outside the white-flecked foam of the ship's wake, reflected the island, still as in a mirror.

Once, Bill's father might have seen it like this from the deck of a small boat. He'd have made passage, as Bill had, at night. He would have arrived off-shore just after dawn, as Bill was doing. Who had met his father in that dawn of long ago? To what remote hiding place had they taken him?

Bill's father, Roger Thomas, had been a cautious man – so cautious he'd left his affairs in perfect order when he'd joined the Army. The factory Roger Thomas had founded and made such a success was to be managed by his brother, who'd been turned down by the Army. A trust fund had been established for the young boy Bill, who had been evacuated to America. Only when all these preparations were completed had Roger Thomas reported for duty. He'd been given a commission after OCTU training, and then, to the surprise of everyone who knew him, he'd volunteered for Special Services. This much Bill had already discovered from official War Office records. The cold, official word ended with two entries. Posted to Special Liaison Duties on Crete. Missing in Action, presumed Killed.

During Roger Thomas's time on Crete someone had seen fit to recommend him for the Military Cross. He'd been awarded it posthumously, and Bill was carrying the medal in a box in his luggage. He was travelling to Crete, at last, to discover how his father had earned that medal. Where he had died, and how. Where he had been buried.

And, somewhere along the way, Bill hoped also to discover something else. Something about *himself*. Something to help him fight what had become his constant craving for drink. He was going to try to answer questions Anna had said he ought to have asked himself years ago.

He was going to try to find out what kind of a man his father had been, a man so cautious in some respects but also bold and adventurous enough to join the Special Services.

'Find out about your father,' Anna had said, 'and perhaps somewhere along the way, who knows, you might find out about yourself!'

Bill looked down at his knuckles, white where they clutched the beer bottle.

'You'll find a world of a sort in the bottom of a bottle,' Anna had said. 'I found one for a month or two. That's how long it took me to realize it wasn't the sort of world I wanted. Don't you think *you* should give it a try, Bill?'

Bill held the bottle of beer at arm's length over the rail, aware that the man next to him was watching him closely. Bill drew the bottle in and gave it back to the man.

'*Nein, danke*,' he said.

The German took it, looked at it and threw it over the side. They both watched it plummet down to the water, then vanish beneath the spume without a trace.

'*Ja, wirklich schoen!*' the German said and walked slowly along the deck, sucking the neck of the other beer bottle as if it were a baby's dummy.

Bill looked down at his hands. They'd stopped trembling. For the moment.

Captain Roger Thomas, commissioned in the Royal Welch Fusiliers but now seconded to Special Services, looked back over the stern of the black rubber dinghy they had launched from the Greek Navy submarine that had brought them from Alexandria. Already most of the conning tower had submerged and the decks were awash.

He felt again the familiar pulse of adrenalin that always came once he was committed to an operation. He always felt it the micro-second after he jumped from a plane – in that fragment of time before the parachute snapped open. This was the first time he had landed at night from a submarine, but the feeling of commitment was the same, and the knowledge he could not go back nor refuse. After all, until that moment came, each assignment was voluntary.

Brigadier Phelps's face always wore an apologetic look when he outlined a job. He never gave an order – 'You will . . .' He used blackboard and chalk, maps, schedules of radio frequencies, lists of explosives and fuses, details of weaponry, as if outlining a *possibility*, no more.

'You see, we've put quite a few chaps ashore on Crete, created a whole infrastructure that lets the locals know that, despite appearances, we haven't totally abandoned them to the Germans. Idea is really two-fold, doncherknow. Gathering information and passing it back to Cairo by radio, and building up a stiffened backbone of resistance, ready for when we invade. Bound to reinvade, sooner or later. Simply bound to, after the thrashing the Germans gave us last time round. Matter of principle, doncherknow. Meanwhile, we need a few chaps out there to – sort-of – prepare the ground. Your papers say you took Greek at school and university – they tell me, not that I can speak any lingo but my own, that you can get by on the classical stuff. 'Course, you needn't go if you don't want to. They tell me it's pretty sticky out there . . .'

'I'll go, sir,' Roger had said.

'Good man. Right, we can get on with the bits and bobs, eh?'

The 'bits and bobs' included a radio, batteries, a generator, three rifles, six Smith and Wessons, a box of grenades, a tin of fuses, a thousand cigarettes and two thousand gold sovereigns. The rubber dinghy had been given a specially strengthened floor-boarding to carry the weight of the cargo – also that of the giant of a man sitting the other side of the thwart, paddling with deep powerful thrusts that sent the dinghy spinning to starboard despite Roger's best efforts to keep it straight.

The Cretan, Kostas Dandanakis, staring ahead at the shore-line of Crete, had already forgotten the submarine. It was transport, nothing more nor less, to get him back to Crete after a month wasted in Cairo.

Ahead of them, from a sheltered spot on the rocky cliff-face, a light flicked briefly. The submarine had spent hours lying off-shore, waiting for that light.

When it had come, they had timed the intervals. Ten seconds, ten seconds, fifteen. The Cretans ashore had two codes. One they would reveal to the Germans if they were taken. Ten seconds, fifteen, fifteen. The other – ten, ten, fifteen – they would use if the way was clear.

Ten, ten, fifteen.

It *should* be all right – assuming there was no traitor among the shore party. There had been traitors, and quisling-type collaborators, some planted in Crete even before 1939.

'There it is again,' Kostas said in his thick, guttural Sfakian Greek.

Roger Thomas had been surprised to find how much use he could make of his Classical Greek; he'd spent a month with Kostas, who'd been brought over to Cairo to talk to him, to acquaint him with the district in which he would be living and working. Such simple things can betray a man. Roger had been taught not to be the first to say hello to a passing stranger if he were sitting down – local custom depended on the one who was moving to speak first. He'd learned the correct way to wear his Sfakian breeches and boots, the braided waistcoat, the beaded head-scarf. He'd dyed his hair black from its natural dark ginger and had shaved only certain parts of his face, and that with a blunt razor to give him a weather-beaten, bristly effect. He'd smeared pomade into his moustache and had twirled its ends – now he looked every inch a mountain man from the Lefka Ori.

'Any Cretan will know you're an Englishman the moment you open your mouth, the moment you start to walk,' Kostas had said, grinning. 'But with luck, in the dark, you might deceive a few of the butchers.'

The light flashed again. Ten, ten, fifteen.

The dinghy was a hundred metres off-shore. No moon. The dark mass of the mountain loomed ahead of them; steep, rocky cliff-faces to each side of their landing beach in a small cove east of Aghia Roumeli, almost at the foot of the Gorge of Samaria, the twenty kilometre slash in the White Mountains that so far had defied the Germans' efforts to penetrate and conquer it. The gorge was now the haunt of Resistance workers and criminal bands, mostly wanted by the police for the time-honoured Sfakian pursuit of sheep stealing. The cove was about seventy-five metres long and fifty wide, the landing a fine, stony shingle. The sea around them was still as polished glass; already the dawn was beginning its spectacular deep red smear along the horizon to the right of them.

Roger dug his oar in deeper and pulled harder, to rectify the boat's slewing under the powerful strokes of Kostas's arm. Only fifty metres to go – soon they would know if the light flash was Cretan or German. He held the oar one-handedly while he checked the Smith and Wesson tucked into the folds of the Sfakian cummerbund around his waist, and then, all at once, he smelled the odour coming down the mountain at him; the scent of thyme and rosemary, oleander and night-scented jasmine, mingling with the salt-spray wrack of the sea. He sniffed, and Kostas turned to him and grinned.

'Crete, eh?' Kostas said. 'Now I am at home.'

They rode the rest of the way in silence. When the boat scraped on the shingle there were hands waiting to drag it forward. Kostas leaped from the dinghy and grabbed one of the ropes; Roger sprang out on his side, and together the body of men picked up the dinghy and its contents and ran it smoothly up the minuscule beach to the shelter of the cliff-face.

A light was flicked on and shone on Kostas's face, then switched to Roger's and was extinguished.

Kostas had his arms round one of the men, his cheek laid alongside the man's cheek in a deep embrace. Hands grabbed Roger and pulled him forward into bear hugs. He smelled the strong odours of body sweat and the pungent raki the men had drunk to keep themselves warm during the long hours of waiting, and he could almost taste the lanolin reek of damp wool and leather. Each man seemed to bristle with armaments; rifles of all descriptions were slung over their shoulders, and they wore bandoliers of cartridges, holstered pistols and sheathed knives.

When the hugs were completed, the men stood around, grinning hugely in the beginning morning light like happy boys.

'This is Maleta,' Kostas said, using the code-name Roger Thomas had been given in Cairo, the name he would use all the time he was on Crete. 'Maleta will strike the blows on our knives, and we will carve our name throughout the *nomes* of Crete . . .' He lifted Maleta's clenched fist. 'He is strong, strong,' he said, then added deprecatingly, 'for an Englishman.'

'What do you bring us, Maleta?' one of the Cretans asked, more interested in the contents of the dinghy than the strength of Maleta's arm.

Already Kostas had bent down and was heaving the material from the bottom of the dinghy, distributing it to each man. All had been provided with back-straps; they hefted the loads one by one and, without words, set off up a track that rose steeply from the beach.

Kostas himself took the charging engine, the heaviest load.

Roger protested when Kostas assigned him to the bag containing the sovereigns.

'Save your breath, Englishman,' Kostas said quietly so that none could hear him. 'You'll need it before we get up to the cave.' He hefted the charging engine and turned to go, but then he stopped, turned back again and held out his hand. 'Welcome to Crete, Maleta,' he said simply.

Distance in the mountains to the west of the island of Crete is measured by time since the map's kilometres mean little in territory that climbs and descends fearsome crags and precipitous chasms. From the beach to the cave was six hours, with the runner who led them setting a pace that would not have disgraced a fell-walker, despite the heavy radio he carried on his back, his rifle, his two filled bandoliers of ammunition, his pistols and knives. Kostas had taken the position at the back of the column of eight men; whenever Maleta began to flag Kostas came behind him, urging him on.

Nothing Roger had ever experienced in his training in the mountains of Snowdonia and around Ben Nevis had effectively prepared him for this climb at this pace. They used no roads, and often the tracks they traversed seemed to exist only in the memory of the runner, one of the several Cretan volunteers who maintained contact between the English officers dotted across Crete, acting as liaison with the packs of Cretan Freedom Fighters and Resistance workers, maintaining radio contact with Cairo and arranging parachute drops of weapons, ammunition, leather for vital boots, and clothing. Food was included in the drop only when there was space. The runners were unsung heroes, capable of covering vast distances each day with letters, money, information; they were often in great danger, not only of capture by the Germans but of betrayal by turn-coat Cretans.

When they arrived at their destination, a cave high up in the mountains overlooking the northern slopes descending to Xania, Souda Bay and the ocean beyond, they were greeted by what at first appeared to be three Sfakians. Only after they had been identified and had gone into the cave did one of the men reveal himself. He shook hands with Roger.

'Major Rhodes,' he said, 'but here, naturally, they call me Rhodos. This is Stavros, my runner, and the other – the one there with that silly grin on his face – is Kavra, my wireless operator.'

'Nice to see you, Cap'n,' Kavra said, his voice pure Lancashire.

Roger smiled at the incongruity of that voice coming out of that face, wearing the costume of a Sfakian that somehow made him look more piratical than all the natural-born Cretans. He reached out his hand; Roger took it and shook it formally, feeling somewhat foolish.

Stavros had made a soup that seemed to consist of a whole sheep boiled in water with herbs and a few potatoes. The men sat round the fire at the back of the cave, whose smoke was dissipated somewhere in the vaulting above their heads, dug their hands into the pot and picked out chunks of meat and bone. They'd eaten nothing during the climb and had drunk only little of the water they found in the abundant mountain springs.

There were no amenities; the men squatted on their heels in the way Roger had seen them hunker down whenever they had rested briefly during the climb. He squatted beside Kostas who was eating – in silence for once; all the night Kostas had talked to him, encouraging him along the track in non-obvious ways, warning him to be careful on the more dangerous sections, nursemaiding him along. At first, when Roger had realized what was

16

happening, he'd been resentful, but soon he'd begun to appreciate the help Kostas was giving him. Now they hunkered side by side, dipping hands into the pot and chewing silently.

Major Rhodes squatted beside Roger. 'I had hoped to be able to stay with you a couple of weeks or so to give you a better briefing,' he said when they had finished eating and were sprawling on the sweet-smelling bed of scrub that carpeted the cave, 'but I'm afraid our unit south of Rethimnon has been blown – Diaghilev is in the bag – and I have to go across there and start again.'

'How did it happen?' Roger asked.

'Usual thing. They were betrayed. This one was a sheep-stealer who informed the Germans to try to get out of the hands of the civilian police. The Cretans shot him – the sheep-stealer – three nights ago. Not that that's any consolation to Diaghilev. You'll have to be damned careful. You've found yourself a good man in Kostas – damned good radio operator. He was in the Navy, you know, before the war – Merchant Navy. How do you fancy having Pakrades as your runner?' he asked, indicating the man who'd brought Roger up the mountain.

'Seems a good chap.'

'Believe me, he's one of the best. Only problem is that he fancies the girls a bit. He'll get to any place faster than any other runner we have, but he tends to dawdle a bit on the way home.'

They could have been discussing the chances of a horse in the Derby.

Roger looked at the inside of the cave that would be his home for so long as it remained undetected by the Germans. He looked at the men he'd be living and working with, the hard Cretan mountain men of immense stamina and fitness. To see them sitting around the fire, laughing with each other, slapping each other's backs, listening avidly to Kostas's doubtless exaggerated stories of his sexual successes in Cairo, one could form no idea, no possible conception, of the rigours and dangers of their daily lives. He looked at the floor-covering, remembering the nights he'd spent in the open in the wilds of Scotland, sleeping on a bed of sweet-smelling heather and bracken, but remembering also the times he'd woken with a twisted branch sticking in the small of his back, knowing that in time he would become so accustomed to sleeping that way that a soft bed would become anathema to him. He looked at the cooking pot, smelling its strange odours; they'd warned him in Cairo there was a shortage of food and that he'd go hungry for days on end. That, too, was something to which he would grow accustomed. Three meals a day has become a habit of civilization, he reminded himself, not a necessity.

But how would he match up in the other ways? In sheer manliness. Roger knew he had always been a cautious man – he'd built his pre-war life and business on caution. So far, he hadn't regretted it. He'd seen too many people ruined in their private and business lives by imprudence. These Sfakian men had nothing of caution in their make-up. They were bold, daring adventurers. Sfakia had never been totally conquered throughout the island's turbulent history. Latterly, the Turks had tried and failed. No-one believed the Germans would succeed where so many had failed. But could he rise above his own nature, his habit of caution, to adopt the reckless ways of these men?

'When are you leaving?' he asked Rhodos.

'Tomorrow morning,' Major Rhodes said. 'I'm sorry. I'll try to get over here, sometimes. If I can.' He looked anxiously at Maleta. 'Think you can manage?' he asked.

Roger looked frankly back at him. 'I don't know,' he said firmly, 'but I'll try. Now, you'd better brief me about things, hadn't you?'

Rhodos saw the quiet strength and noted the total frankness. 'You'll manage all right,' he said, with a silent prayer.

'I have to, haven't I?' Roger Thomas said.

Sam Birntin weighed two hundred pounds now and tended to sweat a lot, especially in the palms of his hands.

Once he'd been a Category Alpha operative with Special Service credits in knife, hand-gun, garotte and close combat. In those days he'd stripped at 168 lbs, winter or summer. He could swim half a mile under water, climb a mountain in snow and run a thousand yards at near Olympic speed. He was lean, hard and muscular, like a middle-weight champion on the night of a big fight. But that was before a love of hamburgers and Budweiser beer had got to him and had slowed his reflexes and clothed those fine-honed muscles with fat he couldn't shed.

They'd sent him to Army boot camp where the master sergeant was well known as a sadistic bastard who could guarantee to lick any civilian into fighting shape. Sam broke training and was found in the local drug-store eating the Double King-sized Whammy Special, with onions and French fries.

They even sent him to a psychiatrist, who explained to him that overeating, especially of one chosen food, was only a projection of the death-wish with Freudian overtones. He'd gone to health farms and had taken the fifteen-hundred-dollar special cure, living on lemon juice and yoghurt, all to no avail.

For the rest of his life, Sam realized, he was going to be 'that big fat guy'.

But he was a good administrator. They brought him in and gave him the job of second-in-command to the director. Behind a desk, he reversed the process and began to shed a few pounds, but he never went below two hundred.

Now he was sitting behind his desk and wiping his

hands on the seam of his trousers. He looked at 27 appraisingly.

'You realize this is another Limited Objective Contract? I've managed to get you a ten per cent raise, but that's all I can do.'

'I had hoped for a full staff job by this time,' 27 said.

'Maybe I'll be able to get one for you after this!' He laughed. 'With a retirement pension . . .'

'Screw the pension. I just want to be on the inside. One of the boys!'

'So you will be. But you have to be patient. Let's face it, you only finished training six months ago.'

'And came out with straight A's in combat, weaponry, political appraisal, case organization and procedures, use of electronics, surveillance and counter-surveillance.'

'An impressive result. Okay, I'll file a paper on you recommending an immediate staff job when this LOC is done.'

'So, where is the job?'

'You accept it? You know the conditions? Once you're out, you're running. And that means you see the contract through to the finals, irrespective of what happens. And we don't bring you in again until it's completed.'

'I *know* that! Look, Sam, this is my third LOC. I did all right in Chile, didn't I, cleaning up that mess? Of course, they won't get an extradition, so it'll never come to trial, but that's not my fault . . .'

'That wasn't part of your brief. You went in there to clean up the mess the CIA had left behind. What the legal beagles do now is not your concern . . .'

'And I did all right in London, cleaning up the mess that defector left behind, that double-double . . .'

'You did. The way you gave him back to the Russians, that was neat. I said so to the Director. That, and the fact you speak Greek, is what got you this present assignment.'

'So, give it to me, eh?'

'Just one thing. It's another 5311.'

'So?'

'You don't have to pull any triggers yourself. You'll have hired back-up.'

'Expendable, I hope.'

'Completely!'

'Good. I had too much trouble with the hired help in London. Having to bring him in was worse than having him take the subject out. More messy, I mean. He was such a damned amateur!'

'It's getting harder and harder to find good professionals these days. Too many of 'em are working for the multi-nationals, cleaning up *their* messes.'

'Okay, so when do we start briefing?'

'Didn't I tell you? We've already started! The assignment is on your own island . . .'

'Crete . . .?'

'That's it. You were a kid when this one happened. During the war. The full colonel involved was a friend of Hoover, goddamn him. He left a mess behind. There's a local guy involved, and now he's.putting pressure on Uncle Sam. Trouble is, we have to help him. We can't put out a 5311 on him for a reason I'll tell you later. There's also some documentation involved. We tried to solve this one through the archives, but one copy of some papers is missing. You're job is to find those papers and destroy 'em!'

'And you've no idea where they are?'

'Yes, I know where they are. Somewhere on Crete!' Sam smiled at 27. 'And I needn't tell you what a damned big island that is.'

He took a man-size kleenex from the box and used it to mop his face, then screwed it into a ball and threw it, with others like it, into the waste paper basket.

'You know, Sam,' 27 said, 'you'd be a good-looking guy if only you'd lose some weight. You could do with losing about forty pounds. I have this fantastic Mayo Clinic diet.

21

Eggs and grapefruit juice. And you get to eat fish and steak . . .'

'You don't say! Now tell me, what in God's name has my weight got to do with a briefing about a job in Crete. Tell me that, will ya?'

Bill Thomas found a room in a pension overlooking the old port of Xania. Simply furnished, it contained a bed, a cupboard, a lamp and a chair. Decorating the walls were artefacts the pension owner's father, a former sailor and fisherman, had brought back from his travels. The light above Bill's bed, fashioned in copper, had been taken from a ship that had foundered on the rocks west of Xania in the fierce storm of 1962. The large windows gave on to a minuscule terrace, three metres by a metre and a half.

Bill took the room because of the terrace; he knew he could sit there and observe the people walking below, among the crowds but not part of them. If he should want to descend onto the quay which ran around the harbour, he could mingle with and be absorbed by the passing parade, sit at a table at one of the fifteen or so restaurants and *kafeneion*, drink a coffee or, perhaps later when he was more confident of himself, a glass of local wine or beer.

What had Anna said? 'You haven't controlled drinking until you can take a drink, one drink, whenever you want to. Just stopping drinking is a truce, not a victory.'

He unpacked his bag and laid in the cupboard his shirts and pants, his pair of sneakers, extra socks and handkerchiefs. He turned back the cover of the bed, trying to decide whether to have a couple of hours sleep. His sleep aboard the *Kydon* had not satisfied him; all night he'd tossed and turned in the heat of the cabin. Restless now, he went to the door of the balcony and stepped outside into the brilliant morning sunshine. The semi-circle of the harbour below him glinted with the phosphorescence of morning; four fishing boats were moored almost beneath his window, and already people were walking purposefully between the restaurant tables and the quayside. Some boats had been dragged up on the slip of the sea-wall opposite, which ended at the light-house, making a sheltered mooring for fishing boats. A couple of them were just leaving the harbour, the thud thud of their small diesel engines echoing over the water. A larger, ten-metre fishing boat was just returning after a night's work; its bow creamed the water before it, cutting the tiny waves with a sureness of movement. No clouds in the pale blue sky but a thousand swifts raced overhead, whirling frenziedly, catching flies, cleaning the air of insects with a ruthless silent efficiency.

Bill sat on the chair, took out a cigarette and lit it, dragging its smoke deep into his lungs. 'Okay,' he told himself, 'time to make a plan.' First, he must locate the war graves and find any records there might still be of the men buried there. He recognized that the records might be incomplete, untrustworthy. But it would be a start. Ioannis, the pension owner, had told him the best source of information would be the Tourist Information Office in the Turkish Mosque at the other side of the harbour, whose bulbous dome he could see gleaming in the morning light. The office opened, so Ioannis had said, at nine o'clock. He glanced at his watch – an hour to go.

If the war graves yielded no information, where then? Try to find some Cretan who had been involved with the Resistance during the war. He had one or two names from the books he had read, many written by British Army officers in the Navy, the Commandoes, the Air Force, based in Cairo. Some of them named small villages up in the mountain; these villages couldn't be too large for him to locate some man, one man, who knew what had been happening thirty-five years ago. Undoubtedly, many of the men involved in fighting the Germans would be dead by now, but the books had spoken of young men, some not even in their teens, who had been active. Bill had taken a Classics Degree, following his father's footsteps, and his Greek, he had already discovered, was quite adequate; he and Ioannis had spoken it together and they had had no difficulty understanding each other. He might fumble a

24

little for words up in the mountain villages, because of the native dialects, but he had confidence that he would succeed in making himself understood.

He heard the knock on his door, walked across the room and opened it.

'I go for one coffee,' Ioannis said. It was an invitation.

Bill shut the door behind him and they went out together to a *kafeneion* at the corner of the square. He sat with his thick, acrid Greek coffee in its tiny cup – he'd asked for one only slightly sweetened and now regretted it – and the glass of ice-cold water.

'I have spoken with my father,' Ioannis said. 'He was a *palikari* during the war. He says that first you must look in Galata, five kilometres from here along the coast to the west. It would help, however, my father says, if you know the name your father used when he was here . . .'

'Name? What name would he use other than his own given name?'

'Everybody had a code-name during the war, especially the English officers. My father was known as Exodus – because that is what he worked for, the exodus of the Germans, all the Germans, from Crete.'

Bill cursed silently. The War Office records had said nothing about any code-names but it made sense, didn't it? Doubtless no one on Crete knew his father as Captain Roger Thomas. How the devil could he connect the code-named man with the real one? Suddenly, the whole concept of his self-imposed mission here on Crete seemed foolish to him, ill-conceived, a waste of his time and energy.

'Damn!' he said. 'Damnation!'

Ioannis had been thinking. 'I will ask my father again,' he said. 'Perhaps he will know somebody who knew the code-names *and* the true names. You should go to Galata. See the parish priest and ask him. He is an old man. If anyone can give you knowledge, he can.'

Bill went to the street that contained all the car-hire companies. On his way he passed through many streets devoted still to one craft, one trade. The street of the leather workers, the street of the barrel makers, the street of the wood yards, the fish shops, the vegetable stalls. He looked at each of the car-hire companies and finally selected the most central one, called Hermes. Its name seemed appropriate to his quest. They gave him a map with the car and pointed to Galata. It took only fifteen minutes to reach it, driving first along a main road heading west and then two kilometres into the foothills of the mountains. The village sat on top of a hill; to the north it looked out over an ugly concrete development at Kalamaki to the sea beyond, yet if one turned one's back on this modern vandalism, one could see the green fields, the orange and lemon groves, the eucalyptus trees, the fields of corn and maize that had made this area into a garden of luxuriant growth.

The road wound slowly, with tortuous bends, into the centre of the village which appeared to contain about two hundred houses clustered around the church. Before the church, a small area had been paved and a monument erected; Bill read the inscription to the Fallen Heroes without particular emotion – so far, he'd not yet succeeded in identifying his own flesh and blood among them – they were just meaningless names in a meaningless list.

The parish priest was sitting in the *kafeneion* next to the church, reading a newspaper and sipping occasionally from a cup of coffee similar to the one Bill had drunk in Xania. Bill stood awkwardly beside the table and waited until the priest lowered the newspaper and said, '*Kalimera!*'

'*Kalimera!*' Bill said, and indicated the vacant chair.

'Please sit down,' the priest said.

Bill noted his long, dark, blue-black robe, stove-pipe hat and feet incongruously clad in leather sandals. The priest's dark face had the texture of old leather; his eyes were almost black, the light blue of the pupils flecked with the blood-lines of age.

'May I speak with you?' Bill asked politely.

'If you wish to do so. Most people wish to speak *to* me, to tell me something. I suspect you, on the other hand, wish to ask me something?'

The old man's eyes smiled with the wisdom of his years; his words had the presumably desired effect of setting Bill at ease.

'My father came to Crete thirty-six years ago,' Bill said. 'He died on Crete. I would like very much to find out where he died and where he was buried!'

'Thirty-six years is a long time to spend without looking for the grave of one's father!' the priest said, his voice mildly reproving.

'I was in America for much of that time. A young boy, in school. Later, after my university eduation, a young man making a career for himself.'

'Finding a wife. Being married . . .?'

'That, too . . .'

'Making children . . .?'

'Mercifully no . . .'

'Mercifully . . .?'

'My wife died.'

The priest was silent, waiting for the almost inevitable question, why? Why did God permit the loved one to die? Even harder to answer, why did God *cause* the loved one to die? There could be no answer, except to a man of faith.

'And now you see no immediate future, so you search the past. You seek, at last, the grave of your father, hoping there to find the image of yourself?'

'That's right, I suppose,' Bill said humbly.

'Your father was here, during the war? What was his name?'

'Captain Roger Thomas . . .'

'No, his code-name . . .?'

'I don't know it.'

'A problem, certainly, but not necessarily insuperable. If he was listed officially among the dead, his true name will be among those recorded. I have a list in the church

27

of those who fell nearby. Do you know where your father worked?'

Bill had to shake his head, feeling foolish. He knew how naïve his questions must seem – Crete was a large island and the partisans had been active over all of it.

'Can you describe your father?' the priest asked. 'Perhaps you have a photograph of him?'

Again, Bill had to admit defeat. His father had not been a man to have his picture taken, and, in Bill's frequent talks with his uncle, he had never thought to ask, How did my father look? His uncle had never thought to say, Your father was this and this height, this and this weight. Whenever they'd talked his uncle had described in detail, believing it to be important, what *sort* of man Bill's father had been. He'd described his gentleness, his essential goodness, his care and consideration for others, his caution that didn't mean cowardice. But he'd never thought to say – your father was six feet one inches tall with clear blue eyes, ginger-brown hair, long, delicate fingers with well-tended finger nails; that because of his height he always seemed to stoop slightly so as not to tower over people shorter than himself.

'No, I have no photograph of him. I have seen his Army records – he was one metre seventy-five high, weighed one hundred and five kilos, had blue eyes, and no distinguishing features, no identifiable scars.'

The priest crinkled his nose in a gesture that could, in another man, have been taken for contempt. 'Not much knowledge on which to base a search,' he said. 'A tall man with brown hair and blue eyes . . .!'

'I'm sorry . . .'

Without speaking, the priest rose and left the *kafeneion*. After a few minutes he returned with a book whose pages had yellowed on the outside. He opened the book and Bill looked at the Greek characters, his mind in such a depression that at first he could not comprehend them. Where the characters referred to a foreigner, the name had been painstakingly printed in Roman characters. Lieutenant-Colonel James Pethridge, DSO, Sergeant Timothy Hawkins, Major Jonathan Rhodes, Lieutenant Roger – here Bill's heart quickened for a moment – William Blandford, MC.

The priest watched while he ran slowly down the list, painstakingly examining each name in turn. Many names were only one word, and obviously code-names. Little Bear, Malvolio, Manoletto, even Tiziano, doubtless a relic of the Venetian Occupation of Crete hundreds of years ago. He closed the book finally, with a sigh. The priest reached across and touched the back of Bill's hand. His finger was hard but cool; a benediction.

'Have faith,' he said. 'What it is intended you shall know will be revealed to you if you have faith.'

'God moves in His mysterious ways, His wonders to perform?' Bill said, unable to keep the scepticism from his voice.

The priest smiled at him, his eyes wrinkling at the corners in a kindly way. Here he was on safer ground. He could argue the polemics of religion with any man at any time. Religious callisthenics, he called it privately. This man didn't want argument; he was as hungry for factual matter as a summer sheep for winter pastures.

'The list of names I have given you was compiled over many months at the time of the German Occupation. Most of those men are not buried here. Some were taken by the Germans, tortured cruelly and killed. Some died in mountain villages as a result of injuries received from German bullets. Some men, of course, were captured by the Germans and taken back to the mainland, presumably to be shipped back to Germany itself. We have another list of the men who were killed here when the German parachutists first invaded – most of those men came from New Zealand. From what you tell me your father came later. Perhaps you would do better to return to London, search the records of the military, find out exactly when your father came to the island and by what means, what code-name had been assigned to him. With this information . . .'

He waved his hand in a gesture that promised nothing but indicated possibilities.

Bill felt utterly frustrated. He didn't want to return to London just yet. Not empty-handed, not with failure to project him back into the state of mind where alcohol became once again a necessity . . .

The priest examined his face, seeing the disappointment it failed to conceal.

'I will ask questions for you,' he said. 'I will seek a tall man with blue eyes and brown hair. If he was active in the *nome* of Xanion, with God's help we will find him.'

'The work we do here is very simple,' Kostas Dandanakis said to Maleta. 'We gather information about the movement of German troops throughout the area and send it to Cairo by radio. We arrange for parachute drops of arms and ammunition, food and clothing. We ask Cairo to send us transport for the troops still in hiding throughout the island and then help to convey those troops through the mountains to the south coast, where a submarine, or a boat, comes to pick them up at night. We help the local people to establish bands of guerillas, ready for the day when we will strike!'

Roger Thomas, Pakrades the runner and Kostas were sitting on rocks outside the cave in the morning sunshine. Below them stretched the fertile plain of the north coast of Crete; in the distance they could see the ocean, Xania and the long tongue of the Akrotiri. The war seemed a million miles away.

Roger had slept very deeply and had been confused at first when Pakrades woke him with a whispered, 'Maleta, it is morning,' shortly after dawn. It would take him some time to get used to his code-name. He had a set of forged papers that would help him if he were stopped by a German patrol; the papers carried his photograph and said he was Giorgio Stafanakis, that he had a weak heart and was therefore ineligible for forced labour, that he lived in the mountain village of Kaprisses where he had been born.

Any Cretan-speaking expert among the Germans, any quisling policeman, would know the papers were false when 'Giorgio' began to speak his classical Greek!

They had breakfasted on a plate of rice, with meat balls in it and many herbs. Rice was like gold since the German invasion, but Pakrades, Maleta would soon learn, was a genius when it came to scavenging!

'You haven't mentioned any guerilla activities,' Maleta said. 'Any sabotage of German installations, any raids on German outposts!'

Kostas's face clouded over and he looked at Pakrades. 'There you have one of our problems, Maleta,' he said. 'You know that every time one of the guerilla bands strikes, the Germans take a terrible revenge on our people. They burn villages and kill the entire population in reprisal. Of course, the guerillas carry on their work of harassing the Germans every way they can, but many of the villagers are against them.' He spat on the ground. 'There are many men on Crete,' he said bitterly, 'many *kapitalists* who would rather give the whole island over to the Germans than risk losing one sheep, one kilo of wine or sugar!'

'When victory comes,' Pakrades said, 'we will remember the *kapitalists*.'

Maleta nodded his head, thinking. He'd been dropped into Europe several times to blow up railway bridges and sabotage trains, factories and installations in order to hamper the German war effort. Many times he'd run across locals who didn't welcome him with his explosives, knowing what would happen in their district once the Commandoes went away.

'What do we do today?' he asked, to change the subject. He knew that eventually he would be drawn into the island politics but wanted to postpone the moment as long as he could.

'Today,' Kostas said grinning, 'I take you to Manoletto.

He is the guerilla leader to the west of Omalos. A Sfakian, like me. But watch out, *Englesos*, he eats Englishmen for breakfast! When there are no Germans available!'

Bill left the priest of Galata with none of the confidence that wise and holy man had tried to instil in him. For an hour they had talked, at Bill's request, about the lives of the English soldiers who had come to Crete during the war. The priest himself had been active in the Resistance and had known many of them, including the legendary Patrick Leigh Fermor, Jack Smith-Hughes, Xan Fielding, the runner George Psychoundakis. He'd described the rigours of a life spent hiding in caves in the mountainsides, walking immense distances, often hungry, being chased by Germans, sometimes betrayed by self-interested Cretans and Greeks from the mainland who had come to the island with the Germans, seeking to ingratiate themselves with the local population. Such men, he'd explained, could pray for only one thing when the Cretans uncovered them – a quick death and a speedy burial.

When he arrived back in the old port of Xania, he parked the car at the water's edge in front of the pension, went and sat in one of the leather-covered chairs of the nearest *kafeneion* by the Hotel Lucia and ordered a Nescafé. He couldn't face the prospect of another strong Greek coffee. He'd been sitting there for five minutes when a short, fat man, wearing the standard uniform of a shirt open at the neck and a pair of dark worsted trousers, eased himself into the chair beside Bill.

'*Kalimera*,' he said.

'*Kalimera*.'

'You are Bill Thomas?'

Bill turned and looked at the man. He'd be about sixty and had close-cropped, grey hair. Bill noticed at once that the ends of three of his fingers were missing.

'Stavros, my name,' the man said, speaking a heavily-accented English. 'Ioannis from up there told me to speak to you.' He beckoned with his finger towards the pension. 'I met your father once.'

Bill felt a surge of feeling which elevated him instantly from the depression his visit to Galata had induced in him.

'If your father was Captain Roger Thomas?'

'He was,' Bill said excitedly. 'He was!'

'Yes, I met him. We knew him as *Maleta*!'

'Where? When? What can you tell me about him?'

'I only met him once.'

'Tell me,' Bill said, 'tell me all about him!'

'It was a long time ago,' Stavros said. 'I remember him only vaguely now.'

'Don't worry,' Bill said, 'tell me *anything* you can remember, any small thing.'

'It was in the village of Kaprisses . . . you know it?'

'No. I've only just arrived on Crete this morning!'

Bill's spirit soared. He had only been here a short time and had already met a man who knew his father! Somehow it seemed incredible; more logically, the reaction of the priest – his strong suggestion that Bill was on a foolish wild-goose chase, trying to back-track thirty-five years of forgetfulness – was the appropriate, inevitable, one.

'I remember a tall man . . .'

'Yes . . .?'

'With blue eyes – I remember his eyes because not many Cretans have eyes that colour. They were disturbing eyes, that seemed to be able to see right through into your soul . . .'

'Yes . . .?'

'His hair was black . . .'

Bill felt instantly deflated. The Army record had been quite specific. Captain Roger Thomas had brown hair.'

'. . . but I think he must have dyed it. His moustache was not exactly the same colour . . .'

Hope again! Of course, his father would have dyed his hair if he were living in the mountains and trying to pass

33

as a mountain man. The Cretans Bill had already seen all had *black* hair, or grey, or silver.

'What was he doing in the village of Kaprisses?'

'Waiting for me in the *kafeneion*. I was a runner in those days, for Manoletto. I used to take messages to an Englishman called Rhodos, who was later killed by the Germans in Rethymnon. One day, I went and found a new Englishman with Pakrades and Kostas Dandanakis. The Englishman was Maleta. Pakrades told me his real name was Captain Roger Thomas. I took him a message from Manoletto and he gave me a message to take back, with a bag of gold sovereigns. They had a radio somewhere but I do not know where it was at that time. The radios were always being moved around, you know, and the men, too. I gave him the message, we drank a glass of wine together and I left. I met many of the Englishmen during the war. I was with Michali when he kidnapped General Kreipe.'

That moment had obviously been the high point of Stavros's life – he glowed with pride as he spoke about it. Bill listened impatiently; he wanted to hear more about his father but knew he owed it to this man to hear him out, to let him live again, in memory, his moment of glory.

'And Maleta, Captain Roger Thomas?' Bill said when the recital that must so often have been repeated finally came to an end. 'What can you tell me about him?'

'Only what I have already said. I went to the *kafeneion*. Pakrades was sitting outside, on guard. Inside was Maleta. With Kostas Dandanakis. Sitting at a table, drinking wine. Maleta greeted me and held out his hand. I took it. I said, I have come from Manoletto. He said, Good. How is he? I told him. Then gave him the message. He reached inside his pocket and gave me an envelope. He also gave me a small piece of cloth, a strip, and I could feel the weight. I tied it round my waist, under my shirt. That's always how we used to carry the sovereigns. He asked me if I had a gun, and I said, no, but my strongest desire was to possess a gun to kill Germans. Kostas reached inside his shirt and pulled out a gun which he gave to me under the table so that no one could see. There were some men in the *kafeneion* – I do not remember exactly how many. Kostas also gave me some bullets for the gun, in a box. It was the first gun I had ever had. I was only young in those days, you understand.'

'It was a long time ago. Tell me, how did my father *look*?'

Stavros thought for a moment, scratching his head. 'How did he *look*?' he asked himself. 'Strong, I suppose; powerful. You know how it is, there are rams and sheep. He was not a sheep!'

Now that Bill had met someone who had actually seen his father, had actually spoken with him, he was hungry for any scrap of knowledge.

'Help me, Stavros,' he said, 'to make a picture of my father in my mind . . .'

Stavros scratched his head again. 'I'm not very good with words, Mr Bill,' he said. 'With marble I am very good – that is how I earn my living. With words, eh? Your father was sitting down when I arrived . . .'

'How was he dressed . . .?'

'Like a Sfakian . . . you know, long black boots – though I didn't see them until he stood up – and breeches, you know. Nothing on his head. Thick black moustache and those blue eyes. Long hands – now I remember – like a doctor, though not quite so clean. One thing gave him away, apart from his voice. When he blew his nose, he used a cloth he took from his pocket. I had never seen that before. Now I know many foreigners use a cloth, and many Cretans, too, but in those days we blew out our nostrils to the ground. I mentioned it to Pakrades on my way out of there. Pakrades said he'd told Maleta many times, but it was a habit Maleta couldn't get rid of.'

The image of his father's persisting in using a handkerchief helped Bill enormously. 'And this was in Kaprisses?'

'Yes, up in the mountains . . .'

'In 1942?'

'Yes. There was snow in the mountains. The month was September. Crete was not a happy place to be that winter . . .!'

Roger Thomas woke suddenly, as he had now learned to do, and lay still, trying to identify the sound that had woken him. He heard Pakrades stir in his sleep next to him, wrapped in his overcoat against the cold. The fire in the back of the cave would be cold ashes; he felt the icy blast that came in the mouth of the cave and lost itself in the high vaulting – they needed that draught of air to carry away the firesmoke and, more importantly, the fumes from the charging engine. Without that, the batteries would be useless and they would have no communication with Cairo. Or with the other radio stations scattered throughout Crete.

Kostas Dandanakis was breathing deeply on his bed against the wall of the cave; he'd made the bed himself from the pliable twigs of a mulberry tree, plaiting them together to be as soft as a spring mattress. He'd offered to make one for Maleta, but Maleta had declined. They wouldn't be able to stay in the cave much longer – too many people already knew where they were. The Cretans were so hungry for any news of activity, any proof the Allies had not just abandoned them to their fate, that inevitably the presence of an Englishman was bandied about. In those bad days of 1942, it was a panacea to say, The Englishman is up in Kaprisses, therefore something is being done to help us . . . And, equally inevitably, some of the ears on which the news fell were not entirely friendly . . .

The noise came again; a clink of metal on stone echoing from a short distance. He heard the snicker of a sheep, quickly stopped.

Roger slid out of his bed in one movement, took the pistol from his belt and slipped off the safety catch. He went across the cave and woke Kostas by touching his nose. Kostas came instantly awake, his hand flashing down to his waist.

'Germans,' Maleta whispered. He sped across the cave again and woke Pakrades with the same message.

Kostas had gone to the mouth of the cave, and Maleta joined him. Immediately below them the ground fell away, the last hundred metres in front of the cave a steep rise. Boulders had fallen to the left of the cave; Kostas slipped out and hid himself among them. Roger sensed Pakrades standing beside him.

'Quick,' he said, 'we must draw them away from here. With luck, they won't find the radio equipment.'

The transmitter and the charging engine were both hidden at the back of the cave behind stones – he knew, however, that the beds would give them away, and the cooking fire. He slipped left, behind the rocks. Pakrades followed him silently. When they drew near to Kostas he held up an admonitory finger.

'Five of them,' he mouthed, 'with a girl.'

Roger moved left, flattening himself against the contours of the rocks. When he had gone twenty metres, he could look down the slope immediately below the cave mouth to the pasture below.

The girl was running in terror. The five soldiers were chasing her, making fun of her, forcing her farther and farther up the side of the hill. As she whirled and tried to pass one of them, to flee back downhill, he'd grab some part of her clothing and tear it. Already she'd lost most of the blouse she'd been wearing and her skirt had been rent to the waist.

At the far end of the pasture below a patrol of fifty or so Germans was watching, shouting encouragement.

Suddenly, a figure Maleta had not previously noticed rose from the ground and continued up the hill. A second girl, who must have flung herself down to gather her strength for one final dash, now ran forward, screaming. Maleta noticed the Germans had left their rifles behind them and had unbuttoned their tunics. They moved fast, and Maleta saw the Fallschirmjaeger flashes on their arms. The killer élite of the German Army here on Crete.

Pakrades had moved alongside Maleta. 'Just come a little closer, you bastards,' he said as he pointed his pistol. 'Just a little closer!'

Kostas gripped Pakrades's wrist. 'Are you mad?' he said. 'Look down there!' He pointed to the troops watching from below and the half-track vehicle on which the Spandau was mounted.

The first girl gathered herself for the last stage of the wild run for freedom. Up the steep slope and into the cave, hoping, no doubt, to lose her pursuers in there.

Maleta could have told her the cave had no rear exit. Once inside, both girls would be trapped.

The second girl had reached the foot of the steeper incline; one of the soldiers came close to her, reached his hand forward and ripped her skirt from her body. She stumbled, picked up a large stone and whirled, smashing it forward towards his face. He roared with laughter as his hand grasped her wrist, stopping the stone within inches of his nose. With his other free hand, he reached out and tore off what remained of her clothing. Two of the other soldiers drew level, reached in and seized her ankles. They picked her up between them, carried her to the side and dropped her on a patch of grass, her legs spread wide.

Pakrades let out a deep moan. 'Let me shoot,' he pleaded, but Kostas held his wrist even firmer.

'If you shoot, we all die!' he said.

'I'd rather die than watch this happen!' Pakrades hissed.

'We have to think of the Englishman!'

Maleta felt a shock of shame that he should be the cause of their inactivity. Certainly it would be suicide to interfere in what was happening but his entire sensibility was outraged.

'Don't bother about me,' he said. 'Let's get on with it.'

The three of them, with the advantage of surprise, would be able to kill the five unarmed Germans with ease. And then would lie in wait for the other fifty to come up the hill with the benefit of mortars and the covering fire of the Spandau.

'Wait,' Kostas said. He'd seen the first girl go into the mouth of the cave. 'Pakrades,' he said, 'go back in and bring her out. Be quick! But don't make a sound.'

They heard the prostrate girl scream as the first of her violators entered her. The pain in her voice ripped through their minds.

Pakrades skittered along in the protection of the rocks and reappeared a few moments later, pushing the girl in front of him. 'Quick!' Kostas said and led the way along the rocky path, no more than a sheep track, that wound round the side of the mountain face. They moved hard and fast. After about ten minutes, they heard a burst of machine-gun fire; Maleta expelled the breath from his body, guessing what was happening, knowing they'd be using the girl's body for target practice. No doubt she'd rather be dead than suffer again what must already have happened to her five times.

They went on for two hours before they felt justified in stopping and taking a breather. They gathered together in a small hollow in the rocks, where a carpet of grass grew. The girl went modestly behind a rock, suddenly aware of the torn state of her clothes, and did the best she could to knot the garments together. When she re-emerged, shyly, Kostas looked at her and growled.

'That is better,' he said, 'now you look like a good Cretan woman instead of some German whore!'

It was rough, but effective, therapy.

'German whore!' she said, spitting at him. 'Evangelina and I left our village only because we overheard the Germans talking about the Englishman, the radio, the engine, with Dollimenides, the traitor. We came to warn you to stay put where you were.

'What's your name?' Maleta asked, his voice more soft and gentle than Kostas's had been.

His soft gentleness was an error. The girl reacted to his kindness with tears, as she suddenly realized the full horror of what she had miraculously escaped. Pakrades clumsily put his arm around her shoulders to comfort her, but nothing could stop her anguished sobbing for some time. Maleta took his handkerchief from his pocket – no-one knew how he managed, even living rough up in the mountains, always to have a clean one available. He gave it to the girl and she used it to dry her eyes.

'My name is Elvira Brandakis,' she said. 'Evangelina is my sister.'

'Evangelina is dead, Elvira,' Maleta said softly. 'It's better that way!'

She moaned, and her face creased with pain, though she had no tears left in her. She made the sign of the Cross on her breast and sank back onto a rock, wringing the handkerchief between her hands.

'Why did you come to tell us to stay where we were,' Kostas asked brusquely, 'if you knew the Germans were coming for us?'

'Because Dollimenides had the story wrong!' she said with an angry toss of her head. 'He told the Germans you were in the cave below the Three Widows. Rhodos used that cave two months ago; we knew he would have left traces behind him and Dollimenides and the Germans would believe you *had* been there but had left the district!'

'And the Germans saw you leave the village and chased you?' Maleta asked.

The girl's eyes flashed with what must have been her usual spirit. 'We led them a dance, you can bet,' she said.

'Why did you come towards our cave?' Kostas asked.

'So that they would believe we were heading *away* from where you were. They fooled us when that half-track appeared – we had meant to go down the mountain but they blocked that way. We had no alternative but to continue upwards!' She looked at Maleta. 'You, *Englesos*,' she said, 'you are a soldier. You have seen people die. How is it?'

He knew what she was asking. 'Very quick,' he said. 'Just a flash and then it's over.'

She was crying again, but this time the tears fell slowly from her, washing out her misery.

'Pakrades,' Maleta said, 'go back towards the village. Question everybody you meet, to find out if the Germans discovered our radio. You, Kostas, go towards Omalos and find Manoletto. Tell him to get a message to Rhodos to say what has happened. And inform him about Dollimenides being a traitor – he'll know what to do about that.'

Kostas was worried. 'What about you, Maleta? Where will you go? What will you do?'

'I shall go back to our camp near Kaprisses and wait there for news of you. Rhodos can arrange a drop for us above Kaprisses, on the plain. We shall need another radio, batteries, a charging engine. If the Germans have not found the one in the cave, we can bring that out again, but not just yet. If Dollimenides knows, others know, too. The Germans are not stupid. Already they may be moving more troops in to search the whole parish thoroughly. We cannot take that risk.'

'And the girl?' Kostas said truculently.

His orders were to stay with the Englishman, to look after him until he found his feet. Kostas thought of himself as being in command of their little group. But Maleta had matured fast; he had learned the topography of their area very quickly, and now, it seemed, he was ready to take charge.

'The girl cannot go back to her village just yet,' Maleta said firmly. 'They'll be looking for her. She will be arrested and put into the Gestapo prison, and interrogated to tell them what she knows about us.'

'You will take her with you?' Kostas asked.

'Yes. I will look after her, and she can guide me through the pass to Kaprisses.'

Elvira had been watching and listening to the dialogue between the two men, her head tilted to one side to understand the Englishman's classic Greek, which sounded impossibly stilted to her ears. Kostas looked angrily at her.

'Go away,' he said brusquely in Cretan dialect. 'Let men talk together, woman, without your ears soaking up each word like dry bread mops up soup!'

She turned away without question and went to where Pakrades was preparing for his journey, lacing his boots tighter over his thick woollen socks.

Kostas faced Maleta squarely. 'This thing with the woman, Maleta,' he said 'is not good. The woman should go back to her village. She is grown and not yet married, though she has been asked for. She has too independent a spirit, that one. Only bad can come to you from such a woman, Maleta, believe me when I speak.'

Maleta was exasperated; he accepted that here on Crete he must follow the Cretan way of life and must abrogate certain Northern European concepts of debt and duty. But, dammit, the woman had risked everything to warn them; her sister Evangelina had *died* a most horrible death because the two sisters had tried to warn them. He owed Elvira something; he couldn't in all conscience send her back into that village to fend for herself, at least not until the traitor Dollimenides had been eliminated. Manoletto would send three men over; they'd come into the village, tap Dollimenides on the shoulder, then blow out his brains. Justice in the mountains was crude, instant but totally effective. Only then would Elvira be safe.

'Look, Kostas,' he said, 'I'm prepared to take your advice in most things, but in some things I have to do as I believe. Some things I can change, some I cannot . . .'

'Like the cloth for blowing your nose, eh?'

'Yes, like the handkerchief! But we're not dealing with the matter of blowing my nose. We're talking of debt. I owe that girl a life since she risked hers to warn me. I cannot abandon that debt, Kostas.'

'She is a woman, Maleta. She did what she had to do.'

Maleta knew it was useless to argue the philosophy of womanhood with a Cretan, just as it was useless to expect Kostas to understand his point of view.

'It will be as I say, Kostas,' he said with quiet but

43

unshakable authority. 'Pakrades will go back towards the village, you will go to Manoletto, and the woman and I will go to Kaprisses. When you have seen Manoletto, when Pakrades has informed himself about the situation in the village, you will both come to me and I will tell you what is to be done.'

There was no possibility of argument – it was a command.

Kostas knew that, from that moment, the Englishman had established his authority. In a sense he had issued a challenge: Kostas could turn round and walk away to join some other unit, he could pull out his knife and they would fight it out or he could obey.

'Watch the woman, Maleta,' he muttered. 'She is a lioness waiting for cubs. Offer one finger, she will take your hand; offer your hand she will take your arm; offer your arm and she will take your senses.'

'I think I can look after myself,' Maleta said, smiling benevolently in victory. 'I had a wife who owned my heart. When she died, she took that heart with her.'

Kostas snorted at the naïvety of the Englishman. 'When grass fails to grow in the springtime, Maleta, when there are no flowers to brighten men's eyes, then we will talk again about your heart. In the meantime, remember, Kostas warned you not to take the woman . . .'

'I will remember, Kostas,' Maleta said.

Sam put his thumb on the concealed panel in the door. The built-in sensor read his thumb-print, verified it via the Data Base and operated the lock mechanism. The door opened. He walked through the detector-scanned lobby to the far door where he waited.

If the powers-that-be ever moved him up to the status of director, he thought to himself, he'd rip out all this gimmickry. He'd have an open-plan office where everybody could see everybody else at work. He'd de-classify most of the stuff they handled interdepartmentally and make everything available on demand to everybody inside the Centre.

The green light came on. He spoke to it, feeling foolish. 'Sam Birntin,' he said. 'Facetious!'

He grinned at the door. 'Facetious' had been his own contribution. The word contained all the vowels in their correct order and gave the voice sensor something to bite on.

Once again the lock was pulled and the door opened.

The director was sitting at his desk, facing across the room. Sam marched across the carpet, halted at the front of the desk but didn't salute. Twin flags on the wall behind the director fluttered in the air movement Sam's march had caused. One was the Old Glory, the other told everyone the director was a Yale man.

Sam was a Harvard graduate but bore no grudges. A man couldn't always decide for himself where he would be educated.

'You sent for me, Director?' he said.

The director coughed to clear his throat, one of his many nervous habits. 'Sit down, Sam,' he said. 'You look like a Marine standing there.'

'I *was* a Marine,' Sam reminded him as he pulled the chair forward.

'*Was*, Sam, *was*. I've been going through the papers on this Theseus affair. One aspect of it worries me. 27. I hadn't realized the close involvement that exists between 27 and the case subject . . .'

'Neither had I when I gave out the LOC. It's a fortunate coincidence.'

'Are you convinced it's fortunate, Sam?'

'It gives us an inside track we didn't expect.'

'And is bound to put extra pressures on 27.'

'I know that. But I think 27 can take it. Straight A's, don't forget.'

'That was training. This is field work. I don't need to remind you there's a world of difference.'

'No, you don't, Director, but you will . . .'

'You've made arrangements for a cut-out if anything goes wrong?'

'Yes, Director, I have.'

Sam sat there patiently, knowing that Worry-guts would have to go through his routine.

'You know you can't bring 27 in until the job's completed?' the director said, as if on cue.

'I know that, Director.'

'You have a 5311 standing by on 27 if necessary?'

'Yes, Director, I have!'

Standard procedure. Everybody expendable, once they were out and running. No untidy ends left lying about. As soon as the job was completed, you got out the rake and scooped them all in again. But not before. The rules were as inflexible as Grand Master chess; everybody knew it and had to accept it without demur to qualify for the game.

Sam got up to go and started to cross the carpet again. If and when he was director, he'd have an office a quarter of the size, with windows all round it so that he could see everybody, everybody could see him. He turned.

'One thing, Director?' he said softly.

'Yes?'

'You got a 5311 out on me?'

'Of course,' the director said. 'You know the rules.'

Ioannis took time off from managing his pension. He was bored with catering for the whims of tourists, who demanded to know why the water wasn't boiling at all times, why he didn't serve breakfast, why they couldn't bring boy/girl friends into their rooms during the night and hold riotous, drunken parties, and longed for the vast silence and peace of the Lefka Ori, the White Mountains. When Bill asked him if he'd care to come to Kaprisses, he readily agreed, put up his NO VACANCIES notice and climbed into the hired car.

The road to Kaprisses branched off the main Xania–Chora Sfakion road, climbing to the right around the tortuous bends of the mountainside, often with nothing to the right of them but a sheer drop into a valley. Mercifully there was little traffic on the road; from time to time they would pass a donkey carrying a burden of *horta* or a peasant on its back, urging it lazily along with a not very enthusiastically-wielded stick. Sometimes a youth would roar past treating a 50cc Honda as if it were a Grand Prix racing bike, its rasping snarl sufficient warning for Bill to pull well to the side of the road.

Tourism came late to Greece and even later to Crete, Bill thought, but when it finally did arrive it brought all the worst excesses of the so-called civilized countries. Already the Cretans were abandoning their finely-carved wood furniture in favour of modern plastic-covered chipboard; many of them passed over local *tsikoudia*, as the Cretans call raki, in favour of excessively priced, imported whisky and gin; and pizza parlours were springing up everywhere, even in the relatively untouched Xania, in which the active Archaeological Society had banned the high-rise hotels that had blighted so much of the eastern north coast.

Here in the Lefka Ori, tourism had been restricted to the daily hordes who tramped from Omalos, squirming like ants down the twenty kilometres of the Gorge of Samaria. Ioannis beckoned and Bill stopped the car on a wide bend. They came out of the car and looked along the mountain.

Kaprisses clung to the side of the rock as if glued there countless ages ago by a giant hand. Many of the houses seemed to hang directly over the chasm below. The houses were all old with tiled roofs faded over the centuries from constant exposure to sun and wind. They huddled together, as if for mutual self-protection, each building blending into the next. Colour splashed everywhere from myriad blossoms improbably seeded in every nook and planted in every possible manner of container, from old olive tins, *feta* cans, to pottery vases and glass jars.

'You see why no-one ever was able to take Kaprisses,' Ioannis said. 'The Turks tried to build a mosque there but every night the work they had done that day seemed to shift downwards towards the chasm. When the Mosque was finally completed, it was leaning to the west. After the Turkish celebrations, the mosque finally collapsed into the gorge, taking twenty Turkish leaders with it. The Turks had built it, it seems, over a cave. The cave hadn't been there when they started. While the Turks were building over the ground, the Cretans were working in the ground, expanding the depth of the cave but propping it up with timber. When the mosque was completed, they set a slow fire to the timber . . .'

Bill laughed. 'It seems to me from what I know that the Cretan excels in one thing – in the creative thinking he brings to his villainy!'

Ioannis smiled. 'It is a philosophy,' he said.

Bill knew he meant philosophy in the same way an Englishman would mean – a way of life! A way of thinking, of acting, with a delicious, unperverted creativity.

The *kafeneion* was crowded when they arrived in Kaprisses, with what looked like the entire male population

49

of the village sitting at the tables, drinking coffee from thimble-sized cups, playing *trapola* with raucous shouts as they slapped the cards on the table, casting the dice onto *tavli* boards with the deft flicks of experts and moving the pieces round the board with no uncertain pauses, a confidence bred of many games. Every Cretan considers himself a champion at the three games that turn backgammon into *tavli*, and no game is complete without the vociferous slanging match, the fist shaking argument, that follows every throw.

The *kafeneion* fell silent as Bill and Ioannis walked in.

'Greetings,' Ioannis said to the room in general.

No one replied. All eyes were fixed on Bill; they didn't see many foreigners in Kaprisses, and, historically, those who had come in the past had been invaders. Suspicion dies hard in sealed communities.

The man behind the counter was about the same age as Bill but his figure and his face had been hardened by a lifetime of mountain living. He looked at the older man sitting behind the counter when Ioannis called for two coffees – the older man nodded slightly and the younger one poured two glasses of water from a carafe he took from the modern refrigerator that was the *kafeneion*'s only piece of formal equipment.

He brewed the coffee in copper pans on an antique gas stove fed from a gas bottle, poured it with one deft flick into the cups and brought them to the table with the glasses of water.

Bill looked around the room. The walls were once white but hadn't been painted for years and now were blotched where the plaster had peeled away. The wall decorations were calendars, photographs of footballers, a picture of a *pappas*, a snap of a wedding couple, now almost completely faded. The floor was made of the rolled and polished composition containing flecks of variously coloured marbles; the tables, a motley assembly of woods painted crudely in different colours, had worn American cloth on them. The high ceiling of the room was old, browned wood supported by thick pine beams now almost black from the smoke of ages.

It was a room in which men sought companionship, not decoration; where men could talk and play together, throw their cigarette ends on the floor without some woman constantly sweeping up after them; where they could drink coffee and water, eat sunflower seeds and spit the shells out without regard for where they fell.

'German?' the man asked when he'd put their coffees on the table.

'English!' Bill said in Greek.

The man smiled, and suddenly the room came back to life as card games and *tavli* were resumed. *English.*

A man who'd been sitting by the counter, alone at a table, got to his feet and lurched across the room towards them. Like most of the men in the *kafeneion*, he hadn't shaved for a day or two. He was grinning as he weaved towards them, revealing a mouth almost devoid of teeth. His grey shirt was torn at the shoulder and his trousers were held round his hips by a knotted tie that had once been blue and silver.

'English?' he said as he drew near. 'English very good!'

'Thank you!' Bill said.

'Me. War. Much boom-boom!' He opened his mouth wide revealing his bare gums, with one almost-rotted tooth in the top, two in the bottom. 'Much boom-boom!' he said, or tried to say, holding his mouth wide open.

'Shut your mouth, Andonis,' the waiter said. 'They don't want to hear about your boom-boom!' He turned to Ioannis. 'He was a prisoner in Retimo during the war,' he said. 'The Germans took his teeth out one by one without anaesthetic. The English rescued him and twenty others. He has never forgotten, poor devil. When we got him back up here, his mind was a bit touched. We look after him.'

'Was he in the Resistance?' Bill asked eagerly.

'Yes. He was a good man . . .'

'Here in Kaprisses?'

Andonis had wandered back towards the table in the

corner, still muttering 'boom-boom'. The card and *tavli* players threw words at him as he passed, like a man eating will throw a fish-head to a friendly cat.

'Yes, he was here, in Kaprisses. Here, there, everywhere, I understand. You know, I was born the year the Germans were kicked out of Crete, so I didn't know. They christened me Victorio, to celebrate!'

Bill could hardly contain his excitement. 'Could you ask him if he knew an Englishman here in Kaprisses?'

'Which Englishman? There were several here during the war.'

'The one called Maleta . . .'

Victorio called across the room. 'Andonis,' he said, 'do you remember an Englishman here called *Maleta*? During the war?' He turned back to Bill. 'What year was it?' he asked.

'1942 onwards. Maleta was my father.'

'1942, Andonis. Remember a man called Maleta? An Englishman? This is his son.'

The noise of the *tavli* games was suddenly stilled. The card players whispered to each other, and one by one the games stopped. The quiet voices shivered through the room like rustling silk scraped by fingernails.

'Victorio, give Thanakis a coffee!' the old man behind the bar shouted, his voice cutting through the room like a blade.

It was a command to be obeyed instantly. Victorio looked at Bill in some confusion, then turned to look at Ioannis and Andonis. Ioannis's eye-brows were raised; he didn't understand it, either. Victorio shrugged and went back behind the bar. The older man said a few words to him, quietly, and Victorio's sun-beaten face flushed even darker. He flung the makings of the coffee together in a sudden onset of anger, clattering the copper pan onto the gas stove, splashed water into a glass, carried the coffee and the water across to a table and banged them down in front of one of the card players, who whispered sibilantly at him.

Ioannis looked quickly round.

A man sitting at a table in the centre of the room, aged about thirty, said in an unnaturally loud voice, 'Come on, let us get on with the game.'

Bill caught the words the others muttered. 'Shut up. Stay still!'

Ioannis looked back at Bill, then at Victorio standing by Thanakis's table and biting his lower lip in angry indecision.

'Come on, Bill,' he said in English, 'let us get out of here.'

He fumbled in his pocket, produced a 20-*drachmae* coin and put it on the table. Victorio let out a shout like a jabbed bull, raced across the room, and before Bill could get to his feet, picked up the glass of water Bill had only one-quarter drunk and threw the contents into Bill's face. Bill pushed his chair over backwards, his feet entangling themselves in the table legs, but felt Victorio's fist thump into his breastbone, driving him backwards and down into the chair itself. Ioannis started to come round the table to his assistance but suddenly found himself grabbed from behind by two of the card-players. As he recognized the word they uttered, his eyes opened wide and he pushed his chair back from the table and sat on it.

Bill felt his legs flailing about, drew back his knee and lunged forward. He felt his shoe thump satisfyingly into Victorio's leg. Victorio howled and hobbled backwards. Bill scrambled to his feet and stood there weaving, wondering what the hell could have caused this unprovoked attack.

Victorio came in again, his shoulder forward, a bull of a man with a kill-or-be-killed lust in his eyes that Bill could instantly recognize, knowing with dread that he was no match for the fitter, younger man. The year spent on the booze had sapped his strength; he knew it had weakened him and made his flesh and muscles flabby. The first onslaught hit him solidly in the chest and he cannoned backwards, his legs cycling uselessly as he fought to keep his balance. He whammed his closed fists sideways and in, clapping Victorio's head between them, but Victorio merely shook himself and slammed both *his* balled fists inwards and upwards into Bill's booze-weakened gut. Bill felt the air driven out of his body like a punctured football; his head spun and his belly was seared by pain. He tried to bring up his knee in a desperate attempt to get Victorio in his most vulnerable part but felt his knee kicked contemptuously aside.

Balancing on one foot, blinded by pain and trying to gulp even a fragment of air back into his body, Bill saw Victorio's arms begin a windmill almost as if in slow motion, knowing that this time he would be finished, this would be the end of him; once he were down, nothing could prevent the infuriated bull of a Cretan from kicking him to death. The two fists came round and under and up, brushing Bill's futile arms aside like sticks, and then Bill felt the contact with his abdomen and his lower ribs bend in, the pain of the blow driving through his belly to his back bone, lifting him and slamming him backwards, up and back at the same time. He was already unconscious when his body fell on the floor of the *kafeneion*, when the back of his head smacked down and when Victorio reached in, grabbed his arm and dragged him across the floor to throw him through the opened door like the carcase of a dead dog.

When Bill recovered consciousness, he was sitting on the ground, his back propped against the rented car. Ioannis squatted in front of him. Bill's hands had been clutching his middle while he had been unconscious; he could feel the throbbing pain in his abdomen, reaching up into his rib case. Gently he probed the two bottom ribs; they hurt but didn't appear to be broken. He struggled to his feet, using the car for support.

'I will drive,' Ioannis said.

Bill shook his head. 'We're not leaving here,' he said firmly. 'Not yet.'

'You are not going back into the *kafeneion*?' Ioannis could not keep the alarm from his voice.

'Are there any other *kafeneion*? And shops?'

'Yes, I think three shops.'

'Good. That's where we are going . . .'

Ioannis was patently worried as he walked slowly beside Bill, his brow corrugated with doubt. 'I do not know what we have run into, Bill,' he said, 'but I advise you to leave it alone for the moment. Let me find out in a day or so exactly what is happening . . . I'm Cretan; they will tell me!'

'I'm English, but they'll damned well tell me, too!' Bill said, his anger giving him strength.

They went together into the first shop; a small general store, it had shelves of tinned and bottled goods, and sacks of rice, corn, maize, salt, sugar standing on the floor. In the back Bill could see the tins of feta cheese, the barrels of olives, of oil, and the local wine, *krassi*. There were crates of Alfa beer, and lemonade, open boxes of vegetables, tomatoes, onions. Over it all hung a smell of paraffin and camphor, and that indefinable odour of small grocery shops everywhere.

The man standing behind the counter was unmistakably a Sfakian who had forsaken the mountain slopes for the life of a shop-keeper; the shop fitted him as badly as an unpressed suit.

'A packet of Karelia,' Bill said, asking for the most popular brand of cigarette.

The man produced the packet from the shelf, and Bill paid his 17 *drachmae*, taking his time to count the coins, assessing the Sfakian. Bill reckoned he'd be around sixty – old enough to have been alive during the war and active with the Resistance. He had decided in favour of the direct approach since the counter was between him and the Sfakian.

'Did you know a man called Maleta during the war, here in Kaprisses in 1942?' he asked suddenly.

The Sfakian looked at him. 'Maleta? 1942? Here in Kaprisses?'

'Yes, an Englishman!'

The Sfakian looked at him from beneath bushy eyebrows. 'Damn war,' he said. 'I was not here on Crete. I was stranded with the Cretan Brigade on the mainland when we came back from Jugoslavia. It was 1944 before we came back here, just a few of us. I was in the south, in Aghia Roumeli.'

Bill felt deflated, his pain returning to him with increasing vigour. He knew he ought to leave it, to go back down the mountain to Xania, to rest in his bed in the pension. But the beating he had suffered infuriated him. He knew there was no point in returning to the *kafeneion* to be beaten again by Victorio. Not until his strength had returned and he'd got rid of his booze-induced weakness. Then he'd take Victorio on again, but this time give a better showing of himself.

He went into the second grocery shop, almost a carbon copy of the first one except that the person behind the counter was an old crone, dressed all in black, her silvered hair drawn tight to her skull, her mouth almost as empty of teeth as that of Andonis. Bill bought another packet of Karelia.

'Were you here during the war, Mother?' he asked.

'Yes, I was. Why do you ask?' The woman looked at Bill and then at Ioannis, as if suspecting them of being policemen trying to trap her.

'Don't worry, Mother,' Bill said. 'I only want to know something that perhaps you can tell me. Were you here in 1942?'

'You speak funny,' she said. 'I was here, all during the war. I had my family to look after, my man to feed.'

Bill was determined not to let himself hope. 'Did you know a man called Maleta?' he asked. 'An Englishman?'

'I did not know any men!' she said firmly. 'I was a good

woman. I had my husband! I lived in the house of his father and mother. How would I know a man, especially an Englishman, did you say he was?'

'Yes, an Englishman.'

'We had many Englishmen here, at different times. They all had strange names. Mostly they slept outside the village, but they used to come to the *kafeneion* in the evenings. Some of the women used to take food in to them – poor rascals did not get much to eat. Not that anyone had much, you know. The Germans used to come and forage for food. We used to hide it.'

He could see he had opened the flood-gates of her memory. She rested back on her seat and clasped her hands together.

'They were very cruel,' she said. 'The women used to hide to keep out of their way. They did bad things. Gave girls babies and then left them. Sometimes the girls would come here from other villages to have their babies, for the shame. Some of the babies went over the cliff, you know. And their mothers, too.'

'Did you ever hear anyone speak – do you remember the name – of Maleta? An Englishman?'

'I remember one called Rhodos. He was very jolly and used to make all the men in the *kafeneion* laugh. We always knew when Rhodos was here. Some of us used to sneak in the back door of the *kafeneion* to look at him. He was very handsome . . .'

'*Maleta?* You don't remember Maleta?'

She held out her hand and he put his hand beneath it, since that was apparently what she wanted.

'You are young,' she said, 'and I am old. You called me Mother and I thank you for that. Forget the past,' she said. 'Some memories bring only pain. Each time you let the memory occupy the space in your mind, it brings back more pain with it. Remember only the good things, like Rhodos laughing . . .'

'You remembered the girls having babies and throwing themselves and their babies over the cliff from shame . . .'

57

'I did not say the girls threw the babies over the cliff, or themselves. The *family* sometimes would come here and find them, and they would throw them over. Not the girls. The girls wanted to have the babies – no matter who the father. It was the family who would not permit it. You understand. I would not have remembered any of these things if I had known they would mean much to you. The past is dead, young sir. Look, the Germans come now into my shop, as you have done, and I give them beer and cigarettes, and don't even overcharge them one *drachma*. The past is dead, young sir. Let us who remember it have peace.'

'So you won't tell me about Maleta.'

'I will tell you this, since it seems to mean much to you. I saw Maleta in the *kafeneion*, in the street, once outside the village. I was tending the sheep; he was sitting on a rock cleaning a pistol. We did not speak – that would not have been proper and I was always correct. With me, and all the other girls of this village, he was always correct. I never believed the things they said of him after he went away. Never.'

She took her hand from his. 'Now,' she said with quiet dignity, 'go away from me, from this village. Too many old bones are safely put to rest beneath too many stones. Let us be that way, I beseech you.'

She pushed the 17 *drachmae* he had put on the counter for the cigarettes back towards him.

'Keep your money,' she said, 'and let us keep our memories.'

Sam Birntin clipped the earphones round his head, the pencil-slim microphone bent near his mouth.

27's voice came through clear and strong, considering it was being bounced off a satellite from a public telephone.

'I've found someone who could be a great help. It's the most fascinating coincidence. An Englishman, brought up in America, looking for his father who was parachuted in here during the war. He'd make a very good cover? Should I recruit him?'

'Wait.'

Sam pressed the button that tested the line all the way from Washington to the satellite, back down to Souda Bay on Crete, out from there to a public telephone in a mountain village. Line clear. He activated the surveillance system that would sound a beeper if that intact line were broken by tapping.

'Okay audio your end?' he asked.

'Sure, no one can overhear me and I'm direct dialled into Comtelsat. Look, I know what I'm doing . . .'

'Yeah, straight A's, I remember.'

'Do I recruit? There isn't much time.'

'How much?'

'Minutes.'

'Okay, don't recruit yet. Keep filing situationers on him. And let me have a run-down via Souda. I'd rather not recruit, if possible.'

He heard 27 chuckle. 'That means going facetious, doesn't it?' 27 said. 'For more authority. You wouldn't like that!'

'Okay, 27. So you listen to the scuttlebutt! But don't get smart, eh? That was a good situationer you filed on Theseus. You do good work, but you get a bit lippy sometimes. I'm just giving you a friendly word, okay?'

'Okay. I met 272 today. A good pro, I'd say.'

'The best. One of the best free-lancers we have.'

'But ice-cold.'

'So's Alaska, which is where your next assignment will be if you don't learn to button it. G'bye.'

After his conversation with the old lady, Bill temporarily lost heart in his search. He longed to find a bottle of something – beer, wine, or some of the local *tsikoudia* – and lose himself in it.

'Are you a drinking man, Ioannis?' he asked as they got back into the car.

'I take a drink sometimes . . .'

'That means you're not a drinking man!' Bill looked at his hands gripping the steering wheel and saw them shake a little when he loosened his grasp.

'They say alcohol makes you forget your troubles,' Ioannis conceded. 'If you would like a drink, we could stop somewhere. We ought to think about eating anyway.'

'Alcohol makes you forget nothing!' Bill said. 'It's the great multiplier. If you're abundantly happy, it makes you more happy. If you're sad, it throws you down a pit of depression. Believe me, I know!'

Ioannis eyed him carefully. Cretan men, with very few exceptions, are not big drinkers. They already have too much life in them, too much happiness, to need the stimulation that comes from excesses of alcohol.

What had Anna said, 'You haven't licked it until you can take a drink any time you like . . .' Well, today would be as good a day as any to try. Bill had never been more desperate to belt a few back; if he could manage today, he'd know he was cured.

'Okay,' he said, 'let's drive down the hill and find a restaurant . . .'

It was the wrong decision and part of him knew it. He was in no mental condition to try to restrict himself to the one drink Anna had stipulated. He turned the car in the narrow street that led from the square of the *kafeneion* where Victorio worked, drove past it and headed north towards the steep decline from the village, back the way they had come. Already Bill could taste the wine he'd have and his hands clasped and unclasped the steering wheel in anticipation.

As they were about to leave the village, they came to a bend on which stood a large tree. He had to slow down to pass the tree on the dog-leg turn where the road narrowed.

Suddenly a girl stepped from behind the tree and stood in the middle of the road. He had no alternative but to stop. The girl came to the driver's side of the car to where Bill had the window open. She was wearing jeans and a mannish, light-coloured shirt with the collar turned up. A light scarf frothed at her throat and her dark hair was pulled severely back from her face and fastened behind with some sort of large wooden pin. She looked Cretan but not Cretan, local but international. He would have estimated her age at just over thirty, but, without realizing it, he would have been a few years out.

'You were in the *kafeneion* just now,' the girl said, speaking English with a slight American accent.

Bill looked at Ioannis, uncertain whether or not to agree. Damn it, he'd had enough of local customs and taboos for the day – all he wanted now was lunch and that bottle of wine. Ioannis shrugged his shoulders to show he had no special knowledge.

'Yes, we were,' Bill said. 'But only for a short time. Since you know we were there, you may have heard we left rather suddenly . . .!'

'Can I get in the car, and will you drive me a short way down the road?' the girl asked. 'It's better we aren't seen talking here.'

Bill reached behind him and opened the back door. The girl climbed in quickly, and Bill drove down the road for a couple of miles, with no one speaking until he reached a wide bend, recently enlarged and resurfaced, where he could pull the car off the roadway and park beneath pine trees, overlooking the long valley below them.

'This do for you?' he said, turning on his seat.

'Fine.'

'We could start by exchanging names,' he said. 'This is Ioannis. My name is Bill, Bill Thomas . . .'

'Mine is Maria. Maria Stafanakis.' She looked at him as if the name should mean something special to him, but apparently it didn't.

'Stafanakis . . .' she repeated.

61

'A good Cretan name,' Ioannis said.

'It was the name of your father at one time,' Maria said. 'When he came to Crete in 1942, he was given papers in the name Giorgio Stafanakis. His code-name was Maleta. His English name, Captain Roger Thomas.'

Bill hadn't realized he'd been holding his breath until suddenly he exhaled. All thoughts of alcohol, of the bottle of wine with his lunch, had fled from him.

'Let's start backwards,' Bill said. 'You speak American . . .?'

'I have lived in America for a number of years. I was married there. It didn't work out, so I came back to Crete to pick up the pieces.'

Bill was shaking his head. 'I was married in America,' he said. 'My wife was killed in a car I was driving on the Van Wyck Expressway. It was my fault . . .' The sentence came running involuntarily out of him – words he had said to himself over and over again, drunk and sober, since it happened. 'Sorry,' he said, 'I didn't mean to go into the details . . . Tell me who Stafanakis is . . .'

'. . . was,' Maria said. 'He's dead now. He was my father. He had four sons, all of whom were killed during the war. He gave the identity papers of one of his sons to your father, so that he could pass for Cretan. My father was a *palikari*, or so my mother told me. He was killed in 1943. My mother died in 1960; that was when I went to America to work as an au pair girl, and later I met my husband. My mother told me about the Englishman who'd lived in our family home as one of her sons. The *kapitanio*, she used to call him.'

Now Bill felt again that terrible hunger for more information, for any details about his father. In particular now, he wanted to know why mention of his father's code-name had caused such a violent reaction in the *kafeneion*.

'Tell me everything you can about him,' he pleaded. 'Everything your mother told you over the years.'

Maria laughed. 'That would be a tall order,' she said.

'My mother was very fond of him, apparently. Treated him as the son she'd lost, I'd guess.'

'If only your mother weren't dead!' Bill said wistfully, then realized how tactless his remark was. 'I'm sorry,' he said. 'That's a thoughtless thing to say!'

'I understand it,' Maria said. 'I was just as hungry as you are to learn all about *my* father. The reason I stopped your car was that there is a man still alive who knew your father. I remember him and my mother sitting together, talking about my father and yours. When I returned from America I asked about him. He's still alive, but he's become something of a recluse. He lives all year round up in the mountains, as a shepherd – people send their flocks up to him in the spring and bring them back again in the autumn. God knows how he survives all winter.'

'What's his name?' Bill asked trying to control the eagerness of his voice.

'Kostas,' Maria said. 'Your father knew him as Kostas Dandanakis. He was your father's wireless operator.'

When the telephone rang the man answered it with his usual, cautious, 'Yes?'

He had not heard the voice on the other end of the telephone for a long time.

'I'm calling from Kaprisses as you asked,' the voice said. 'An Englishman turned up in the *kafeneion* asking about his father who, he said, was here during the war.'

'Did he give his father's name?'

'Yes. Maleta!'

Theseus expelled his breath in a long hiss; all these years he had been afraid something like this might happen.

'What did you tell him?'

'Nothing. Victorio was there. He beat up the Englishman, then threw him out in the road. Apparently he then went to the shop of Katerina, but she sent him away without telling him anything – she asked him to leave her in peace. It's my belief he will come back, asking more questions.'

'Did you find out where he is living?'

'No, but he was driving a car from the Hermes Rent-a-Car company in Xania.'

'Good. I can trace him through the car.'

The voice at the other end of the telephone sounded frightened. 'I think he will be back!'

'He will not return; you can take my word for that!'

Bill and Ioannis had returned to Xania where Bill stretched out on his bed, his body a mass of aches, his stomach throbbing with pain. Ioannis offered to call his doctor to examine him for broken bones, but Bill declined.

'I'll be all right in the morning,' he said. 'I have to be if I'm going to climb a mountain to look for the shepherd.'

Ioannis's face clouded with doubt. 'I cannot come with you tomorrow, Bill,' he said. 'Tomorrow the tourist police come to look at the pension. I must wait for them to be here when they arrive. I do not know what time they will come.'

Bill looked up at this kindly Cretan, whose face was wrinkled with concern. He held out his hand and Ioannis took it.

'You are a good friend,' Bill said, then quoted one of the oldest Cretan sayings – 'It is my good fortune to have met you.'

He withdrew his hand, fatigue creeping over him.

Ioannis seated himself in the chair beside the bed. 'I want to give you a word of advice,' he said. 'Crete is an island,' he said, 'in more senses of the word than one. The people here are very insular. Many times Crete has been invaded and she has always suffered badly. Memories are long on Crete, and people are passionate in their beliefs. I do not know what happened in Kaprisses all those years ago, but I saw what happened today and recognized the symptoms. You appear to have opened a barrel, Bill; a barrel that should perhaps remain closed. I ask you to think about this. The woman in the shop was very troubled when she asked you to leave her in peace. The man in the *kafeneion* was very troubled when he deliberately provoked a fight with you. I have never seen a Cretan do such a thing, except when there is some kind of vendetta. If there is any possibility of your being involved in a vendetta, Bill, I urge you strongly to go away, to stay out of it. Even now, in these modern days, men are still killed because of some old vendetta, especially in Sfakia. The government tried to stop it many years ago – they sent many men from Sfakia to the other end of the island, to the *nome* of Lasithi, to try to end these old feuds. But without success. Think about this, Bill. I have known you only a few days but already I think of you as a brother.'

Bill knew the Cretan was sincere. Though they had known each other only a short time, he, too, felt a bond of affection.

'I will think about what you say, Ioannis,' he promised, already half-asleep.

He slept for the rest of the day and most of the night, waking at five in the morning feeling refreshed, with most of his pain gone.

He remembered the many times he'd woken in the night from a drunken sleep, his mind craving a drink even when he was unconscious. He got out of bed and took a shower in the bathroom on the back terrace, sheltered from wind and noise. When he went back through his room to stand on the terrace, he saw the first stirrings of life along the old port water-front as the waiters started putting out the cushions for the metal chairs that would later attract tourists and Cretans alike. He watched two fishing boats coming back in, one an eight-metre, the other a tiny four-metre. Both, he knew, would have been out all night.

During the night he must have been thinking, while asleep, about what Ioannis had said. He could feel that he was getting into something bigger than he could understand, some long ago dark story of tribal differences. But he knew he must continue, irrespective of the risks he ran. One factor alone impelled him. So far he had thought of his father in war-hero terms. It had sounded so noble that his father had landed on Crete clandestinely to help an embattled nation, a Quixote tilting at the German windmills. But could he now be so sure his father had proved to be a consistent hero? The reaction of Victorio, logically analysed, would seem to indicate that Maleta had been such a man that the very mention of his name would provoke violence, not admiration. Bill was determined to find out why. And if, in the process, he discovered that his father was not a hero but a coward, not a knight in shining armour but a despicable character, then Bill would have to learn to live with that fact. But he could not bear not to know. One way or the other, he had to find out for himself. He had to be certain.

Maria had caught the six o'clock bus that came down the road past Kaprisses, bringing the villagers in to the Xania market. Bill had parked his car by the Venetian Armoury in the port and was waiting when Maria arrived. She was wearing cord trousers, heavy walking shoes and a mannish shirt, and had a sweater tied round her waist. She examined him critically.

'How do you feel today?' she asked as he let in the clutch and began to drive.

'Fine. I ache a bit, but that'll go once I start to use my muscles again.'

'It's a hard journey,' she said.

'I'll manage.'

On the way she told him what she could remember of her mother's talk about the Englishman, Maleta. Mostly they were inconsequential stories, remembered because of the humour of them. They formed a mosaic Bill would have expected, given the circumstances. Maleta had slept mostly in caves in the mountains; he had come to Kaprisses from time to time to clean up, to eat a cooked meal, to rest and relax by the wood-fired stove, to sit in the *kafeneion* – that same *kafeneion* where Bill had been beaten – to chat with the men. Many of the stories had to do with Maleta's incomplete understanding of the Cretan dialect. Nothing in them gave any reason for a vendetta. Whatever had caused the violence of Victorio's reaction to Bill had not been discussed by Maria's mother. Was that because, at the time, Maria had been a young, innocent girl, shielded from harsh realities? Crete is a land of male chauvinism to this day, Bill thought. All those years ago the women and the girls must have been protected from any sort of unsavoury talk.

By the time they arrived at the high plateau in the Lefka Ori where they would leave the car, Bill had fixed in his mind a vague shadowy outline of his father, a man of good humour prepared to be the butt of other's jokes, a courageous man, an instinctive leader. But the picture lacked definition; it had no real detail to bring it to life.

Bill parked the car beneath a pine tree and locked the doors, though he knew no one would touch it. During the drive up through the mountains they had seen few other vehicles, mostly lorries delivering sacks of the ubiquitous cement for concrete or the small three-wheel trucks driven by a motor-cycle engine that carried local produce. A large Mercedes had come past them, but they could see no sign of it when they parked. Presumably it had continued over the hill and down the other side of the mountain.

They started up a track to the right. It wound round the mountain, climbing steeply all the way. The first kilometre had been cleared, and stones had been roughly laid on it to make the going easier. Bill saw evidence of primitive road-making, where rock faces had been hammered down to widen the track. After the first kilometre, whoever had been working on the road had given up, and now it became an animal track, winding its way haphazardly around larger boulders, through gullies. The air became colder with every step they took; they were above the tree line and the only vegetation was a garigue of scrub and springy mountain turf cropped close, smooth as a billiard table. The way was littered with old animal droppings. Once Bill turned a corner and came to a small clearing, ringed by rocks in which someone had built a primitive shelter containing a stone fireplace. He could imagine a shepherd crouching there, his charges all about him, when the deep snow drifted across the face of the mountain and when the winds for which Crete is well known blew about his ears. Bill stopped there for a moment to catch his breath. He and Maria had not spoken much on the steep climb. They sat on rocks, half-facing each other, content for the moment to breathe the mountain air and to let already aching muscles relax.

'We're about a third of the way there,' Maria said.

He noticed she was not breathing deeply and appeared to be taking the climb completely in her stride.

'I suppose as a young girl you used to do this all the time?' he asked.

'Yes. I finished school when I was eight. It was a waste of time, everyone thought, to give *girls* an education when they could be out on the hillsides tending sheep and goats, bringing home firewood. I went to school in America, after I was married.'

'And yet you came back here . . .?'

'Yes. I was homesick!'

Bill looked about him at the mountain range, the rocks in their shades of mauve, ochre, brown, gold, the dark brown-green of the garigue.

'I can imagine one could be homesick for a land as beautiful as this,' he said.

'The beauty's only skin deep,' she said. 'Life is hard here in the mountains – even now, when much of the lower part of the island has been taken by the tourists, the mountain men still have a hard life. Lots of the younger ones leave and go to work in Aghios Nikolaos, Heraklion.'

'But you came back . . .?'

'Yes, I was – am, I suppose – one of the few . . .'

They set off again on the last part of the steep climb. Here the going was even more rugged, the path often a feature of the imagination, animal droppings the only reliable clue. As they climbed, Bill's eyes were taken by a score of different wild flowers, many growing, it seemed, from the very rock itself; all having a precarious hold on life but blooming perhaps the more vigorously and beautifully because of that. Now it was definitely cold and Maria put on her sweater. Bill, wearing a cotton windcheater, was hot from the climb, but he knew he would be chilly if he remained still for any length of time.

After an hour, they topped a rise and found there the flat, high plateau dotted with sheep and goats, a sea of grasses of several kinds interspersed with shrubs of herbs and small bushes of some flat pine. The mountain continued its rise on the far side of the plateau; fresh water came down and wound its way across the flat ground, carving out a mountain rill where the water ran crystal clear over darkened stones. Bill glanced at his watch. They had been climbing for three hours. Almost beneath the towering peak of the mountain, a hut had been built about ten metres above the plateau height; from its doorway, a shepherd would be able to oversee the whole plateau.

The entire mountain top seemed to glisten with a special radiance that Bill knew must come from the total clarity of the air. The sun was high above them and, to his surprise, the plateau was warm and gentle as a valley meadow. A flock of large birds swooped down the sheer face of the continuing mountain. Bill couldn't recognize them but guessed they might be egrets, young eagles, flying joyfully in sport. They banked when they reached the shepherd's hut, flattened their flight path, then turned and soared back up the rock, maintaining precise formation.

Bill and Maria walked across the plateau towards the hut. The sheep skittered when they approached but went quickly back to munching the grasses. As they neared the hut, Bill saw two donkeys tethered on long ropes; the donkeys bore the marks on their backs of the wooden saddles the Cretans used for carrying heavy loads.

The hut was, in fact, two huts. One was little more than a shed, open on one side to the wind. One side of the shed carried a long low bench that appeared to have been made from stones, crushed and flattened and now covered with the small pine branches of the shrubs of the plateau. On the bench were round discs wrapped in straw. A flat stone pressed the top of each disc, and from the straw a thin whey was still dripping. Bill had eaten the cheese the mountain men made from ewe's milk and found it delicious.

As they drew near the second hut, attached to the side of the cheese-making shed, they saw the unglassed opening that served as a window and, inside it, the head and shoulders of a man. His face was deep-cut by wind and weather and tanned the shade of dark brown leather. His hair was grey and grizzled in tiny curls. He wore a white beard that he had obviously trimmed at regular intervals; he'd also shaved since his cheeks were smooth up to the hair line of his beard and moustache, which had been twisted and waxed at the ends.

Even sitting down, with only his head and shoulders visible, he gave the impression of a powerful man. His features, if anything, were larger than life, carved rather than moulded, formed by strength from within and violence from without. It was the face of a man who had suffered but had never been defeated, who had known extremes of emotion, who had loved and hated with a fierce passion, who had arrived at peace only through turbulence. He looked through and beyond them, as a man will see without looking, will hear without listening.

Maria opened the door and she and Bill went into the hut.

'We greet you,' she said formally, and the shepherd nodded his head.

He was sitting at a table rough-hewn from the trunks of trees. His chair, however, was incongruously like the chairs film directors use on the set, though its seat and back were of animal skin, not canvas. There was a bench – half a tree trunk supported on two rough-hewn logs.

On the table stood a pottery mug and a plate. Beside the plate was a segment of cheese and a piece of pan-fried corn-bread. Behind him the pipe of a stove extended to the ceiling, but to judge from the temperature in the hut it had not been lighted that day. Without speaking, he used the long knife on the table beside the plate to cut a piece of cheese for each of them and a section of the bread. Maria, without speaking, took two more pot mugs from a shelf above the door and placed them on the table. The Sfakian reached down, brought a glass carafe covered in straw from beneath the table and poured a little of its contents into each mug. He raised his mug and waited. Each of them took his own, and the Sfakian said 'Good health', without attempting to clink his mug against theirs. The mountain water was tastier than any wine would have been.

Only when she had taken a bite of the cheese and the bread did Maria speak. 'Kostas Dandanakis,' she said. '*Kirios* Kostas, I bring the Englishman to you.'

Kostas waved his hand quickly to silence the girl with a gesture of dismissal. His eyes were looking deep into Bill's features, as if trying to mesmerize him. Bill could read no expression on that gaunt, cleaved face in front of him. He stared back without blinking, without shifting his gaze, telling himself he must not permit himself to be intimidated.

A look of intense sorrow came into those dark eyes, a deep pain unlike anything Bill had ever seen in a human. It was the look a man sometimes sees in the eyes of a much loved dog, a look that says, 'I hurt and there is nothing you can do for me.'

'Get out,' Kostas Dandanakis said. He half-rose in his chair and, with shock, Bill saw the fresh blood on the man's trouser leg.

'Get out!' he said, his voice the rumbling of rocks. 'Get

71

out of here and leave me in peace. I know who you are. I can see your father in your face. Get out. Go away!'

He had risen to his feet and Bill could see another pain flit fleetingly across those patrician features. This was the normal pain caused by a wound. Now he could see the blood and the torn cloth of the man's trousers.

'You're hurt!' he said. 'You've hurt yourself!'

'What is that to you, *macropantalonades*!' Kostas said. Long trousers! – the term of contempt of all mountain men for those who come from the plains.

Maria had risen to her feet in fear.

Bill got up. 'Let me have a look at your leg for you,' he said.

The shepherd shouted, his deep bass voice thundering round the small hut, 'I do not need your help! Get out and leave me in peace!'

He started to come round the table towards them. Maria clutched Bill's arm and drew him towards the door. Bill backed slowly away from this giant man who was stumbling towards him and then suddenly found himself on the top step of the three that led from the hut to the ground beneath. He and Maria went down the steps and retreated a few metres from the hut. Kostas appeared in the doorway, waving a hand as mighty as a club at them.

'Go back down and leave me in peace,' he shouted, jerking his hand in the air to emphasize his words.

The violent action was his undoing. It caused him to twist in the doorway, to lose his precarious balance on his damaged leg, to fall headlong down the three steps, crashing his head on the flat stone of the path that led to the hut.

Bill and Maria ran forward. Kostas lay there inert, knocked unconscious by the violence of his fall. Bill looked at the leg which had twisted under the Sfakian. He pulled the cloth aside and looked with dismay at the end of a broken bone, protruding from the flesh. The Sfakian had broken his already damaged leg in the fall.

'Oh, my God!' Bill said. 'What are we going to do?'

He looked up when Maria didn't reply. She had her back towards him, looking towards the sky.

'What is it?' Bill asked.

She turned back to him, her face troubled. When he looked past her he saw the black clouds that already had filled half the horizon and were now racing across the sky towards them. As he watched, he saw a distant flash which he recognized as lightning.

The wind, which appears so suddenly on Crete, without warning, had already begun to lash across the plateau. The sheep were running, flocking together to seek protection at the base of the mountain. The tinny bells of the goats sounded as they ran to join the sheep; only one, tethered, could not move and began to bleat plaintively.

Within seconds, the first knife-like icy flurry of snow swept across the plateau in anticipation of the storm. The large flakes settled everywhere at once, though Bill knew that soon they would melt, taking the heat of the ground with them.

He looked at the donkeys; both were staring wild-eyed at the source of the storm, tugging at their tethers.

'If we could get him on the back of one of the donkeys,' Bill said, 'perhaps we could get him down to that other shelter – you remember, the one with the fire place – before the worst of the storm comes.'

'Perhaps we should stay here, safe in the hut?' Maria said. 'We never try to move in a storm.'

Bill looked at the leg, cursing his lack of medical knowledge. But something told him he ought not to let the man stay in that condition a minute longer than he could. He thought of gangrene, the loss of a leg. What would that do to a proud Sfakian, compelled to hobble about for the rest of his life on a crutch. The wound itself already looked dark and ugly. Kostas must have fallen somewhere on the rocks to gash himself as deeply as that; with no flesh to protect him, the fall from the hut, though short, had been sufficient to snap the exposed bone, doubtless brittle with age. He felt responsible; if he had not come to the plateau to disturb the shepherd's peace, the fall would not have happened. No doubt the mountain men had their own ways of curing superficial cuts and abrasions, even ones that went as deep as this one.

'We must try to get him down,' he insisted, 'or he will lose his leg.'

'You know the dangers?' Maria asked him. 'This is going to be a terrible storm. Not even a Sfakian would venture out in it. The first storms of the year are often the most violent.'

'We must try,' Bill insisted. 'We must. Or rather, I must. If you want to stay up here in the hut, I understand. There's no point in both of us running a risk. Just help me to get him up on the donkey, that's all.'

Maria looked at him and shook her head. The wind was howling now and the thick wet snow-flakes were falling all about them. She brushed them from her eyes.

'I can see you're stubborn,' she said. 'Come on. I'll help you. I'll go down with you.'

They lifted Kostas onto the back of the donkey, after Bill had tied his leg to a stick with a twisted head, the traditional shepherd's crook of Sfakia. Kostas's body was bent forward; using the string that had been hanging from the donkey's saddle, Bill tied his hands forward to keep his body more or less erect.

Maria gave Bill a stick. 'You'll need that,' she said. 'I don't know if you've ever tried to drive a donkey into a storm!' She took the donkey's bridle and led it forward. 'If it won't move,' she shouted back to Bill above the clamour of the wind, 'poke the stick up its arse!'

Bill had to do just that to get the donkey to start to move across the plateau; with Maria leading from the front with a tight halter and Bill occasionally jabbing the stick up the donkey's arse, they managed to get it across the plateau and on the start of the long, downwards trail. The donkey was more surefooted than they were and seemed to know the path by instinct. They would never have found it – already the flocculent snow had obliterated all obvious traces of it. Maria had moved to the side of the donkey's head when they had started the downward plunge; she held the donkey's ear with one hand and steadied Kostas's body with the other. Bill walked further back, his stick ready should the animal refuse, but once headed downwards, the donkey seemed to recognize it was going home and set a cracking, often dangerous, pace, sliding down part of the track, banging into rocks.

The side of the mountain was completely exposed to the full force of the wind and the snow, which covered them all from head to toe. Bill brushed the snow constantly out of his eyes, his limbs already numb with cold, his ears tingling with the sting of the violent blast.

Maria seemed better able to cope than he was; doubtless lessons learned in her childhood were coming back to her. She seemed able to hunch her head forward so that the impact of the snow on her face was lessened and to memorize the next short stretch of path so that she didn't need constantly to keep her eyes open forward. When the impatient donkey skittered too incautiously, she pulled its ear, often steering it out of danger by sheer force. Bill realized that he, too, was a passenger, that Maria was taking the brunt of the journey; without telling him, she had chosen the hazardous role. If the donkey were to slip uncontrollably, it would fall on Maria and could push her and crush her against a rock.

The wind howled viciously through the canyons they were traversing. Bill had lost all the feeling in his hands and his body, and was stumbling forward by instinct. He realized he was no longer urging the donkey forward but hanging on, being carried by the animal's lunging. When they reached the small grotto in which he'd seen the fireplace, Maria pulled the donkey into the partial protection of the overhanging rock. Bill reached up and wiped the encrustation of snow from Kostas's face. The Sfakian blinked his eyes open.

'You are fools,' he said. 'You ought to have stayed in the hut. The storm will last only two days.'

'In two days,' Bill snapped angrily, 'you would have lost your leg. Now shut up.'

Maria was rubbing her limbs with snow, trying to bring the circulation back. The temperature had dropped to freezing, all the heat taken from the air by the vicious blast of the wind coming across from the high mountain, the wind from the north. All the countryside was covered in that white, swirling cloud of death that blanketed all life.

'Will we make it?' Bill asked Maria.

The next section he remembered was the most steep, the most winding. They'd had enough trouble climbing some of the 45-degree slopes, moving cautiously from one foothold to the next. How they'd manage going down, not able to see the slope, let alone the footholds, he couldn't tell.

Kostas laughed, a deep rumble in his throat that cracked the snow from his upper lip. 'You've come so far,' he said, 'you must continue. If you stay here, we will all freeze once darkness comes. You are a brave fool, *Kirios* Thomas, like your father. Why are all the English such foolish adventurers?'

'You wouldn't speak of my father up there!' Bill said angrily. 'If you had talked with us, we would have still been in the hut with a fire going.'

'Get me down,' Kostas said. 'Let them mend my leg and I will talk to you. Then I'll tell you all you want to know about your father. I have seen the lust in your eyes. I can know why you are here. You want to find out the truth about him. Well, only I, Kostas, know the truth. I was with your father all the time, except once when he sent me away. I warned him what would happen but of course he would not listen to an ignorant Cretan. When they have put my bones together again, I will talk to you. That I promise. I will tell you everything I know. I owe you that, for your foolhardiness in bringing me down so that I would not lose my leg!'

The effort of speaking cost him dearly and he would have fallen off the donkey's back when he slumped forward, unconscious, had they not tied his hands to the pummel of the saddle. They set off again, but this time Bill insisted on taking the forward position, determined to do his share.

It was a nightmare journey with the donkey lunging forwards, often uncontrollably, sliding down the steeper passages often with its arse touching the snow, its voice braying, its eyes looking wildly about it. If the donkey had not instinctively known it was going home, nothing they could have done would have controlled it. Bill held on to its ear, trying to steer it during the worst slides, but often his feet slid from him and he went down the precipitous slopes on his back. Often only his grip on the donkey's ear prevented him from slipping to the bottom of the incline. Whenever he could be sure of his footing, he released his hard grip on the donkey's ear, stroked it, patted its snow-covered muzzle, breathed and talked into its ear, trying to soothe the excited, frightened animal. Gradually its braying ceased, almost as if the donkey could hear his words and understand the comfort he was trying to offer in their joint adversity. It settled into a determined rhythm of movement, taking more care to place its feet, angling its bulk round the worst of the rocks, occasionally pushing him into a safer track out of danger. Now Bill rode with his arm round the donkey's neck, completely exhausted, hanging on to the animal, drawing warmth, comfort and strength from it.

Bill looked back frequently: despite her mountain heritage Maria seemed to be faring little better than he and was hanging on to the animal's rump and the back of the saddle. The bulk of Kostas loomed over them, slumped forward in the wooden frame, his shoulders bending with each step of the way like thick rubber. His chin was down on his chest; his head a complete white cap of snow.

When they reached the village of Aghios Voutros they were too exhausted to do anything except stand by the donkey, in a total daze, unable yet to accept that they had made it through the storm. Men rushed out of the *kafeneion* and cut Kostas from the donkey, then helped Bill and

Maria up through the storm into the inside of the *kafeneion* where they had laid Kostas on a table.

Bill struggled with the arms holding him. 'The donkey?' he said. 'Look after the donkey!'

The Sfakian men laughed. 'The donkey will look after himself,' they said.

Bill wouldn't accept that. Despite their laughter he struggled back outside and went to the side of the *kafeneion*. The donkey was squatting beneath a wooden platform, lying on the ground protected from the storm, contentedly munching a handful of *horta* someone had kindly thrown to it. The donkey snickered when it saw him. Bill felt a fool as he bent his head under the shelter and breathed in the donkey's ear, the nearest he could get to saying thank you.

They telephoned from the *kafeneion* for an ambulance to take Kostas to the hospital in Xania. He had revived in the warm atmosphere lying on the bare table next to the stove in which a wood-fire was blazing. He'd drunk two glasses of *tsikoudia*, the strong liquor distilled from grape-skins, but was barely conscious of his surroundings. Bill and Maria had thawed out when the ambulance with its flashing blue light pulled up outside the *kafeneion*. Bill wanted to ride into Xania with Kostas but Maria dissuaded him. He didn't take much persuading; he was in no condition to travel anywhere at that moment. Now that the feeling had returned to his body he became aware of the many cuts and abrasions he had suffered on his way down the mountain. One of the Sfakians gave him a plastic bottle of merthiolate, and he went into the lavatory, stripped and smeared the red liquid on his cuts, none of which was very serious. But they all stung like hell!

He and Maria sat at a table and drank a couple of *tsikoudias*; the fiery liquid burned its way through them. The owner of the *kafeneion* brought them a *mezedes* of hard bread, cucumber and a piece of *feta* cheese. Gradually Bill felt the energy flowing back into him. When it finally returned, he felt better than he had for a long time.

Suddenly, with an almost physical shock, he realized he

had drunk *two* glasses of alcohol and was not craving for more.

The storm outside continued unabated and a festival atmosphere developed inside. One of the men produced a lyre from the back room and another a mandolin. The card games were forgotten, the *tavli* boards abandoned, and then one by one, as the drink flowed, the men began to dance. One man, a slight and almost unSfakian thin man they called Thanakis, began to dance a wild *sirtos* in the ring of men, leaping into the air, twisting his feet together in what seemed to Bill to be impossible contortions, reaching down vigorously and slapping his ankles with the flattened palm of his hand. The music grew wilder and wilder. Someone threw a plate into the centre of the ring of dancers and it smashed; there were whoops of joy as the men danced round the broken plate shards, and then another plate went in, then another. Bill sat there, mopping it all up in his joy, his ordeal down the mountainside temporarily behind him. And he realized that, after the first two drinks of the reviving *tsikoudia*, he hadn't taken – hadn't *wanted* – a single drink, even though almost all the men present had tried to pour some kind of liquor into his glass. He'd put his hand over the top at first, but they insisted. He'd let one man fill the glass with *ouzo*, but now the glassful of liquid was sitting there. Each time someone approached and said 'Good health', clinking the two glasses together, Bill returned an enthusiastic 'Good health', raised the glass to his lips but didn't drink. He didn't want a drink; he didn't need one – he was drunk, in a sense, on the relief of their escape from what must have been a frozen death, and in the warmth of the companionship of these men in this *kafeneion*, so unlike the welcome he'd been given in the *kafeneion* of Victorio.

He reached out his hand impulsively and Maria took it, gripping it tightly. Now that he had an opportunity to study her more closely, he could see she was older than he had first thought her, a mature woman only a year or two younger than he was. Now that they were closer together, he could see the lines on her face and could sense that she had suffered, that her maturity had been fire-forged by unhappiness.

'What went wrong with your marriage?' he said.

Some questions are better asked without preamble. After that struggle down the mountainside, he knew they would always feel a special closeness, two people who have survived death interdependently.

'My husband took our two sons on a trip round Washington by car. One holiday. He was going to show them the White House, the Monument, the Memorial – you know, all the usual tourist stuff. They got involved in a demonstration that had nothing to do with them. The car was turned over by a group of Communists and set alight. They were all burned. They were just tourists, passing through – the boys weren't old enough to know anything about politics – they didn't even know what the word meant!'

She was able to say it now but he could read on her face the suffering it must have caused her at the time. He squeezed her hand more tightly.

'I'm sorry,' he said, 'I ought not to have asked.'

She shook her head. 'It's okay now,' she said. 'At the time you feel bewildered. There's nothing you can do. You long to smash faces, to go out and do something active and aggressive to pay the bastards back!'

Thanakis pirouetted to their table. 'Come on, Englishman,' he said, 'come and dance with me.'

But Bill laughed ruefully. 'Dance, Thanakis? I'm lucky I can even walk, let alone dance.'

Stefano cursed the snow which piled onto the windscreen wipers, carrying a solid white wedge from side to side, preventing him from seeing the mountain road down which he was driving the ambulance with great care. The heavy Daimler's good tyres held the road as firmly as any vehicle could in this weather. Soon they would put on winter tyres with a thicker tread, but the storm had caught them all napping.

He pressed the switch for the hot air blower, trying to warm the windscreen sufficiently to melt the snow; so much was falling directly on to the windscreen that no hot air blower could hope to cope with the sheer volume of it. He leaned forward, squinting through the small space the wiper cleared each time. Yanni was sitting in the back with the patient. The wound in the man's leg was a nasty one; Yanni had almost been sick when he'd seen the ends of broken bone sticking out through the flesh. He, Stefano, was made of stronger stuff. 'Put the heater on full blast,' he'd said, 'but don't touch that wound except to cover it lightly with a gauze. With luck we can keep it partially frozen until we get him there and then the butcher can sort him out!'

'Butcher' was a term of affection; the bone doctor in Xania was one of the best on the island – if anyone could mend the Sfakian, he would.

Damn the snow! Damn the road which wound precariously. Luckily, the storm was keeping everybody indoors. Only one car had passed them, a big Mercedes that had blasted its way past them on the straight stretch, the damned fool of a driver risking his life to squeeze past.

If the driver of the Mercedes kept driving like that, they'd be picking *him* up at the side of the road and taking *him* down into the hospital.

The right of the road was a continuous slab of mountain rock; to the left of them nothing but the open chasm below. Stefano kept as far to his right as he could, though he was scared of encountering a fallen rock. Snow worked its way into the cracks, froze and thawed – a natural force as strong as a pneumatic drill; big slabs of rock always fell on the road during and after a snow storm.

He changed down for the bend, angled to the right.

Damn, the Mercedes was parked to the right of the road, its lights gleaming due to someone's foot on the footbrake.

Stefano eased to the left, near to the chasm, going slowly. He was level with the Mercedes when it started to move forward, pulling to the left, forcing the ambulance over.

Stefano hit the button that sounded the klaxon.

'Mother of God,' he muttered, 'is the damned fool drunk?'

He pressed the accelerator to bring himself clear of the Mercedes. The engine roared and the back wheels spun on the road as the ambulance leaped forward. The Mercedes roared, too, and swung to the left.

Stefano swung left. It was a mistake. He shouted loud, in frustrated anger, in the sure knowledge of his own error. He heard the crunch as the Mercedes hit the side of the ambulance, felt the left wheel dip, hit the brake but knew he was too late, tried to slam the gear into reverse but was too late, tried to swing the steering wheel to the right but was too late: the ambulance plunged over the edge of the sheer side of the rock, starting its somersault, then turning over and banging the side of the rock face, twisting, screeching as the metal body ripped, dropping from stone to stone, bouncing off the ledges, to finish up on its side, crushed, a hundred metres below the level of the roadway.

The Mercedes stopped and the driver climbed from it. He peered over the edge through the swirling snow. Already the cab of the ambulance was partially covered. Within minutes, he knew, it would be totally concealed from view in the ravine below.

He got back into the Mercedes, lit a cigarette, then slowly engaged the gear and drove down the road.

The wind howled after him; the snow flakes scurried down; the ambulance lay twisted on its side, immolated in the all enveloping storm.

Everyone in the *kafeneion* fell suddenly silent when the door opened, admitting a flurry of snow-flakes and a policeman, wearing a motor-cyclist's helmet, high black boots, striped trousers, and a black leather jacket. The policeman lifted his goggles to his helmet and peeled off his gloves. Outside, they could hear the muffled squawk of the radio on the police motorbicycle.

'Who called the ambulance?' he asked, his voice harsh in the silenced atmosphere.

'I did,' Thanakis said. 'At least, I was the one who used the telephone. But the ambulance has gone. At least an hour ago.'

'Who was the ambulance for?' the policeman asked.

Bill stood up. 'I brought a shepherd down from the mountain,' he said. 'He'd broken his leg in a fall. We brought him down, this lady and I.'

The policeman crossed to his table, then took a note-pad from his pocket, and a biro pen.

'Though you are a foreigner, you speak Greek!' he said, making it sound like an accusation.

'I learned it at university.'

'Ah, an educated man. Then perhaps you can tell me where the ambulance has gone, educated man.'

'To the hospital in Xania . . . ?' Bill said, perplexed. 'It took the shepherd, Kostas Dandanakis, to the hospital to have his broken leg mended.'

'What is your full name? Where are your papers?' the policeman asked.

'My name is Bill Thomas, and here is my passport,' Bill said, fumbling in the pocket of his jacket. 'But I don't see what that has to do . . .'

He was silent under the policeman's stare.

The policeman laboriously copied the details from Bill's passport into his note-pad. He checked every page, looking for the date of issue, the date of arrival in Greece, the physical characteristics. He held the passport next to Bill's face, checked the photograph against the face several times, then put his fingernail under the photograph and tried to prise it off, as if it were a false picture that concealed the true one beneath.

No one else in the *kafeneion* spoke.

'Look, tell me what this is all about?' Bill said firmly. 'Why are you examining my passport?'

The policeman ignored him. 'You telephoned for the ambulance?' he said to Thanakis.

'Yes.'

'Name?'

'Thanakis Sirkondakis.'

The policeman wrote that, too, laboriously in his book, then turned back to Bill. 'You say you brought a man called Kostas Dandanakis, a shepherd, down the mountain?'

'Yes.'

'In this storm?'

'Yes!'

The policeman's air of disbelief was obvious. 'Did anyone witness this?' he asked the room in general.

Maria spoke from the table, contempt in her voice. 'I came down with him,' she said. 'I am Maria Stafanakis. *Stafanakis*. Don't bother to write that on your pad. I'll ask my uncle, who is police chief of Maleme, to telephone it through to your officer. Now tell me, policeman, why are you asking these questions.'

He snapped his pad shut and put it in his pocket. 'Because, *Kiria* Stafanakis, the ambulance never arrived at the hospital. The ambulance does not answer its radio, and I have searched the road between here and Xania, looking for it, and can find no trace of it. I want to make certain the ambulance had been correctly called because of a genuine accident and not because of some wild game of the mountain men. Once a police car was stolen. We found it on the top of the mountain where it had been carried by hand. It took us two days, with a half-track crane, to get the car back again.'

The men of the village were grinning. All knew the exploit well. The men of the mountains have a high sense of humour and little respect for authority – anything that seems like a good practical joke is manna to them. In so many ways, they react to the hardship of their environment

84

to become almost like juveniles – it wouldn't have been too far-fetched for them to call out an ambulance and devise some high-spirited prank involving it.

'The ambulance left here with *Kirios* Dandanakis in it,' she said. 'You have my word for that. Perhaps the storm was so bad he couldn't get through. Perhaps he is parked somewhere waiting for it to subside . . .'

'*I* got through,' the policeman said pointedly.

No one could bring himself to put the other alternative into words – that the ambulance had gone over the edge of the cliff. But all were convinced that was what had happened.

Bill sat down, banging himself into the chair. He slapped his hand, palm flat, onto the table top, making the glasses jump. He picked up the glass of *ouzo* and looked at it. All that effort wasted. If he'd taken Maria's advice and they'd stayed on the mountain top . . . Kostas would most probably have lost the leg but, dammit, he'd still be alive . . . He bent his arm, brought the glass of *ouzo* near to his mouth, saw the bottle on the counter from which he could get another drink, then another drink, then another, until he could forget the face of that patrician Sfakian . . .

Then he felt Maria's hand on his wrist, the soft but determined touch of her fingers, and flung the glass of *ouzo* away from him, to bang and shatter against the wall, spraying its liquid wide.

'We'll walk down the road,' he said. 'We'll examine every inch of the way. If the ambulance went over the side, there must be some trace of where it left the road.'

They all went, knowing it was a futile search but unable not to make it.

Bill was lying on his bed in the pension that evening, trying to gather strength to go round the port to eat a fish supper with Manolis and Yannis, who kept a small taverna at the far end of the port where the fishermen brought part of their fresh catch. Ioannis had taken him there the first night he had arrived; they'd eaten sardines and salad, drunk lemonade. Tonight, Bill knew with certainty, he could drink a glass of wine.

He heard the timid knock on the door. 'Come in, Ioannis,' he said.

The door opened but the man who came in was a stranger. He was dressed in a suit and wore a tie. His suit was dark worsted and seemed to have been newly pressed, and his tie was tied with a small old-fashioned knot in the collar of a pure white shirt. His shoes had recently been polished.

'Mr Thomas?' he asked. 'Mr Bill Thomas?'

Bill swung his feet to the floor. 'Yes, that's me. Who the hell are you?' After the events of the day, he was in no mood to be polite.

The man seated himself on the second bed in the room, lifting his trousers fastidiously to avoid ruining the crease. 'I have one of those long, complicated Cretan names,' he said, 'so please just call me Petro and I will call you Bill.' His English was quite impeccable, without the slightest trace of an accent. 'You will be more interested, not by *who* I am but by *what* I am. I believe my equivalent rank in the Metropolitan Police Force, at Scotland Yard, would be detective superintendent. Today you were in a sense responsible for calling out an ambulance. That ambulance subsequently disappeared. I would be grateful if you would tell me everything that occurred prior to that ambulance leaving the village for Xania.'

Bill told the story as completely as he could, though he didn't deem it necessary to tell the superintendent *why* he had sought out the shepherd. He did not make any mention of his father, nor of the events in Kaprisses, none of which seemed relevant.

Petro listened intently, not interrupting except to clarify a point. 'And that is all you can tell me?' he asked when Bill had finished.

'I'm afraid so.'

Bill had described to him how they had walked the road for five kilometres until it became obvious even to him that they would find no traces until the snow had ended. The blizzard had continued until six o'clock, by which time Bill was back in Xania. As if to compensate for the violence of the day, the air was now quite warm for October. Bill noted that the superintendent did not appear to have brought a top coat with him.

'Isn't it rather strange that a man of the rank of superintendent should be investigating the loss of an ambulance?' Bill asked, suddenly intrigued. 'In England, that would be the job for a detective sergeant or an inspector.'

'In England, doubtless you have more men available than we do,' the superintendent said. 'As a matter of fact, two of my inspectors at this moment are in London, attending a course with Scotland Yard officers. I am taking this case only because we have a shortage of men today. And because the case intrigues me.'

'I think, sad though it may be, that the ambulance has gone over the edge of the cliff,' Bill said.

'Ah, what makes you think that?'

'I can't see any other logical explanation.'

'Ah, the well-known English love of logic. And if I were to tell you that you are correct . . . ? The ambulance *did* go over the cliff. I understand from what you said that you all made a search with the aid of my policemen but could see nothing because of the powdered snow. What if I were to tell you that, after your search ended, the snow stopped falling but the wind increased its velocity to a point at which it blew the powdered snow off the edge of the road, scooped it out of the valley, you might say, like a vacuum cleaner in reverse. We found the ambulance an hour ago. It had gone over the edge, as you believed. The three men in it were killed instantly in the fall.'

'Thank God for that,' Bill said bitterly.

So, he had been right. If only he'd left the Sfakian in the

hut, stayed up there with him, three lives would have been spared.

'I suppose the driver missed the road in the snowstorm?' Bill asked.

'Again, your English logic. Yes, that is the way it looked. But let me tell you a curious fact and ask you to explain the logic of it to me. When that ambulance left the hospital it was almost new, unmarked. The man who cleaned it this morning tells me there was not a single scratch or mark on the ambulance. Apparently he takes a great pride in it! I have been down that chasm and have examined the ambulance. I was taught forensic examination methods in England and America. There is a scratch down the side of that ambulance. The scratch was made, not by a rock, but by the impact of another car. The other car was painted black. It was going in the same direction as the ambulance. It is my belief the ambulance was pushed off the edge of that road. Now, what is your logical answer to that?'

After the superintendent had gone, Bill sat on the small balcony that abutted his room. The evening *volta* was well under way as the hundreds of people from Xania walked up and down along the strip of roadway between the numerous restaurants and tavernas and the water's edge. Mercifully motor cars and the ubiquitous ear-shattering motor-bicycles were banned from this part of the town from sundown to midnight; the scene below reminded Bill of the paintings of Lowry or of Breughel, as the myriad moving people formed and reformed an endless variegated swirl of humanity.

He felt from what the superintendent had said that the accident to the ambulance had been deliberate. Petro had not taken such a strong line; using Bill's own logic against him he had pointed out that it could have been nothing more criminal than careless driving in a horrendous storm, a single act of stupid thoughtlessness. Motor cars, like

88

telephones, had come late to the Cretans; the rate of traffic accidents is as high as anywhere else in the developing world. Petro said all his men had been alerted to look for a car that had been involved in a recent collision. The ambulance had been painted white over green; the car that hit it must have been marked by the white and green paint combination. He didn't offer much hope; cars are very expensive on the island of Crete and old models are kept in service longer than elsewhere. The Cretan hasn't yet adopted the habit of the weekly clean and polish, of eliminating every scratch, and most cars bear the marks of their passage through the streets.

Bill heard what Petro said but couldn't accept it totally. It had been his own experience that people driving in a storm were ultra-careful, not careless. Though he could find no logical reason for it, he was convinced the collision had been deliberate.

But why? And against which of the three people in the ambulance was the collision intended. Could it be a vendetta against the driver, Stefano? The medical orderly, Yanni? It seemed hardly likely that Kostas, living alone on a mountain-top out of touch with the world, could have provoked such savage feelings.

Bill took the papers he had brought with him from London out of his briefcase. The photo-copies of his father's Army records, the citation he had received, his personal documents. A name leaped at him from the citation. General Spiros Orfandakis. Old soldiers never die! The line of the jingle came back to him. He went quickly downstairs to where Ioannis was sitting in the reception room of the pension.

'Does the name of General Spiros Orfandakis mean anything to you, Ioannis?' he asked.

'Yes. He was very big in the last war. Now he lives in the *nome* of Lasithi. A great leader of the *palikari* of the Resistance. Everybody on Crete knows that name – it is like saying "Monty" to an Englishman or "Ike" to an American. He was a strong Royalist!'

'You say "was". Is he dead?'

'Not that I have heard. In the time of Venizelos, he retired from the Army and left politics. I believe he lives in Aghios Nikolaos, at the other end of the island – I seem to remember he opened a restaurant that does very well with the tourists. Why do you ask?'

'He knew my father well enough to recommend him for a medal to the Army Command in Cairo. If he is still alive, he may be able to tell me things about my father. Tomorrow, I'll go to Aghios Nikolaos to see if I can find him.'

While they were sitting there, talking, the telephone rang. Maria was on the other end of the line, calling from a *kafeneion* in Kaprisses.

'I wanted to ask how you are?' she said. 'After your ordeal today?'

'I'm okay,' Bill said. 'How are you?'

'It all comes back. I remember the many times I was caught in such a storm as a young girl, how afraid I was. Once, I disobeyed the rule and tried to get down through the storm as we did today, but I had no donkey. I got lost and spent the night huddled between two of our sheep. I was thinking about those days and wondered how you were.'

'Tomorrow,' Bill said on impulse, 'I'm going to Aghios Nikolaos to try to find General Spiros Orfandakis. He was one who recommended my father for his medal. Would you like to come with me?'

'I would love to,' Maria said with immediate enthusiasm. 'How will you go?'

'I'll drive the car.'

They arranged to meet in the village of Vrisses, on his way to Rethymnon along the new road that is virtually a motorway along the north coast of the island. They stopped for lunch on the way and reached Aghios Nikolaos by six o'clock in the evening. A tourist policeman was standing near where Bill parked the car. Bill asked him if he knew the present whereabouts of *Kirios* Orfandakis.

'He will be in his restaurant, I expect,' the policeman said. 'Usually he sits just outside the door, organizing the waiters with military precision and drinking ouzo or wine.'

'What sort of a man is he?' Bill asked. 'May I approach him to speak with him about something that happened in the past?'

The policeman laughed, looking at Maria. 'If you can get close to him,' he said, 'for he has many friends who stop to talk and drink an *ouzo* with him. You have good means of attracting his attention. The General has always had an eye for a fine woman!'

Maria laughed, too, and full of hope she and Bill walked to the restaurant the tourist policeman had indicated. It commanded almost the whole of one side of a small inlet in which many tourist boats were parked. The terrace of tables and chairs at street level was fifty metres long and ten metres deep. Steps rose to the interior of the restaurant, which had long deep glass windows closed at this time of year. The main tourist boom had ended but there were still sufficient people to populate the quayside, though most were wearing some kind of woollen sweater or pullover.

The table just outside the door was empty.

'I guess the General takes a siesta,' Maria said. 'No doubt he'll arrive later now that the high season is over. We could sit down somewhere? Take an ouzo?'

She looked sideways at him. On their way from the *kafeneion* yesterday, he'd told her the whole story of the death of his wife, the way he still blamed himself. His return to London to live, his slide into alcoholism, his arrests for being drunk and disorderly, his accidental meeting, in Bow Street Magistrate's Court, with an old school chum who had become a probation officer. And Anna, the probation officer's wife, who herself had been in a car accident, damaging her spine, and now would spend the rest of her life in a wheel-chair. Seeing the courage with which Anna had coped with her problems, including her own drinking, had helped him enormously. It was

Anna who had suggested he come to Crete, to search out the story of his father. 'Perhaps, when you find out who and what your father was,' she had said, 'you'll know who and what you are!'

'I can take an *ouzo*,' he said lightly, 'but I don't particularly want one. I'd be happy to drink a lemonade while you take an *ouzo*!'

She put her hand in his. It seemed to fit naturally.

'Let's just walk,' she said. 'I feel a bit stiff after the long ride; a walk will stretch our muscles.'

They wandered for an hour around the small inlets and bays of Aghios Nikolaos, past the fishing port and the ferry embarkation port. Mostly they talked about their lives in America, to which Bill had returned after his university education. He'd drifted professionally, working with a TV network in New York, a publishing house in Boston, an advertising agency in Chicago, where he'd met his future wife. They'd gone together to the Coast where he'd taken a teaching post in Berkeley.

As he talked, describing what he had done, Bill realized that all his adult life he'd been unsettled, moving from one job to another, never certain in which direction his future lay. Of course, he'd always had the income from the trust fund his father had set up and this, in a way, had promoted his instability. He'd never had to worry at the end of the month; he'd never had to struggle to earn his livelihood in the face of fierce competition. Had this, perhaps, contributed to the ease with which he'd fallen into alcoholism after the death of his wife?

The figure of the general was unmistakable when they returned to the restaurant. Most of the tables in the upper room were already filled, though the hour was early for eating on Crete. The tourists came first; later the tables would fill with Cretans and Greeks from the mainland.

Spiros Orfandakis was unmistakably a Sfakian, far from his native mountains. His features bore so much resemblance to those of Kostas Dandanakis that Bill drew in his breath. Despite his apparent age, the general's hair was still jet black and his deepset eyes had the penetrating gaze of mountain men everywhere. He was sitting with his back to the door beside the wall, his eyes flicking. Every waiter who passed him received some instruction, some admonition. 'Bread on number seven, quickly,' he'd say. 'More *krassi* for twenty-five.' He was a military overlord with his eye on the ebb and flow of the battle. Two other men were sitting at his table, drinking *ouzo* with him and eating the inevitable small *mezedes* of a sardine, a shrimp, a piece of cucumber, tomato and cheese with the hard-baked bread.

As Bill and Maria walked up the line between the outside tables, a dozen or so of which were occupied in the warm-for-October evening, the two men rose, extended their hands and left. Bill seized his opportunity and walked up to the general's table, Maria trailing behind him. He saw the general's eyes flick over and beyond him, fixing over his shoulder at the face of Maria.

'*Kalispera*, General Orfandakis,' Bill said.

'*Kalispera*. But it is Spiros Orfandakis. I hung up my baton many years ago.'

Maria added her good evening, and the general half-rose in his seat with great courtesy when he returned her words. 'Will you sit and take a glass of *ouzo*?' he asked.

It was the last complete sentence he spoke during their entire conversation. Bill quickly learned to interpret only the phrases which related to them, ignoring the spattered commands strung like pearls along the general's speech pattern.

'This *ouzo* . . . Clear Number 7, you dolt . . . comes from my own . . . Will you let Number 9 die of thirst? More *krassi* . . . vineyard. I hope you like it . . . Take those shrimps back and put a slice of lemon with them, you savage.'

'I have come from Xania to see you,' Bill said.

'Then you've either . . . heard of my moussaka . . . which I doubt . . . or you are a military historian . . . in which case I am at your disposal . . . though I assure you I know nothing . . . but I am happy to talk to anyone . . . who

93

brings such a beautiful woman . . . to grace an old man's table.'

'My name is Bill Thomas,' Bill said. 'My father was Captain Roger Thomas. His code-name on Crete was Maleta. You recommended him for a medal.'

The general thought, though the stream of instructions from his mouth did not abate. 'I remember your father,' he said. 'I might not have done so, but you bear a strong resemblance to him – it might almost be Maleta sitting opposite me at the table. How may I help you?'

Bill felt a wave of relief. 'I want to find out everything I can about my father. I know I have left it a long time, but I want, if possible, to learn what kind of man he was. I want to get to know him.'

'That will be very difficult,' the general said.

'I intend to find as many people who knew him as I can. If they will all talk with me I shall be able to put together a picture from the mosaic of their words . . .'

'Ah,' the general said. 'Your father also was a good man with words. Without meaning to be so, he was a great charmer. We were not always together here on Crete during the war, though we avoided many of the problems of the mainland. But here, too, we had our Royalists and our Socialists, and very often they seemed to be fighting for different things rather than combining to fight the common enemy, the Germans. Your father helped me a lot with his charm. He could negotiate very well between the Communists and the Royalists.' The general chuckled. 'Sometimes, again without meaning to, he used his charm to his own advantage . . .'

'How do you mean?' Bill asked.

'The girls of Crete were very susceptible in those days,' the general said, still chuckling. 'There are many small episodes in my life I am going to have to talk to the priest about before Charon gets me!'

This was a new aspect of his father that Bill hadn't thought of. He'd concentrated, in a sense, on the story of his father as a hero or a coward, a strong man or weak. He hadn't thought of his father as possibly a womanizer, a charmer, a negotiator between two hard military factions.

'How long will you stay in our village?' the general asked him.

Bill looked at Maria. 'Just as long as it's necessary,' he said.

Maria nodded. 'I'm in no hurry to get back,' she said.

The general waved his arm. 'You can see how it is here,' he said. 'And from now on the pace increases. It is better if you come to my house tomorrow morning. There we can talk. There, also, I have papers, some drawings, even some old photographs. I believe one or two of them are of your father . . .'

'I'd want especially to see those,' Bill said, his eyes gleaming with anticipation.

'Come to the house at ten o'clock – no, eleven. I will look through my cabinets for a few things I think will help and interest you, and then we can talk. Your father was that rare thing, a brave and frightened man. That is why I recommended him for the medal. Any stupid fool can be brave if he doesn't know fear, doesn't know the dangers involved. The man who knows fear, who conquers it and is brave, then he is a hero . . .'

'And my father was a hero . . . ?'

'That is something, my young friend, that you must find out for yourself. Just as I found out for myself, in that spring-time of 1943, over there in the *nome* of Xanion. I remember, spring came early after the worst winter we had known in my lifetime. Or perhaps that was just our impression, after two years of occupation by an enemy who proved himself more evil, more vicious, more cruel than even the hated Turks . . .'

The Germans had established an observation- and gun-post high in the Lefka Ori from which they could control several of the mountain passes used to smuggle escaped prisoners down to the embarkation points of the south, Chora Sfakion, Loutron, Aghia Roumeli. The gun-post was on a mound outside a village; using forced labour throughout the long arduous winter, the Germans had built a concrete emplacement with a 360-degree view of the mountains.

Maleta lay on the flat surface of a rock, his glasses in his hand shielded from reflection. Pakrades lay behind him, Kostas Dandanakis to his right.

'You say they've laid mines round the block house?' Maleta asked.

'Yes. The bastards did that themselves after they had driven all the workers away, in case anyone made a note of where each one was placed.'

'But the Germans make a passage through the mines, twice every day. Once in the morning when they go on duty, once each evening when the night patrol takes over.'

It wasn't a question; Maleta himself had been lying on this rock for two days and two nights, observing. Pakrades had cooked food for him and had struggled up the mountain path to bring it, unobserved, to him.

Maleta had sent back a message; Kostas had coded it and had sent it to Cairo, giving information about the bunker. Cairo had sent its directive which Kostas had uncoded and had brought up to Maleta. He took the paper from his pocket and read it again.

'The village must be evacuated, the bunker destroyed. There will be a drop of explosives for your use at FLYBLOWN shortly after dusk on the evening of the 8th. General informed.'

96

General, Maleta knew, was the code-name for Spiros Orfandakis, the man who controlled the partisan side of their activity in the *nome*, a man of whom even Manoletto was afraid. *General* was a Sfakian, a man of immense personal strength and political power.

Now that he had received his instructions, he could end the observation. He scrambled back from the rock and went down the path that led to a cave behind and below them. They'd been using the cave for a few weeks as a headquarters for meetings with the men of the village, Manoletto, even the general himself.

They were sitting round waiting for him when he arrived.

'What does Cairo say?' the general asked without preamble. 'I have asked that fool of a man of yours, Kostas, but he would not tell me even though I threatened to beat it out of him!'

Maleta looked at Kostas and grinned. He and Kostas had achieved an understanding during the past few months and he knew the Cretan's loyalty to him was unswerving.

'Cairo says we must evacuate the village and destroy the bunker,' he said.

Elias groaned; he'd guessed what the answer would be.

'We have twenty old men, forty women, and sixteen children there,' he said. 'Two of the old men and four of the old women can no longer walk.'

'Then they must be carried.'

'Carried, at dead of night, with Germans everywhere? We have no donkeys; the Germans, no doubt anticipating something like this, have driven them all away. They have killed all our sheep. The villagers are starving, but still they want to remain, even to die, in their own houses.'

'They must be made to move; the weak must help the strong to carry those who cannot walk,' Maleta said.

'Who will take the explosives, Maleta?' Manoletto said. 'It will not be easy, crawling through a minefield with explosives in your hand. The Germans drop the shutters on the slits at night; the explosives will have to be placed

97

inside by hand. My men will storm the barracks in the village as soon as the block-house is blown. We will kill every last German in there, but who will carry the explosives to the block-house?'

'I will,' Maleta said quietly.

And so the plan was made. The explosives would come from Cairo on the 8th. The block-house would be attacked on the 9th. The evacuation of the villagers would begin at dusk, though some with legitimate reasons would walk quietly away from the village during the daylight hours and not return. Many of the young women would go into the fields during the day to pick spring *horta* and would not return. At dusk, the exodus would begin.

'No one will take anything,' the general said. 'It will only need one German to catch one person carrying something of value and they will guess there is to be an exodus. Everything will be left behind!'

Elias didn't like that. 'It is enough, surely, that we make people leave their homes without forcing them to abandon the simple treasures they own, the piece of embroidery, the photographs of departed ones . . .'

'Everything!' the general roared. 'If I catch one man, one woman, carrying anything, I will shoot that person as a traitor!'

Only when the exodus was completed would the partisans of the Resistance move into the village, surrounding the German barracks in the school attached to the church. Everyone knew what would happen the moment the block-house was blown. The German armoured columns would storm up the road from Vrisses and the German dive-bombers would take off from the Akrotiri; within an hour the village and anybody still left in it would be burned or blown to death. Most of the villagers would disperse over the mountains to Arevitis, Vatoudiares, even as far as Drakona and Therison.

The exodus began on time; approximately thirty percent of the residents of the village had managed to leave by dusk and the rest left soon after. Those who could not walk were carried between four people on improvised stretchers; during the day, one by one, they'd been moved to houses on the edge of the village to make their escape that much easier.

The village force was commanded by Major Gsteinoff, a hard-line Prussian career officer who hated the demotion his assignment up in the mountains had meant. He'd spoken out of turn about the softness of the garrison force in Rethimnon; this distant posting had been his reward. He was a swaggering brute of a man, always impeccably dressed, demanding military-style subservience from all the villagers.

The village priest had invited him and his senior officers to dinner on the night of the 9th. He wanted to serve them a twenty-years-old local wine and to discuss ways in which local collaboration with the German forces could be achieved. At least, that was his story. On a signal from the block house, the priest would retire from the room into which Manoletto's men would toss a bunch of hand-grenades.

Maleta watched the German officers walk from their quarters in the priest's house on their nightly tour of inspection. When it was completed, they went back and the light was switched on in the priest's dining room. The watch had already changed in the block-house. Ten men occupied it during the night and mostly spent their time reading and playing Muehle or cards. Elias had arranged for the Germans to find a cache of *tsikoudia* that day; the Germans had confiscated the barrel and it had been opened during *Abendbrot*. The Germans going on duty were maintaining their steadiness under the major's inspection with some difficulty. Elias had estimated the last person would leave the village by ten o'clock. From ten to half past, the partisans would take up positions around the barracks.

Maleta felt the light tap on his arm that said go. He was lying on the ground behind a rock at the edge of the block-house perimeter. Behind him the cliff-face of the back of the mound fell sheer. The explosives were in a sack on his back – three metal cylinders, each four inches long and one inch in diameter, the largest size that would fit through the block-house slits. He started his crawl across the mined ground, fear drying his mouth like blotting paper. As he crawled forward, lying flat on his belly, his hand searched the ground in an arc in front of him.

The night was black, with clouds hiding moon and stars alike, the darkness before him so intense he couldn't even make out his own hands, stretched on the ground in front of him. He probed carefully, left and right in an arc, remembering lessons learned in the Commando training in Achnacarry in Scotland. Then, it had all seemed a game; and no one had ever thought that one day he'd be lying on his belly playing the game for real. And for keeps. One mistake and there'd be nothing left of him.

The ground over which he was crawling was uneven and consisted mostly of rock. Here and there, however, were the pockets of earth you find in any mountain landscape, often no more than a sifting of finer material into a fissure, the home of a bulb, a flower clinging precariously to life, wild garlic, a minute thyme shrub.

Nothing. After he'd completed the arc once in each direction, he humped his body forward, keeping his feet together, trying to compress his body into as thin a cylinder as possible. Nothing again. Hump forward again. He was wet through with fear-sweat that clogged his face and eyes, and drenched his arm-pits and arms, his crotch. It's true, he thought. When you're really afraid you do want to shit yourself. He knew a small amount of piss had leaked from his bladder the first time he'd come to an obstruction he thought was a mine head. It turned out to be a piece of stone.

The object his fingers had just felt wasn't a stone. It felt too cold for that. Too regular. He could feel the hard edges of it, estimated it to be circular, about two centimetres. Gently he began to remove the soil around it; the looseness of the soil was another clue. You could hardly expect a mine-layer to tamp the soil around his mine with his foot, like a gardener planting. The cylinder of metal was vertical in the soil. He slowly cleared soil, then hefted himself further forward so that his face was only inches from the mine.

The smell came suddenly, foetid in the night air. Damn, he'd shit himself! He felt a flush of shame, knowing he'd have to face the other men, soiled, if he managed to escape. For a wild moment he wanted the mine to explode, to save him from the contempt he felt he'd read in the Cretans' eyes.

As he tickled the soil away, the cylindrical metal object slipped to the side. Damnation, a booby trap. Even though he was so close, he flung his hands over his head and pushed his face into the ground, already counting.

Most of them have instantaneous fuses, especially if booby-trapped, as this one must have been.

Nothing. The stink of his body. Nothing. From somewhere, the sound of water gently running over rocks. Nothing. Men inside the block-house laughing, and still nothing. The chink of a boot on a stone behind him, and finally it came to him the object he'd found had not been a mine-head but a piece of iron from a concrete reinforcing rod . . .

'He put it in his pocket,' Spiros Orfandakis said to Bill, 'and brought it back with him. He was wrong about one thing. We didn't despise him for shitting himself. It proved to us what a *man* he was, to be able to do what he did and still feel the fear to shit himself. He kept on crawling. The gods of war were kind to him; Charon kept his distance and your father found no mines in his path. He lobbed the three cylinders through the windows; they were a new design with an instantaneous heating fuse wound round inside them. The canister, two seconds after lighting, became a sticky mass no man could lob back. He cleaned out the block-house; we killed all the officers. We took Gsteinoff out of the village with us; the major died slowly and *he* messed *his* pants, but your father knew nothing of that. He was swimming in a mountain spring, cleaning himself!'

The general was seated in his study, looking east over the end of the island of Crete. He could see lights moving along the road to Elounda; beyond them a fishing boat out in the Gulf of Mirabellou, heading home from the island of Psira, showed the red, the green and the white at mast head.

The papers were spread all about him, the photographs he had promised to select to show to the son of Maleta. How the young man had brought memories back to him! Memories of his youth before Crete had known the tourists who now provided his income. He felt a nostalgia for the Lefka Ori where he had been born; the peaked, rugged countryside, the high mountain range that separated the north from the south, the boys from the men! Because no man of the mountains, and of the south, would admit to kinship with these softer men from the flat plains of the north!

All those war years spent hiding in the mountains and moving constantly whenever they suspected their locations had become known to the Germans. Always, endlessly it seemed, waiting for the Allies to move, to organize an invasion. He'd trained his men well; they would be ready for the invasion when it came. He'd had his problems; some of his men were not up to standard, some of them not entirely trustworthy. And then he had difficulty with the ELAS men, the militant wing of the Communists, who wanted to place themselves ready to take the towns of Xania, Rethymnon, Heraklion.

He'd got on all right with Theodor Karfounis. Tomorrow, he noted, he must give the young Englishman all this material he had on Karfounis. He'd known Maleta was supporting Karfounis; it hadn't taken the wily old general – well, young as he'd been in those days, but still wily – long to work out that Maleta was playing a double game, no doubt on orders from Cairo. Maleta was trying to bring the Communists and the right wing together, and damned well succeeding. Look how he'd brought the general and Karfounis together. If any man could unite the two factions, it was Maleta; this shy, diffident but iron-rod hard man who'd dropped in among them – well, actually he'd arrived by boat – as a raw young man. And, on first sight, it looked as if his son, Bill, were made of the same tough material. Yes, he must definitely talk to Bill about Karfounis.

Whatever happened to Karfounis? the general mused.

He heard the knock on the front door. Dammit, this evening he was alone in the house. His manservant and wife had been given permission to attend a wedding. He got up and walked slowly to the door, opened it wide and looked at the man standing there.

'Do I know you?' he asked.

The man shook his head. The general noticed the man was wearing white cotton gloves. That is odd, the general thought. It is not cold enough tonight for gloves.

'No, General, you don't know me,' the man said. 'But maybe you'll recognize this?'

He reached into the pocket of his jacket and produced a gun.

The general had seen enough guns in his time to know when the hand holding it belongs to someone who means business.

'Yes, I recognize it,' he said. 'It is a Colt ·45. I had one during the last war. I have still got it.'

'But not on you, I hope. You see mine is in my hand, and loaded.'

'If you are going to rob me, then be quick and get about it. I have 100,000 *drachmae* in a wall cupboard in my study. Plenty of things around the house of value on the market. You had better come in, I suppose,' the general said.

'You still have your military appreciation, General,' the man said, smiling. 'If you can't halt the enemy advance, draw him forward, keep him on the move, cut off his retreat, hit him while he's off balance and least suspects it . . .'

'Something like that. Okay, come in. I'll go first into my study and sit down. You can tie me to the chair or whatever you do. I don't want to be hit or shot. Not for a miserable 100,000 *drachmae*. I can see you're not Cretan. This is the first time I've known of any crime in Aghios Nikolaos. Occasionally a young man runs away with a motor-bicycle or even someone else's car, but that's either high spirits or there's a girl involved . . .'

Keep on talking, the general thought. Keep him off-balance. Inside the door of his study was the iron bar he used for propping open the shutter; if only he could reach that, step aside, grab it and swing. The shot would go past him; by the time this intruder had recovered his balance, the general would have smashed the iron bar into him. And then he'd show the miserable bastard just how a Sfakian can fight, even one so old as Spiros Orfandakis . . .

But the man was a professional, and a good one, cold as ice. He stepped to the side of the general and kicked him hard behind his knee, where the blow wouldn't show. The general lurched forward, off-balance. The professional moved in and caught the general's lower arm, pulling it backwards. The general spun, falling forward, completely off-balance, and his forehead smashed into the wall with all his weight behind it. He was out cold when the professional bent over him and dragged him into his study. He saw the iron bar behind the door and laughed – he'd expected something like that – the general shouldn't have flexed his right hand as he walked along. He lay the general out on the floor behind his desk, took a quick look at the photographs and the documents with which the table was littered. They meant nothing to him.

In one corner of the room, behind the general's desk, was a stove on wheels that gave out a modest blast of heat. He lifted the top and saw the gas bottle which fitted there.

The house was old, with a wooden floor, wooden beams, a wooden ceiling. The furniture it contained was all wooden. He took a bent-wood chair which had iron fittings. The fittings would not burn; they'd be found near the metal of the stove during the forensic examination. He placed the chair within inches of the stove, which he turned up to full heat. Then he piled papers on the seat of the chair and on the floor beside it.

He lit one paper, and when it was sufficiently charred he blew out the flame. The heavy smoke rose as he held the paper near the general's nostrils; the general's deep breathing sucked the smoke into his lungs. When he began to stir, the professional clamped his hand around the general's wind-pipe and quickly strangled him.

If they found enough of the body left to conduct an autopsy, they'd find traces of smoke in the general's lungs, positive proof, they'd say, that he'd died as a result of the fire.

When the paper on the chair, which was already smoking, caught alight with the heat of the gas stove, he drew the curtains on the window, noting the cars passing along the road below and the fishing boat sailing across the water before the curtains swished closed.

Then he let himself out by the front door and walked unhurriedly down the drive, towards where he'd parked his car in the entrance to a citrus-fruit grove about a kilometre away.

Bill and Maria ate in the general's restaurant, then checked into the pension that occupied two floors above it. They found a pharmacy still open in the streets behind the port and bought toothpaste and brushes, a comb, soap, a face-cloth.

The room they'd been given overlooked the port. They sat on the terrace and watched the life ebb out of the night, holding hands, talking only inconsequentially about the people they could see walking below. The violent storm of the previous day had not touched this end of the island.

The night air was warm for October and balmy with the odours of the ocean, the scents of the plants and, from time to time, the more earthy smell of frying fish and the smoke from charcoal grills.

It was well past midnight before they could bring themselves to go into the tranquil cave of the room. When they stepped inside, he took her tenderly in his arms.

'I came looking for my father,' he said softly, 'looking for myself. And found you!'

'We found each other,' she said.

'I want you.'

'I want you, too.'

'There hasn't been a woman in my life since my wife died!'

'There have been men in my life, but they weren't important.'

He pulled two of the single beds together, and they undressed in the soft night light.

When they held each other close, in the bed, with only a sheet to cover them, neither felt an immediate lust. Just a desire to hold and be held, to wrap their arms about each other and join their skins in comfort. When he kissed her there was no immediate passion, only a strong desire for a deeper union than mere skin contact. But soon their kisses turned subtly into a questing hunger. He caressed her breasts and found her nipples hardening, just as the flesh of his body was hardening with want.

When they lay together and he entered her, she gave a long shuddering sigh of pleasure. They made love gently and generously, each seeking to take and to give the maximum of pleasure. Bill knew he would need to learn all over again; loving one woman, and one woman only, leads to a singular technique, its tested actions producing known responses. With Maria he was anxious to try everything, prolonging the pleasure and the agony, withholding the final part of himself for as long as possible in the exquisite sensation the knowledge of her body gave him. Maria shared this feeling; when some movement he made proved too dangerously tempting, too orgasmic in its potential, she would murmur, 'No, no, not yet.' They became like two people on a swing, daring each other to go higher and higher without toppling finally over the edge into space.

But then neither could delay it any longer; the rhythm became pulsing and regular, driving onwards inexorably towards the single point of flashing explosion with both of them gasping and exclaiming simultaneously as his hands dug into her shoulders and he felt the sharp clutch of her fingernails. And, for a while, for both of them it seemed as if the shuddering release of their joint orgasm would never end.

They lay side by side, exhausted, their arms and legs still awkwardly intertwined where they had fallen apart but still together. Both lay without moving, but then the circulation in his arm began to go and he was obliged to move to avoid cramp. As he liberated his arm from beneath her shoulders, he bent over and kissed her, finding her face as wet with perspiration as his was. He reached across her and took the towel from the night table, wiping her face gently with it and then his own.

Side by side but intertwined, they fell asleep.

When they arrived at the general's house the following day they found it surrounded by a crowd of more than five hundred people. The fire brigade had brought its two pumping engines and a unit of the army had turned out, but none of their efforts had been able to save the building, which had been completely gutted by fire.

The general had died in his sleep, no doubt asphyxiated by the smoke.

His manservant, a former sergeant who'd looked after the general for forty years, had been granted a night's leave of absence to go with his wife to the wedding of his grandson. The house had still been blazing when he returned, at six o'clock, to make the general's breakfast coffee. He'd dashed into the blazing building to try to rescue the general but the flames had beaten him back. Now, with the hair on his head singed and third degree burns on his arms and shoulders, he was in the hospital in Aghios Nikolaos and not expected to live.

Bill felt sick as he stood with Maria, looking at the still smouldering ruins. Though he'd only met the general once, he could feel the loss of such a fine man, the unnecessary waste of such a purposeful life.

Maria crossed herself as she stood there, tears streaming down her face.

'Come on,' Bill said. 'Let's go back to Xania.'

Bill arrived in Xania in the late afternoon. Maria had insisted he drop her at Vrisses so that she could catch the afternoon bus back to her village. He had wanted to drive her but she'd laughed and said, 'That's not necessary. Here on Crete, we're used to taking the bus and, to be frank with you, after driving an American car, I'm happy to take a back seat . . .'

'And let us do the driving . . .' he said, recalling the Greyhound slogan.

Despite the great sadness of the death of the general, they had been very happy together that day, happy in the companionship each gave the other and the sense of closeness with another person that both, without defining it, had missed for some time.

'I have to go back to my village,' she said. 'I want to go back, on my own, to think about you, among other things. I knew what I wanted to do when I came back to Crete after living in America. Perhaps start a business of my own, go back to womanly things like weaving on a loom. Now that I've met you, I'm not so sure what I want any more. I'm going to have to think about it. And that's best done on my own!' She'd touched the side of his face. 'You have a much stronger personality than you know,' she said; 'at least, to me. I find you very disturbing. I'm not yet sure I want my peace disturbed.'

Bill stretched out on his bed. The pension was silent and there was no sign of Ioannis. He was drifting off into sleep when he heard the tap on the door.

'Come in,' he called and was surprised to see the detective superintendent, Petro.

This time, Petro was wearing a pair of khaki cotton trousers and a white shirt open at the throat. Sandals on his feet and no socks. He could have been a fisherman or a tourist, anything but a policeman.

Bill struggled upright on his bed, rubbing the sleep from his eyes.

'I am sorry if I disturb you,' Petro said.

'That's all right. I was tired – I've just driven from Aghios Nikolaos.'

'It is a long road,' Petro said sympathetically. 'How did you like that end of the island?'

'Not very much. I like the mountains of the Lefka Ori better.'

'That must be why you look so sad . . .'

'No. I met a man down there, last evening. Today I discovered the man was dead, killed in a fire in his house. Although I only met him briefly last night, it seemed such a tragedy.'

'You mean Spiros Orfandakis . . . ?'

'Yes.'

Bill guessed the news of the death would have been broadcast on the Cretan radio, since the general was such a well-known public figure.

'It *is* a tragedy,' Petro said. 'Spiros Orfandakis was one of the great men of Crete. We cannot afford to lose men like that. You know we have elections soon. Some people were hoping to persuade Spiros Orfandakis to come back into public life, as the right-wing candidate. He was wasted, running that restaurant in Aghios Nikolaos. You went alone to see him?'

'No. A girl came with me.'

'Maria Stafanakis? A tragic story. I hope she finds happiness back here among her own people.'

Though Petro's voice was sympathetic, Bill felt a flush of annoyance.

'Is there anything, anyone, you don't know?' he asked, exasperated. Now he could realize that in his own subtle way Petro had been questioning him – he had been asking him what he had been doing, and with whom. 'What did you want to ask me?'

'I wonder,' Petro said, quite unperturbed, 'how long you intend to stay on Crete . . . ?'

'I didn't know the detective branch was concerned with immigration,' Bill said. 'Surely, my entry stamp is in order? I believe I am permitted by the government to stay for three months before I must apply for a renewal?'

'Of course, my dear fellow. I am merely taking a friendly interest in your plans. Though the fact does not seem to have occurred to you, you are having a somewhat turbulent passage through our country. You go to a *kafeneion* and a fight ensues; you visit a man on the high mountain and that man dies later in an ambulance. You visit a man in Aghios Nikolaos and that man is suddenly killed in a fire. The Cretan people are very simple in their beliefs. Many are convinced, even to this day, that Charon sometimes takes on human form. Charon is the god of death, you perhaps know . . .'

'I know,' Bill said angrily. 'And I also know you're talking a lot of rubbish. I had nothing to do with either death. I was far away from each one at the time, in the presence of witnesses.'

'The same witness each time, I believe. Maria Stafanakis. Her uncle, perhaps you know, is the police chief of Maleme . . .'

'I know!' Bill stood up, paced across to the window and looked out. He turned back and saw the superintendent watching him with a smile on his face.

'What are you suggesting . . . ?' Bill asked.

'I am wondering if perhaps it might be better for you to give up this search for your father and to leave Crete . . . ?'

'*Leave Crete?*' Bill asked, astounded.

'Yes.'

Bill stopped his pacing and stood in front of the superintendent, who continued to sit on the bed with that superior smile fixed on his face.

'Let me get this quite clear. Are you officially, as an official policeman, kicking me out of Crete?'

Petro shook his head. 'No, Bill, I am not. Apart from anything else, I do not have the power for "kicking you out". I can recommend to the appropriate people that you be put on a plane. Perhaps they will take my recommendation, perhaps they won't. You can get yourself a lawyer, and I would not have a case to bring against you since I would be obliged to prove criminal malfeasance. Whatever else you might have done or been while you have been here in Crete you have not, so far as I am aware, become a criminal. The British authorities have no outstanding charges against you; you have been convicted, I believe, three times on charges of being drunk and disorderly . . .'

'You've checked on me, with the British police . . . ?'

'Yes, I have checked . . .'

Bill was stunned. 'But why? Why the hell are you checking on me? What the hell are you *doing* here? I think I will just take that piece of advice and get myself a solicitor. You have no right . . .'

The smile was wiped from Petro's face. 'I have every right,' he said, 'to investigate my cases in any way I see fit. I have every right to put in a legitimate enquiry about *everybody* who might be involved when I have valid reason to suspect a crime *may* have been committed. Do not try to tell me, *Kirios* Thomas, what my rights are and are not. You came to this island as a tourist. You have become involved, on two occasions, in enquiries outside the area of tourism with people who subsequently have died. I have investigated your background in England and, at this moment, I have a telexed enquiry with the FBI in

Washington and the State Police of New York, Illinois, and California . . .'

'You forgot Massachusetts,' Bill said, his anger quietly simmering. 'I also lived and worked in Boston one time!'

'Thank you. I will telex them as soon as I return to my office.'

'You'll *what* . . . ?'

'You have heard me!' Now the velvet glove was off, and Bill could see the iron hand beneath. This man was no fool – certainly not a man to be taken for granted.

'Listen to me, Bill,' he said, his manner softening a little. 'I do not know what is happening here. But I have what I believe in England you call "a copper's nose"; I smell that something is out of place. Somehow, and I have no idea how or why, you are involved. I just want to make certain that you have strength enough to carry on with something you may have started. This is all conjecture. I cannot give you any reason for any of this except my copper's nose. But, if you are turning over stones, are you strong enough, are you determined enough, to face what-ever mess you may find beneath them? If you are, stay and see it through. If you are not, if the drunk and disorderly charges in London mean you have no courage, then get out of Crete now. Before I find a valid reason to put you on the next plane.'

The postman lumbered up the steps the following morning, carrying his heavy bag on his shoulder, a perplexed look on his face.

'Beel Tioma?' he asked.

Bill recognized the Greek version of his name. 'Yes, that's me,' he said. The postman handed him a letter which bore an Aghios Nikolaos postmark. Puzzled, Bill tore it open and read it.

'Memory sometimes fails me,' the note said. 'In case I forget to tell you when you come to the house tomorrow,

I am writing this note. A man who knew much about your father now lives in Heraklion. On your way back from Aghios Nikolaos, you must not forget to call on him. His name is Angelos Stavakis and he has a house on Chrisostomou – anyone will tell you where it is.' Beneath the message the general had signed his name, and then had added a postscript. 'Your arrival here this evening disturbs me and opens the box of Pandora for us all. I urge you to be as careful as I myself intend to be.'

The word *careful* had been underlined three times.

Bill set off immediately for Heraklion. He thought for a moment about taking the note to show it to Petro but then resentment at the *ipastinomos*'s peremptory manner overcame him and he tucked the note in his pocket and left.

The tourist map showed him the Chrisostomou leading south outside the city wall, virtually a continuation of Evans Street, named after the man who reconstructed Knossos according to his own beliefs. He stopped at a *kafeneion*; a half-dozen men inside all gave him directions for the house of *Kirios* Stavakis. Though the directions all varied in points of detail, on one thing they were unanimous – the house was the largest on the road, surrounded by a garden of immense proportions, and Bill, they all swore, 'could not miss it'.

It was as large as they had said, and the garden was as immense. Two men were working in it, tending the vines, the fruit trees, the sea of flowers. Three sprinklers were at work – the garden must consume enough water daily to nourish a small village, Bill thought.

The house was not modern. It had a tall elevation with high windows contained in dark-painted woodwork. The stone work was a mixture of ochre wash and natural colours that was pleasing to the eye and restful.

'*Kirios* Stavakis?' Bill asked one of the gardeners. He'd parked his car in the gravelled area outside the large gate.

The gardener beckoned towards the house without speaking.

Bill walked up the drive, lined with a mixture of oleander

113

bushes and pine trees, and found a bell on the massive, unpainted door. He heard the bell ring inside. The door opened after a few minutes and revealed a lady all in black, short and fat, with silvered hair drawn neatly back.

'*Kirios* Stavakis?' Bill asked. 'I was told to come here by General Orfandakis.'

The lady crossed herself when he spoke the name but, as Bill had imagined it would, it served as an introduction, an open sesame. She pulled the door wide and he followed her into the cool dark hall. She pointed to a room on the right and he went in. The room looked out over the whole of the city of Heraklion since the house was poised, like an eagle's nest on an eyrie, on a promontory of land. The road was some distance below, and the sound of passing traffic was inconspicuous.

He stood looking out of the window for some minutes before the door opened again and a man came in. He was dressed in a dark pin-striped suit that had an Italian cut. His white shirt had double French cuffs, and his shoes were either Gucci or Pucci – Bill could never remember the difference between the two. His thin black hair curled across the skin of his scalp; he wore his sideburns fashionably long, curling back behind his ears and shining with some sort of pomade.

'My housekeeper has told me my dear departed friend, Spiros Orfandakis, sent you to see me,' he said. 'You know of his tragic death?'

'I was in Aghios Nikolaos when it happened,' Bill said.

'A great loss. There'll be a state funeral tomorrow, of course. I shall preside. The four *nomakis* will be there, all the *thimakos*. Athens is sending a deputation; Karamanlis himself might be here – I'm waiting for a telephone call from Athens to confirm it. The Neo-democratia Party will be well represented – I have used my influence there, of course. Passok and the Communists of KKE will want to show up, if only to attach a little of the General's glory to themselves, but I shall make certain they take a back seat.'

He sat on a chair as if preparing to give an audience.

'Now, make yourself comfortable and tell me why the General sent you to me. What can I do for you? Any recommendation of my dear departed friend is a command . . .'

Bill sat on the nearest chair, found the light from the window in his eyes. Stavakis had seated himself with his back to the light, not missing a trick.

'The General told me you knew my father,' Bill said. 'I've come to Crete, rather belatedly I admit, to find out what I can about my father's life here during the war. The General was going to talk with me, to show me some documents and photographs, when he had his unfortunate accident . . .'

'Unfortunate? Ah, I see your British understatement – you are British, are you not? – it was, is, will be a tragedy. For Crete, for Greece, for the civilized people of the world!'

The politician in Stavakis had come to the fore; he was making a speech to a Chamber of one.

'My father . . . ?' Bill said hopefully.

'Your father was a great man. He worked with me, was one of my most trusted lieutenants . . .'

'You know who I'm talking about without my giving his name?'

'Of course. Your name is Thomas, is that correct? Captain Roger Thomas, whom we knew as Maleta, was one of my right-hand men in the terrible struggle against the Germans.'

'Can you describe him to me?' Somehow, Bill didn't altogether trust this glib man – any man who worked with *him*, who'd been selected by *him*, would by definition be a great man.

'Physically? He was very tall, with black hair, blue eyes and a habit of always bending his shoulders forward slightly; he looked at men as if he could see through them at a glance. I told you, he was very valuable to me; I do not know what I'd have done without him. He left me free to conduct the higher strategy of the Resistance, in association with the General, of course, while your father attended to the details. Of course, I kept in the background as much as possible. I always believe in letting people who work for you get on with the job you give them – too many small-minded men are unable to delegate responsibility . . .'

Small-mindedness was obviously not one of the faults of *Kirios* Stavakis, Bill thought. He doubted he would get any sort of reliable opinion from this egotistic politician – the only information he'd gain would redound to the politician's credit.

'Can you tell me where my father was buried?' he asked.

Stavakis made a temple of his fingers. 'In those days, you understand,' he said, 'I was not always able to insist on my men observing all the niceties. I would have liked to have been able to give every man who died a decent burial, in consecrated ground, with a cross and a headstone, but it wasn't always possible. When I served as Mayor of Xania, I opened many graves where men had hastily been buried, and transferred the remains to more decent places. Many relatives came to me with tears in their eyes to thank me for that. Then, when I was *nomakis* of Xanion, I continued that work so far as I was able. Alas, your father's body was not one of those I was able to find, to exhume, to give a decent burial in a proper graveyard. No, Bill, your father – please think of it this way – your father still lies where he fell in the service of Crete, the service of mankind. Who knows beneath what rock in what mountain your father lies entombed. I am sure he would approve of it being that way. Your father loved the Lefka Ori; it is fitting that he should die and remain there. Believe me, his spirit, his memory, is a reminder to us all of human dedication, human decency, human dignity in the face of adversity . . .'

Bill knew he should have felt awed and humbled by the image this man was offering him. Who knows in what corner of some foreign field . . . Rupert Brooke had put it with such clarity, hadn't he? Then why did Bill feel slightly sick? It took a considerable effort for him to ask another question.

'Were you there, did you know, how and when my father died?' he asked.

'I was there. I do know. Do you want me to tell you?'

'Yes. Please.'

'It was, as I have said, in the Lefka Ori. In the summer of 1943. I think the Germans already knew they were defeated, not only here in Crete, but on the mainland of Greece, in Russia, in Europe, in North Africa. We had a beautiful summer in the White Mountains that year . . .

The message had come from the German High Command, the office of Field Marshall Hans Weberlich, Iron Cross, himself:

'Any village harbouring one terrorist, one English criminal, one escaped prisoner, any village found to contain one rifle, one round of ammunition, one piece of explosive no matter how small, will be burned to the ground, the stonework of the shells of the houses obliterated by bombs, the inhabitants – except those young girls able to give relaxation to our troops – killed.

There will be no exceptions to this order.'

The village of Mavroti, high up in the Mavri mountain, was such a case. A German patrol of four men carrying a radio had been fired on from the village. They'd been pinned down but had sent back a signal. The four men had been massacred and their bodies thrown down one of the gorges between Mavri and Korda. But the signal had got through, and an 'extermination' order was issued.

Aleko was working in the office of the police chief of Retimo and saw the order. Excusing himself from duty he left the office and gave the message to his cousin and namesake. Little Aleko set off at once. With luck, he'd be at Mavroti at dusk; the Germans would arrive at dawn.

The *palikari* happened to be meeting at Arevitis; he stopped on his way to inform them, and a plan was quickly devised by General Spiros Orfandakis. They would evacuate all the women and children from the village; the able-bodied men would stay behind in ambush and the German column would be wiped out. Mavroti, they knew, was doomed, but at least they'd have the satisfaction of taking a whole German extermination squad with it. Manoletto had a hundred men only two hours away; Theseus had twenty men close at hand. Maleta was sent into the village to supervise the evacuation, with Pakrades and Kostas Dandanakis to lead the women and children to safety up the Mavri. Once they'd passed the Gorge of the Angels, the Germans would not be able to follow them except in single file and on foot, an easy target for the Sfakian Resistance snipers. When he had seen them safely past the Gorge of the Angels, Maleta would return with Kostas and Pakrades to play his part in the ambush.

It didn't work out according to plan. The Germans had somehow learned about the ambush and had mounted a two-pronged flanking action. One flank attacked the Resistance fighters from the rear; the other set off in pursuit of the women and children, all of whom were trapped at the entrance to the Gorge of the Angels and slaughtered. The Resistance fighters suffered heavy casualties in the scattered, fragmented actions that developed. When they reassembled to count the dead, Maleta was among the missing.

'After the Germans had burned and bombed the village of Mavroti, and had left the area,' Stavakis explained to Bill, 'we went looking for our dead. We found many friends cut down by the German bullets. Many of us, including Spiros Orfandakis and myself, were wounded, but despite the intense pain, I laboured to bring all the dead Cretans down into a small place where a chapel had been built, a shrine to the shepherds. We gave them a simple burial there in the shade of a eucalyptus grove. I said a few prayers for them . . .'

'But you didn't find my father?'

'No, I regret to say we did not, though, I assure you, we sought him with the same unselfish diligence we sought our own. Of one thing you can be quite certain: your father died a brave death in a good cause. In every sense of the word, he was a hero.'

Stavakis stood and opened his jacket. He was wearing red braces on his trousers with small gold clips. He unclipped one side and pulled out his shirt. The gash in his side was long and had been deep; it had been crudely sewn together.

'Many of us achieved heroic deeds that day,' Stavakis said. 'I like to think humbly that even I acquitted myself with some honour!'

Bill went for dinner that night to the restaurant of Manolis and Yannis in the fishing port. He had a craving for fresh fish, simply cooked, and for the companionship, the laughter, the cheerful irrepressibility of the simple fisherman community. Manolis put a table outside the door for him and he sat looking across the iridescent mauve-purple water at the sunset, wondering what to do, where to go next. Should he take Petro's advice and leave Crete? Surely, he'd found out what he wanted to know. His father had lived a hero's life and died a hero's death up in the White Mountains. His body had fallen behind some rock and by now had been consumed by rain and wind. What did it matter when a man died, where his mortal remains rested if the manner of his dying was so heroic?

Somehow, Bill could not be content with this explanation. He wanted to know more; he wanted to find out not only how his father died, but how he had lived. He'd finished his plate of delicious small fry fish and was eating a slice of *feta* cheese when Petro slid into the seat beside him. In a way he was pleased to see the *ipastinomos*; Petro held the one thread of consistency in all he had experienced.

'*Krassi?*' he asked, offering the bottle into which the local wine had been poured.

Petro nodded – Manolis was hovering in the doorway,

looking at Bill with a troubled expression on his face. Bill signalled for another glass and Manolis brought it at once.

'Fish?' he asked. 'Bread, a salad?'

'No, thank you. I have eaten,' Petro said. Pointedly he waited until Manolis had left before he turned to Bill, raised his filled glass and said, 'Good health.'

Bill replied with the traditional Cretan 'S'eguia' but didn't clink the glasses. It was obvious this wouldn't be a suitable occasion.

'You went to Heraklion today,' Petro said.

Bill no longer bothered to wonder how Petro knew; he'd realized the policeman was probably having him watched.

'You went to the house of Angelos Stavakis!'

'Yes. He knew my father during the war. He was able to give me a lot of information about where and how my father died.'

'Tonight, Angelo Stavakis attended a meeting in Heraklion in connection with the state funeral of General Orfandakis.'

'He told me he was arranging things.'

'Angelo Stavakis is a very important man in Crete. I do not know if you realize how important. You have heard of Venizelos, of course?'

'Who hasn't . . . ?'

'Venizelos was a liberal, the first of our liberals. Though he held no official office – he was not a *nomakis* of any of the regions – he managed to unite the people of Crete as no man has ever done. Crete will shortly hold its elections. People who know are predicting the Socialists, even the Communists, will gain control of Xania and Heraklion; the left wing will hold the two largest and, some say, the most important regions of Crete. Angelo Stavakis, the wartime hero, has the personal influence to stop them, to keep control of Crete in the hands of the Neo-democratia Party. Stavakis has an enormous war-time reputation – only Spiros Orfandakis had a bigger one and now he's dead. After the war, Stavakis became a business man and now wields tremendous commercial as well as political influence. Without him, the left wing would have an easy victory in Crete.'

'Very interesting, but I don't understand why you're giving me this lesson in politics?' Bill said.

'You went to see General Orfandakis, another man of tremendous right-wing influence, and he died shortly afterwards. When Stavakis came from his meeting tonight, having been delayed, he found that his car had exploded! If he had left that meeting at the time he planned, he would have been halfway home when the bomb went off. Angelos Stavakis is no fool; many people in the past have made the mistake of writing him off as an egomaniac, a man who thinks only of self-aggrandisement . . .'

'I got that impression very strongly,' Bill confessed.

'You are not alone. But in both business and politics, any man who falls for that line is as good as dead. Stavakis is a power to be reckoned with on all levels. Starting from nothing after the end of the war, with only his reputation as a war-time hero, he has built himself a business and political empire that has no equal on Crete. He is an extremely wealthy man and extremely ambitious.'

'Is he married? I saw no signs of a wife at his house.'

'He did not marry. Perhaps he regarded that as a waste of his time and energies. Stavakis dedicates himself to only one thing, the right-wing business and political empire he has created here on Crete. He hates the Socialists and Communists with a passion but works like a snake, silently and insidiously, often destroying them from within. Last night, someone tried to destroy him. We are not used to these gangster methods, Bill. We are not used to ambulances being pushed off roads, people's houses being fire-bombed, cars being wired with time fuses. All this seems to be happening as a result of your being here, in the wake of your enquiries. Who exactly are you, Bill? What is your real purpose for being here on Crete?'

Bill had been staggered by the news. Could all these 'accidents' be coincidence? No, that was patently impossible. Stavakis had escaped death but the effect on Bill was the same as if he'd died.

'The left-wing movement has become international,' Petro said, all his attention focussed on Bill. 'And not all of it comes from Moscow. Has someone sent you here, Bill? If so, who is the next target?'

Bill was not angry. He could see the *ipastinomos* had legitimate grounds for suspicion.

'There's nothing I can say to *prove* you're wrong,' he said. 'But I had no hand in any of this. The person who sent me here is sitting in a wheel chair in London. She had become a drunk, just as I had, and she conquered it in her own way. She believed that by coming to Crete and looking for my father, I might conquer drinking my own way. So far, she's been right. You're going to have to take my word for it, but other than that, I have no motive for being here. I have no political affiliations in any country – I never even voted for anyone except the president of the university union, and that was years ago!' He laughed wryly. 'And he didn't get in!'

He started to take a sip of wine but self-consciously put the glass back on the table.

'We take our elections very seriously, Bill,' Petro said. 'I am not speaking about presidents of university unions. Every town mayor is voted in by the people. It is a hard fought contest in each case. The young people are becoming more and more interested in controlling their own destinies, as they call it. They want distribution of wealth, often without work.

The Government in Greece nominates four men to control the four *nomes* of Crete. A *nomakis* is an important man, appointed by the government. The *nomakis* meet regularly, in Xania, and they discuss the affairs of the country. But even *nomakis* are human beings, and they depend for their success on influence. They get that influence from politicking with the business and commercial community, the popular leaders.

'The reason I mentioned Venizelos earlier was because

Venizelos was a man of *influence*; he held neither elected nor nominated office. And yet he went on to be the leader of all Greece and our best known statesman.

'There are two such men today, Bill. One is Angelos Stavakis. He is well-known as a former war-hero, a man wounded in the Resistance. Now he is a leader of the business community – there is no pie on Crete that doesn't have the finger of Angelo Stavakis in it. Stavakis is a right-wing supporter.

'The other man is Ioannis Skiamnakis. Skiamnakis is young and already has had a varied career. He is a man of the people, especially of the younger people. He started his adult life as a fisherman, which gives him impeccable origins. He has also been a footballer, which gives him popular appeal. His name is better known among our young adult men than even that of Karamanlis. For a while, he became a folk singer and appeared on television and on the radio many times. His singing style is simplistic and not as committed as that of Maria Faradouri. But the people love it.

Now he very rarely appears on television but he is still well-known. And influential. Recently, he's done a bit of politicking himself. Not seeking elected office but appearing on behalf of candidates of Passok, the Socialists. You could say at this moment that we have an internecine fight between Stavakis and Skiamnakis – and only Stavakis's reputation as a war-time hero keeps him solidly out front. It occurs to me there must be many people around who would like to see Angelos Stavakis dead and Skiamnakis as the real influence behind the scenes of Crete. Somebody *tried* to kill Stavakis. And failed!'

'And you think it might be me?' Bill said, self-consciously.

'No, that is not at issue.' He was studying Bill closely. 'You can probably guess what I am thinking, Bill,' he said.

'Yes. That whoever is responsible for these deaths is somehow connected with me and my search for my father . . .'

'And that you, yourself, might become the next victim. You have considered that possibility?'

'I was just beginning to,' Bill said.

Petro looked at his wrist-watch. 'A plane is leaving the NAMFI base in an hour,' he said. 'Its first stop is Germany. I can put you on it.'

Bill was tempted. Germany early in the morning, a quick flight to London. He could send a telegram to Maria, asking her if she'd like to join him there. They could work things out together. Dammit, his father was a *hero* who'd died an honourable death. He didn't need any further knowledge about him. And he'd cured his drinking habit. Okay, he'd had three glasses of local wine this evening and would probably be on his fourth if Petro hadn't turned up, but that didn't mean to say he was back on the bottle. He'd lost his craving, his *need* for alcohol. The glasses of wine he'd drunk had merely served to relax him after a day of driving.

Only one thing still troubled him; if he left now, he'd never know why Victorio had provoked that fight with him. He'd never know why the woman in the shop had pleaded with him to leave them in peace. And he'd never know why the general had said in his letter – 'be careful, as I intend to be'! It seemed the general hadn't been careful enough, if one believed, as Petro was implying, that the house fire was not an accident.

'They've conducted an autopsy on the General?' he asked Petro.

'Yes, on what remained of him. The fire was very hot – the house had wooden floors, wooden furniture, wooden ceilings, all very old and dry.'

'Did they find anything wrong?'

Petro shrugged. 'Part of the General's skull had been staved in. It could have been the traditional blunt weapon – or it could have been one of the beams falling on his head.'

'I'm not leaving,' Bill said. 'I'm going to carry on with my enquiries.'

Petro heaved a sigh of relief. 'I hoped you would say that,' he said. 'I have the feeling that you are the small piece of grit on which the pearl grows in an oyster. No grit, no pearl. But I warn you, you will be in grave danger. We will be able to keep some sort of an eye on you, of course, but only from a distance. If we get too close to you, if the grit is too closely protected, the pearl may not form . . .'

'I'll be careful,' Bill said.

'Where will you start?'

'I'll start again where I started before. I shall go to Kaprisses, to the *kafeneion*. And this time, I shall be ready when Victorio takes a swing at me . . .'

The windows of the *kafeneion* were steamed over from the inside when Bill parked the car conspicuously outside the door. Though he was trying to look confident, to put a swagger in his steps, he feared he would be no match for the strong, fit Sfakian. But he was determined to go inside, come what may.

He opened the door, went in, shut the door behind him to keep out the cold night air and stood with his back to it. Only three tables were occupied. At one a man was reading a newspaper, focussing through a pair of glasses he held in his hand as if he'd borrowed them. At another table, two men were playing *tavli*, and one man was watching them. Four men were playing cards at the third table. It was all very quiet, very tranquil.

Victorio was standing behind the counter, reading a newspaper. He looked up, looked down again. Bill realized that, in the doorway, he was standing in deep shadow. He walked deeper into the *kafeneion* but no one took any notice of him. He began to feel foolish, his courage ebbing with every step. He forced himself to continue to the counter. A half-dozen water glasses stood on the counter beside a bent-over pipe with a tap on it. He held one of the glasses under the tap and three quarters filled it with water. Victorio glanced at his hands but didn't bother to look up.

Bill took the glass and with a flick of his wrist threw the contents into Victorio's face.

Victorio let out a roar of astonished shock; when he'd wiped the water from his eyes he saw Bill for the first time, let out a yell and started round the counter. Bill was too quick for him; he grabbed the bunch of Victorio's shirt at his throat and pulled him half across the counter top, then hit him on the ear with a round-house swing that must have set off an explosion in Victorio's head.

The *tavli* players were silent, but none moved; no one tried to interfere. All knew this was a private fight. The Sfakian is accustomed to minding his own business especially when a feud or a vendetta is involved.

Victorio was stunned with surprise at the attack, and that gave Bill the advantage he so desperately needed. He banged his hand in again, this time hardening the blade, and smashed the side of Victorio's neck below the ear so hard his hand buzzed with pain. Victorio staggered. Bill changed his grip, caught the front of the Sfakian's generous hair, lifted his head and banged it down on the counter top. He lifted it up and banged it down again, seeing the blood spurt over the wood. Victorio thrust his arms down and used his sheer brute strength to lift himself off the counter. He staggered as he came round the corner, but Bill knew he'd lost any advantage he might have had. From now on, it would be a rough-house, with strength and muscle against him.

Petro had helped him. 'Do not try to outfight him,' he'd said. 'He will pound you. Try a police trick – go for the pressure points, under his ears, his throat, his wrists. Use his own weight against himself but, whatever you do, do not kill him. And do not repeat this conversation we have had.'

Victorio came round the counter like a bull, roaring with pain and rage, his hands outstretched to grab Bill, to tear him limb from limb. Bill didn't allow himself to think, to be afraid, to hesitate, or he knew he'd be lost. He danced in, grabbed the Sfakian's wrist and swung first up and then down with all his force. He felt the crack as Victorio's arm was jerked in its socket, knowing from what Petro had said that that arm would be useless for several seconds. He slipped to the side, caught Victorio's other arm and swung the great bulk of the Sfakian forward like a baseball bat, propelling the bigger man by his own weight, reeling forward to smash against the wall with a thud that shook the building.

The other men in the *kafeneion* were standing up, roaring approval.

Victorio started to turn away from the wall and Bill jumped up in the air. With both feet he kicked the Sfakian in the small of his back and the back of his knee; he slumped forward and his knees and his face hit the wall together. He buckled slowly like a tree and started to go down but he wasn't yet finished. As he went down he twisted. Bill had made the mistake of standing too close and the breath was driven from his body by the pile-driver Victorio slammed into his gut; he staggered backwards, winded, tripped over a chair and sprawled. Despite the blood streaming down his face, Victorio, crouched like an animal, came forward and picked Bill off the ground by his leg and his shoulder. Bill tried to turn in that grip; the arm he had whip-lashed was obviously less useful than the other and his head was nearer the ground than his legs when Victorio threw him like a sack across a table. The corner banged into Bill's back with excruciating pain but he had no time to consider that; the Sfakian was using his good arm and fist like a mallet pounding the fibres of a steak into tenderness. The table cracked across the middle and Bill fell among its remains; the breaking table took Victorio by surprise and he stumbled forward and fell into the maelstrom of flailing arms and legs. Bill saw his chance as if in a freeze action snap-shot; Victorio's chin was twenty or so centimetres from his foot. He kicked out with all his force and felt the crunch as his shoe-sole hammered the side of the Sfakian's neck, his face, his chin.

The blow was the last of which Bill was capable; he lay there inert, only partly conscious, his body a pulsing mass of pain and ache. The spectators saw the fight was over; one of them fetched a glass of water and threw it into Bill's face. Bill struggled away from the broken table into a sitting position, his head in his hands. They dragged Victorio out of the broken wood and propped him with his back against the wall, two metres from Bill. Victorio was given the cold water treatment; one eye opened, blinking, and then the other. When he focussed on Bill, he let out a muted shout and struggled into a kneeling position. He shook his head violently from side to side, as if to clear it, and then shambled forward.

Bill squatted helplessly there. Okay, he'd given a good account of himself, hadn't he? He'd knocked the bastard out, hadn't he? He knew he had no more strength; the Sfakian would come in and finish it off and there wasn't a damn thing he could do about it. When Victorio was within a half-metre, Bill tried one last ineffectual gesture. He flung out his right hand; it made contact with what felt like the iron rod of the Sfakian's hairy paw and was seized in a bear hug he couldn't break. Slowly the Sfakian forced it down until it lay, helpless, on Bill's knee. The Sfakian's other hand came slowly round towards Bill's head. He saw it coming but didn't even have the strength left to duck. The hand went round the back of his head and drew him forward and suddenly he could smell the Sfakian's sweat, hugged tight to his body in an awkward embrace.

'Okay, Englishman, you did it,' Victorio said. 'But don't try it again, eh?'

Bill was too exhausted to speak. A half an hour later when he'd cleaned up but was still feeling groggy, Victorio was moving easily round the tiny kitchen behind the counter frying tiny meatballs and chunks of octopus leg, and envelopes of pastry containing cheese and spinach. He made an enormous plateful, garnished it with the iron-hard baked bread chunks known as *paximada* and served it on a table with a carafe of local wine.

'Ten years old,' he said. 'That will put the meat back into your balls!'

Bill didn't feel the first glass go down, nor the second.

When he paused after a sip of the third, the plate of food was empty and he had no memory of eating any of it. But he was feeling considerably stronger. Victorio was sitting at his right hand side; the *tavli* board was busy again but the card players and the man reading the newspaper had left. Bill looked at his watch, surprised to see the time was only eleven o'clock. It felt like four in the morning.

'Okay, Victorio. Now tell me what it's all about,' he said.

Victorio smiled at him. 'I guess you've earned that,' he said. 'Here in the mountains we have long memories and the son must suffer for the father. Accept those two apparently unconnected customs, Bill, and you will understand why I had to hit you. When I was a baby, I was brought up with a girl I believe you know – Maria Stafanakis as she is now called, since she left behind her husband's name . . .'

'I know her.'

'Then you'll know that her father was a *palikari* who gave his name to your father . . .'

'I know that, too!'

'Now I am going to tell you something you must tell no one, not even Maria. I want your promise on that . . .'

'You have my promise,' Bill said.

'The father of Maria, the *palikari* Stafanakis, and the wife of Stafanakis, were not the blood father and mother of Maria. The mother of Maria, like my mother, was killed by the Germans. They came from the village of Mavroti . . .'

'Where my father died . . . ?'

'You've been very quick in digging out information. Your father did not die in the village; he died outside it, in the mountains. The Germans had been ambushed, but they had discovered the ambush in time, had circled round and cut off the guerillas. They found the women and children . . .'

'In the entrance to the Gorge of the Angels . . .'

'And slaughtered them.'

'I was told all this,' Bill said, 'today in Heraklion.'

'Then you must have been to see Angelos Stavakis.'

'Yes. He was at the Mavroti fight.'

'Yes, but even he does not know this. Not everyone from the village of Mavroti was massacred. One lady escaped, with two babies. That lady took the babies of two of the women of the village and carried them out, over the mountains, hiding in shepherds' folds, in stone huts. She brought those two babies to Kaprisses. One baby she gave to the wife of the *palikari*, Stafanakis, who had lost her four sons. That baby was Maria . . .'

'And the other baby?' Bill asked, already suspecting the answer.

'That baby was the man you fought tonight.'

'And my father . . . ?'

'We believe your father was the man who disclosed that ambush to the Germans. We of Kaprisses think your father was a traitor – a traitor to Crete, a traitor to his country, a traitor to our people. Once, when I was younger, if I had met you I would have killed you, in memory of your father!'

'And now . . . ?'

'Now we fight. I give myself the satisfaction of punching you. You give yourself the satisfaction of punching me, and then we forget the past, eh? Crete has lived too much in the past. Now we must make a country in the modern age. We join NATO; we permit them to foul the skies above our mountains with their jet planes, to make gunnery practice on the Akrotiri; we encourage the Germans to come back again, this time, as tourists, and in most places, we accept them. I want to forget the past, Bill, and yet you come here to try to bring it all back. And when you are beaten, you go back to your lair like a wounded animal and then, later, you emerge again full of fight. Well, I have

130

had my fight, you have had your fight, so let us quit, eh? Let us lay all these memories to rest . . .'

'The lady who brought you up, the one who carried you over the mountains, is she still alive?' Bill asked.

'Yes. Still alive. She was never completely fit after her mountain ordeal – that was why she gave Maria away – she suffers terrible rheumatism and arthritis. Now she lives in a house in Xania. I go to see her every week and take her some things. I am going there tomorrow. Would you like to come with me?'

Bill hesitated. As Victorio had said, perhaps the past should be buried. What point could there be in reminding the old lady of the terrible past, of the ordeal in the mountains that had left her an invalid for life?

'Do you think that's wise?' he said. 'I don't want to reopen old wounds.'

Victorio laughed. 'She will enjoy seeing you,' he said. 'Her mind is as clear today as it was the day she escaped from death. She likes to remember those days. She was, alas, very fond of your father – I understand all the women were – and I am certain she will enjoy meeting his son. She has so few pleasures these days, it would be a kindness for you to give her an hour of your time . . .'

The house in Xania was the annexe to the hospital. Evangelina needed frequent treatment for her arthritis and it was easier for her to live in the house than in Kaprisses, with the painful bus journey three times a week for the X-ray and deep heat therapy that were the only way to prevent her limbs entirely locking together in pain. She was a cheerful, quiet person who loved nothing better than a long gossip. She had obviously been looking forward to the arrival of Victorio; she'd combed her yellowish hair starkly back and had fixed it with a comb. She was wearing a black satin dress with a bodice embroidered in black thread. Her skin had reverted to a baby-like smoothness.

Her eyes were bright, her hearing acute, and she still had all her own teeth. Sitting in her chair, with a piece of embroidery in her hands, Bill could sense a quiet authority about her, a firm dignity and resolve.

'I have brought a boy-friend for you,' Victorio said, teasing her. 'He's going to take you away with him to England . . .'

'Do not be vulgar,' she said. 'Remember your manners and introduce the *Kyrios* to me properly.'

Bill held her hand, gnarled and twisted almost out of recognition by the arthritis working insidiously in the joints of her knuckles, her fingers swollen like iris roots. Acting on impulse, he bent over her hand and kissed the back of it lightly. She smiled with pleasure.

'Ah, there's a gentleman,' she said, 'not like that lout of a son of mine. And he speaks Greek, I hope?'

'Yes, I do,' Bill said, 'and I am very honoured to be introduced to you!'

She gave a little squeal of pleasure. 'Such a fine voice,' she said. 'I remember only one person . . . you speak in the same fine manner as someone I used to know. But that was long long ago.'

'Maleta?' Bill asked her. 'Are you thinking of an Englishman called Maleta?'

She smiled, looking at him with an enormous warmth. 'You are Maleta's son,' she said. 'You have his eyes. One can always tell by the eyes. And you have his voice, also. Your father was a fine gentleman, just as you seem to be. Once he kissed my hand, just as you did now. I think it is the old way, eh? The British way?'

Bill didn't want to disillusion her by saying it *was* old-fashioned but French in origin. They gave her presents of fruit and chocolate. Bill had bought a small bunch of flowers from the market.

'Do you, by any chance, have an English cigarette?' she asked shyly.

Bill produced the packet from his pocket. 'Please keep them,' he said. 'I smoke so seldom!'

She lit one with obvious enjoyment, holding the match in her twisted fingers with surprising grace. He glanced at the fine embroidery and wondered how anyone so crippled could do such delicate work. He had wanted to light the cigarette for her but she'd thanked him and said, 'No, I can manage. It is good practice for me.' She settled back in her chair, taking the smoke deep inside her lungs, obviously enjoying it, holding it there until she exhaled it with infinite pleasure from between her pursed lips. 'When I was a young girl,' she said, 'we were not permitted to smoke. But we used to do it! If only the men had known how many things we did that were not permitted . . .'

'Such as . . . ?' Victorio asked, grinning.

'I am not going to tell you a girl's secrets,' she said. 'You will notice the *Kyrios* doesn't ask . . . Too polite. You should take lessons in manners from him. But then, he has the advantage of his father's blood!'

That was something Victorio couldn't take. 'His father's blood!' he said contemptuously. 'We know what that was made of . . .'

'Do not speak badly,' she said sharply. 'You were too young to know. And then, you grew up with all those lies about you. I can see you've both been fighting. Men are such fools. Especially Sfakian men. Looking at your face and your hands, *Kirios*, if you will pardon my forwardness, I think you are not much better!'

Bill nodded shamefacedly, feeling ten years old again. 'You said *lies?*' he asked. 'What lies?'

'Some story the men put about. None of the women, not one, believed it. They said the Englishman, Maleta, was a traitor; that he had betrayed the village of Mavroti to the Germans. Bah! I was there and lived to tell the tale. They called me a foolish woman. Maleta helped me escape from the Germans. Is that the action of a traitor? Lies, all lies! And the men have carried those lies with them until this day, it seems. Well, now you two foolish boys have had your fight. Perhaps now you can put the fighting and the lies behind you and become friends. You have much to offer each other, perhaps,' she said.

Bill had seated himself in front of the old lady, Victorio to the side. 'I have been told something about that terrible day up in the Mavri,' he said. 'Would it pain you to tell me about it? You were there after all. The man who told me was there, but I suspect he was in the background and not in the thick of it . . .'

'I can tell you only about the journey to the Gorge of the Angels,' she said.

'It won't pain you?'

'Why should it? I came away with my life and my boy. Though I scold him all the time,' she said, laying her hand on Victorio's knee, 'he has been a good son to me, as good as if he had been conceived in my own body!' Victorio had covered her hand with his. 'Also,' she said, 'I think this is perhaps the time for everything to be said.' She placed her other hand on Victorio's. 'The doctor from Athens was here again yesterday,' she said. 'I have been having pains in my chest. He says the problem of pumping the blood through my bad joints has placed a great strain on my heart. He says I must not make any plans for the long-distant future . . .'

'Mother!' Victorio said, his voice anguished.

'Come, Victorio. You are a grown man – no, you will be when you stop being so foolish and find yourself a wife! One thing I have never told you. Now I think you must learn it, even though it will give me pain to tell, and you pain to hear!'

She turned back to Bill. 'It was an afternoon like any other, that day in Mavroti,' she said, 'but that the men were all talking excitedly, like little boys, about the German patrol they had shot and had thrown down the gorge. In those days we were used to killing in Mavroti; the two principal families had been fighting for fifty years, neither giving an inch of ground. Fifty years before, one of the men from one family had drunk too much *tsikoudia* and had gone to the house of the other family. He had forced

134

open the window of the bedroom of an unmarried girl of that family and was about to climb into her bed when the family, alerted by the noise the pig of a man was making in his drunkenness, caught him. They cut off his private parts and that was the start of the feud. That story is not important now but only to let you know what we had grown up with in Mavroti.

It was an afternoon like any other. I was weaving and dreaming that one day the bedspread I was making would go on my own marriage bed. I could hear my father coughing and spitting – he had a bad chest. I could smell the bread my mother was baking in the fire-oven, I can even remember the crackle of the sticks she kept feeding into it. My friend, Alicia, brought her ewe down the street outside our house – I heard its clatter on the stones and knew she was taking it for milking. And then, I heard a strange shouting, in a voice I did not know; the voice as I later learned, of the young man we called Little Aleko. He was shouting, "Everyone come to the church, everyone come to the church at once, everyone . . ." '

'Everyone come to the church at once,' Little Aleko shouted as he ran into the village of Mavroti. Though he'd come up the mountain side at a jog-trot, he was still full of breath and his shout carried through the closely packed houses and the stone alleyways of the tiny village that clung so perilously to the mountainside. The church, as he called it, was a small chapel about six metres by four that had been built long before the Turkish Occupation; in front of it was a bower of grape vines and benches made of logs on which it was permitted for young lovers to sit for an hour in the evening under the benevolent, sanctified gaze of the Almighty. The village meetings, such as they were, would be held there, and the village courthouse, too, dispensed its rough justice beneath the vines, the geraniums, the oleander that defied nature by blooming so high.

One by one, the people came out of their houses and gathered in the place before the church; ten minutes after Little Aleko arrived, the great *palikari*, whom all recognized, came with the Englishman, Maleta, to address them.

'The Germans are coming,' he said, 'to kill you all and to set fire to your houses in reprisal for the four men you killed. How many times must you all be told never to shoot a German if he carries a radio box? This time, the Germans managed to speak over the radio box to the other Germans and they are coming to wipe you out. So, you must all leave. The men will gather all their rifles, all their ammunition, all their explosives, and come with me. We will set a trap for the Germans and kill as many of them as we can. The women, and the children, and the old people, will go with Maleta up the Mavri. You will take all your donkeys with you to carry the old people who cannot walk, and you will climb the Mavri to the pass through the Gorge of the Angels. In the gorge we will post men to hold the Germans back, should they succeed in following you up there. Is that clear?'

'It is clear,' the old man of the largest family, traditionally the village head man, said. 'We will take with us only what we can carry.'

'Good. Tell the young men to come to me down the road. We will set the trap around Kiptsis – if we can get them into the defile there, we can wipe them out . . . And you, Maleta, go fast for the gorge. Drive them mercilessly on. If any cannot keep up with you, then leave them behind.'

They were forty – old men, old women, younger women, babies in arms, toddlers. They had a total of seven donkeys. Three of the old men couldn't walk, and two of the women. Some donkeys carried three people, some an old man, an old woman and as many kids as could hang on. Maleta walked with the strongest, including Irena and Elvira. They both put their babies on the donkey with Katerina and walked, one each side, making the noises mothers will. The column left the village, moving slowly at first since the donkeys were not used to walking after sunset. Mikhail, a lad of ten, led the way. He'd wanted to take his dead brother's rifle and go down to fight with the men at Kiptsis but Maleta had flattered him.

'Come on, *palikari*,' he'd said jokingly, 'you're the only one can lead us safely and surely up into the Gorge of the Angels!'

Maleta walked near the back, with Evangelina, Irena and, of course, Elvira. Motherhood suited her; she'd lost much of her wild tempestuousness. She and Irena were opposites – Irena was small and chubby and quiet; Elvira was tall, slender and anything but quiet – but they got on very well. They'd arrived in Mavroti together, both very obviously pregnant. They told of how their husbands, two brothers, had been killed by the Germans. The villagers asked no questions and took them in; Evangelina let them share a bedroom in her house while she slept on the sofa. She'd never been married and it was a rare treat for her to share her life with two mothers-to-be. She took more interest in their babies, when they were born, than even their mothers did. Evangelina would bathe the babies, cradle both on her knees, sing the old Cretan lullabies to them, while the two mothers were out in the mountains tending Evangelina's sheep and goats. She came of a rich family; when she moved to Mavroti, it took two carts to carry all her possessions. Many of the village men had courted her, and the men from nearby villages but none had been successful.

'I like my own bed,' Evangelina said to the two mothers. She didn't tell them that as a young girl she'd fallen in love with a man from Athens . . . ! Or that she was no longer a virgin . . .

'We must get your babies christened,' she said to the two girls but looking at Maleta. He grinned at her.

'After the war is over!' Elvira said. 'The day the Germans are driven from Crete, we will christen the babies together.'

'You have names for them?'

'Maria and Victorio,' Irena said, as shy as ever.

'Victorio? What kind of a name is that . . .' But Evangelina was pleased when Irena said, 'You will be godmother to both of them!'

The climb to the Gorge of the Angels was four hours by day for a healthy shepherd. At night, with the burden of the old people and the babies, it seemed to last for ever. They were on the last stretch, however, well after dawn, when the Germans appeared from the gorge itself.

They were paratroopers.

Maleta had heard the plane go over in the dark, about an hour before dawn. It had been flying low, but he knew they would not be seen and had not even dispersed the column. On the far side of the gorge, the narrow pass widened to a mountain meadow. The Germans must have dropped there and infiltrated the gorge before light came. The column had no hope; within minutes they were surrounded. The Germans ordered them all from the donkeys; some of the women were crying, clutching their babies and young children to them. By Maleta's right hand was a large rock – beyond it, a small opening of a cave mouth. Evangelina had taken the two babies in her arms. He looked at Elvira and Irena, motioned with his head. Elvira could see it would be impossible for the two women with the two babies to get into the cave. She bit her lip, bent and whispered to Irena. Then she looked back at Maleta. Who could read everything on her face at that fleeting instant in time? Evangelina saw the look and glanced at Maleta. He knew what Elvira was saying. 'No!' the shake of his head said. 'No!' But Elvira turned away, suddenly screamed and, with Irena beside her, also screaming, ran into the thick of the paratroopers, tearing off the thick jumper she wore. She raced up to the Feldwebel, grabbing for his schmeisser. He was taken momentarily by surprise at seeing this bare-chested woman come racing forward, but he recovered quickly, slammed the butt around into the centre of her breast-bone, reversed it quickly and fired at point blank range into her belly.

Irena was holding Elvira as her body jerked back, blood and froth foaming from her mouth. She let the body drop and jumped for the Feldwebel, an angry mountain cat. She raked the side of his face with her fingernails; he turned the gun, pushed the muzzle into her lower belly and held it there. Then, one at a time, holding her hair with his other hand, he fired five bullets into her, then let her drop, still alive but a bloodied dying mess, to the ground at his feet.

He looked around. 'Now,' he said, 'everybody against the rock. Let us end this business.'

As soon as Elvira had started her scream and had run forward, diverting everyone's eye-line, Maleta grabbed Evangelina's shoulders from behind and slid her sideways behind the rock, pushing her towards the cave. She tucked the babies under the thick shawl, tied in a knot round her waist and crawled like a dog into the depth of the rock.

Maleta followed her. The fissure was about two metres long, growing slightly wider, then it turned a corner and climbed up into a narrow chimney. The exit hole was too small for a human body to pass.

Evangelina turned to Maleta, a look of hopelessness on her face. He pushed her as far up the chimney as he could, then went back and squatted near the bend in the fissure, his pistol in his hand. He heard the rattle of the schmeisser, Irena's scream, the chatter of the gun as it fired again. He heard the shouted commands, longing to go out there with his gun blazing but knowing he wouldn't last five seconds.

And then they heard the long-drawn-out tattoo as the massacre began. It seemed to go on for ever. Nobody screamed, nobody shouted, and Maleta could imagine them all facing death with the same courage they'd brought to their impossibly difficult lifes. He felt sick at the needless deaths of all these innocent people and shuddered as if with a deep ague when he thought of Elvira and Irena, who had sacrificed themselves when they had seen even the faintest possibility of their babies escaping alive.

He heard the Feldwebel shout, 'Make camp here,' and knew they would be confined to the cave for as long as the Germans were out there. Alone he and Evangelina could have survived, but what would happen when the two babies began to cry, as inevitably they must when they woke and hunger overcame them? He beckoned for Evangelina to stay where she was and crawled slowly forward round the dog-leg bend in the cave. The morning light flooded the cave's entrance. He drew himself upright hearing a noise he could not grasp at first. He eased himself forward a millimetre at a time, holding his breath, until he could look round the side of the rock face.

A German paratrooper was standing in the cave mouth. He was trying to be sick but nothing would come from him except a thin stream of bile that ran down his chin. His belly heaved with deep convulsions, but there was nothing left for the constricting muscles to hold.

He could only be twenty-two or -three, Maleta thought,

but his body was lean, doubtless battle-hardened. The section of the gorge behind him was empty but Maleta could hear the quiet sounds the rest of the unit were making as they prepared to make camp.

He saw the stark shadows as two of them walked down the gorge. The boy in the cave mouth moved so rapidly he took Maleta by surprise, sliding himself back deeper into the cave until he was only a metre away.

Maleta could have killed him, quickly and silently, with one chop below his ear, but what then? Where could he hide the body? And could he guarantee to kill the man absolutely silently? He held his breath and waited; the German was too pre-occupied with his own sickness, his need to hide from the other soldiers. Maleta could guess the treatment the poor young kid would get if his comrades-in-arms knew his weakness – they would despise him, deride him unmercifully.

He reached up his hand to start to back off; it was a mistake. His hand caught a loose stone which fell, clinking, to the floor. The German whirled round and saw Maleta. His eyes opened wide.

At that moment, Evengelina, hearing the stone, called softly, 'What's happening, Englishman?'

Maleta knew the German had heard and had understood. He prepared himself to leap forward, taking a chance on killing the German silently so that the two whose shadows he could see outside would not hear but knowing, however, he didn't have much hope.

The German glanced behind himself rapidly. Maleta noted professionally that despite his sickness the paratrooper had hunched his body into a defensive posture, exposing none of his vulnerable points to attack. It would not be a rapid fight.

Then, to Maleta's great surprise, the German held his finger across his lips in the universal gesture for silence. He flicked his hand as if to say. 'Be quiet, go back'. Maleta did as the German said; the German followed him, crouching, back into the cave. Evangelina gave a soft moan as she saw the bulk of the German but Maleta reassured her, whispering. 'Be quiet. It's all right.'

'I've never been so frightened in all my life,' Evangelina said to Bill and Victorio, 'as when that German followed your father back into the cave. We stayed there for a long time, it seemed, until the Germans settled down and then the boy helped us to escape, coming with us part of the way. He told us his name was Hans Ohlman and that he came from Hamburg. He was totally sick of the war, with the terrible brutality he had encountered on Crete. He'd joined the Army and had volunteered for the paratroopers as a very young man who'd done well in the Youth Movement. He said that like many other young Germans, he'd been betrayed, misled by the Hitler propaganda into believing he was fighting to make life better for people throughout the world. But then, when he came to Crete, and they started to massacre the people of the villages – the women, children, babies – he was sickened by it all, nearly driven out of his mind by disgust with himself and his fellow men.

'If it hadn't been for him and your father, I would have died with Maria and Victorio that day on the slopes of the Mavri in the Gorge of the Angels.'

Victorio and Bill had listened to her account of that terrible day without speaking. When she stopped, Bill laid his hand on her gnarled knuckles.

'You did a wonderful thing,' he said, 'to bring those two babies safely out of the mountain.'

Victorio's face wore an anguished look. 'You said there was something you would tell me?' he said. 'Something I would not like.'

Evangelina freed her hand from Bill's and grasped Victorio's. 'On the way up the mountain,' she said, 'Irena talked with me. She told me we were all in danger – I knew that, of course – but that we might die. She didn't want to die with something bad on her conscience. She made me hear her confession and asked me to carry that confession with me if I should live and she should die and one day pass that confession on to another. Now the doctor tells me I am coming to the end of my life, and I have never made that confession. It is time for me to speak. I will not tell anyone else but somehow, I want to tell you. With Bill here to listen since Bill's father, Maleta, helped save my life. Irena told me that she and Elvira had both told lies when they came to the village of Mavroti, when I took them into my house to live. They had not been married to two brothers. They had not even been married. Irena knew, somehow, that she would not survive the war. She had what you might call a premonition. She didn't want to die a virgin. So, one day when she was tending her flock in the mountains and a young man chanced by, she gave herself to that young man!'

Victorio was looking deep into Evangelina's face, seeking to understand.

'Who was that young man, Mother?' he asked quietly. 'Come on, tell me!'

'He was a German,' Evangelina said. 'A German soldier.'

At four o'clock in the morning of the same night, Evangelina was sleeping soundly in her bed in the hospital annexe, under the influence of the sleeping pills the doctors were now prescribing for her, when the door handle turned slowly. The room was flooded by moonlight; the light of the corridor was lost as the door opened and the man came in. He was wearing rubber-soled shoes which squeaked faintly on the polished wood floor but not sufficiently to disturb Evangelina's deep slumber.

He closed the door carefully behind him then turned towards the bed, moving slowly but purposefully forward. Once he stopped for a moment, hearing a sound from the corridor outside, but then moved forward again until he was standing beside the bed. The moonlight gleamed on the syringe in his right hand, on the barrel filled with liquid and the thin needle which protruded from the end. He turned the covers back gently, exposing Evangelina's shoulder beneath her night-gown; he drew the gown across the shoulder so that her upper arm was exposed, then puckered the skin between his thumb and forefinger, readying it to receive the needle.

The light click on and a voice said, 'Don't move or I'll shoot you dead.'

He whirled round. The *ipastinomos* was standing in the cupboard behind the opened door with a gun in his hand levelled at the intruder's chest.

The intruder was quick; he jumped sideways, the hypodermic syringe clattering from his hand onto the floor, and jumped for the window. Petro took careful aim at the back of the intruder's leg. The man, however, slipped on the floor and went down, and the bullet intended for his calf caught him in the back of his head, killing him instantly.

The door opened and Vassili, Petro's *enomotarxis*, flung himself in. He scudded across the room and briefly examined the body lying on the floor.

'He is dead, Chief!' he said unnecessarily.

The sound of the shot had woken the hospital and a great babble of voices sounded in the corridor.

'Get that syringe,' Petro said, 'but be careful not to smudge the prints. Take it to the pathology laboratory and tell them to analyze the contents – no doubt it will be an excessive dosage of some kind of drug.'

He heard the policemen in the corridor and outside the window telling everyone to be quiet and to go away, marvelling at the ability of a crowd to materialize anywhere, it seemed, at any time of day or night.

He crouched beside the dead man, searching his pockets.

The wallet contained money, an American Express card and a Diner's Club card, both in the name of Walter Mecklin. A passport in the same name. Once the man must have looked like the passport photograph, but his face was now unrecognizable. The passport was American, the clothing the man wore looked American to Petro – white and grey striped chino pants, a dark shirt made of sea island cotton, a belt. Petro took the wallet and the passport and left the body where it lay.

Evangelina stirred in her sleep – not even the sound of the shot had penetrated the double sleeping-dose the doctor, at Petro's request, had given her.

'Clean up,' he said to his *enomotarxis*, 'before she wakens. Be sure no one talks to her about it.'

'Yes, Chief,' Vassili said. 'Do I send for the murder squad?'

'Of course! He was about to commit a murder, was he not?'

Bill caught the six-fifteen plane for Athens where he changed terminals and found a flight leaving in one hour for Frankfurt. There, he could change onto the local Lufthansa flight. For Hamburg.

He arrived in the centre of Hamburg at three o'clock and went straight to the Central Police Station. The receptionist listened to him, found an *inspektor* who listened to him, and twenty minutes later Bill was in the Military Records Office annexe on the Hohluftchaussee, a short distance from the town centre. The records clerk was a roly-poly man wearing a dark suit, a flamboyant shirt with a twisted collar, an old-fashioned tie and thick glasses. He had the appearance of a mole more used to burying himself in dark mounds of paper than walking in the sunshine. His eyes gleamed when Bill told him what he wanted. It was a challenge and Willi Baier loved challenges.

'We have much to go on,' he said, 'though your information may seem scanty to you. Firstly, the boy's name, Hans Ohlman. Secondly, that he came from Hamburg. Thirdly, that he was in the Youth Movement, and fourthly that he was selected for the Fallschirmjaeger. Fifthly, of course, that he was posted to active duty on

Crete. It should not take us very long. First, we start with the name!'

The files were in dark green boxes on shelves which extended deep into the bowels of the building.

'We used to be in the centre of the town,' he said, chattering as he searched, 'but the cross-referencing meant we needed more space, more space, always more space, until finally the Amt kicked us out. Go find more space for yourselves, they said. I knew about this building – it used to be a warehouse for a book publisher, you know – and so I negotiated for it and was lucky to get it . . . Ah, yes, O for Ohlman. One "n", do you think? Makes it more easy. Ohlman, like all German surnames ending in "n", is usually spelled with two.'

'You speak good English,' Bill said, making conversation with this efficient but caricatured twinkling man.

'We had to learn English, you know, in the school. Now, I get so many enquiries from America and from England, I seem to speak it all the time. Only the Americans and English want to know what happened to their relations in the war. The Germans do not bother to ask. They're afraid it might turn out that Uncle Friedrich had been an officer of the Gestapo. To me, it is all the same. There are good and bad, inevitably, on both sides of any fence, *nicht wahr?* My only concern is to get the documentation right. If the man was a corporal in the Sixth Panzer Regiment, then the documentation should show that precisely, not that he was a sergeant in the Fifth Panzer. That would be as bad as assigning the wrong K number to a Mozart work . . . Good. Ohlman, with one "n". We have twenty-seven!'

Bill groaned.

'We have Ohlman, Adolf, four. No. No. Ah, here we are. Ohlman, Hans, only three!' He drew three sheets of paper from the file, carefully inserting in their place a green slip, a bunch of which grew out of his top pocket like iris leaves.

'All from Hamburg. All in the Youth Movement. Hmnn, and all trained as Fallschirmjaeger! Now there is yet another of those many coincidences that make my life so fascinating. But only this one served on Crete.'

He was reading off the information on each sheet of paper from a set of symbols as meaningful to him as shorthand to a secretary. 'You see this symbol "K" is for Kreta,' he explained.

'Is that him?' Bill asked.

'Do not be in such a hurry,' Willi Baier said, mildly disapproving. 'This information has been lying undisturbed for over thirty years. We must bring it back slowly, carefully. Now we look at file 274/15/2745.'

'What is that?' Bill asked.

'With luck it is the life story of Hans Ohlman, the man you are looking for.'

They found it; the age was right, the qualifications were right, and there was another suggestive pointer.

Willi Baier chuckled as he read it. 'One of those, eh?' he said. 'The human race is never short of surprises . . .'

Bill was impatient to know.

'Your friend Hans,' Willi said, 'started off his life in high enthusiasm for the National Socialist principles. He became a member of the Youth Organization and won commendations. He joined the Army as soon as he was able; he even joined the Nazi Party, which was not, of course, compulsory. He was offered Gestapo training but turned it down in favour of active duty with the paratroops – it was no doubt a more glamorous unit for a young man – won immediate recognition and was posted to a crack unit. Went to Crete. There, however, things seem to have gone wrong. He was reprimanded three times for being drunk on duty. Was given military punishment in the category known as "severe". Was eventually charged with cowardice and sentenced to death. His superior officer intervened on his behalf, because of his record, and he was posted to a labour battalion on the Russian Front. He never joined that battalion . . .'

'Does it say why not . . . ?'

'Yes. He was imprisoned in military hospital in Augsburg . . .'

'Why was that . . . ?'

'It does not say here on the record. Now that is a bad thing – someone ought to have picked him up from the hospital files; he ought to have been cross-referenced. Wait till I find out who was in charge of that file. I will make it hot for them, you can mark my words . . .'

Willi's eyes gleamed with zealous anger.

'Does it say *anything* about his life in hospital?'

'No, only that he was discharged. In September, 1945.'

'You said he was *imprisoned* in hospital. That is an unusual word to use in the English language. We usually say "admitted" . . .'

'I know what I am saying, my good sir,' Willi snapped waspishly, obviously still angered by the failure of his cross-referencing machine. 'He was *imprisoned*. There were two hospitals in Augsburg. This one was destroyed by the Americans when Germany was defeated. It was used by Himmler's men. For experiments in genetic engineering . . . !'

Hans Ohlman lived in the poorer part of Hamburg in a Government rent-controlled flat that had not been repaired since the day it was thrown together hastily in 1953. Bill glanced at the furniture; the odd tables and chairs, the cupboard and sideboard, both carefully hand-painted, the standard lamp that once had graced the drawing room of a large mansion before the shade became tattered. It had been sewn carefully but not very expertly.

Hans Ohlman noticed the direction of Bill's gaze. 'Each month, in Hamburg, people put out the things they no longer want. Anyone can go round and collect what they need. Young people setting up home on a budget tour the city on that particular evening. Anything left over, the city authorities take away and burn.'

Bill had been shocked when finally he'd met Hans

Ohlman at the address Willi had given him. He'd formed a mental picture, based on Evangelina's description of the tall, handsome, fighting-fit paratrooper. The man who'd confronted him when he'd knocked on the door had white hair, the sallow complexion that comes from internal disorders and the drawn features that speak eloquently of a life-time of suffering. Though his shoulders were stooped, he still, however, retained an air of dignity, of pride. Bill saw that his suit, though frayed at the cuffs, had been carefully if somewhat clumsily repaired. The tiny flat was impeccably clean. Though the walls and the woodwork had not been painted for a decade, they had been washed; the curtains at the window were bright, through a little tattered at the seams.

A plate on the table carried a small piece of ham, an end of a loaf of coarse-grain bread and an end of cucumber. A cracked pot tureen carried a thick pea soup which steamed and smelled deliciously.

'You are welcome to share my supper,' Hans said with a natural dignity, as if the food on the table were a banquet fit for a gourmet.

Bill had to admire the man's style; though he'd obviously been down on his luck for a considerable time, he made no apology for the sparseness of his surroundings or the frugality of his table.

'I have just eaten,' he lied, 'but please do not let me stop you.'

'It can wait,' Hans Ohlman said. 'What can I do for you?'

Bill accepted the invitation to sit in a chair. 'You once saved my father's life,' Bill said. 'I wanted to come and thank you.'

Hans Ohlman smiled. 'I am afraid you will have to tell me a little more about the circumstances,' he said. 'I know I should remember something as important as saving the life of another man, but . . .'

'It was on Crete, during the war,' Bill said quietly.

The grimace that came to Hans's face was as if Bill had

punched him violently in the stomach. He took a handkerchief from his pocket and used it to wipe his lips.

'I'm sorry to speak so brashly about something I can guess must be hateful to you,' Bill said. 'I've been to the Military Records Office. They gave me your address before the war and then helped me find your new address. They showed me your Military Record . . .'

'It is a sad thought to know that one's actions have been recorded for all to see,' Hans said. 'But I suppose that is the inescapable nature of modern life . . .'

'I have recently experienced the same thing,' Bill said, thinking of Petro's search through his history. 'I too was punished for drunkenness.'

Hans smiled. 'It is a foolish way of seeking oblivion,' he said gently. 'Can you remind me of the circumstances of my meeting with your father. I presume I *did* meet him, if I saved his life?'

'It was a cave in a place called the Gorge of the Angels. High in the Mavri mountain. My father was hiding with a woman and two babies . . .'

Hans immediately remembered it. 'That was the day of my conversion,' he said sadly. 'The day I allowed myself to forget all the dogma the National Socialists, the Nazis, the Military Authorities, had pumped into me. The day I allowed myself to *think*; to look about me and, for the first time, to *see* what was happening. I was never the same after that day. In a way, I think I could say that your father saved *my* life. He was such a tender and gentle man; he was so gentle with the Cretan lady with the two babies!'

'That lady is still alive; I saw her only yesterday. It was she who told me how good and kind *you* had been.'

Hans smiled. 'I thought the rest of the world said the only good German is a dead one! The moment my eyes were opened, I knew how wrong I had been. How innocent, if I dare use that expression. How overly simplistic. I believed that good would triumph, that perhaps we had to use evil in the day as a means of securing good for the morrow. That in the end all the killing, the torture, the brutality, would be justified by the result. Your father awoke a spark in me that has never since been extinguished.'

'You've suffered for that?' Bill said.

'Yes, that is true. As you know from having read my record, I could never bring myself to take part in military actions again. For a time I used drunkenness as my means of escape, but then they sent me back. They had had enough of a paratrooper who was always too blind drunk to jump. They sent me back to Germany, before assigning me to a labour battalion in Russia, but, in the assembly prison in Klagenhofsburg, I had the misfortune to meet a soldier I had once despised. I had known him in the Youth Movement – even there he was a rat. I had done my duty as a good Nazi and informed on him to his superior. He never forgave me. When I returned from Crete, like the rat he was, he'd nibbled his way into a position of responsibility and had even been made an officer in the Gestapo. It was he who sent me to Augsburg.'

Hans fell silent, remembering, seeing a parade of places and faces, of men who were pleased to give a downwards shove to this former paragon, the élite paratrooper who'd been sentenced for cowardice.

'Don't say any more,' Bill said quietly. 'I had no desire to stir up bad memories.'

'I have learned to live with these things. Perhaps, after all these years, it will be like therapy to face up to them again. In Augsburg – the special war-time hospital, you understand, that was destroyed by the Americans after the war – they were conducting genetic experiments. Trying to improve the race, to eliminate all those bad "human" tendencies that crop up in all men. They needed sources of raw material. I became such a source. After all, despite my cowardice and my drunkenness, I came of good Aryan stock. The testicles, the liver, the kidneys, the pancreas, the thyroid glands all came in for special treatment. Sometimes the surgery involved was crude; they weren't, after all, trying to cure me as much as to extract every milligram of usable biochemical. Medically, I am told, my insides are a disaster. But, since there are no records of what went on in Augsburg – the hospital commandant took pains to destroy them just before the Americans arrived – I cannot prove I was a patient and not an orderly. I do not, therefore, have a pension. Sometimes – in fact, most nights – I cannot sleep very well. I am very tired during the day and have never been able to hold on to a regular job. Now I have a job of sorts. I have two, three, sometimes four *kneipes* where I can go after they close, to clean the floors, wash the tables. I earn enough to live that way but not, you will appreciate, for luxuries!'

All this was said without a single trace of self-pity. It was not a plea for help, for pity. Merely a statement of the facts of the matter.

'Do you think we could talk for a while about my father?' Bill asked. 'I'm so very anxious to question everyone who met him, however briefly, anyone who can cast light on his character, his personality.'

'One of the things that impressed me when I first saw him was the fact that he could have killed me but didn't,' Hans said thoughtfully. 'Perhaps he had many reasons for not doing so but in my unit we were taught to kill instinctively, without counting the reasons. Kill first, kill quickly, or you yourself will be killed. Your father must have had none of that kind of training. When we came from the cave, even though we were nominally enemies, he was friendly towards me and very gentle to the woman and the babies. I can see them both now, the tiny mites, bundled in clothing, two leather wallets hanging round their shoulders like knapsacks. They were so alike I believed them to be brother and sister, and the woman who carried them so bravely to be their mother. I stayed with them as we skirted the parachutists' camp, in case any of my fellow paratroopers should see them. I planned to say I had taken them prisoner, to avoid their being shot on sight. It was your father who told me the woman was not the mother of the babies. He told me how the two real mothers had sacrificed themselves so that he and the babies could escape with the woman. The way he told it, I felt so terribly ashamed and yet, in a way, proud that humans could be so self-sacrificing. If you like, it was the knowledge of the true nobility of those women, whom I would never know in person but whom I had seen brutally murdered by our Feldwebel, that started me on my path of self-analysis, self-criticism.

'I was with your father for one hour only. During that time, I came to respect him. And then, when the time came for us to separate, for me to return to my unit, so far as he knew, to more killing, more brutality, he didn't try to stop me, to lecture me, to kill me. He could have done this. Once we were away from the camp we talked as we walked along. I remember now, he told me about his son living in America in safety, saying thank God that you would never know anything of the horror and sordidness of those years. You must be that son; how strange but, in a way, how complete that at last I should meet you.'

'And that was the last you saw of my father? Heading away across the Mavri with the woman and the children?'

'Yes. I often wondered what happened to him. If he survived.'

'He was killed shortly after he left you,' Bill said. 'He left the woman and the children and headed back to the battle lower down the mountain, where your other unit was supposed to be ambushed. But, of course, you knew about the ambush, didn't you? And you trapped the villagers and the Resistance fighters and killed most of them.'

'Yes. We stayed in the camp in the gorge for three hours, and then we went down the mountain. Our B Company had slaughtered most of the fighters; then we went in to finish matters. I pretended to fall on a rock, twisting my ankle, and that way stayed out of the battle. I never fought again.'

'Can I ask you one more thing? You knew my father, if only for one hour. Recently I met a man on Crete who said many men believed my father was the traitor, the one who betrayed the villagers of Mavroti to your unit. Do you think from what you discovered about my father that that was true. Don't try to spare my feelings; if he *was* a traitor, I want to know . . .'

Hans was smiling. 'Your father, a *traitor*! Quite impossible!'

'But how can you be so sure?'

'Because I knew who the traitor was. He used to meet my major clandestinely. I always went along as one of the major's bodyguards. I never saw him face to face, you understand, so I cannot describe him in detail except that he was a much smaller man than your father, much heavier built.'

'Do you know who he was?'

'Yes,' Hans Ohlman said. 'He was a Resistance fighter who believed the Germans would win. A *palikari*, I seem to remember they called the leaders of the Resistance. He knew all their plans. His code name was Theseus.'

Bill stayed the night in Hamburg at the railway hotel by the main station. It offered simple comfort. He could not forget the image of Hans Ohlman, that brave man struggling with a life that must have become almost impossibly hard to bear; his body in total disorder, racked with nightly pain, and unable to hold down a regular steady job. They'd talked into the evening about Hans's way of living. He read a lot, in German, English and French. He'd even tried to learn Greek, but his instincts had given him a mental block.

Bill's sleep was troubled and several times he got out of bed and sat in the chair of his room reviewing the knowledge he had gained since he went to Crete. As usually happens, he fell sound asleep around six o'clock and was woken by the room-maid bustling in at nine. He

154

hung the Do Not Disturb sign on the door-knob and slept soundly until midday.

Then he made two telephone calls. The first one was to London, to the solicitor in Gray's Inn who handled the trust fund his father had set up all those years ago.

'How is the fund, Victor?' Bill asked.

'Very healthy, now that you seem to have come to your senses and are no longer drinking it away.'

'Is there any way it can provide a capital sum?'

'To you, no. Your father was very skilful about that. He wanted you to have the income. It will provide capital for your heirs when they achieve a majority. Why?'

'I want to split the fund. There is a man who deserves part of that money. I'd like to see him get a share. Look, I don't need it all; I'll be getting another job soon . . .'

'And keeping it how long, Bill? You don't have a very good record in that respect.'

Bill told the solicitor about Hans Ohlman. Victor was Jewish; somehow it helped him understand.

'What I can do, Bill, is to borrow from the fund's income against the fund's capital. I can effectively pay Mr Ohlman ten thousand pounds equivalent immediately and then see that he gets shall we say ten thousand *deutschmarks* a year for the rest of his life. It'll cut your money for a few years . .'

'I don't mind that. I have much more than I need right now. One thing, Victor, let him know the money comes from my father, and not from me, eh?'

The other telephone call was to Boston. Greg Faraday hadn't yet left for his office. 'Bill, for Christ's sake, I haven't heard from you in years. Where are you, what are you doing? Looking for your old job back?'

'No, Greg. You remember I suggested, just before I left, we ought to have somebody in Germany reading all the trade magazines and sending us extracts as part of our market-intelligence department. Has that been set up?'

Greg's voice was hesitant. 'You know how it is, Bill. I have so much on my plate, I've just never got around to it. I use an agency in New York, but they miss half the stuff.

If I could find our own guy . . . The board has approved a job allocation.'

'I've found just the man for you,' Bill said. 'His name is Hans Ohlman.'

'Great, Bill. Where does he live?'

'I'll get him to write to you. I think he may be changing his address any moment now . . .'

When Bill arrived in Xania that night, after changing planes in Athens, he realized that the nature of his enquiry had changed. Somehow he was only interested now in clearing his father's name of the accusation of treachery. Though the events had occurred thirty-five years ago, he still thought he might be able to back-track them. After all, he had the code name of the real traitor – Theseus – hadn't he?

He came from the plane deep in thought and, without any luggage other than the small shoulder bag he'd taken, was able to avoid the crowd and head for the rank of taxis on the other side of the small terminal. He had his hand on the taxi door when he felt his arm being clutched. He turned; the man standing there had that unmistakable aura of coppers everywhere.

'The *Ipastinomos* would like to see you, *Kirios* Thomas,' the man said. 'I have a car waiting.'

Bill left the taxi and climbed into the Fiat 133 that was parked in the non-parking area. 'VIP treatment?' he said, making conversation.

The policeman grunted but said nothing then nor all the way in to Xania. He'd used his radio, saying several code-words meaningless to Bill. As they drove past the National Bank of Crete he spoke to Bill for the first time.

'You going to stay in Zorba's pension again?' he asked.

'Yes. I didn't give up my room.'

'We know.'

He drove Bill to the side of the Lucia Hotel in the old

port. 'The Superintendent says stay in your room until he gets here,' he said.

'Am I under arrest?'

'Not so far as I am aware. Just stay in your room!'

Petro arrived five minutes later. 'Where have you been?' he asked. 'I have had half my force out looking for you. It is only when we checked the Olympic flight records that we found you'd flown to Athens, en route to Frankfurt.'

'I thought you were having me watched,' Bill said. 'I supposed your men would spot me leaving and report to you . . .'

Petro had the grace to appear sheepish. 'We *were* watching you. The fool of a policeman on duty that night has a sweet tooth. When the pastry baker opened that damned idiot, thinking you safely tucked up for the night, went off and spent an hour stuffing his fat belly! Meanwhile you took a taxi from the square to the airport. The taxi driver took his next fare to Heraklion and decided to stay there for a couple of nights. We located him this afternoon!'

'I'm flattered,' Bill said.

'You will not feel that way when I tell you what has happened since you left Evangelina. Somebody came into her room and tried to inject a massive overdose of insulin. It could have killed her within minutes, and the doctors would have believed she died of a heart attack!'

'You said "tried to" . . .?' He wasn't successful . . .?'

'No. I was standing in the cupboard watching him at the time! I shot at him to try to bring him down. He stumbled and the bullet hit his head. Do you know the name Walter Mecklin, from your days in America?'

'He was American?'

'He had a US passport. We are checking with Washington, but so far we have no information about him. He also had American Express and Diners Club cards. We have checked with those companies; their bills were settled automatically by the Chemical Bank of New York. They apparently have no permanent address for him. From time to time they receive deposits from banks from many different countries – he appeared to be a man who travelled a lot. He could be a hired assassin.'

'But why, why use him against Evangelina?'

'The answer to that question should be obvious to you. Because she talked to you. Do you not realize, Bill, that somebody is tracking your movements? Everybody who talks to you ends up dead!'

'Is Maria Stafanakis okay?'

'Yes, that was my first thought, that they might also get to her. Victorio is unharmed too. We have put Evangelina under constant guard, and one of my interrogators is getting her to repeat everything she said to you, everything she can remember about your father. If you know anything, Bill, anything you have not yet told me, please . . .'

'I think this may be it,' Bill said, excited. 'I went to Germany to see a man called Hans Ohlman – oh, my God, can we get in touch with Hamburg immediately?' He gave Petro Hans's name and address, and Petro despatched one of his men with rapid-fire instructions.

When he'd gone, Petro said, 'Please, the details . . .'

'Hans Ohlman is a German. He was a paratrooper who grew sick of the killing here on Crete. One of his jobs was bodyguard to an Army major, the contact for a *palikari* who was also a German sympathizer. And a traitor!'

'Please, Bill,' Petro said, exasperated. 'Give me a name, a name, damnit!'

'Theseus!'

'Who Theseus?'

'That was his war-time code-name!'

Petro was silent, thinking deeply. 'That is it!' he said. 'After the war, the code lists of all the *palikari* were destroyed. They linger on only in the memories of the older people, the people who were actually there in the mountains fighting. Somebody does not want anyone putting a real name to the code-name, Theseus . . . And he is prepared to hire assassins to prevent it from happening!'

He got up from his chair. 'Where are you going?' Bill asked.

'To see Evangelina. You had better come with me!'

On the way through Xania, the radio telephone in Petro's car sounded his code-symbol. He picked up the microphone and identified himself.

The message was concise. 'On that call to Hamburg, Chief. We talked to the police. Hans Ohlman was killed early this morning by a hit-and-run driver, on his way back from a taverna where he'd been working . . .'

Petro looked sideways at Bill, who was numb with shock. He lifted his hand, then smashed it down on the top of the dash-board. 'Damn and blast it,' Bill said. 'Damn, sod and blast it! That poor bugger. He was so brave; they'd made such a mess of him but he was trying so hard to keep himself decent. If only I'd stayed away . . .'

'You cannot reproach yourself, Bill,' Petro said. 'From what you have told me, life could not have been all that good for him.'

But Bill did reproach himself. He couldn't obliterate the sight of that brave but shattered man, with his plate of food, his patched suit, his basic inner decency that wouldn't let him complain.

'I'll catch the bastard who's doing this,' Bill said angrily. 'If it's the last thing I do!'

Evangelina was having a good time talking endlessly to the police interrogator, who was taking down each word with great care. She'd never known such a good audience. On the table in front of her chair was a tape-recording machine whose microphone was picking up every sound she made; she squealed with delight when he played it back to her every time he'd missed a word in his shorthand.

Petro came straight to the point. 'Evangelina,' he asked, 'who was the *palikari* known as Theseus?'

'Theseus? Theseus was General Spiros Orfandakis. He was the greatest *palikari* of them all . . .'

Bill went back up to Kaprisses with his head buzzing. It didn't make sense, did it? The general a traitor? They'd questioned Evangelina again and again but nothing would shake her conviction that Theseus was Spiros Orfandakis. But Orfandakis was one of the several who'd died. How could a dead man plant a bomb in Stavakis's car, arrange the murder of Hans Ohlman – Bill was certain that was no accidental hit-and-run accident – and even arrange the attempted muder of Evangelina herself?

When he arrived in the village he realized he didn't know where Maria lived, though he knew he could easily find her. Victorio was in the *kafeneion*, a changed man now he had learned the truth about his father. He was no longer boisterous and overt, and greeted Bill listlessly.

'When you escaped over the mountain,' Bill said, 'you and Maria, you carried a leather satchel round your shoulders. Evangelina tells me the idea was your mother's. In the bag she'd put a few personal possessions. It would seem that even when she started that trip she had some kind of premonition. By any chance, do you remember that leather satchel, and do you know what happened to it?'

'I still have it somewhere,' Victorio said without much interest. 'I have not seen it for ages.'

'Could you find it?'

'It must be somewhere around the place.'

'Could you look for it?'

'Yes, I will find it sometime . . .'

'Not *sometime*, Victorio,' Bill said. 'Not *avrio*. Now!'

Victorio waved his hand around the *kafeneion* which was three quarters full. 'And who will look after my customers? Friend, Bill, I told you once there is no point in searching the past. The past is dead and buried. I have a busy *kafeneion*; I earn enough to keep myself alive. What the hell does the past matter? Go away, Bill. Take Maria with you and go away and leave us all in peace!'

'Look, Victorio. You didn't have any say in the matter

when you were born. We don't choose our own parents. What does it matter who your father was . . .'

'You can say that. Your father was married. He was a great hero! My father and mother were not married, which makes me a bastard, and my father was a murderer, not a hero!'

Bill knew he'd do nothing with Victorio until the pain of the knowledge he'd gained about his antecedents had faded. He went in search of Maria and found her in the cottage that belonged to Evangelina. The cottage was set back from the road behind a wall with an open gate. Inside Bill could see a small, long courtyard, covered by a vine, with many pots of carefully tended geraniums, hibiscus, basil. The geraniums were still blooming. The courtyard took and retained whatever warmth was in the October day; it was a sun-trap of delicious appearance.

From a low room off the courtyard, Bill could hear a sound he couldn't identify, a steady rhythmic clack that stopped every so often, then was resumed. A radio was playing softly a sad Cretan tune of lyre and bouzouki, with a woman's voice singing a plaintive melody.

He called softly. 'Hello?'

There was no answer. He went through the door into the courtyard and was immediately seized by his wrist. His arm was forced up behind his back; he felt something hard press into his back and cursed himself for falling so stupidly into a trap. Of course, whoever was doing the murders would expect him to call on Maria; he would simply stand in wait for him.

The man behind him spun him round. 'Oh, it is you,' he said.

He was the policeman who had given Bill his lift from the airport. Bill was flooded with relief when he realized Petro was having Maria guarded.

'She is in there,' the policeman said, indicating the room from which the clack still came.

Bill went forward, stood in the doorway and called. 'Maria.'

'Come in,' she said.

He went in. She was sitting at a loom and the clack he had heard was the shuttle flying backwards and forwards across the material as she pulled the handle above her head. She was weaving a fine cotton material; on the roll in front of her were many coloured threads. When she stopped the shuttle, she bent over the weave with a needle, sewing the threads into the pattern of the material. He looked over her shoulder.

'I won't be a minute,' she said, 'but if I stop now I'll forget the pattern!'

She worked the shuttle a couple more times, banging the threads tight into the weave. The loom was over two metres wide; the cloth would be a very fine material with an inlaid pattern Bill had seen on many rugs and pieces of cloth in the shops, but never so delicately woven.

'Evangelina taught me this,' she said. 'I used to come in here from our house to watch her. She made such wonderful things until her arthritis stopped her!'

He bent down and kissed the nape of her neck, feeling her shiver. She forgot the weaving, turned round on the bench and put her arms around his neck, drawing his mouth to hers in a long, deep kiss. Her mouth tasted like mountain spring water after a long hard journey.

'I was going to be so happy here,' she said, 'sitting at Evangelina's loom, weaving my cotton and woollen fabrics, perhaps even selling them in a shop in Xania. And then you came along and this suddenly seems like a prison to me . . .'

'I've got to talk to someone, Maria, and I'd like it to be you!'

Something in his voice stopped her romantic mood quickly. 'You'd better come into the other room,' she said.

She poured him a glass of home-made lemonade, and she told him everything he'd discovered. Except the fact about her mother being unmarried.

'Do you remember the leather satchels, Maria?' he asked, when his story had ended.

As he'd recounted the information about each death her eyes had opened wider and wider. When he'd told her about Hans Ohlman, the man who'd helped save her life, she began to cry. He put his arm round her to console her.

'I didn't remember him,' she said, 'but Evangelina told me about him and how he helped her to escape. She told me about how my mother and Victorio's mother deliberately sacrificed themselves so that we could get away in Evangelina's arms . . .'

'You knew Stafanakis and his wife weren't your parents . . .?'

'Yes, I knew that long ago. Poor Victorio. When we were young here together, he tried so hard to protect me, like a big brother. I think if it hadn't been for that brotherly feeling, we would have had an arranged marriage together – I know he's always been fond of me. When I left to go to America, it was largely because I wanted to get away from him for a while, to test my feelings about him. You know the result. That poor man, Mr Ohlman! To survive all that and then be murdered by a hit-and-run driver, alone at night on a cold Hamburg street!'

'That leather satchel could be important, Maria,' Bill reminded her.

'I know; that's what's so sad. I had it with some other things in my suitcase in New York once. The suitcase was stolen from the trunk of the car! More than anything else, I missed that little leather purse. It had been everywhere with me!'

'Can you remember what was in it, Maria?'

'Nothing very much. A fuzzy picture of my father and mother standing near a wall in the sun. A locket made of brass, with what I took to be hair in it. A gold ring . . .'

'Any inscription in it?'

'No, nothing. It looked well-worn, I remember. There was also a scrap of yellowed paper on which someone had written, in funny Greek characters, a few lines of a poem, written I would say by an amateur, an amorous girl perhaps!'

Bill was disappointed. Somehow, he'd placed great store by the leather satchels and their contents. 'Victorio says he still has his somewhere. We must get him to find it . . .'

'He's very stubborn. He always was. But I could usually talk him round. Shall I try?'

'If you would.'

'They won't like me going in the *kafeneion* and taking the *horofilakas* with me. The men of the village have the traditional mistrust of the police, you know.'

'Perhaps I can persuade him to stay here while I look after you,' Bill said.

The *horofilakas* was happy to stay in the comfort of the courtyard drinking lemonade. Bill didn't hear what Maria said to Victorio; he sat at a table just inside the door, feeling slightly melodramatic, while they talked behind the counter. When Victorio went into the back room, Maria made coffees and served glasses of water as the *tavli*-playing men called for them. Several made jokes which Maria parried with deft ease, but mostly the *tavli* and the cards gripped their attention. When Victorio returned, he was carrying a newspaper-wrapped parcel.

'Take the damned thing away,' he said, 'and do not bring it back. I do not want to see it again.'

They took it to Maria's house and opened it. Inside, yellow with age, Bill found a diary bound in calf-skin with a brass lock, about an inch thick with gold-leaved page edges. The key was in the satchel with it. There was also a folder containing three photographs. One was a man on his own, dressed in Sfakian clothing, carrying a Sfakian shepherd's crook somewhat self-consciously. The second photograph showed the same man with a slender, bright-eyed girl, who wore a defiant look on her face. The third photograph showed the girl and the man, and between them, a baby.

Bill's heart lurched as he held the photographs to the light. Despite the years that had passed since the photograph was taken, he could see the features quite clearly. The man and the girl unquestionably were the father and the mother of the baby. Both carried that familiar look of self-satisfied pride.

'I must go back to Xania,' he said. 'Will you come with me?'

Maria shook her head. 'No, Bill. Not yet. I don't want us to start like this, if we *are* going to start. I want you to finish this business on your own, without me. I've bought a little car; it'll be delivered later today. So I can come and see you even when there are no buses. But first, you must take care of this business. I couldn't bear the thought if I should stand between you and the wretched people who arranged the death of that wonderful man Mr Ohlman. Aren't you going to read the diary before you go? It might tell you something important.'

'I'll read it after I've had another word with Evangelina.'

Evangelina was still telling her story to the shorthand writer, who was beginning to get a glazed look to his eyes.

'Could you wait outside for a moment?' Bill asked him.

The man left, grateful for the respite.

Bill took the leather satchel from the newspaper wrapping.

Evangelina wept when she saw it. 'I have not seen that for so long,' she said. 'Maria took it to America with her and it was lost. Where did you find it?'

'This is the satchel of Victorio, not Maria,' Bill said, handing it to Evangelina.

'No, surely not. This one has these silver coloured rings on it. Victorio's had brass coloured rings. The girls got different rings so they would always be able to tell them apart.'

'I got it from Victorio,' Bill said.

'Victorio?' Evangelina asked, puzzled. 'I could have sworn . . .'

Bill had seated himself near Evangelina. He reached out and held her hand. 'Just as you could have sworn that

Theseus was Spiros Orfandakis? Can you look at this photograph for me?' He showed her the picture of the man alone he'd taken from the satchel.

Evangelina looked closely at it, then turned to Bill. 'It was all so long ago,' she whispered.

'Who is it, Evangelina?' Bill asked softly.

'I think you know who it was, young man.'

'I want you to tell me the name.'

'You understand, I said what I did to protect you and Victorio . . .'

'You pained Victorio very much by telling him the lie that his father was a German soldier. His father was that man in the photograph. His war-time code-name was Maleta. Roger Thomas. The girl in that picture was Elvira, not Irena. My father is the father of Victorio, with Elvira his mother. It was Irena who went with the German and gave birth to a *girl* child, Maria. Irena was a romantic; she even wrote poems to her German lover and Maria had those poems until her bag was stolen in New York!'

'It was all so long ago,' Evangelina said. 'Things were different then. I knew the girls were not married when they came to the village but in those days unmarried mothers suffered badly. Sometimes, if it was suspected the girl had been with a German, the baby was thrown over the cliff, and many times the girls, too. The first time Maleta came to the village and spoke with Elvira, I knew the baby was his. A woman can tell these things. That was what made things so bad in the Gorge of the Angels. That the *mother* had to sacrifice herself for the baby when the father had to stand by, helpless. I did not tell you but when we were in the cave, Maleta asked me to look after the baby and told me he would be back after the war to care for the baby himself, perhaps take the child to England and send him to a fine school.'

'And the hatred in the village, when I first arrived and said I was his son?'

'You have to remember how it was in those times. Elvira was thought to have been married to a fine Cretan boy who had died fighting for his country. She had given birth to his baby, so everyone thought. And then this Englishman comes and starts paying attentions to this war-widow. Once, someone even saw them kissing and that caused a great scandal. They thought a foreigner was tampering with a war-widow!'

'And since Elvira had no kin in the village . . .'

'Everyone in the village took it upon himself to be her protector, her father-figure, her brother-figure. You were fortunate the entire village did not rise against you when you arrived — twenty years ago they would have stoned you to death to atone for the offence of your father . . .'

'And the lady in the shop, who pleaded with me to go away?'

'She is my greatest friend. You understand, I had to talk to someone about this great burden I was carrying. She and I are the only two who knew the truth, until you came along weaving together all the fine strands . . .'

Bill went back to the Pension Zorbas and lay on his bed, reluctant to carry his investigation further until he had assimilated the knowledge he'd already gained. He'd established to his own satisfaction that Evangelina's memory was faulty, but that she had such a love of talking that she was prepared to carry the narrative of those war years along with scant regard for the actual truth. Who was there to question her word? It had been an innocent deception, until she had tried to manipulate the facts to protect one person. She had not realized there is a balance of truth; any attempt to interfere with that balance can only result in good for some, evil for others.

The brass lock on the diary gleamed on the night-table by his bed. He couldn't ignore it. He took the key and opened the book carefully. The spine crackled and a musty smell came from the pages.

The diary had been bought in a shop in St James's,

London. The title page had been printed in flowing script. *This is the diary of Captain Roger Thomas.* Beneath that was printed – *Time and the Hour runs through the roughest Day.*

1st January, 1941. Private Brian Cargill reported for duty today. Before the war he was a waiter-cook. Promises well for eating!

Bill closed the diary, the emotional strain of reading his father's words and of looking at life through his father's eyes was too much for him to take in one sitting. He'd heard of the events at Mavroti from several different sources – was he now to see and feel, through the pages of this book, an eye-witness account?

He sat upright and deliberately forced himself to reopen the pages and read the entries one by one. His father's literary style was factual rather than poetic. He gave details of fellow officers and of the men who trained with him, with often only a thumb-nail, subjective, sketch.

He told of his posting to Cairo, his transfer to Alexandria, his uneventful journey across the waters to Crete, his landing, his first few days with Kostas Dandanakis and Pakrades, his first trip up into the mountains. His account of the first day he'd spent in the Lefka Ori had a certain natural simple charm; he'd obviously fallen in love at first sight with the scenic grandeur, the hardened characters, the rugged, rustic lives of the people he met.

He described some of the actions in which he became involved. The destruction of a bridge and the way they'd strewn the area with British Commando detritus to make the Germans believe a force had landed, blown the bridge, and then departed without help from the Cretan people. Sometimes, it appeared from the diary, the Germans were deceived by the parachutes they found stuffed behind rocks, the remains of meals of British food, the empty packets of Players Navy Cut cigarettes. They even deposited bus-tickets marked London Transport, dated a few days before the action.

Sometimes, the Germans were not deceived and the diary painfully recorded stories of massacres, of the destruction of whole villages.

15th July 1943. I ask myself sometimes, to weigh the rights and wrongs of one bridge destroyed at the expense of twenty-seven hopeful young lives. It's an equation not even God can help me balance.

Only rarely did Captain Roger Thomas philosophize in the pages of his diary, but then the agony could be felt strongly.

17th August 1943. We will lose this battle unless we realize and accept that man has an innate capacity for bestiality. We must not play the game according to a set of rules of our own invention, truly, but if we descend into that same pit of horror, that same Styx, by what miracle will we resurrect ourselves.

All the *palikari* were mentioned often. Manoletto seemed to have been a big shambling bear of a man with a childish sense of humour, a predilection for practical jokes, an enormous appetite for food and drink and, strangely, a courteous fear of 'the ladies'.

Spiros Orfandakis was a philosopher-soldier, an educated man who drew examples from the past to plan his strategies of the Resistance fighters' war. He was excessively polite but had a command of iron when necessary. It became apparent that everyone, including Maleta, admired him immensely.

Theseus was small, fat, ubiquitous. Maleta dismissed him as a 'counter-jumper', a term Bill remembered vaguely from the novels of H. G. Wells as someone who started life humbly behind a counter and managed by diligence, and often by fawning flattery, to secure promotion to the other side, the manager side, of that social barrier.

It was obvious to Bill that once again Evangelina's memory had been suspect. But if Theseus *wasn't* Spiros Orfandakis, then who *was* he?

The entry which followed the first mention of Elvira stretched over the pages of two consecutive days. It had obviously been written on the evening of the second day.

How can I describe the emotions I feel as I sit down to write. Elvira is cooking the rabbit I caught earlier, with herbs found on the mountain and water from a spring, using the last of the salt from my pack. It was my intention to go to Kaprisses and deliver her to safety there. Why have I delayed? The only answer can be Elvira and the shameful carnality she has woken in me. I thought that part of my body dormant for the duration of the war. How could Elvira so quickly awaken and stimulate those forgotten feelings? And how could I become so quickly a victim of my sexual appetites. Don't say you love me, Elvira pleaded, only that you desire me, you find me attractive, you want me. I suppose that having seen her sister defiled, she wanted to reassert the beauty of clean desire. Am I so English that I cannot accept sexual relations outside of love and marriage? Such a prig? Elvira teased me by calling me a cold English fish. Is that true? I think not. I enjoyed lying with Elvira. I enjoyed being naked in my sleeping bag with her naked beside me and beneath me. Oh, God, when will this war come to an end. Why doesn't Cairo send the troops they have been talking about. An invasion of Crete would be so simple to mount, so decisive. The Cretan people are ready to fight any day. We could kick the Germans off this island in a week. And then I could be posted elsewhere, anywhere my mind and body are not so perturbed . . .

The last entry bore no date and followed several blank pages.

I must leave Evangelina alone with the children but now she will be safe. She is a fine woman and an inspiration. I have talked with this curious German boy. He is such a mixture of German dogma and frustrated humanity. I hope he will not suffer for his kindness to Evangelina and the children. I think from what he has said that I know now who the traitor is who has so bedevilled us these last few months. I will go back down the mountain to confront him, to kill him if necessary. I will leave my diary with the baby and not risk putting the name in it, lest I suspect the wrong man. I pray to God I will return.

Bill closed the book, his mind deeply troubled by the image he had formed of his father, this simple, cautious man caught by emotional, military and political forces he could not understand, a man of basic principles who had suffered the shame of desire. He realized quite clearly that his father came from a world which died after the war ended, a world with rigid values. He shuddered to think what his father would have made of the modern, permissive, drug-and-sex addicted world. He knew how much his father would have despised *him* for the ease with which he had coupled with Maria, the use he'd made of alcohol to forget his woes, the lack of personal strength – his father would doubtless have called it moral fibre – that had caused him to sink so low before Anna had started him back on the upward path.

On instinct, he opened the diary again and riffled through the back pages.

Something was missing, wasn't it?

He found what he was seeking; two pages had stuck together at a corner.

This is a supplementary clause to the will which has been drawn up by my solicitor, Victor Pallman, of 32 Gray's Inn Close, London. In addition to the bequests that will stipulates, I hereby add a wish that Evangelina Stogakis, of the village of Kaprisses in the Nome of Xanion, Crete, be provided with the sum of one thousand pounds a year for the rest of her lifetime, the money to be used in any way she sees fit for the benefit of herself and my child, as yet unchristened, by Elvira Brandakis (deceased). After the death of Evangelina, the capital sum from which this income is dervied is to be given without reservation to my son by Elvira Brandakis. I make this bequest while of sound mind and in full possession of my faculties.

Only one man could now help him, Bill felt. He took his car and drove to Heraklion, to the house on the Chrisostomou. Angelos Stavakis was drinking an *ouzo* on his terrace, looking out over the whole of Heraklion, and invited Bill to join him.

'I heard of the incident of your car,' Bill said. 'I want to tell you how sorry I am. It seems that disaster follows me everywhere I go on this quest to find the facts of my father's life!' He told Stavakis about the attempt on Evangelina's life and the murder – or so he felt it to be – of Hans Ohlman. 'Evangelina is now being guarded by the police, and so is Maria Stafanakis . . .'

'Our police can be very efficient,' Stavakis said. 'Who do you deal with in Xania? You realize I am not without a certain small influence there, if you need help.'

'The *ipastinomos* seems very efficient,' Bill said, thanking him.

'I know Petro,' Stavakis said. 'I have always thought he would be a good *astinomos* when the present man retires, as I believe he will shortly. Please tell your friend what I say.'

'Perhaps you can help me,' Bill said. 'I feel I have gone as far as I can in my investigation of my father.' For some reason, Bill had said nothing about the diary. 'Now my sole intention is to clear his name of being a traitor. You were a *palikari* in those days. You knew everyone. Did you know the man whose code-name was Theseus.'

A look of pain crossed Stavakis face. 'Yes, I knew Theseus,' he said quietly. 'But why do you ask?'

'Because I have reason to suspect Theseus was the man who betrayed the villagers of Mavroti. If I can prove that, then I can leave Crete a happy man.'

'Surely you can leave Crete a happy man now,' Stavakis said. 'What better knowledge can a man have than that his father was a hero?'

Bill shook his head. 'It won't work like that,' he said. 'I'm afraid I've inherited my father's stubbornness!'

Stavakis thought for a long moment. 'Please take an *ouzo*,' he said. 'And some of this cucumber. Here on Crete, we always eat something when we take strong drink. Our violence is in our emotions, not in our appetites; do you understand this?'

'I think I do.'

'Then perhaps you can understand something else. The war was a long time ago. Many things had happened which we regarded in a very violent way at the time. A classic example is the hatred we bore for the Germans who tried to break our spirits.'

'And now, as a lady in a shop in Kaprisses said to me, you take them in as tourists without reservation.'

'That is correct. We like to forget the past. Once, people

here lived so much in the past that the future was in jeopardy. Many innocent people were killed in vendettas that began so long ago that everyone alive had even forgotten the reason . . .

'You have asked me if I knew Theseus. Yes, I did know him. He was a *palikari*, like me. He worked with me many times, with Spiros Orfandakis, Manoletto, your father Maleta, with Kostas Dandanakis.

'Theseus was a thinker, Bill, and like so many thinkers, he let his head pervert him and rule his heart. He believed that what the Germans were trying to do was good. He saw the success Adolf Hitler had made in Germany, with full employment, a resurgent economy; he looked at Crete, which in those days was a poor island with many people living barely above subsistence level, and thought it would be a good thing if the German Fatherland success could be repeated here.

'Yes, I knew him. I did not know he was a traitor. Your father's runner, Pakrades, knew he was a traitor – or at least he suspected it from something your father must have said when he came down the Mavri to where the fighting was going on, though many of the men had already been slaughtered.

Do you remember I told you that after the fighting, when the Germans had gone away, I scoured the battlefield looking for dead men, hoping to find some who were still alive? Well, I found one who was barely alive. Pakrades. He was in the mouth of a cave. "The traitor Theseus is in the cave", he said to me. I went in and the sight was horrible. Pakrades and a couple of Manoletto's men had taken Theseus into the cave and there they had exacted a terrible revenge. Please do not ask me for the details – I used to have nightmares about it. When I came back out again, Pakrades had died. It was obvious to me that the men had been so intent on destroying Theseus they had not heard the Germans approach the cave. Theseus had been screaming; the Germans heard and threw grenades into the cave. Everyone but Pakrades was killed outright, and somehow he crawled outside.

'That moment was perhaps the most horrible one in my life. I forced myself to crawl back into that cave and to rearrange Theseus to hide the evidence of his own countrymen's butchery. When he was decent again, I laid him out next to the others, all together in a row. There was a risk that someone else might see what I had seen and might know the terrible truth I had learned about Theseus. The man was dead – why defile his memory? I gathered dry brushwood from the hills about, stacked it on those corpses and set it alight. When the fire was blazing, I fled from that place. When the bodies were found, they were all beyond recognition. We buried them together in one long grave, there in the foothills of the Mavri.'

Stavakis tossed off the remains of his *ouzo*, grabbed a piece of cucumber and ate it voraciously, as if to stem the rising tide of the bile of his memory. 'Let them rest in peace. Let their memory remain intact. Each of those men had family. Let them all live at peace with their souls, believing, as you should now believe, that their fathers, brothers, sons, cousins, uncles, were heroes, who died for their country.'

Bill didn't know what to say; he gazed out from the terrace, moved by Stavakis's eloquence, more powerful because of the simple way he'd expressed these horrible things.

'What is your job?' Stavakis said finally, obviously trying to change the subject, to be a gracious host.

'I have no job at the moment,' Bill said. 'I have a classics degree; I've worked in publishing, advertising, public relations . . .'

'I could use a man like you,' Stavakis said. 'Your Greek is excellent and with a little practice would become quite modern. I have many interests in Aghios Nikolaos you could look after for me. I find it so difficult to travel the full length of the island, even though we now have the motorway.'

'Are you offering me a job?' Bill said.

'Yes. I am offering you a chance to settle here on Crete. There would be a house and a car with the job, of course, and a generous salary. Your working here among us would let you see the new Crete some of us are trying to build; it would help you to forget the ways of the past . . .'

The message was quite clear. Forget about Theseus, and you get a salary, a house and a car. It wasn't the first time Bill had been offered a bribe. 'That's something I must think about,' Bill said.

'Yes, you must do that. Before your visa runs out and the authorities ask you to leave the country . . .'

Bill went to Kaprisses, feeling he was getting to know every inch of the mountain road. He found Victorio sitting in Maria's parlour, a glass of beer on the table by his hand. It wasn't the first one he'd drunk.

Maria shook her head as if to say, 'He'll be all right.'

Bill looked around the room that must have held so many memories for them.

'I suppose you lived here until you moved into the *kafeneion*, eh?' Bill asked.

'Yes.' The answer came out neutral, flat.

'I noticed you still call Evangelina "Mother".'

'I have always called her "Mother". It seems to be another of the many things I have been wrong about in my life.'

'Does it matter so much to you who your father was?'

'You ask me this? You have spent time and money answering that question for yourself. God, I wish you had stayed away and kept your nose out of our affairs!'

'Doesn't the truth interest you, for itself?'

'Look, Englishman,' Victorio said, turning the word into an epithet, 'I do not have the education for a philosophy like yours. I work in my *kafeneion* which Evangelina bought for me. I earn a living and pay back

175

Evangelina's loan, because that's what I insisted it be. I do not give a damn about what you philosophers say or do, just that you leave simple people like me alone to live our lives . . .'

'All these years,' Bill said, ignoring the outburst, 'you've lived with a lie in your heart. You've believed the man Maleta was the man who betrayed the people of Mavroti, including your mother and Maria's mother, to the Germans. I have proof it was not Maleta . . .'

'What do I care for your proof? What do I care for Maleta?'

'You should care a lot,' Bill said. 'I also have proof that Maleta, and not a German soldier, was your father. Just as he was mine. I have proof, Victorio, that you and I are brothers; same father, different mother!'

Victorio's head came up. 'What are you saying?' he whispered. 'If this is another of your stupid philosophies, this time I will kill you!'

Bill got out the photograph. 'This was in your satchel. You must have seen it a hundred times without knowing who the man was. I've just shown this picture to Evangelina. She has identified the man as Maleta and the woman as Elvira. And the baby, Victorio, is you! There was also a diary, written in English. It tells everything. One day, if you want me to, I'll translate it into Greek for you. That way you'll come, as I did, to know a little bit more about *our* father!'

Victorio leaped up and charged across the room. 'Is this true, Bill? Swear it is true! Swear it . . .'

'It's true,' Bill said then he was swept up in the air, held in the bear-like grip he'd felt before. But this time, the grip was one of love, not hate; of pleasure, not anger. Victorio couldn't contain himself; he whirled round, swinging Bill off his feet, knocking over the chair and the table that carried the beer.

'Bill,' he was shouting, 'my brother! My brother! The same blood!'

·When he put Bill down, both turned to Maria. 'You

know what this means, you two clowns,' she said. 'That my old man was the German soldier. Both of us are bastards, but my old man makes me the bigger bastard of the pair of us. What the hell – what do I care who and what my old man was? At least my mother must have felt something for him at the time, or she wouldn't have written that sloppy love poem to him. "You are straight as the chyparis, firm as the mountain, sweet as the herb, pure as water from the spring's melting snow . . ." Thank God she didn't marry him; imagine me, a well brought up little *fraulein* wearing a dirndl skirt and papering my walls with *deutschmarks* . . .'

She laughed bitterly and briefly, but there were tears at the corners of her eyes.

Bill went across and put his arm round her shoulders.

'Somebody wins, somebody loses,' she said.

'Nobody loses,' he said and kissed her forehead.

Victorio came and put his arms round both of them. 'It's still the three of us,' he said, 'isn't it?'

She shook the tears from her eyes. 'Yes, I guess it is,' she said.

They broke apart and Bill went back to the chair in which he'd been sitting. 'I've been to see Angelo Stavakis,' he said. 'He offered me a job in Aghios Nikolaos, with a house, a car and a good salary. The condition is that I stop trying to discover the identity of the traitor, stop trying to back-track my – our – father's activities. There's also the implied threat that if I don't stop, if I carry on investigating, he'll have me thrown out of the country. I want to ask you both what you think I should do . . .'

'Go on,' Maria said immediately.

Victorio held up a hand to stop her. 'Bill has found out what he wanted to know. And he has helped us find the truth about ourselves. Maybe he should stop now!'

'What do you think, Bill?' Maria asked.

'I want to go on,' Bill said. 'There are one or two questions I want answered before I quit. Okay I run the risk that Stavakis may be able to kick me out, but it's a risk I'm prepared to take!'

'Then we're two to one,' she said.

'I have only said – maybe we should stop now,' Victorio said. 'I am happy to be talked into it. If Bill is kicked out – and we must expect that Stavakis will do what he says since he is a powerful man – then I can carry on where Bill leaves off. Stavakis can not kick me out, can he?'

They heard the knock on the door and Maria called, 'Come in.'

The door opened and the *horofilakas* stood there. 'Are you thinking of going out, miss?' he asked. 'If not, I'd like to go down the road for a bite of supper.'

'You can go back to Xania,' Victorio said. 'From now on, I will look after the lady. Giorgio can mind the *kafeneion*, and I will camp out here!'

'I will have to telephone for instructions,' the *horofilakas* said, obviously pleased at the prospect of ending what must have been a tedious assignment.

'You do that!' Victorio said, assuming command.

The change in him since Bill had spoken was astounding. Now he was a complete man again, a proud Sfakian. After all, hadn't his father been a hero of the Resistance?

'What will you do next, Bill?' he asked when the *horofilakas* had gone.

'I think the time has come to cover my tracks a little,' Bill said. 'I'm going back to England.'

Maria glanced quickly at him. 'I thought we'd agreed the investigation would go on?' she asked.

'So it will,' Bill said, 'but I shall start it again where I began before. In the War Office, in London.'

Captain Rupert Williamson, of the War Office Records Office, was as helpful as he could be.

'Look,' he said, 'I don't have minutes of *every* meeting that ever took place. Certainly I have minutes of the meetings that took place in Cairo and Alexandria on the Cretan Question, but quite a lot of that material was given a classification that says that not even I may read it, let alone procure it for you to read. I have records of your father being posted to Crete – the ones I showed you when last you were here, and of your father's medal recommendation. I have accounts of him coming out of Crete – he came out a total of three times – and the discussions he had with the Cretan Section. But I don't have everything. What I *can* give you is the name of Colonel Bythorne. Jack Bythorne was in charge of the Cretan Committee. I'm not supposed to say this to you, of course, but if you go to see the Colonel, perhaps he might tell you something I can't. Sorry to be evasive, old boy, but regulations, you know . . .'

Bill thanked him and left with Colonel Jack Bythorne's address in a village in Northamptonshire.

The village was a two-hour drive from London in the car Bill had rented. The house occupied the centre of the village, a long, low building made of the deep ochre stone that contains so much iron. The French windows on each side of the main door gave direct access to the driveway of gravel; the door itself had that lustrous patina of old wood. A housekeeper came to the door, holding her hastily removed pinafore behind her.

'Bill Thomas,' Bill said. 'I telephoned to the Colonel last evening for an appointment.'

'Ah, you're the gentleman from London. You'd better come in. The Colonel's expecting you and told me to ask if you'd like coffee?'

'Yes, thank you,' Bill said and followed her into the hall. Door to the left, door to the right, an old wide staircase leading off the hall.

The colonel rose as Bill came into the room. Bill noticed that though he tried to stand erect, he had to push his weight on his stick to help support him.

'Damn silly gout,' the colonel said. 'Stops me moving about as much as I'd like to. Trouble is, you say you've got gout and everybody treats it as a joke and makes farcical comments about port and pheasant, neither of which has ever appealed to me.'

He held out his hand; Bill took it and noted the firm grasp. He estimated the colonel would be about eighty years old, but his eyes were still keen. His thinning hair was neatly brushed back and his face had the pink scrubbed look of public schools and the Army.

'Sit yourself down!' the colonel said. 'Did you tell Maisie about coffee?'

'Yes, I said I'd like some . . .'

'Good,' the colonel said as he seated himself laboriously, his leg propped out in front of him. 'She's a good girl. She'll bring two cups with the pot. I'm not supposed to have any, but Maisie obliges me when we have a guest. Right, you said you wanted to talk about Crete when you telephoned last evening. You writing a book or something?'

'Not exactly,' Bill said.

'Not exactly? What does that mean? Either you are writing a book or you aren't. Which is it?'

Bill saw he would need to be precise in what he said. The colonel's mind was obviously not impaired by his age.

'I'm not writing a book. I'm trying to collect information about my father and his part in the war. Your question made me think that perhaps I might one day set it all down on paper!'

'Too many damned books been published about the war. Still, I suppose it's a good way to keep the generals out of mischief in their dotage. Luckily I don't have that problem. This damned gout brought me out before the fun started!'

'But you were in Cairo?'

'Yes. I had the gout pretty badly even in those days. They gave me a desk job. I hated it.'

'You were in charge of the Cretan Committee . . .'

'Yes. Convener, we used to call it. I used to arrange all the meetings, look after the records, bring all the people together who wanted to talk. Mostly it was a lot of hot air – you could have floated balloons on it if you'd wanted. I also used to pass messages backwards and forwards between London and Cairo on the Cretan question. You know, Winston was very keen on it at the time. Eden was supposed to get cracking on it but he had other things to occupy his time . . .'

'You met my father. Captain Roger Thomas . . .?'

'Yes, I did. When you called last evening, I searched my memory a bit to see what I could find for you. Spend too much time these days thinking about the damned roses and chrysanthemums, you know. Good to remember chaps like your father again. He was the right sort, altogether the right sort!'

'I believe you met him three times?'

'Whoever told you that wants to go back to school. I met your father five times. I was the man who briefed him before he went in. And he came out four times.'

'*Four*? The War Office said *three*!'

'They only know what they're told down there. Don't tell the War House everything. Never did, or you'd be inundated with telegrams telling you not to do what you've just done, and to do things you knew were just downright impossible. Your father was a fine chap. What do you want to know about him?'

'I've read his diary of those years . . .'

'Ah, kept one of those, did he? Not supposed to, you know, by Army Regulations, but a lot of the chaps did. Most of 'em were nothing but a list of the young ladies they'd seduced . . . But I guess your father wasn't like that, eh? Very fine chap, your father.'

'He appears to have done his share of philandering . . .'

'And why not, young man. Don't hold that against your father. People were having a damned bad time in those days . . .'

He broke off when the door opened and Maisie came in bringing a tray of coffee.

'I've brought a cup for you, Colonel. I thought that seeing as how you have a guest, you might want to be polite and join him.'

'That's very kind of you, Maisie,' the Colonel said gravely.

'And Mrs Bythorne says I'm to ask discreetly if the young man's staying for lunch because there's only two chops and it'll mean you having cold pork pie, and don't offer him any sherry because it's only the cooking and the Vicar's expected this evening . . .'

The colonel turned to Bill. 'Would you care to join us for lunch,' he said. 'You've heard about the menu! And don't worry about the sherry – there's plenty of gin.'

Bill shook his head. 'I was hoping to get back to London as soon as possible,' he said.

'Good. I hate pork pie! You heard, Maisie? The gentleman declines our invitation to lunch. Now get about your business, eh?'

She bobbed and left the room.

'You'd never believe it,' the colonel said, 'but that young lady is sixty years old and has never been out of this village. Now, as I was saying . . .' he said, continuing without a break in his memory, 'people were having a damned bad time in those days. We who had to send them in were very conscious of the splendid work they were doing. Your father was one of many, of course . . .'

'In his diary,' Bill said, 'he asks often what has happened to the projected invasion of Crete. He makes the point quite strongly that he thought an invasion was being planned. He even had a code-word to use when the invasion began, with a list of strategic targets ready for sabotage by the team of men he'd collected together so secretly he hadn't, apparently, told the other Resistance fighters about them. They were men he'd recruited himself, with only Pakrades and Kostas Dandanakis aware of what was going on . . .'

'I was aware of it, too,' the colonel said gravely. 'I didn't suspect he was writing all that down in his diary.'

The colonel looked away from Bill, staring out of the window, his thoughts a long way, a long time, away. When he turned back, Bill was surprised to see his face had changed, had somehow become more haggard, as if he'd aged in those few seconds. When he spoke, his voice was low and husky.

'You're after the truth, is that it? Not some flim-flam you can put in some cheap newspaper to make yourself a bob or two, eh? You want to know what part your father played in the war?'

'Yes, Colonel, I do want to know the truth. And I don't write flim-flam for newspapers – that's not my style.'

The colonel chuckled, but it took an effort. 'No, I can suppose a son of Captain Thomas wouldn't go much on flim-flam. Your father was a stubborn chap, but he had a very strong sense of right and wrong. You surprised me earlier by saying you'd found him philandering – that wasn't your father's way. I talked a lot with his Brigadier before he was sent – we needed a chap who'd be scrupulously honest and fair in his dealings with the local people; your father qualified on all counts. Plus he could speak a sort of Greek – more than enough to get by!'

The colonel looked at Bill, searching his face, as if it were Bill and not his father who was being selected for a delicate, important, mission.

'You'll do,' the colonel finally said. 'Look here, young chap. What I'm about to say to you would get me cashiered if I were still a serving officer. Perhaps it will help me to get the whole mess of my chest to someone I can trust – Lord knows, I've carried the burden of it long enough. You know the situation on Crete when your father went there?'

'I've read the official histories.'

'Good. The Allies had been on Crete, mostly New Zealanders by an unhappy accident, and had been kicked off by the German paratroopers in a brilliant exploitation of the new German war techniques . . .'

'The *blitzkrieg* . . . ?'

'Something like that. Well, a lot of chaps stayed behind. Some were imprisoned on Crete, some were shipped out to the mainland of Greece and then to Germany. Quite a number escaped and made for the mountains. The locals were damned good and gave them food and shelter. We sent a lot of chaps in with radios to help the locals, get them all together, feed information back to Cairo, make an escape route for the poor devils who were starving!'

'Men like Rhodos.'

'That's right. He was one of the best. It was a great tragedy when he was killed. He was responsible for uncountable numbers of chaps crossing the country and getting to the south coast where we could pick them up by submarine and boat. Damn War Office – they should have given him a VC but they didn't. Meanwhile we were working on a plan. For the reinvasion of Crete by the Allies. Malta and Crete would have been the lynch pins of our Middle East strategy!'

'So, you *did* have a plan to invade Crete, just as my father says in the diary . . .'

'Damned right we had. And a good plan it was, too. It would have been a success. It had the total support of the British General Staff.'

'So, what went wrong? Why was the plan never put into operation?'

'Now I have to digress a little. But it concerns your father. You know there were problems on the mainland of Greece with the Communists. You know that the Communists wanted to take the opportunity to seize control of Greece after the war? That they were as active fighting the Greeks who didn't subscribe to their views as the Germans. Well, we had a similar situation on Crete. It was your father's job to try to reconcile the two factions, to lay the groundwork for an effective *Cretan* uprising when the invasion began. But, of course, he had to do his liaison work with the *palikari* without letting them know he was also dealing with the Communists. That was vital, and your father handled that brilliantly. I personally am convinced that, if we had gone ahead with the invasion, with the inside help your father's chaps would have provided, we would have been successful. We would have had a firm presence on Crete. The invasion of Europe would have taken place that much earlier, with luck the war would have been shortened.'

'But the invasion never took place,' Bill said. 'Why not?'

The colonel sat back in his chair. 'Politics,' he said. 'Damned politics. How we were bedevilled by the politicians! The scheme we'd prepared went into the Joint Liaison Committee which met in Cairo. It was a very good piece of military planning. The JLC threw it out.'

'Why,' Bill asked, 'if it was so good?'

'Because the Russians on the Committee, consulting directly with Stalin in Moscow, said *Nyet!* If there was to be an invasion anywhere, they said, it must be on the land mass of Northern Europe, to divert some of the German attention from the invasion of Russia. Now, that was the official reason and I believe it. I also believe the Russians were in contact with the left-wing partisans and wanted to give them more time to prepare for a post-war coup.'

'But surely, the Americans also sat on that Joint Liaison Committee? Surely the Americans and the British together could have outvoted the Russians?'

'The Americans didn't want an invasion of Crete either,' the colonel said sadly. 'It will never be known exactly who pulled Roosevelt's strings during the war. Remember, he was a sick man, a dying man. The anti-communist spectre was uppermost in the minds of the planners in the Pentagon. Some say Hoover had more say with Roosevelt than is generally known. Eisenhower wanted all the manpower he could get concentrated on his own personal – i.e. American-approved – battle plan. It didn't include liberating what one American general called to me: "That goddam bunch of Commie rats on Crete. Let 'em stew in their own juice," he said. "Maybe the Germans'll kill a few more of 'em for us . . . !" The next message I received from your father told me his network of left-wing fighters had been infiltrated and that the bulk of them had been trapped in a village and slaughtered by the Germans.'

The colonel was silent. Bill was shocked by the awful truth that lay behind what the colonel had just said.

'You think . . . no, it's impossible.'

'I've never voiced that thought to anyone,' the Colonel said. 'I'm not going to voice it to you now. I am telling you the facts and you must draw your own conclusions. One thing I can tell you, however. One thing I've never told anyone else. Your father rescued one man from that village and sent him over the mountains. He had radioed to me in Cairo; I sent a submarine. The man was brought to Alexandria and I had him put in a ward by himself in the hospital. I visited him a couple of times and he slowly recovered. Shortly after that, my gout became too painful for me to carry on my duties and I was sent back to England. Some time after the war the War Office forwarded to me an envelope containing a postcard. The message on the card simply said, in French, "Thank you for everything. Please do not reply." I didn't, of course, and later burned the card. The envelope had been posted in a small village in Provence called Frojane.'

'The man's name?' Bill asked. 'Will you tell me that?'

'I can trust your discretion absolutely?'

'Absolutely.'

'We used a code-name on Crete, you know.'

'I know.'

'His real name is Theodor Karfounis. If you see him, give him my regards.'

Theodor Karfounis rose as the door opened and, through
the swirl of smoke from the grill in the centre of the room
and the acrid fumes of the men's own-grown, hand-rolled
tobacco, he saw the Englishman.

'Be quiet, all of you,' he said, stifling the growl that had
arisen when the men identified the late-comer.

Maleta came in and stood near the grill.

Theodor took a plate from the stack on the table, and a
fork, speared a piece of the mutton on the grill and handed
it to Maleta. He beckoned for Ortis to get *krassi* from the
barrel; it came out dark red, like blood.

Maikhis was muttering in the corner as the Englishman
took his mutton and chewed on it.

'Be quiet, Maikhis,' Theodor said firmly. 'Let the man
eat first, then you will get your turn.'

Maleta chewed slowly, savouring every bite of the tough,
roughly-cooked meat. He hadn't eaten for twenty-four
hours; it had been a long climb over the mountain.

'You came alone?' Theodor asked.

'No. Pakrades and Kostas came with me.'

'Do they need food?'

'They are waiting outside the village to see what sort of
reception you give me.'

Maikhis snorted with derision. 'They are women,' he
said contemptuously.

'And if that is true,' Maleta said unperturbed by the
implied insult, 'you, my friend, are the arsehole of a ewe
dropping pellets of shit everywhere you go . . .'

There was a roar from the corner as Maikhis sprang to
his feet, pulling his opened clasp knife out of his belt.

The men gathered around the grill scattered, opening a
space into which Maikhis threw himself. Maleta handed
his plate to Theodor, wiped his hand down the side of his

trousers and then, with the speed of a snake, slapped Maikhis open-handed across his face. Maikhis's eyes bulged with rage and surprise.

'Take out your knife, Englishman,' he hissed.

'In England, we only use weapons when we fight *men*. Children we slap.'

He sprang in again, slapping left and right in rapid succession, the open-handed insulting blows bringing tears to the Cretan's eyes. Maikhis brought his curved clasp-knife in and up in a slash that would have disembowelled the Englishman in one go.

This is why they trained you, Maleta thought. To fight bare-handed against a man with a weapon. At first, they'd taught him the relatively easy trick of taking a rifle and bayonet away from a charging infantryman.

The final lesson had been how to take a hand-held knife away from a man experienced in its use. Speed and an unerring aim, the courage to face the razor-like blade, the deftness and technique to use the man's own strength and momentum against him. But that was training, the instructor standing by ready to advise. Here was no instructor, the knife wasn't a dummy and Maikhis had lived with it all his life.

Right hand down, grab the wrist. Turn left, sliding the forearm along the flat of the blade. Drop on one knee. Shoulder under the arm, left hand up to stop the knife if it comes backwards by wrist action. Use your shoulder for leverage, pull and throw.

Maikhis went over Maleta's shoulder, somersaulting with the momentum of his own forward thrust, shouting with the pain in his arm.

Maleta grabbed the knife handle and wrenched the weapon out of Maikhis's hand. There was a sudden smell of burning cloth as the Cretan sprawled on the hot charcoals of the cooking fire.

Maleta stamped on Maikhis's chest, grinding his back down into the embers.

'That's the best place for a ewe's arsehole,' he said. 'On the fire.'

He stepped back, looking at the clasp-knife. Then he threw it, like a dart, to stick in the chyparis tree stump on which Maikhis had been sitting.

The Cretan came up from the fire, coals sticking to his back, roaring with pain. Those nearest brushed the coals from him; Ortis threw water from the wooden bucket to douse the flames.

Maikhis turned and faced the Englishman, hate in his eyes. 'You will not do any more of your fancy tricks on me,' he said.

Theodor grabbed his arm. 'This is not a circus,' he said. 'We are here to have a meeting, not a brawl. At meetings you talk, and everyone listens. Everyone gets a chance to talk. Including the Englishman. If we do not do it this way, if we allow ourselves to brawl instead of talking, we might just as well hand Crete back to the Royalists. So, sit down and shut up, or get out and go back to your village.'

Others shouted the same advice. Maleta stood ready, not knowing for certain if the Cretan would ignore them and jump. He knew he wouldn't fare well in a slugging fight against the heavier bear of a Sfakian. Sometimes you have to take a chance. He stepped forward and reached out his hand.

'I fight for the honour of my men. I let no man insult a man of mine. You fight for your own honour. Now we are equal.'

It was touch-and-go. Maikhis looked at the extended hand as if he would crush it and break the arm to which it was attached. But then he spread his arms wide and brought them in, one at a time, slapping Maleta's hand in a gesture old as Crete.

'*Endaksi!*' he said. 'We talk.'

He went back to the tree stump and flicked out his knife before sitting down. Everybody put away his plate. Ortis flicked a coarsely rolled cigarette to Maleta who caught it, squatted down on the ground and lit it with one of the fire's embers. The remains of the mutton had been salvaged; it lay forgotten and still smoking on the table top.

'What do they say in Cairo?' Karfounis asked.

'They say we must be patient. They are making plans to invade with many men, many machines, many airplanes, many boats, many guns. But it will take time!'

'And what do we do meanwhile?'

'We train, we plan, we train again, so that when the invasion comes we will be ready.'

'This training, how do we do it without weapons?'

'The weapons will come.'

'Last night there was a drop on the plain of Omalos. Manoletto and his men got everything. I hear there were many guns, much ammunition, many explosives, even food. Yet here, we have only the weapons we can steal from the Germans, and the food we steal from the Cretans. The ewe came from a *kapitalist* in Vrisses who sells lambs to the Germans. When the time comes, we will remember him.'

How could Maleta explain to these simple people the involved politics of the people in Cairo. These men were desperate to end the Royalist's grasp on the island of Crete and what they saw as the injustice of inequality. Nature's simple law says to him who has shall more be given. A man with twenty sheep grows richer faster than a man with only two. The brand of Communism, Socialism, the left-wing beliefs of these men had nothing to do with Russia, Marx or Lenin. It had nothing to do with political theory. It sprang from inequality; from poverty, sickness, starvation. In peace-time these men tended sheep on the slopes of some of the hardest mountain territory on the island; they worked vineyards carved out of the mountain slopes, terraced to retain the handful of soil that gave nourishment to the vines. These men saw the German invasion as a perfect opportunity, since the country had been thrown into chaos, to build a future in which more of the benefits of the island would be distributed among more of the people. But first, as every man in the room was aware, the blood of Cretans would need to flow. The authorities in Cairo saw this clearly, 'We cannot, in all conscience, supply arms to partisans knowing those arms will be turned, not against the Germans, but against their own people,' the Brigadier had said.

Captain Thomas would not let himself be put off so easily. 'You asked me, sir, to go to Crete with special assignment duties. While appearing to be carrying out the normal liaison functions of the other Englishmen on Crete, I was to set up a network that could spring into operation the moment an invasion came. This I have done. In some parts of Crete, the only men with whom I could set up such a network were left wing, are left wing, I freely admit. But if the network I've created is to be effective, it must have arms and ammunition; it must have supplies of explosives!'

'For use against whom, Captain?'

'For use against the *Germans*. This whole business of Cretan fighting Cretan is a myth, a chimera born in the Joint Liaison Committee. If I can show these Cretans of mine the good faith of the Allies, if I can give them weapons and ammunition, as I have requested repeatedly, I can control them. But without that expression of good faith, no one can predict what will happen. The Cretan, Brigadier, is *not* a Greek. He's not even *like* a Greek. He's emotional, childlike, yes, but he's intensely loyal and generous to a *friend*. If you can earn the friendship of a Cretan, you have it for life. If we send them arms and ammunition, if we send it equally to both sides, the left-wingers and the right-wingers, we will show good faith; we will earn friendship. And in that situation, I can exercise some control. One man in particular can help me. Theodor Karfounis is very well respected by these left-wing elements. Let him be given an appointment by the Greeks here in Cairo . . .'

'They'd never agree to it. The King would never permit it.'

'One day quite soon he may *have* to agree to it,' Captain Thomas said sombrely.

Theodor Karfounis had sipped his Vichy water slowly as he talked, as he told Bill what his father had reported that day in Mavroti on the slopes of the Mavri.

'My father had known the village before the massacre?' Bill asked.

'Yes, of course. It was our principle meeting place. When he returned from Cairo he came straight there. He had his fight with Maikhis – that was inevitable. He had to fight one of us because there was so much anger. Time after time we'd seen the *palikari* of the other side receive parachute drops of everything they needed. Yet, when we asked for it, we received nothing. And yet, when the invasion came, we would be the key men in that whole *nome* of Xanion. I had men ready to take control of the port of Souda, of Xania. We could take Maleme, Kastelli. Other units that would seize Heraklion, Rethymnon and the principal roads along and across the island were already in position, many already supplied through your father with the arms and ammunition and the explosives they would need. And we got nothing!

Your father was a *filos*; he spoke frankly to us that night and hid nothing of what had been said in Cairo. I trusted him, for a while, but of course my men could not understand what he was saying. Most of them were simple peasants like Maikhis, used to fighting for what they wanted, used to taking it with their bare hands. To them, the Englishman, as they contemptuously called him sometimes, was a man who spoke with two voices. And then, suddenly, we were betrayed. Only three men knew where we were. Pakrades and Kostas Dandanakis, two Cretans, and your father, an Englishman. That was when I withdrew my friendship for your father.'

Bill had travelled to the South of France after his

meeting with Colonel Bythorne in England. It had been a simple matter, in Frojane, to find Karfounis. He was living in a small cottage, with a couple of acres of vines growing around it, a couple of dozen chickens, a cow for milk. Obviously, he lived frugally on the produce he could grow himself in the hot climate of Provence. He was wearing patched-denim overalls of the type French workers used before the promotion of modern-day 'jeans'. It had been early evening when Bill arrived by car from Nice Airport. At first, Karfounis had denied that anyone of that name lived there.

Mention of the name of Colonel Bythorne had opened the door.

Karfounis had looked at him. 'I know you, do I not? I have met you somewhere before?'

Bill had smiled at the wizened little man, the flesh taut on his bones from a perennial lack of food, his eyes sunk deep into his boney sockets, his hair, now white, twisted into tiny springs.

'No, we've never met before,' he said, 'but you knew my father, Maleta.'

He saw the poignant look that flitted across the man's face at the mention of Maleta's name. 'Ah,' he said, 'in some ways you resemble your father. Not in all ways, I hope. I have lived here for many years in solitude and safety. The locals accept me as one of them – they no longer call me the Greek! I do not have much more time to live – it would be a kindness to a harmless, juiceless old man to let me live the rest of my days in peace.'

Bill stayed in the cottage overnight, sleeping on the bed which ran across one wall, smelling the work smell of the older man in the bedding. Karfounis spent the night in his chair, sitting, as old people can, with his body slumped into a sleeping position.

Karfounis was up at six o'clock the following morning; he lit a fire in the cast-iron stove, fetched water from an outside well and made coffee. Bill woke with the smell of it in his nostrils; when he came to drink it, he realized it was thin and meagre. Karfounis drank only water and ate a plateful of crushed oats, scalded with water and heaped with salt.

'The cafe in the village serves breakfast,' he said gruffly.

Bill shook his head, then went outside to urinate in the footprint lavatory and doused his head with water drawn from the well.

When he'd dried himself, the one-time Cretan was already at work, digging the ground in his garden. Bill went and stood beside him.

'You will be going now,' Karfounis said. The implication was obvious.

'I want to talk some more,' Bill said. 'I want to ask you some more questions.'

'Too much talk is not good for a man,' Karfounis said. 'I do not have any more answers . I want only to be left in peace.'

Bill couldn't bring himself to leave. He walked across to the wall and squatted on the ground with his back to it. The scent of Provence came to him from the houses about, the acrid smell of tomatoes on the vine, the odour of cooking garlic, the musty tang of grapes left to sweeten and shrivel. Karfounis had found peace here. Bill could get the tangible feel of it. A life of simple natural rhythms, as changeless as the seasons following ineluctably, one after the other, with death the only punctuation. Again, Bill was assailed by doubts. What right did he have to disturb this man's peace by reawakening old memories, scratching at old sores?

He had made up his mind to go away, to return to England and invite Maria to join him there, when Karfounis threw down the long-handled spade with which he was digging and came to squat beside Bill.

'So, I will tell you and then you must go away. Maleta said we could make a personal appeal to Cairo. A small team of men dropped in at night by parachute; we met them outside Epanochorion. One British lieutenant colonel, one American major and a Russian. We talked with them all night and, by my oath, we kept politics out of it as much as we could. The British officer hardly spoke; the American seemed to take the lead but I could tell he didn't like many of the answers I and my men gave him. He asked if I would serve in a combined unit with General Spiros Orfandakis – I said that though I respected the General, I would not accept his leadership. Then the Russian started questioning me, and again my answers seemed to be the wrong ones. In the end, when dawn came, I knew we were no further forward, so I left. Maleta, Pakrades and Kostas took the officers away and I never saw them again. Three days later, we were betrayed to the Germans. If you want to know what happened, I'll tell you. The men who fired on the German patrol to provoke the destruction of Mavroti were not our men. I think they were placed there deliberately by your father, so that the Germans would attack as they did!'

'Why would they want to destroy Mavroti if *you* and your left-wingers were the target?'

'That is simple. We had a large cache of guns, ammunition and dynamite buried in one of the graves in the churchyard. The guns were old, mostly First World War relics; some of the ammunition was so old it was risky to fire it. But they knew that when the time came we would. I think the mission that parachuted in said to your father, Get rid of Karfounis and his men, and he chose to do it by means of the Germans.'

'Someone has said to me that the traitor was not my father but a *palikari* whose code-name was Theseus. Do you know who Theseus was?'

'Yes. That was the name Spiros Orfandakis used . . . !'

There it was again. Orfandakis! Bill still couldn't conceive of the old general as a war-time traitor.

'Do you believe it was Orfandakis who betrayed you . . . ?'

Karfounis was shaking his head. 'No, I do not believe that,' he said decisively. 'The General was extreme right wing and as such he and I did not get on. But to betray us to the Germans would not be his way. I can tell you. He would give us all a trial, then put us against a wall and shoot us. Maleta, on the other hand, had to maintain relationships with the rest of the *palikari*. He could not be seen killing Cretans. He had to do it by subterfuge – and what better scape-goat could he have than the Germans . . . ?'

He reached out his hand and squeezed Bill's knee. 'Don't take it so badly,' he said. 'What does it matter what your father was? I have learned that, here in France. Sometimes I think the Cretans set too much store by family and, since your father was on Crete, you have been affected by that. Live your own life – How old are you, thirty-nine, forty? – forget the past, as I had until you came here.'

'I can't,' Bill said. 'It's as simple as that. I think this whole affair must have become some kind of obsession . . .'

'All right. I will tell you everything I know, and then, please, you must go away! I had heard about your father before I met him. I had heard a new Englishman had dropped in to take part of the territory of the Englishman, Rhodos. At that time, the English were trying to help us organize ourselves; they were setting up units to which we could give information about the location and movements of the Germans; they were in contact via radio with Cairo. We all thought they were working towards the future invasion of Crete by the Allies. Then, one day, Pakrades, your father's runner, came to me and said the Englishman Maleta wanted to see me. We set up a meeting in Ebrosneros, just off the road to Vrisses. There is an old Venetian ruin in the village; I knew we would be safe there. The village is built into the side of the mountain; from almost any one of its houses, we could keep the valley under observation . . .

Maleta came over the mountain to Ebrosneros, using paths the shepherds and their flocks had made for hundreds of years. One by one, Pakrades picked out the Cretans in their hides, guarding the village from surprise. Maleta and Kostas had talked about Karfounis. 'He is a difficult man to understand,' Kostas had said. 'His head is full of philosophy. But he has a good heart.'

Many of the houses of the village had been built to take natural advantage of the rocky terrain; often a room would be in a cleft, roofed over, with a floor of natural stone chipped flat. They'd see a terrace, covered with vines, a hand-dug well, a shelter for animals and humans. Each house had its opuntia patch, its carob trees with the dark brown fruit hanging from the branches, the walnut trees, the carefully nurtured cacti, some of which climbed five metres high. Everywhere was the evidence of sheep and goats, but not one of the animals was visible – the German food foragers descended quickly, without warning or time to gather in the wandering animals.

Ten or so men were standing round the entrance to the ruin when Maleta arrived; they recognized Kostas and several greeted him. Maleta smiled at their appearance – if he'd been a German, he thought, he would have been frightened to death by looking at these lean muscular men with their dark hair, searching eyes, muscled bodies laden with guns of all descriptions and knives bristling from them. Many seemed giants; all wore the clothes of mountain men like a uniform: breeches tucked into high boots, dark shirts with waistcoats over them, silk-like handkerchiefs on their heads. All had well-developed moustaches, many of which had been waxed at the ends.

Pirates, brigands, Maleta thought. Any of the descriptions would fit. And yet, living among them, he'd already found them to be tender-hearted; they could shed tears for the loss of a friend, fight over a glance thrown at the wrong woman at the wrong time, and dance with an extraordinary agility, leaping wildly into the air, slapping their ankles, without appearing the least bit effeminate or demasculated. They treated their women abominably, according to Maleta's British standards, using them as beasts of burden and bed-warmers. The women's faces and figures showed it; they were mostly trodden down by years of the hardest labour in the stubborn mountain groves, by fetching and carrying primitive loads that would make even a donkey blench. Maleta had often seen them walking the tracks, the husband riding the donkey in front, the woman walking behind with a monstrous load of kindling, a sack of carob fruits, a giant pitcher of water.

He nodded to the men and said a general '*kalimera*'. There were grunts and suspicious looks, but he ignored them and strode purposefully forward, knowing any sign of hesitation would be read as weakness.

Karfounis was inside the upper room, which Maleta could only reach by climbing a cut-stone circular staircase so narrow his shoulders touched the sides of the walls.

The room had no roof; through the three Venetian arches, they could see the valley below them, the Lefka Ori to the side, the road snaking up towards them and the other houses of the village with their red roof tiles.

Maleta walked forward and stretched out his hand; the man waiting for him took it and squeezed it in his mountain grip. Maleta squeezed back, his eyes fixed on the Cretan's features. Karfounis was grinning but it was impossible to read beyond that. 'How was your journey?' he asked.

'Like any other, in the mountains.'

Maleta was wearing sand-coloured Army officer's riding breeches and the high, black Cretan boots Kostas had had made for him; his open-necked shirt was dark cotton over a woollen vest. The night journey had been arduous and cold, with the ever-present danger of a fall from a cliff face that would have been fatal. But Maleta knew there was no point in saying any of this to the Cretan. 'Let's hope it wasn't wasted,' he said.

They squatted in the window, both looking out. Maleta could smell meat cooking and see the smoke from a wood fire. A table was being laid beneath a mulberry tree in the ground below.

'How shall we do it?' Karfounis asked. 'Talk first and then eat, or eat first and then talk?'

'Talk first.'

'Good. After we eat, we may not be able to talk . . . We have been many days in the mountains!'

'I want a number of strong men,' Maleta said, coming straight to the point in a way he knew Karfounis would appreciate, 'and an even stronger man to lead them, to control them!'

'To gather information for you to send back to Cairo? This is woman's work, or suitable for *macropantalonades*,' he said, using the term of contempt of the mountain men for the men of the cities and plains who wear long trousers and shoes rather than the Sfakian breeches and boots.

'No. I have another task. I want men who can prepare for an invasion of Crete by the Allies. Men who can train themselves in discipline so that when the Allies come, they can rise strongly and efficiently against the Germans, striking quickly and effectively. I don't want men who will hold a committee meeting before doing anything, who will run like rabbits when a gun is fired at them.'

'And you came to me? Why?'

'Because Kostas Dandanakis told me you are a strong man. That you have many strong men who look to you as a leader . . .'

'Kostas Dandanakis said this . . . ?' Karfounis laughed as if in disbelief.

'Yes.'

'And nothing else?'

'He warned me you have a head full of philosophy!'

Karfounis laughed again, striking his hand against the side of his breeches in amazement. 'That is the richest thing I have heard in months,' he said. 'Kostas Dandanakis, that Royalist, says that I, Karfounis the Communist, have a head full of philosophies.'

'I have no interest in politics, Karfounis,' Maleta said quietly. 'Only in beating the Germans.'

'And what is that, my friend, if it is not politics?' Karfounis asked. 'We beat the Nazis, the Fascists, the Germans and the Italians. What for? So that the Royalists can take Crete back for themselves? And you ask Karfounis, a Communist, to help you do this? That is rich, that is truly rich. Come, we will eat. I will put your proposition to my men, and we will all decide.'

The meal the women of the village had prepared was a feast by any standards; the mountain men had brought two sheep, a goat and three rabbits. The women had found rice in the storehouses, and *krassi*, potatoes and oil.

When they sat down, the women brought around the small glasses of *tsikoudia*; Maleta threw his head back and downed the drink in one gulp according to local custom; the fiery, crude raki bit his throat like acid but he swallowed it quickly.

A plate of small sweet cakes was passed around, each one, as Karfounis said, a tooth-full.

Maleta looked up the hill-side; the sentry looking down the valley waved cheerfully. Maleta admired the military skill with which Karfounis had organized this meeting; safe within the ring of watching men, one couldn't have told there was a war on, with the murderous invaders only a few miles away. He ate the rice piled on his plate that had been cooked in the juices of the meats. Karfounis speared a portion of the rabbit cooked in oil and tomatoes and held it out on the end of his fork to Maleta, who bit a chunk off it.

'Very good,' he said. Then he took up his glass of *krassi*. '*Iss iyia!*' he said.

All the men nearby took up their glasses and clinked them against his. '*Epissis*,' they said, and '*Iss iyia.*'

The lamb had been roasted in chunks, still on the bone;

the goat had been cooked into a stew. They chewed on bread the women had baked, the hard *paximada*, and ate the cheese, semi-hard and tangy. All the time they talked, like kids on a picnic. Mostly they talked about the accidents the Germans had suffered and the way they'd been taught to use the Greek language wrongly and badly.

When the food had been consumed, the men rose from the table when Maleta, who understood their customs, did. He walked across to the base of a fig tree, sheltering beneath its branches while he pissed against the trunk. The men stood beside him, all pissing, talking, laughing, joking.

Karfounis and Maleta joined arms and walked around the village square. Now that the meal had been consumed, the women had disappeared. The three *kafeneion* were empty since most of the older men and boys left in the village were out tending the sheep in their hide-aways or digging the soil for a few potatoes, a few tomatoes and beans.

When they returned from the *volta*, the table had been cleared and carried now a bottle of *tsikoudia*, a plate of dried figs, a bowl of almonds, walnuts. Each man took a ritual *tsikoudia*, but then turned to the more voluminous *krassi*. And almost immediately, one of them began to sing a *mantinadhes*, improvising the rhyming couplets in the tuneless but musical Cretan chant.

Welcome Englishman from afar, come to share our table.

The others sang the chanting reply: *From afar the Englishman comes, to find our welcome.*

Maleta sat fascinated as the age-old singing continued.

We eat in friendship, drinking seals it
Drinking seals the friendship of our food
As brothers we, all together in life and death
In life and death we live as brothers together.

Karfounis was watching Maleta and suddenly, after one of the reply chants, he took up the singing. His voice was low and rich, his singing clear.

The Englishman comes, will he drive out the Germans.

Do the Germans leave when the Englishman comes.
Maleta wants strong men, and a palikari *to lead*
A palikari *to lead strong men, is what Maleta wants.*

Now the smiles were going; now the singing was growing more intense.

Maleta speaks with Cairo, will Cairo listen to his words?
Will Cairo listen, to the words of Maleta?
Strong is a man's arm, but longer the barrel of a rifle.
A rifle is longer than the strong man's arm.
A bad word thrown at a friend hurts the soul, a bullet fired at an enemy kills the body.
Better bullets than bad words.
Will Maleta give us bandoliers of bullets, or garlands of words?
Which will the Englishman give us, bandoliers or garlands.

The singing stopped; the silence was potent.

'Which is it to be, Maleta?' Karfounis said quietly. 'If we agree to help you, to form ourselves with discipline the way you ask, ready to help the Allies push the Germans into the sea, will you give us words or bullets?'

'I will take you to Cairo with me,' Maleta said. 'We will speak with the military there. You will tell them what you need, and they will give it.'

Karfounis rose and held out his hand. 'Maleta,' he said, 'I will go to Cairo with you and we will speak with the military there. And, if I return with bullets we will build you a force that will be as a hammer in your hand when the time comes to strike the Germans.'

'We crossed the mountain,' Karfounis said to Bill, sitting by the wall beneath the sun of Provence in the autumn of 1978. 'A boat landed at night in Loutron and we climbed aboard. The boat took us silently to where a submarine waited. I tell you frankly I was scared to sit in that tin fish below the water but I conquered my fear rather than let your father see it. We went to Alexandria and then to Cairo – they hid us both in great secrecy in a small house and the next day, without delay, we went to the office of the Joint Liaison Committee. They greeted me respectfully, calling me *Kapitanio*. We all sat at the same long table. Pinned to the wall was a large map of Crete. A sheet had been hung over the *nomes* of Rethymnon, Heraklion and Lasithi, which were not of my concern. Maleta stood before the map and talked about the symbols that had been placed on its face. How we would cut the road east and west of Xania, how we would isolate the German force on the Xania to Omalos road, control the routes onto and off the Akrotiri. I remember a girl sat at the end of the table, on a small extension table. As we spoke, she wrote down every word in shorthand. Every so often another girl would come in, take away her shorthand pad and leave a fresh one.

'I told them about my men being ready, men I had collected together from those left on Crete when the Cretan Brigade left. Men who had escaped from the German prisons. Men who had come from Greece to fight for their homeland. Maleta asked me questions to which he, but not the Committee members, already knew the answers. The American on the committee asked many questions, as did the Russian. There was a Frenchman there; he looked bored throughout the whole proceedings. The English officer asked about strategy, and I told him.

'Finally, it was agreed that I would have the help I needed; the equipment of radios, rifles, ammunition, explosives. They would send men to operate the radios to keep us all in touch, so that, when the time came to strike, we could strike as a single force. It was a very good meeting. When it ended we went into another room and a manservant brought drinks. I had whisky, I remember. It was the first whisky I had ever tasted and I enjoyed it very much. Even the Russian drank the whisky. After we had been there about twenty minutes, drinking, the girl returned and brought papers for us all; I remember I was amazed when Maleta translated the paper and I found my own words had been written faithfully. Many times I have tried to write my thoughts in the form of words, but I have never succeeded. "These are the Minutes of the meeting," the English officer said. "I want you to take them away and study them – the Captain will translate them for you. They are the record of our promises . . ."

'And then we drank more whisky, and more. And then, like a fool, I began to talk. About Crete, about my people. All of them could understand me most of the time but where I made too much use of Cretan words, Maleta, who by this time could speak like a Sfakian, would translate for me. As I talked, I gave them my philosophies. I remember I had had four whiskies, and I had never drunk it before so was not used to it, though I was not feeling drunk, only excited by the opportunity to explain something of the *real* nature of life on Crete, a view very different from that of the Royalists. I remember the look on the face of the American when finally he said, "But you're a Communist!"

'I looked at the Russian and realized he had been leading me on, provoking me.

' "You're a Bolshevik!" the American added.

'But I told him, always plain speaking, if by Bolshevik you mean Russian, let me tell you I am not. I owe nothing to Russia, to the Bolsheviks. I am a Cretan. What we are going to do on Crete has nothing to do with what they may or may not do in the Soviet Union!

'Well, even a peasant such as I was knows when he is not wanted. They bustled me out of there pretty quickly. We returned to Crete a few days later; I had my copy of the Minutes with me, the official record of the meeting, and I went ahead with the plans that had been outlined. But Cairo never kept its side of the bargain. Eventually they did send the American and Russian, with the Englishman to Crete, as I explained to you, but shortly afterwards we were betrayed. I think I opened my mouth too wide on that occasion in Cairo; I think your father was a soldier and, like a soldier, when given his orders he obeyed them. And I still believe his orders were, Get rid of Karfounis and his men any way you can!'

Karfounis got to his feet and Bill watched him cross the garden to his house; he returned a few minutes later with an old envelope in his hand. 'These are the Minutes,' he said. 'I have kept them all these years. Read them for yourself and form your own opinion of whether I know what I'm saying or not. And then burn them. I do not want to see them again. And I do not want to see *you* again.

'Those years are painful in my memory. So many good, young men killed. So many of my friends. Because I remained true to my philosophies. And who can blame your father? He was carrying out his orders.'

Bill spent the journey from Nice to Athens and from Athens to Xania reading and re-reading the Minutes at which the Joint Liaison Committee had promised full military support for the establishment of 'a Force of Cretan Nationals, fully trained to commit acts of sabotage with the intention of aiding the Allied invasion of Crete and the expulsion of the German Occupation Force'. The specific targets already agreed by Maleta and Karfounis were listed. The two men, working together, would also seek and examine other targets for which additional supplies as requested would be made available. The entire operation would come under the command of the General Officer Commanding the Allied Forces of the Middle East, Allied Force Headquarters, Cairo.

The message of the Minutes was clear – set up the Force and we will back you with arms and ammunition.

It was equally clear, from what Karfounis had said, that he had carried out his end of the agreement but that the Allies had reneged.

The question troubling Bill's mind was the role of his father in all this – had he, as Karfounis believed, been given an order, and had he, like a good soldier, carried it out? The order to get rid of the Communist!

205

The fact that he had made himself responsible for getting Karfounis out would seem to indicate this wasn't true, though Karfounis believed this was merely another cover-up.

He went straight to Ioannis's pension when he arrived in Xania. Ioannis was sitting in the entrance, talking to a Canadian tourist who'd rented one of his rooms. He followed Bill into the front room.

'How was your trip?' he asked. He looked at Bill's expression. 'Not very successful, I would guess.'

'Too successful,' Bill said glumly. 'I'm turning over stones and appalled by what comes popping out.'

'Maria Stafanakis came by this morning and asked me when you would return. I told her I expected you yesterday. She said she might come by later this evening.'

When Ioannis had gone, Bill got out the diary again and reread the entry that related to the trip Maleta made to Cairo with Karfounis. Puzzled, he reread the Minutes of the meeting. The two separate documents seemed to make no sense. Why, for example, had Captain Thomas written in his diary – *I cannot get them to see the simple military expedient of arming Karfounis and his men, who would be totally effective in the Nome of Xanion when the invasion comes*, when the Minutes clearly stipulated agreement on this very point? He read on and on. Nowhere did the diary show the sort of anxiety his father must have felt if he had been *ordered* to get rid of Karfounis and had betrayed him to the Germans. The entry that related to Mavroti, the massacre of the villagers, the discovery of the identity of the traitor, were all clear and incapable of misconception. The Mavroti incident had come as a total surprise to Maleta. His principal agony had been that Elvira and Irena had sacrificed themselves so that he, the babies and Evangelina could escape.

If I could have foreseen the event, the diary said, *I would willingly have walked onto the German guns myself. I blame myself for not having posted military-minded scouts in the front of our tragic column. My only excuse is that I believed the Germans to be*

behind us and that we were forging on in all speed. But it is a poor
excuse and I shall not cease to blame myself.

Bill closed the diary. Reading it was painful to him especially since he had read the Minutes of the Cairo meeting and had talked with Karfounis.

When the knock came to the door he thought it was Maria and bounded across the room to fling the door open. Petro stood there.

'I thought you had decided to return to England,' he said.

Bill let him in. 'I did return,' he said, 'but I came back again.'

'To see Maria Stafanakis, no doubt.'

Bill's anger flared. 'I don't really see that's any of your business!' he said angrily.

'I freely admit it is not my business. The life and death of your father equally is not any of my business. Please understand that quite clearly. I am conducting an investigation into the deaths of people today, not those of people who died thirty-five years ago. What happened then is history. But what happened to Kostas Dandanakis, to the General, and what nearly happened to Angelos Stavakis and Evangelina is contemporary crime! And my job is to catch criminals!'

'Have you made any progress?'

'Some progress. The car that crashed into the ambulance was stolen from a tourist in Rethymnon. The man seen driving it answers to the description of the man I shot and unfortunately killed in Evangelina's room. A man answering the same description was seen outside the hall in which Angelos Stavakis held his meeting. I also have a description that could be his from the local police in Aghios Nikolaos. The FBI in Washington can give me nothing on him. I had hoped to track him through the American Express and Diners Club cards but somehow he managed to fool both those organizations with forged references – or that is what the FBI informs me.'

'Fingerprints?'

'Nothing on the FBI file.'

'Social Security in America . . .?'

'Nothing.'

'Military?'

'Nothing. So far as the American authorities are concerned, he never existed.'

'And yet, he had a bank account, a passport, credit cards . . .?'

'Yes, very strange, is it not? You have lived in America. Perhaps you understand this matter.'

Bill racked his brains to think of an explanation, but nothing came. 'Of course, if he was a professional hit man, he would have taken some trouble to cover his tracks, wouldn't he? He would have given himself enough documentation to establish an identity that would easily be accepted, and then would have back-tracked, destroying the traces of it . . .?'

'I do not know how things are in America,' Petro said, 'but I know no one could do that here in Greece!'

'Except a member of the police, perhaps?'

Petro snorted with disbelief, shaking his head. 'In the time of the Colonels, perhaps, but not now!' He looked appraisingly at Bill. 'What are you going to do now that you are back among us?' he asked.

'Nothing much. I'm going to take Maria Stafanakis out to dinner . . .'

'You know that I have taken away her guard.'

'Yes, I did know.'

'I am sure you can look after her as well as any *horofilakas* of mine,' Petro said. He turned at the door as he was preparing to leave. 'Take my tip, Bill,' he said. 'Do not get involved any more. Take a holiday; let Maria Stafanakis show you our beautiful island. Take the walk through the Gorge of Samaria, if the water has not yet blocked it. Go down to Chora Sfakion. See Knossos, Phaestos, Gortyna. But leave this matter alone.'

When Maria arrived later, she drove Bill in her new car to the Panorama Restaurant just outside the village of Malaxa. It was well-named; they sat on the enormous balcony and looked out over the breath-taking view stretching from Galata to the left, across the glittering lights of Xania, to the string-of-beads illumination of Souda Bay and the Akrotiri. Maria had pulled her hair severely back from her face; her eyes glittered.

'I've missed you, you devil,' she said.

They had been given a table in the corner, away from the crowds of Cretans eating dinner with families and friends. Bill marvelled again at the way the Cretans keep their children up and out until the small hours of the morning, and pamper and spoil them, according to northern European standards.

When he mentioned this to Maria she pouted. 'You mustn't bring your northern European standards to this island,' she said. 'This is the Mediterranean. You must judge everything here by different values. Anyway,' she added, 'the kids probably had a four-hour siesta this afternoon.' She snuggled her hand into his. 'You're not very romantic, Bill, to come to a place like this and talk to me about what other people do with their kids.'

'Sorry! What would you like me to talk about?'

'Have you no imagination? You could start by telling me, true or not, that *you* missed *me* while you were away . . .'

'You know I did!'

'Knowing and being told are not the same thing, Bill!'

He squeezed her hand. 'Give me time,' he said. 'I haven't had much practice lately.'

She squeezed his hand back. 'I know, Bill. I'm not trying to push you.'

The waiter came and they ordered. A rabbit stew for Bill, moussaka for Maria.

'I think of all those lovely rabbits running round the hillsides,' she said, 'and I can't bring myself to eat them anymore.'

'My father went to Ebrosneros during the war, and they gave him a rabbit stew. Lamb, goat . . .'

'Who did?'

'A man called Karfounis. Theodor Karfounis. He was one of the men my father contacted while he was here.'

'And you've met Karfounis? Where?'

Bill remembered his promise that he'd say nothing about Karfounis's present whereabouts. But Maria was different, wasn't she?

'In France of all places. He escaped there after the war ended. He couldn't come back here, anyway. He'd been a leader of the Communists . . .'

'Where in France?'

'A tiny place called Frojane, in Provence.'

'What's he doing now? Writing his memoirs?'

'No. He has a few acres, tends his garden. I gather he doesn't make much money, barely enough to live on. Strange thing though, he doesn't seem to be at all bitter, even though he thinks my father betrayed him. He wants to forget.'

'And you don't help him by asking questions, Bill.' There was no reproof in her voice, only a statement of fact.

'No, I know I don't. And that makes me feel bad.'

They ate in silence for a while. 'We could take a few days' holiday, Bill?' she asked. 'It would be nice to be able to put all that behind us, if only for a few days.'

'Where would we go?'

'Down to the south coast. It won't be crowded at this time of year, but the boat will still be running between Chora Sfakion and Loutron, perhaps even to Aghia Roumeli!'

'Sounds like a good idea. When shall we go?'

She smiled shyly at him. 'I have a bag in the back of my car,' she said. 'If you wanted, we could go tomorrow morning.'

After the meal she drove slowly down the twisting, winding road back to Xania. The evening was so balmy, neither felt like going indoors. They parked the car, walked slowly round the harbour, hand in hand, looking at the lighthouse so brilliantly illuminated, seeing a couple of late fishermen going out, rippling the surface of the harbour, their engines throbbing quietly in the night.

A shaft of light gleamed from the door of Giorgio's *kafeneion*. Inside, they could hear the soft sound of a mandolin being played. On impulse, they went inside and found Ross, the Irish boy who'd travelled Greece learning its music, playing the lyre, twisting it gently on his knee as his fingers searched delicately for the chords. Giorgio was accompanying him on the mandolin; the two played together in familiarity, serene, composed. Three people sat at the tables, listening to the music, drinking *tsikoudia* and eating peanuts. Bill and Maria sat down; Giorgio saw them, muttered to Ross, and together they changed the rhythm to a lively *pendozalis*, the spirited swinging dance the Cretan males perform with their arms locked together. Bill felt his feet tap compulsively to the insistent rhythm; Maria saw him and smiled.

'Giorgio would teach you to dance if you asked him,' she said. 'There is so much you could learn about life in Crete today, if you wanted . . . Take Ross for example – he speaks modern Greek perfectly and plays our music. Most people think he's Greek!'

Bill looked across the room. Yes, the Irish boy *did* look Greek, wearing the standard worsted clothing of the Cretan artisan, his hair longer than most Cretans wear it, and neither so black nor so springy. If the boy can so absorb himself in local life, Bill thought, so could he. He could find some way to stay in the country; to start a business perhaps in partnership with a Cretan, even with Maria. Presumably if he were to marry the Cretan girl, they would let him stay indefinitely. It could be a good life. If only he could learn to live a modern life and forget the past!

'Have you thought about getting married again, Maria?' he asked when Giorgio had finished playing and had brought them a glass of *tsikoudia* each, with a small plate of peanuts. Then he and Ross had gone back to playing quietly, almost as if for themselves rather than for the late-night audience.

'I have, several times,' she said.

He felt a pang of jealousy.

'In theory only, you understand!'

That made him feel better. 'What conclusion did you reach?'

'That it wouldn't work for me. I've learned to be independent and self-sufficient . . .'

'And that's not possible when you're married to some-one?'

'Not if you love that person. Your desire to look after them, to serve them – to use that old-fashioned word – makes you pervert your own independence and self-suffi-ciency. After a while, you find yourself living for them and not for yourself . . .'

'It needn't be like that . . .'

'It usually is, Bill. At least, in northern Europe and North America.' She shivered. 'It's late, Bill, and I'm getting tired. Can we go back to the pension?'

They walked back round the harbour and into Pension Zorbas. All the lights were out, but they fumbled their way up the steps, giggling as they stumbled, until they reached his room. The short walk seemed to have dissipated the mood that had fallen on both of them when they discussed marriage. They went to bed together and made love with a gentle and caring passion until they both fell asleep in each other's arms.

When he woke the next morning, he remembered the night, turned round to touch her and found the bed empty. He got up and showered, wondering where she could be. Her car was no longer parked on the quayside below his window.

When she returned, about a half an hour later, she had brought yoghurt from the market, deliciously creamy, a couple of peaches and croissants from the cake shop.

While she had been away, he'd idly examined the leather satchel in which he was keeping his father's diary and now

212

the Minutes of the Joint Liaison Committee meeting. When he'd emptied everything out, something had seemed bulky beneath its silk lining. When he'd pushed in the diary with its brass lock, the lock had caught on the lining and ripped it.

Beneath the lining was another envelope, so old and dried out it crackled when he withdrew it from its hiding place. The envelope contained the Minutes of a second meeting of the Committee in Cairo. This time, neither Karfounis nor Captain Thomas had been invited.

With the Minutes was a note which read, 'You know the risk I am running, sending these to you. Please take care of them and of yourself.'

The note was signed only with the initials J.B. 'Colonel Jack Bythorne,' Bill said to himself as he settled down to read them.

What he held in his hand was a verbatim transcript of the proceedings of a meeting. Much of what had been said had been crossed out by pencil and amended to make the 'official' expurgated transcript. For purposes of speed, however, the shorthand writer had not given the names of the speakers, only their national origins.

USA: Well, I think you all know why I've called this second meeting. That guy Karfounis must be crazy if he thinks we're backing him. And frankly, Colonel, I can't think what your Captain is doing, bringing a rabid rebel like that for our approval.

USSR: Let's make one thing clear – are you objecting to the man because of his politics or because of his 'rabid rebel' quality? I would have thought that what we needed on Crete, assuming we need anything at all at this moment, is someone with exactly that rabid rebel quality.

GB: Gentlemen, I don't think we should permit our discussions to deteriorate into political considerations. For my part, I'm impressed by the man Karfounis. I have the utmost faith in Captain Thomas and will support him to the hilt in his choice. If he believes the man is the one best qualified to lead an insurgency in the *nome* of Xanion, then I think we should stick to the resolution of the previous meeting and support him. What do you think, François?'

FR: The man impressed me, *bien sur*. His politics are his own affair. Certainly, if we could secure Crete, we would speed up matters in this part of the Mediterranean, and the sooner get back to the Free French project of an assault on the South of France. Anything that accelerates our return to France is to be welcomed and supported. I'm certain that General de Gaulle would agree with what I say.

USSR: Even if it meant delaying the fight against the Germans across the north of Europe. May I remember you, gentleman . . .

GB: We say, *remind* you, gentlemen . . . Ilyanovich.

USSR: May I remind you, gentlemen, that we are bearing the brunt of this war? That daily, many thousands of Russians are being killed on the soil of the Motherland. I have a very clear message for you all from General Stalin, since we are talking of our leaders. Certainly I am here to give you promise of the assistance of my country but not at the expense of the Second Front which your Winston Churchill, Colonel, and your President Roosevelt have already promised. Certainly, a limited quantity of arms can be supplied to the free people of Crete fighting in the national cause . . .

USA: You mean the damned Communists . . .

UK: Gentlemen, let's restrict ourselves to discussions of tactics or arms and supplies and leave out the politics.

USA: I don't see how we can do that. I'm here with a brief that comes directly through the Army from the White House, the Pentagon and the Department of State. We're not going to supply a bunch of Communists with weapons so they can go around murdering their own people, so that Crete, when this war is ended, can become another Communist outpost . . .

USSR: I must protest.

USA: You can protest all you want. And while you're protesting let me remind you of one thing. The Allies have agreed on a thrust on the western end of the African coast. General Eisenhower himself will direct that action. Any support the Americans give in the Mediterranean is going to take first account of that largely US action . . .

UK: You forget, old lad, that the plan for the invasion of Crete is in front of the full meeting of the Joint Liaison Committee, not just this Cretan sub-committee. If the JLC says, in all its wisdom, that we invade, then we're going to need men like Karfounis on the ground. And they'll be no good there if they haven't been supplied with arms and ammunition, if they haven't trained with them.

USSR: Anything that detracts from the invasion of Northern Europe, my friends, is not according to the wish of General Stalin. The scheme for the invasion of Crete will never pass the full meeting of the JLC. I would have thought you knew that.

UK: Gentlemen, I think we are wasting time on polemics. We cannot anticipate what the full meeting of the JLC will or will not say. Our job is to arrange the background feasibilities. I propose, therefore, we abandon this meeting and that we go back to our previous position, i.e. full support for Captain Thomas and Theodor Karfounis with such arms, ammunition, explosives and supplies as can be procured, according to the list already discussed.

FR: I second that motion . . .

USSR: May I remember our friend from France . . .

UK: *Remind*, Ilyanovich.

USSR: Thank you. May I *remind* our friend from France that his function here is informational and advisory and that he cannot propose, second or vote any motion.

USA: Okay, I'll propose a motion. That we don't go along with Karfounis. Nor with Captain Thomas. That we get rid of Karfounis as soon as we can, any way we can. I don't think we can rely on your Captain Thomas to do it, so I suggest we get somebody else. In fact, I think we should send somebody in to Crete to make damned certain it gets done.

USSR: Karfounis, active on Crete, could certainly be a danger. He seemed to me the sort of man who could start a unilateral action against the Germans, even without support from us. Unilateral action could be dangerous. If an uprising occurred on Crete, we could find ourselves compelled to support it, to divert troops to that purpose at a time when we are not ready for this. I support your motion.

UK: Gentlemen, we haven't had a motion, only a lot of vague waffle . . .!'

USA: Okay, this is it. I vote we dump Karfounis, anyway we can. And I vote that Captain Thomas not be – repeat not – informed.

The shorthand writer had appended the notation; motion carried, two votes to one.

'There we have the positive proof I've been looking for,' Bill raged to Maria while she tried in vain to get him to eat the breakfast she'd been out to buy. 'My father knew nothing about the betrayal of Karfounis.' He opened the diary and scanned the pages hurriedly. 'Here it is,' he said: ' "*Runner from G in Loutron with envelope JB.*" Look, Maria, see for yourself. He got the envelope as he was on his way to climb the mountain to the Gorge of the Angels. He wouldn't have had the time to read it . . .'

'We don't know it was the same envelope, Bill!'

'What other envelope could it be. The runner for G, whoever that was, brought the envelope which had probably just arrived from Cairo by boat, with more men; the note says – you know what a risk I'm taking *sending* this to you . . .' He was pacing the room in his excitement.

216

'Come and sit down, Bill,' Maria said, 'I can't think with you walking up and down.' He sat down and she took his hand. 'One thing you've overlooked,' she said. 'The Military Delegation, when it arrived, may have seen the strength of the Karfounis force and decided after all to solve the problem in the direct, military way. By doing what Karfounis thinks they did. By *ordering* your father to take care of it confident that, as a good soldier, he'd carry out those orders to the letter!'

'I guess that about wraps it up, Sam,' the director said. 'If we now have access to the Minutes of that second Cairo meeting. After all, that's why we went in there in the first place, isn't it?'

Sam was trying hard to be patient. 'Yes, Director. That was the original brief. Find the Minutes of the second Cairo meeting and destroy them. But you're forgetting the additional complication we have over this guy Theseus, and this British guy, Bill Thomas.'

'Now we can put out a 5311 on both of them, right, Sam?'

Sam reached into the breast pocket of his shirt for one of the tissues he always kept there. He'd forgotten to put one in when he left his own office to come to report 27's last message to the director. He wiped his hands down the seam of his trousers, knowing the director would notice again and despise him for it.

'We can't solve *all* our problems with a 5311, Director,' he said.

The director *had* noticed him wiping his hands. 'You ought to see a doctor to help you solve that problem with your perspiration, Sam! They say it's a sign of nervous tension . . .'

'Or frustration . . .? Do you agree with my request, that we leave the Minutes exactly where they are for the moment?'

The director shook his head. 'It's too dangerous, Sam. We're all agreed on that. I'd say that someone has to go in and lift them!'

'Not 27, I hope? That could be a dead give-away. It'd be foolish to risk compromising 27 at this stage of the game.'

'It's got to be done, Sam. I don't care who you use, but it's got to be done. I want those Minutes out of there as soon as possible.'

Colonel James Quentin Hassler, who was known as Jimmy when on active duty with the Rangers, hunkered down outside the mouth of the cave in the twilight, looking out over the mountains, thinking of his native Pennsylvania.

The men said Jimmy had a long back leg; some added that he'd been bred from a mountain goat. The truth was something different; Jimmy had earned his leg muscles running demijohns of illicit mountain 'Dew', often with no shoes on his feet. Finally, he'd run all the way out of the mountains of Pennsylvania, left his crude, tobacco-chewing father and his slatternly mother and had got himself, with fifteen cents in his pocket wrapped in what once had been a corner of his bed-sheet and now did duty as a handkerchief, to Fort Wix.

The recruiting sergeant had taken one look at him and had laughed. The next day, when the sergeant came to the guard-room, he'd found the kid squatting on the dirt road outside the stockade.

'Go home, kid,' he'd said kindly. 'Come back in a couple of years when you're old enough!'

'I'm eighteen,' the kid said.

The sergeant looked hard at him. 'C'n you prove that.' he said incredulously.

The kid pulled a tattered piece of paper out of his pocket. It was a birth certificate. 'This man used to ride the mountains on a horse carrying a Bible. He insisted on baptizing all the babies he could find. To do that, he had to certify the birth. He certified mine, brought me this paper from someplace. I guess it makes me for real, eh?'

'It sure does!'

They took him in, bathed him, gave him a suit of old denims and recruited him into the US Army. They'd never seen anybody like him. The Kid, as they called him, had a thirst and hunger for learning; in three months he could read and write, could clean a latrine better than anybody in the camp, could march with a pack on his back, his boots hanging over his shoulders, all day and never sweat or show signs of being tired.

One day they took him with them on the rifle range, to cart the heavy ammunition boxes. He was cleaning up the firing point after the men had finished when the sergeant lay down to zero the sights of a rifle. The Kid was staring intently at him as he shot. He 'scored' a six-inch group at two hundred yards. 'How's that for shooting, Kid?' he asked.

The Kid shrugged his shoulders, blatantly unimpressed.

The sergeant, nettled, beckoned the Kid down. 'You ever handled one of these?' he asked, pointing to the carbine.

'Nope!'

The sergeant pushed a clip into the stock of the rifle. 'Okay, wise guy, let's see you hit the target.'

The Kid squinted along the barrel. 'Take off the safety catch, here,' the sergeant said, showing him. 'And you don't have to cock the gun each time. It cocks itself. You just aim and fire. Five times.'

The Kid aimed and fired five times, missing the target completely with all five shots.

'You see, Kid,' the sergeant crowed, 'it ain't so easy as it looks!'

Colonel Jimmy Hassler smiled, remembering. He hadn't aimed at the target. He didn't understand why at the time, but he knew instinctively he ought not to hit it. He knew instinctively the sergeant would make his life hell if he beat him on the rifle range. But when they'd all left the range, he walked to the back of the butts to look at the notice glued to a piece of cardboard, posting the hours at which the rifle range would be in use. The five holes in it could have been covered with a dime.

The Kid had learned to shoot in the mountains of

Pennsylvania and could cut the harness of a Revenue hunter at a hundred yards, toppling him off his horse.

He saw the movement in the rocks below him and eased himself to the side of the cave mouth, out of view. You never know who to trust on a mission.

The party of three came quickly up the cleft between the rocks, out of sight of anyone observing from either below or above, keeping away from sky-lines. When they reached the small plateau at the mouth of the cave, they crossed it quickly and went into the cave. Jimmy Hassler smiled. 'Damned amateurs,' he said. He took the grenade out of his belt, opened the base and removed the fuse cap, but put the fuse back in. He screwed the base back, then pulled the pin, holding the lever against the side of the grenade. Then he bowled it underarm, straight into the cave mouth. He heard it clatter against the rocks inside the cave and then the three men came belting out.

He was standing there, holding the gun on them.

'Which one of you amateurs is Theseus?' he asked. 'And don't worry about the grenade – I took out the fuse cap. It'll smoke, but it won't explode.'

'That was a lousy trick, *Americano* . . .!' Theseus said.

'We're not playing games. You guys came up here like a bunch of Boy Scouts. One at a time, slowly. And don't come up the bottom of a cleft; that's the place they always plant the mines. And don't walk into a cave, bunched together. One guy in there with a schmeisser could have cut you to ribbons. Jesus, you guys really need training, don't you?'

They glowered at him as they sat in a circle. Colonel Hassler had his back to the bulk of the mountain and could look out and down protected by an overhang of rock. He projected an atmosphere of total confidence and command.

'Do we talk?' he asked Theseus.

'Yes.'

The colonel looked at the other two men. 'You two,' he said, 'down the mountain a hundred metres. You right, you left. Move it!'

They looked at Theseus, who nodded to them; then they scrambled to their feet and left.

'Now we talk,' the colonel said. 'I know that you like to talk. Even to the Germans. So far, I'm the only one who knows. I run my own shop in Cairo, which has nothing to do with the rest of the Allied Command. I play my cards close to my chest. You don't think I'd let the Germans set up on the island without making sure I knew – I was in a position at all times to know – the sources of their information. I've cracked every code they've ever used – I'm telling you this because I shall know, if they change codes, that you're the man who's tipped them off. And that'll be the last tip off you ever give anybody, Theseus. The next grenade won't have its firing cap taken out!'

Theseus studied this man squatting at ease before him, noting the lean, hard features, the ice-cold, grey eyes. The man spoke abominable Greek with an atrocious, thick, American accent, using it clumsily as if it were a tool he'd plucked off a shelf with which to do a job. He was wearing lace-up boots of a kind Theseus had never seen; his whip-lash legs sticking out of them looked capable of taking him anywhere. He didn't carry an ounce of fat. Theseus knew he himself was hard, but he had the Cretan roll round his waist-line and was sweating from his climb up the mountains.

'Who are you? What do you want from me?' he asked.

'You know Theodor Karfounis?'

'That Communist. Certainly I know him. Everybody knows him and his men. They are all Communists. They fight, not for Crete, but for themselves and victory at the end of the war . . .'

'I want you to talk to the Germans again!'

Theseus's eyes showed his fears. 'Is this some kind of trick?'

'No trick. I want you to talk to the Germans. I hear Karfounis and his men meet in the village of Mavroti. I hear they have weapons, arms, ammunition, hidden in the graveyard of Mavroti. I want you to let the Germans know

222

this. But, it must be done subtly, you understand. It must be done without anyone suspecting that information has been given. I want Karfounis and his men wiped out and the village of Mavroti destroyed if necessary!'

Theseus sat there, silent, trying to understand.

'What is your reason for this?' he asked finally.

'In war-time, who needs a reason?'

'Look, *Americano*. Okay, I have given information to the Germans from time to time. I have also supplied information to the Allies. I work for Crete, in the way I see best. Sometimes, if a small group of men plan to destroy a bridge, a road, a patrol, I inform the Germans in advance, because I know the reprisals that will follow will cost a good many lives. I do not care about the lives of Karfounis and his Communists, but to destroy the village of Mavroti will cost many many other lives. The Communists are hidden throughout the village. The whole village will be destroyed. There are women and children . . .'

'When the Germans bombed Heraklion, they killed women and children . . .'

What the American was suggesting was inconceivable to Theseus. He had betrayed his countrymen, certainly, but only in the interests of preserving the lives of the many by sacrificing the lives of the few.

'If I do not agree to do this . . .?' Theseus asked, already knowing the answer.

'A word in the ear of Spiros Orfandakis and he'll give you a short trial then stick you up against a wall. That way, you'll die in one piece. A word to Manoletto, over on the Omalos plain, and they'll be able to make dolmas out of what's left of you, before you die. Take your pick, Theseus. The choice is yours.'

'And the women and children who die . . .'

'Where I came from, Theseus, a hundred women and children die every year, of ricketts, of malnutrition, of tuberculosis. Fathers rape their own daughters every month, and when that isn't enough, they go out and bugger the animals. Life and death, Theseus, are two sides of a coin somebody else gets to flip. I want Karfounis and his Commie buddies out of the way, and you, poor sucker, are the guy who's going to do it for me, okay?'

Sam Birntin received the cablegram re-routed by normal procedures to appear on his computer display panel. He scanned it rapidly. It seemed to concern the disposal of property. He pressed a series of numbered buttons and the cursor ran across the display panel, scrambling the letters of the message. It ran back again, scrambling them again. After five successive cursor runs, the message appeared in plain language again.

Theodor Karfounis, Frojane, Provence, France. Nat. French.

Jack Bythorne, Little Halstead, Northamptonshire, England. British.

Bill Thomas, Pension Zorbas, Zampeliou 46, Xania, Crete. British.

Victorio Shones, Kaprisses, Crete. Greek.

Maria Stafanakis, Kaprisses, Crete. US/Greek.

The message was signed: 'Theseus'.

Sam Birntin looked out of the window of his office, through the half-silvered glass that let him see out but no one see in. It was shortly after dawn; the sun was rising rapidly over the roof of the White House about a quarter of a mile away.

Washington was slowly coming to life again, to face another day as the self-imposed guardian of the peace of the world. Once, Sam thought, the Brits used to take all the big decisions. Once London was the seat of the responsibility that now had shifted across the Atlantic. You win some, you lose some, and the politicians don't help. The technicians carry the burdens still; despite Watergate, despite the CIA shake-up, despite the revelations of the totally paranoid nature of J. Edgar Hoover and his FBI. There'll always be technicians, he thought.

He got up from behind his desk with its computer print-out facility, its display panel, its instant access to a million technical secrets. He stretched to try to relieve the pain he always felt in his shoulders when he sat too long at his desk. And he'd been there all night, waiting for the message. He reached back over his desk and pressed his intercom button. 'Can you bring me a cup of coffee?' he asked.

'Yes, *sir*!' Leonard could never keep the Marines' snap out of his responses.

When Sam had drunk the coffee, he checked his desk clock. Six-thirty. The director should be in his office by now. He pressed the button on his desk-top marked One; the automatic dialler spun out the intercom number; the director answered.

'I've heard from Theseus,' Sam said.

'What is it this time?'

'A list.'

'Not another.'

'Yes.'

'This programme is getting to be damned expensive, Sam!'

'I know that. Want to review it, Director?'

'No way. We're committed.'

'Then I act?'

'Yes. Check the list first, of course, for crosses.'

'Of course, Director.' Sam put down the phone. Officious bastard, trying to tell Sam how to tighten nuts and bolts.

He activated the print-out again and read the list of names. He tapped a programme onto the computer access terminal by his right hand and watched the letters on his print-out scramble into a meaningless jumble. A tenth of a microsecond later, the names reappeared, with one exception. One name had been removed by data from the computer's 'Memory'.

He tapped a 5311 and it appeared on the display panel. Translated into Action English it said 'Eliminate'. Nobody, not even the computer, uses the phrase 'terminate with extreme prejudice' any more. 'Eliminate' is shorter but means the same thing.

Then Sam Birntin closed his office and went home to his bachelor apartment on Avenue G, Washington D.C. Another technician, going home after the night-shift, doing a job. He scrambled two eggs, soft the way he liked them. Made a cup of coffee, using freeze-dried Maxwell House, the way he liked it, with a lot of sugar and no cream. The eggs tasted like sawdust, the coffee like nothing he could describe politely. It was always the same after a 5311. 'Shit,' he said, 'shit!'

There was no-one to hear, to listen. He took a Seconal, then, on reflection, another one. Then he went to bed.

There was a centuries' old well in the drive-way of Colonel Jack Bythorne's house, with a flat stone on the top on which he'd had a small stone pedestal built, carrying a sun-dial. The sun-dial had been incorrectly fixed and was always two hours slow.

The pedestal stopped the oil company parking its tanker on that part of the drive when it came to deliver fuel for the central heating system located in a small boiler room at the edge of the drive.

The colonel walked the drive every night before he retired, to look at the sky and to ease his gout before settling down to try to sleep. His furthest point was always the central-heating boiler room, to check that the time-clock had clicked out. He'd been having trouble with the programmer that was supposed to turn the boiler on/off twice every twenty-four hours. Sometimes, it ran all night, a wasteful procedure, especially on a retired officer's pension.

He opened the door of the boiler room, switched on the light. 'Damn,' he said, hearing the pump's gentle hum. The programmer had failed again. He hobbled to the wall and pressed the red button of the over-ride *cancel* switch.

The boiler rumbled, the roar of the flame ceased and the room fell quiet. He went outside again, looking up at the stars and smelling the night-scented jasmine that was blooming unseasonally at the edge of the drive. Beautiful night. No moon, of course; he'd watched it wane for the previous few nights. He tried to empty his mind as he started to hobble forward. So many problems and yet what did they amount to? The vicar's wife was being damned officious about the stalls for the winter fair to be held in the schoolroom, but how do you tell a vicar's wife to let the people manage things for themselves?

Young Rupert, damned fool, crashed his motor-bike again and was now in the local cottage hospital, and the father asked 'the Colonel', as they still called him in the village, to have a word. How can you tell a seventeen-year-old, impetuous boy to keep his speed down to what the motor bicycle will safely do, especially on corners when it has been raining.

And tomorrow, dear old Maisie going into that same hospital for another check-up, or so she thought, but young Dr Simmonds had privately told the colonel that the growth was malign, not benign as they'd all prayed. How was he going to tell Maisie she only had another six months?

He was approaching the sun-dial, puzzled because he must have been walking off-line or the sun-dial must have moved, which was impossible, wasn't it? Then he heard his name called softly.

'Colonel Bythorne? Colonel Jack Bythorne?'

The voice seemed to come from his right and he turned. 'Yes, what is it? Who is it?'

Not a voice he could remember hearing, and nobody in the village would use his full name. It'd be 'Colonel'.

No sign of anyone.

He heard the gravel skitter beneath someone's feet. Seemed to be behind him now. Damned kids from Earl's Barton, scrumping the last of his apples? The Coxes he was leaving on the tree for Christmas eating? Caught them the last year, given a couple of 'em a whack with his stick across the backside. Served the damned tykes right.

He felt the blow in the back of his knees. God, that hurt. Felt his stick being pulled away at the bottom as he buckled forward. Saw, at the last moment, the hole open before him that should have been covered by the stone of the well top. He went head first through the hole, his knees banging the sides as he toppled slowly down into the Stygian depths.

Panayottis's eyes gleamed with pleasure as he saw the car carrying Bill and Maria arrive outside the Church. He strode across the intervening space and slapped Bill's hand front and back in the time-honoured greeting.

'Welcome,' he said, his face glowing with pride.

Bill remembered the last time he had seen Panayottis, and the men gathered about him in an awkward group. They had all been in Victorio's *kafeneion* the first night he'd gone there with Ioannis. The night Victorio had beaten him. Panayottis had also been in the *kafeneion* the night Bill had taken his revenge. Word had percolated through every corner of the village – 'The Englishman is okay, *endaksi*!'

The wedding invitation was a sign that Bill had been accepted.

Victorio tapped Bill's arm and beckoned slyly. The other men were grinning. Bill followed them leaving Panayottis standing there, a forlorn figure in his gleaming mountain boots, his full Sfakian regalia including the handkerchief on his head. Proud but forlorn. He would desperately have liked to join the men in a glass of *ouzo*, but tradition demanded he be standing there, waiting, when Stella arrived from the next village.

The men slapped Bill on the back, clinked glasses with him. Once again he had the feeling of what life could become for him should he decide to live on Crete among them, one of them, perhaps even holding his marriage among them in this tiny church of St Nicholas, with its beautiful ikons on the walls and the superb altar cloth the village women had woven and embroidered.

He made the mistake of emptying his glass; it was immediately refilled. He looked round. Maria was sitting with the women beneath the mulberry tree, looking as happy as only a wedding day can show.

The priest was standing in the door of the church wearing his dark-blue robe and his stove-pipe hat; in his hand he held a cigarette and was talking animatedly to a couple of the village boys who would help with the ceremony.

The patriarch from Stella's village was also coming to officiate.

Manolis had banged a third glass of *ouzo* on the table when Bill heard the sound of bells and the excitement grew. The priest threw down his cigarette and went back into the church, taking the choirboys with him.

The women fluttered from beneath the mulberry tree, talking in piercing whispers, their eyes on the road into the village. Bill stood up and saw the three donkeys. The first one had been garlanded with flowers, branches of aromatic daphne, and the ubiquitous basil reported to have been brought to Crete from Jerusalem. Around the donkey's neck had been hung a ring of the goat-bells the shepherds use; the boy leading the donkey was shaking the leather necklace from which the bells hung, making them clatter.

The patriarch sat on the donkey's back, his long legs hanging each side and his feet almost trailing on the ground. He raised his hand on each side, blessing the people as he came. Where the skirt of his robe parted over the donkey's back, his legs were revealed wearing off-white woollen underpants which reached down to his ankles.

Stella was sitting gracefully side-saddle on a wooden seat that had been newly painted and threaded with fronds of mint, oregano, more daphne and basil. She was wearing a white silk gown, gathered into a heap on the pommel.

On her feet she wore white pumps. Her hair had been newly coiffed and pinned into position on top of her head with a bead-studded veil in white. She wore white gloves on her hands, with which she was joyously and childishly tugging the leather necklace of the donkey's bells.

The woman on the third donkey, dressed entirely in black with a heavy black veil must have weighed more than the donkey itself; she was laughing as she rode along, a deep, booming laugh of an inner joy inexpressible in any other way. The rolls of fat around her body bounced up and down with the motion of her heaving laughter; two men walked either side of the donkey, holding her in position and perspiring with the effort it cost.

Panayottis looked shyly at Stella, then walked to the door of the church. She slid delicately from the wooden saddle, arranged her dress about her, plucked at her bodice and walked to stand beside him. Neither spoke to the other. The patriarch was helped from his donkey; he walked to the group of men sitting outside the *kafeneion* and took a glass of *ouzo*, downing it in one gulp. He took another *ouzo*; the boy rushed out of the *kafeneion* with a glass of water; the patriarch downed that in one gulp, too, then made his way across the small square to the church.

Everyone was milling around; the village was filled with strangers Bill had not seen before, many of whom wore the *macropantalones* of the plains, as Bill did. Bill was used to formal weddings, where the people gather silently in the church and where the bridegroom stands nervously by the altar with the best man, waiting for the swelling organ chords that will announce the arrival of his bride-to-be at the main door.

People seemed to be wandering into and out of the church, pushing past the bride and groom without ceremony. Victorio grabbed his arm and dragged him inside. The congregation was arranged in no particular order. Some people were paying money for candles at a small altar just inside the door. Others were standing about in the centre of the church, milling across the altar itself.

The priest and the patriarch came from behind the curtain in the corner, now both robed in what seemed to Bill to be Byzantine splendour, wearing cloaks of red with gold threads and no hats.

Panayottis and Stella came into the church. They had to push through the crowd unceremoniously to get to the front; finally, the *koumbaros*, the best man, shouted and pushed and secured a passage for them. They stood side by side, the *koumbaros* to the right of the bride and the matron-of-honour in the front rank of the crowd gathered in a circle so tight they left little room for the officiating priests.

The ceremony started with the religious chants often inaudible beneath the incessant chatter of the people watching, the scuffles of the children running about between the legs and around the skirts of parents. Bill had never seen such an enchanting occasion. The noise only diminished slightly at the peak of the ceremony, the moment at which the priest placed the *stephania*, the little white crowns linked by a ribbon, on the heads of both bride and groom. The *koumbaros* stepped in, changed the crowns over three times – now the couple were married. There were tears in the bride's eyes but a look, too, of pride.

Victorio was standing beside Bill. 'She is a lucky one,' he said. 'She loves him! And he loves her. I have watched them sitting for hours on the bench, their fingers a millimetre apart . . .'

Bill knew the local custom was still for arranged marriages – fortunate indeed the bride who could have a love marriage!

The two priests joined hands with the bride and groom and began the ritual 'Dance of Isaiah' around the altar; the hubbub increased so loudly that, at first, Bill didn't hear the voice in his ear.

'The *Ipastinomos* would like a word with you and Victorio,' the voice said. 'Can you please leave quickly and quietly, if possible without anyone seeing you?'

Bill was angry. Why the hell couldn't Petro leave him alone. Today of all days, when Bill had practically decided he was going to give up his search and was going to spend some time with Maria, then see if Angelo Stavakis could find a job for him in nearby Xania.

'Where is he?' he asked.

'Waiting in Evangelina's house.'

'I'll be there soon!'

'He said, *now*, *kirios*.'

Bill turned to look at the unfamiliar face of the man behind him. He'd seen the man earlier, standing against the wall of the church. He'd assumed the man was one of the guests from Stella's village. Trust Petro to be watching even so innocent an occasion as a village wedding!

Bill touched Victorio's arm. 'Come on,' he said, 'quickly.'

'We will get a drink later,' Victorio protested.

'No. Come on, please.'

Victorio looked mystified then shrugged his shoulders and together they left the church, skirting the crowd along the walls. When they were outside, Victorio stopped. 'We ought to have stayed,' he said. 'I wanted to give the *koumbaros* a wedding gift for them.'

'You can do that later,' Bill said. 'The *Ipastinomos* is waiting for us in the house. I want to go in there and tell the bastard to get off our backs . . .'

Very angry, Bill marched down the street towards Evangelina's house. The man who'd given them the *ipastinomos*'s message stayed behind at the door of the church, waving them on.

The door to the vine arbour was closed. Bill threw it open. Petro hadn't even had the courtesy to wait outside; he must have opened the door of the house and gone inside. Blasted cheek, Bill thought.

He crossed the arbour to the main door, turned the handle, smelled the gas, heard the click, then saw the rumble of the explosion start in front of him. With only a microsecond left to live, he started the motion that threw him sideways and down. Victorio standing immediately behind him was only partly shielded by Bill's falling body; the crescendo of flame, of explosive violence, the red yellow ball of burning fire hit him full in the chest and he went over backwards, screaming. Bill caught the blast down his left hip and thigh; the side of his body was punched violently backwards, spinning him into the maelstrom of banging burning rubble, the blazing wood, the flaring alcohol from the *tsikoudia* barrel, the gas with which the room must slowly have filled while they were in the church. He felt the searing pain of the burn, the hundred blows of fragmented stone; he was rolled over backwards with his limbs twisted in Victorio's, his nose against the burning skin of Victorio's cheek, his arm bent at an awkward angle against Victorio's ear.

Ioannis was dozing on his chair in the lobby of Pension Zorbas when he woke suddenly, not certain from where the sound had come that had alerted him. Only one room was rented at the moment, the front room of the Englishman Bill Thomas, who had been taken to the hospital after his unfortunate and tragic accident. A taxi-driver had brought the message, with a request that he pack Bill's bag to take to the hospital for him. Ioannis had gone into the room with the taxi-driver and watched him like a hawk. After all, the contents of a client's room were his, Ioannis's, responsibility. And Ioannis was a man who took his responsibilities very seriously.

He stretched in his chair, glanced at the clock on his desk. Midnight already. Tonight he'd eaten early, at ten o'clock. The lamb and noodles weren't sitting too well in his stomach. He got up and walked to the bathroom he'd had built on the back terrace when he'd taken over the house from his father.

The door to Bill's room opened slowly. A figure appeared in the half-light. The man had heard Ioannis's sandals flop on his way to the bathroom. He crossed the lobby of the pension, turned around the head of the stairs and quickly went down. The front foor of the pension was stiff and squawked when he opened it.

As he walked out into the darkened street, he heard Ioannis's voice call from above. 'Yes, who is it?'

The man patted the pocket in which he'd put the envelope from Bill Thomas's room, turned the corner by the Lucia Hotel, and within seconds was lost to sight among the people still promenading along the waterfront.

When Bill regained consciousness, he knew immediately from the smell that he was in a hospital. But he could hear and see nothing, and could feel nothing.

He tried to move his hands, but his arms wouldn't obey him.

He tried to lift his head, but his neck didn't seem to get any message.

He tried to open his eyes, but his lids remained fixed.

'I'm dead,' he thought.

The smell in his nostrils changed to something else he knew but couldn't immediately identify.

He sniffed deeply at it, and then knew he wasn't dead. Unless they provide Guerlain's *Shalimar* in heaven or hell, wherever he might be.

He opened his eyes and saw Maria bending over him. 'You moved your right hand,' she said. She had tears in her eyes.

He lifted his head to look down the bed and saw that his left side was covered in what looked like melting butter. His right side was naked, and he was lying in a muslin tent that enclosed both of them, the bed, the chair beside it, the wheeled trolley across his feet.

'How do you feel?' she asked, her voice small, as if she were frightened by what the reply might be.

'Lousy. My head is splitting open, my shoulder feels as if somebody had hammered it and all my left side feels as if you were rubbing it with a wire brush. Apart from that, okay.'

She smiled through the tears. 'Blasted Englishman,' she said. 'You always have to make jokes . . .'

'How is Victorio?' he asked.

'Burned chest, he's lost half his hair and his prize moustache is a mess, but it seems that you took most of the solid blast. He'll be all right.'

'And Petro?'

'Petro?'

'Petro! Inside the house?'

She looked puzzled. 'There was no one *in* the house. Petro is waiting outside to see if you're all right. The house was empty. Stupidly, I'd left a pan on the stove. The gas must have blown out. The house was full of gas; you must have made a spark when you went in . . .'

'Fetch Petro,' Bill said. 'Fetch him quickly.' He could already feel his senses slipping again as his body and mind sought relief in sleep. He knew damned well he'd made no spark as he went in.

Petro came at once and sat on the chair. Maria squatted on the side of the bed. 'You wanted me,' Petro asked, though looking quickly at Maria as if to say, 'be careful.'

Bill waved his hand weakly. 'If Maria had gone back to the house before we did,' he said, 'it could have been Maria. She has a right to know. That house was a set-up. You'll find some kind of sparking device had been put on the inside of the door.'

'Alas, no,' Petro said. 'The whole wall, the door included, was blown out. You were under it when it fell. You are a lucky man to be still alive.'

'The devil looks after his own! Petro, there was a man at the wedding – when was it, by the way?'

'Yesterday. You have been out for twenty hours.'

'This man was wearing grey trousers with a thin red stripe in them, and a grey cotton shirt open at the neck. He had black hair and a moustache.'

'Forget him, Bill. There were fifty men at the wedding

235

who answer to that description. We will never find him. This was a professional job, like the General, like Kostas Dandanakis.'

Maria's eyes had opened while they were talking. 'Are you saying,' she said, 'that somebody tried *deliberately* to *kill* you?'

'Yes, I am,' Bill said, fighting fatigue. 'He chose the wedding because he knew he could infiltrate the village without being spotted as a stranger. But what I can't understand is that he also had Victorio on his list . . .'

Bill fought it; there was so much he still wanted to ask Petro, but could stay awake no longer. They both watched his head drop back onto the pillow. The doctor came into the tent, swishing the muslin aside. They watched as he took Bill's pulse, checked his heart, glanced at his bandages and the open wounds which had been sprayed with sterile plastic skin. 'He will be all right,' he said, 'but he is going to need rest. Lots of rest. So, the two of you must leave now.'

'I think you and I should go to my office,' Petro said, 'and have a little chat.'

Maria looked at him, but the *ipastinomos* smiled blandly back at her. 'I think you and I might have a lot to talk about,' he said.

Painstakingly, Petro's men had sought out everyone who'd been at the wedding, asking them the same question. 'Was there any one man of whom you could say – *why* is *he* here? Any man you think had no *reason* to be there?'

Three men had been there for the free food. They'd brought their wives and kids with them, had gorged the rice, the lamb, the honey and walnuts, and then had left. One man, a former musician who could be seen every night in one village or other, scrounging drinks, had been there for the alcohol. He'd spent the night sleeping on the bench outside the church.

Panayottis supplied one name. 'Right after the *stephania* had been placed,' he said, 'I saw a man speaking to the Englishman. I have seen this man once before. You know, I took a job in Souda for six months, in the American Naval base. I went to the school in Xania and learned welding – they gave me a six months' job welding steel for buildings. That is how I earned the money for the wedding. I saw this man there a couple of times. Then one day I saw the same man go into a house in Khalepa. He was at the wedding. When I saw him talking to Bill I thought, how nice, he has heard about my wedding and has come to wish me and my bride good luck. Since he was talking to *Kyrios* Bill, I thought Bill must have told him. But I did not see him at the feast afterwards.'

'Can you show me the house in Khalepa?' Petro asked, when Panayottis had repeated his story at headquarters.

They went to the house and quietly surrounded it. Petro noticed the telephone wire going to the first floor window. Like many of the houses in the rich suburb, this one had fallen into disrepair since the days of Venizelos and Prince George, the grand days when Khalepa was a gracious suburb of Xania. Now many of the houses had been divided into apartments, neglected by their owners.

They put Panayottis in the back of a truck with a smoked glass window; he was as excited as a schoolboy. Just before midday, he exclaimed excitedly, 'There he is. That is the man!'

Petro looked at the man who answered Bill's description of black hair and a black moustache. Today he was wearing a sand-coloured suit, a white shirt and a tie, and carrying a briefcase. The van followed him. He went to the Olympic Terminal and there bought a ticket for Athens. When he came out of the terminal, he beckoned for a taxi, though the bus would leave in a couple of minutes. The taxi pulled alongside and he got in. 'Do you fancy a ride to Heraklion,' the man said to the driver.

'Okay by me.'

The real driver, the owner of the taxi, watched it pull

away. 'I hope I will get compensation for loss of work,' he said to the *enomotarxis* standing beside him.

'We will not give you any parking tickets for a week! How is that?' the *enomotarxis* said, smiling.

'Where do you want to go in Heraklion?' the *horofilakas* asked his unsuspecting passenger.

'I'll tell you when we get there,' the passenger said, twisting his body to look out of the back window.

The taxi was speeding along the slip road that led to the Rethymnon motorway when the *horofilakas* saw the unmarked police car parked under a tree at the side of the road, the four policemen bending over it as if doing a deal. He glanced in the mirror and saw nothing behind him, nothing in front of him. The passenger was leaning slightly forward in his seat as if restless.

The driver stamped his foot on the brake and yanked on the hand-brake.

The taxi screamed to a stop almost level with the police car.

The passenger shot forward, his head over the back of the seat beside the driver who turned rapidly and chopped him behind his neck, smashing his throat down on the iron strengthening of the seat back.

The passenger gagged; the driver reached over him and yanked the briefcase.

The four policemen waiting by the side of the road ripped open the back and front doors on that side. One of them grabbed the passenger's arms and forced them behind his back while the other reached in and clipped a pair of handcuffs around his wrists.

'Now we will go and see the *ipastinomos*,' the driver said as two policemen climbed into the back seat, pushing the passenger between them.

He was saying nothing, physically incapable of speaking after the smashing blow his throat had suffered.

Petro beckoned for Maria Stafanakis to precede him into the police headquarters, a four-storey, drab building on the fringes of Khalepa in Xania. They went up the stairs to the second floor and along a corridor, then turned right into the *ipastinomos*'s office. A girl was sitting at a typewriter but reading a strip-cartoon magazine. The *ipastinomos* ignored her and she ignored him.

'Would you like coffee?' he asked Maria, who nodded.

He picked up the telephone and waited. After a minute of silence, he jiggled the instrument. 'Send in two coffees,' he said, 'and Manolis.'

The *horofilakas* who'd driven the taxi came in; close-up one could see the muscles bulging beneath his dark blue cotton shirt, the sturdiness of his body.

'He is Greek,' he said without preliminary, as if there were no one but he and the boss in the room. 'He says he was going to Athens to buy some sheets for his bed, but changed his mind to see if he could find them in Heraklion.'

'What is his background, or *his* version of it?'

'He says he is a car salesman.'

'Who has he sold cars to recently?'

'No one. He says he is looking for a site for a showroom.'

'Where does he come from?'

'He says Patras. We are checking. During the time of the Colonels, he says he left Greece and went to America. He says that is where he learned to sell cars. He had a gun in his briefcase.'

'That was very silly of him. My guess is that he is a damned amateur. I want his entire biography written down, since the day he was born. And you have got an hour.'

'I do not need that long.'

'I want him still to be able to speak at the end of the hour,' Petro said.

Maria was looking at them in horror, discussing the fate of a human being in such a dispassionate way. The door opened and a youth came in with coffee and water on one of those mushroom shaped trays introduced into Crete during the time of the Turkish Occupation. This one was made of grey plastic. The *ipastinomos* with a wave of his hand beckoned for one cup to be given to Maria, a cold impersonal gesture that reinforced his dry relaxed disposal of his prisoner. When the *horofilakas* and the coffee man had left the room, he beckoned to the girl at the typewriter. She put her comic book in her desk and left the room, too.

'We have caught a man who was at that wedding,' Petro said, 'and my instincts tell me he would not have been there normally. If Bill is right, and I am inclined to believe him, the house was set up. As Bill said, you could have been the first one back. You could suddenly have remembered the pan you'd left on a low gas and returned to turn it off . . .'

Maria shuddered. 'Who could want to do such a thing?' she asked.

'What thing?'

'The chances are that the three of us would have returned together after the wedding celebration. We would all have had a few glasses of wine, a few *tsikoudias*. We wouldn't have been as alert as Bill was . . .'

'And not one of you would have been alive today. Maria, exactly *why* did you return from America? Why did you come back to Crete?'

She was perplexed by the sudden shift of question. 'Well, I thought you knew. I came back because my husband and my family had been killed. I wanted a chance to think again about what I wanted to do with my life.'

The answer didn't seem to satisfy him. 'You are a rich woman, presumably, by Cretan standards?'

'I suppose I am. My husband earned good money. We lived careful lives.'

'You did not think to go somewhere your money would be more *useful* to you?'

'I looked around, of course. England tempted me, especially London, but it was too cold, too wet, too inward-looking, if you know what I mean?'

'No, but it does not matter.'

240

'Spain was ghastly – full of phoney film stars and tasteless tourists. The South of France impossible for anyone without a good income. Italy – well, I stayed a while in the Tuscany Hills and that might have been possible, if I hadn't been scared by the Red Brigade . . .'

'So you came back here, to Crete?'

'No, I came back to Sfakia. I found myself longing for the mountains, the clear, clean simplicity of life here . . .'

'What that man tried to do to you yesterday was not clean or simple. Why do you think he tried to kill you, Maria?'

'I don't have a single idea. I suppose it must be something to do with Bill, with my friendship for Bill, I mean . . .'

'You are rather more than friends, I believe . . .'

She could be tough, too. 'You can believe what you like . . .'

'At this moment,' he said equably, 'I intend to believe that you are a recently bereaved Greek-American house-wife, who has returned to her roots to try to forget the pain of her husband's death and to rebuild a life for herself. Who has become involved in matters too large for her understanding.'

'You'd be about right at that,' she said, smiling for the first time.

But he wasn't smiling. 'Do not prove me wrong,' he said. 'I can be a bastard!'

Petro walked into the room in which they were holding the prisoner. The *horofilakas* handed him a folio of papers.

'There it is, Chief,' he said, 'all of it.'

Petro took it and, without glancing at it, tore it across. The prisoner was startled.

'Crap,' Petro said, speaking English, 'all of it crap! You are a hit man. Motor-car salesmen do not carry guns. You are a hood! A paid exterminator. But you made a mistake when you came onto my territory!'

The quaint use of old-fashioned, Bogart-type Americanisms should have been comic but wasn't. It took the prisoner back to the days of Chicago. And the ruthless methods of that era.

When Petro spoke again, he used Greek. 'You are a paid assassin; before you leave this room either for the hospital or the mortuary, you will tell me who paid you, who gave you your orders, who you report to.'

The prisoner sounded defiant. 'And if I don't know?'

Petro smashed the back of his hand across the prisoner's face. The heavy ring he'd put on before he left his own office scored a deep red weal across the man's cheek which slowly began to seep blood.

'Then you will get to the mortuary all the quicker,' he said. 'You are a second-string amateur. I killed the front-line professional. He is dead, do you understand? I will do exactly the same thing to you. Men like you are lice to me. And you kill lice, do you not?'

He spun on the balls of his feet and the back of his hand slashed out again. This time the weal ran down the other cheek. The prisoner's eyes were full of tears.

'In Turkey,' Petro said conversationally, 'they do this to your balls with knives. In Northern Ireland, the British make you stand with your hands against the wall and talk you to death. It is just as painful as knives, believe me! In Russia they do it with injections of drugs! In the USA they bombard your mind with computerised micro-waves. In Libya, they stake you out on an ant-heap and stick honey up your anal orifice. In Brazil, they hang you by your wrists and your knees in what they call the parrot's beak, stick an electric soldering iron up your arse and switch on! I find all these methods fancy, over-sophisticated, unnecessary. I offer my people a simple choice. Do you want to die, to live the rest of your life a cripple, or to tell me what I want to know and take your chances on possible escape from gaol at some future date?'

Petro was right; this man was a second-string amateur. If he'd been a front-rank pro, Petro told himself, he'd have rigged that explosion to go off when Bill and Victorio were back inside the house, and he wouldn't have taken a chance on Bill seeing his face. He'd have rigged some kind of remote device so that he could explode the gas from a safe, unobserved, distance, the way the other man had doubtless killed Spiros Orfandakis.

He drew his hand back again; the spittle formed in the corner of the man's mouth as he saw the preparation for the blow, the cool almost bored detachment on Petro's face.

'Okay,' he said, 'okay! I do jobs from time to time.'

'Who do you work for?'

'I don't always know.'

'Did you know this time?'

'No.'

'How do you get the jobs?'

'I get a phone call. I go to the place they tell me. I find a message.'

'A dead-letter drop?'

'Yes.'

'Giving what?'

'The name and possible location of the target. The method.'

'Come on, what do you mean by "the method"?'

'Some have to be made to look accidental, know what I mean. Some, it doesn't matter. Some have to look like suicide.'

'And then you report back?'

'No, that's it.'

The back of Petro's hand smashed forward and the prisoner's nose spurted blood. 'Nobody pays for that kind of work in advance. You have to make contact to collect your money. How do you do it?'

'Okay, okay. Don't hit me any more, okay? I'm telling you everything, aren't I? I send a letter, *poste restante*. I

243

pick up a letter, *poste restante*. My letter has the money in it.'

'Right. Give me the details. Where does all this take place?' Petro saw the look in the prisoner's eyes and anticipated the lie. He smashed his hand in again. 'And the truth . . .' he said coldly.

'New York City. I live in New York City.'

'He knows the Minutes of the second meeting have gone!'

'Yeah, I suppose that was inevitable, 27,' Sam Birntin said. 'But luckily, he has no reason to suspect you.'

'I want to come in,' 27 said. 'It's all getting too heavy for me!'

'You can't come in, you know that!' The call had been rerouted via the Centre. Sam Birntin had been drinking his freeze-dried coffee black with lots of sugar the way he liked it, when the phone rang.

He'd also been listening to Vivaldi's *The Four Seasons*.

And thinking, for the thousandth time, about retiring.

At first, being a technician had meant something to him. Becoming efficient at holding his fingers on the pulse of the world. It had been easy to remind himself that what he was doing, whatever the cost, would save human lives. Then, he'd start to get worried about the definition of the word *save*. Did it mean *save* in the way a doctor, operating quickly after an auto accident, could *save* his patient? Blatantly not. It meant, save a *way* of life rather than that life itself. It meant, holding back the Communists. Playing games with them, always playing games. Well, a lot of good American boys lost their lives in the 'Nam, trying unsuccessfully to hold back the Communists. And not only the Communists. If Castro could have his way, would Africa be conquered? If the Italian Red Brigade had its way, would more Italians die? Did Baader-Meinhof mean lives saved or lives lost? Who shot Martin Luther King?

Kennedy? Some of it was political, some of it sanity/insanity across an indefinable border.

Franco imprisoned a whole nation and gave them an economy capable of supplying surplus to the other nations of Europe. The Germans annihilated countless Jews and other non-Aryans and then forged the strongest economy in the world, next to Japan, another so-called conquered nation. The pound sterling and the dollar daily took nose-dives when Bonn and Tokyo spoke. The whole goddammed issue had grown too big for Sam Birntin's comprehension, and he was by no means a naïve man. What the hell could it be like for the poor sucker on the street, on the receiving end?

When the Recovery Centre had been founded and Sam had been offered a job, he'd accepted gratefully. He'd been about to put in his resignation, anyway. The Centre offered him some kind of hope. He'd attended the first full briefing of the new staff, by the Secretary, who'd spoken off the cuff but, to continue the metaphor, straight from the shoulder.

'We have established this unit, which will be known henceforth as the Recovery Centre, to do one thing only. The CIA, the FBI, and several other government agencies have been operating for a vast number of years in the USA and abroad, sometimes without adequate supervision, without correct approval. All around the world there are unresolved situations one or other of these agencies has abandoned.

'And now all these former agents are starting to write their memoirs, to cash in on the work they formerly enjoyed doing. Everyone of those unresolved situations is a potential embarrassment to this country. Your job, gentlemen, will be to back-track everything you can find and to clean up the debris!'

Sam had held up his hand and had been acknowledged. 'You mean, like that mess in Angola, Mr Secretary?'

'That's exactly what I do mean. Now the Angolan mess, which as you all know hit front page on every newspaper in the world, was a matter of cleaning up the documentation. Nixon's problem was that he left those tapes just lying about instead of destroying them efficiently and effectively; the Kennedy problem will last forever because a guy lived too long . . .'

That was the first time it had been said. It was never said again in an open meeting. All the staff of the Recovery Agency knew their first priority was to put the lid back on simmering pots the CIA and the FBI had left open. How they did it was left to the discretion of the director of operations.

No files would be preserved. No tapes. And nobody left alive who could talk out of turn.

'I don't expect this agency to be needed for very long,' the Secretary had said. 'You men have been picked because of your proven abilities and your proven discretion. And, dare I use that old-fashioned word, your proven loyalty to your country!'

And Sam had believed it. Every word of it.

'You can't come in, 27,' he said. 'You're on a Limited Objective Contract. When that contract expires you'll be offered another one which you may or not accept. But you can't come in until your contract expires. I know it's getting heavy, much heavier than ever I expected. But you've got to stick with it.'

That was Sam's way. No placebos, no false promises, no bromide. Just straight plain talk. It was a ball game and everybody in it knew the Rules, knew there was no referee to whom you could run crying 'Foul!' Okay, this particular contract had contemporary overtones. Usually the clean up was simple, neat, and effective. This one seemed to involve a lot of guys living round the world. That didn't make the job any the less necessary.

'Give it two more weeks,' Sam said. 'We'll have it by then.'

'And then I can come in?'

'Then you can go anywhere you please, 27. With my blessing. Say the word, and I'll even come with you . . .'

Two days later Bill was sitting up in bed; he couldn't sleep because of the blaring of the vans in the street outside the hospital, with their loudspeakers belching out political propaganda. Each night one party or the other held a rally somewhere in the streets of Xania; all day long the rabble-rousing music sounded, even during the normally sacred hours of the siesta.

Bill was going stir-crazy, confined in his small room.

The prompt action of covering his skin with the air-tight jelly had helped his burns start to heal quickly. Already scabs were forming on the side of his thigh that had taken most of the blast.

Maria had been to see him twice each day but each time she'd sat by his bed, silent and troubled, her mind miles away, as if she were trying to resolve some inner problem. And then, after half an hour, she'd gone down the corridor to see Victorio, though as yet, with his face totally covered by bandages, he couldn't see her. The doctor had told her that Victorio had suffered no permanent damage to his eyes or his ears. 'His hair will grow again,' the doctor assured her. 'We'll make him good as new.'

On the morning of the third day, Bill put on a light cotton dressing gown which didn't rub the plastic skin with which they'd sprayed his wounds and took a walk down the corridor himself. He was shocked when he saw Victorio's bandages – the wounds looked much worse than they were. He seethed with anger when he saw what had happened to his half-brother, an innocent victim of this hornet's nest that Bill had somehow inadvertently over-turned. Bill felt utterly frustrated at the knowledge there was nothing he could actually *do*. He tried hard to analyze the events of the previous weeks to make some kind of sense, some kind of rationale that would account for the murders and the murder attempts, but could find no logical explanation.

On the morning of the third day, Petro came to see him. Bill had just returned from Victorio's room; Maria had just left. Petro smiled when he saw Bill walking carefully to avoid friction between the robe and the coating on the wounds.

'We caught the man who did it,' he said baldly. 'We caught him the following day.'

'And didn't tell me when you were here?'

'We did not want to interfere with your medical condition. If I had told you we had the man in custody you would have been pleading with the doctors to let you out so that you could come and kill him. We needed a few, quiet, uninterrupted days in which to question him. I have *part* of the story . . .'

'Only part . . . ?'

'He doesn't know the rest.'

Petro told Bill what he had discovered. The man was a professional hit man working world-wide. He didn't know for whom, but the 'jobs' he'd done would seem to indicate some supra-national corporation.

'The CIA?' Bill asked, but Petro shook his head. 'They have their own people,' he said. 'They don't go outside the firm.'

'So, what could it be?'

Petro spread his hands wide. 'You tell me,' he said. 'These days it could be anything. You only have to glance at the morality of the modern business world to realize that. Maybe some unsuspecting geologist ran into a layer of oil-bearing rock on the Lefka Ori. Perhaps he found a rare mineral from which one of the large international metal companies can make nose-cones for atomic bombs. Somewhere, in your searches to retread the footsteps of your father, you may, without knowing it, have run across this secret device, this secret process, this "commodity" that has so much value to them.'

'And who might the "them" be?'

'These days,' Petro said sorrowfully, 'it could be anyone. Read *Newsweek* or *Time* each week to realize how much corruption has integrated itself into the thoughts and the methods of big business. If you read the lists of bribes and the people who have accepted them . . . and realize that bribery and corruption go hand in hand . . .' Petro was looking speculatively at Bill. 'How do you really feel?' he asked:

Bill grinned. 'A bit of a fraud,' he said. 'I don't know whether it's the good living here on Crete, but I seem to have recovered remarkably quickly. These burns itch a bit, but I don't have much pain . . . My head's clear again. Of course, I feel weak, but I imagine that's nothing a couple of days in bed won't cure. If only these damn loudspeakers would stop for a while . . . !'

'Election week is always our most noisy – you will get used to it. Sit down, Bill, I want to talk to you.'

Bill swung his legs back on the bed and pulled back the robe to expose his wound dressings. Petro drew the chair across until he could sit close enough to be able to speak in a low voice though the amplified racket outside the windows would have made it impossible for anyone to hear what he was saying.

'The hit man has described the whole set-up to us. We know how he gets his assignments, how much he is paid, how he collects his money.'

'How much was he going to get for me?'

'Twenty thousand dollars . . .'

'That's a scandal. I'm worth a lot more than that!' Bill said.

'To me, yes, you are. He received a quarter of the money in advance; three quarters will be payable when they receive news of your death . . .'

'So the poor bastard is out of luck. My heart bleeds . . .'

Petro had taken a newspaper cutting out of his back pocket. 'Read that, Bill,' he said.

It was from the local newspaper. The cutting told of a house in Kaprisses that had exploded because of a leakage of gas. Two men had been killed in the explosion, one an Englishman who had lived in America for some years. Next of kin were being sought. The newspaper, which was printed in Greek, of course, added an editorial warning to all users of gas to store the bottles *outside* the house.

'I gave that to the newspapers,' Petro said. 'We have five in Xania. They all have published it! I have no doubt a copy of one of them has somehow found its way to the appropriate people.'

'What about Maria?' Bill said. 'She could have been one of the victims.'

'I know. That's why I've had her in protective custody ever since. She is living in your room in Pension Zorbas. One of my men is in the lobby day and night. Every time she comes to the hospital, two of my men travel with her in a car. The only time she is not under surveillance is here in the hospital.'

'So, whoever originated this scheme, whoever hired that assassin, will now believe me and Victorio to be dead.'

'That is exactly right. Now the assassin goes back to New York. In ten days, he leaves a letter in a bar on 45th Street, addressed to B. Vogel, *to be called for* with a copy of one of these cuttings. The following day, he returns to the same bar and picks up a letter addressed to Thomas Samson – one of the names he uses – which contains the balance of his money. My guess is that the bar is a "Company" meeting place, a safe house probably owned and operated by the Company under a shell management!'

'God, I'd like to be in that bar to meet this chap Vogel!'

'I was hoping you would say that. Look, Bill, I can do all this through the New York Police, Interpol, FBI. I could even go there myself and get their cooperation. But you do not know the bureaucracy I would have to go through to get any action. Especially since we have no proof, only the unsupported word of a man whose only provable crime is carrying a gun. If I start that process, the lawyers will be brought in; assuming this man is working for any kind of organization, they will have lawyers standing by – I will not stand a chance. Somewhere along this chain is some evidence I could use, some evidence not even a battery of high-priced lawyers could ignore. I need someone, Bill, who knows enough about

New York to be able to go to that bar and be waiting when this B. Vogel turns up . . .'

'I'm on my way,' Bill said, happy now that a chance of positive action was being offered.

'Bill, it will not be easy. I cannot give you any support. Any authorization. You will be on your own, you realize that?'

'Eventually, Petro, every one of us is on his own. I'd like to take Maria to New York with me. It might be useful to have someone I could trust on the other end of the telephone . . .'

'I think that is a bad idea, Bill. I want you to go on your own. One thing I have to say – I get the feeling – call it my copper's nose again – that matters are coming to a head. I think whatever you do will have to be done quickly . . .'

'Okay, Petro. Get me out of here. Let me go up into the mountains where I can get twenty-four hours of undisturbed sleep, and then I'll be ready to go!'

'About money, Bill?'

'No problems. I still have plenty!'

'Good! The police budget here in Xania is ludicrous – I can not even give you taxi fare to the airport, and I dare not send you out there in a police car since we do not know who will be watching.'

They took care of the details. Petro arranged for someone not known to be with the police to get travellers' cheques and air-line tickets. Bill was put on a stretcher into an ambulance with Maria riding beside him, and they took off for Omalos. Petro had booked *all* the rooms of the pension above the restaurant that looked out over the Gorge.

'You will be peaceful there,' he said, 'and if you cannot sleep, you can always go out on the terrace and listen to the *agrimi* whispering to each other . . .'

The Gorge of Samaria stretched in front and below them,

a large, slashed ravine of tumbling rocks, soaring cliff-faces, inhabited by *agrimi*, wild rabbits, sheep and goats, and the lion-hearted men of Sfakia who tended them. Once the village in the centre of the gorge had been inhabited; no road could get to it and everything had to be carried in on the backs of the families who lived there and their few donkeys.

Now tourists came throughout the season to walk the eighteen kilometres from Omalos to Aghia Roumeli; it was arduous with the first three kilometres almost a vertical descent, but somehow the grandeur of the chasm's formation inspired people to succeed where perhaps they would have flagged in less awesome surroundings. They came at all ages to walk 'the longest, deepest Gorge in Europe' – as the guide books called it. And somehow, no matter how footsore, how weary, they all made it to Aghia Roumeli and the boat that would take them home in comfort.

'I can't stop thinking of my father's runner, Pakrades,' Bill said to Maria, 'walking through this gorge, once in each direction, in the same afternoon. I can picture him, stepping easy from rock to rock with a smoothness, a lack of effort, born in him. I can see them taking the escaped prisoners over this lip, down this steep descent. Looking down into the gorge like this, from this balcony, it all comes alive to me. I seem to see my father, Kostas Dandanakis, Pakrades. Do you know what I mean?'

He turned to look at her when there was no reply. They'd eaten supper in the dining room behind them, the only customers. They'd had lamb and potatoes in a rich stew, potatoes boiled on the side, bread, wine. Simple countryman's fare but infinitely satisfying. Now they were sitting out in the night air before going to bed. Ever since his arrival, when not eating, Bill had sat relaxed on the terrace watching the play of light and shade on the purple-mauve-ochre rocks of the gorge, seeing the tree shadows move with the winter sunshine, following the flights of the soaring eagles.

'You weren't listening to me?' he said, though without reproach. She'd been silent most of the time since they'd arrived. The *krassi* they'd drunk at dinner, the three *ouzos* she'd tossed down fiercely before, the three *tsikoudias* afterwards, seemed to have done nothing to take away her moodiness, her thoughtful introspection.

'You're not peeved because Petro and I agreed it would be better you didn't come with me to New York?'

She turned towards him and he was startled to see the formation of a tear in the corner of her eye. 'No, I'm not peeved,' she said. 'Whatever you have to do there can best be achieved without me around.'

'Then what is it, Maria?' he asked gently, not wishing to intrude into her right, the right of any individual, to privacy.

She grasped his hand tightly, sitting there beside him. He could feel the tenseness within her as if she were steeling herself to do, or not to do, something she could regret. Almost like an angry man who is impelled to strike out against the source of his anger but restrains himself. Or a coward screwing his courage to a point of hated but necessary violent action.

'Oh, Bill,' she said. 'I had everything worked out so well before you came along!'

He smiled at her. 'That's the nicest thing you've ever said to me!' he said deliberately lightly, trying to help her by his tone. 'But, surely, life can't be "worked out" in advance. Every person we meet changes us a little, everything meaningful we say and hear influences and affects other people. I'm not claiming any special wisdom, Maria. I feel myself changed by knowing you. For the better, I hope. I don't think, for example, that I would have the courage to go on with this business if I didn't feel your encouragement and support.'

Now the tear had detached itself from the corner of her eye and others followed it down her cheek. He bent across awkwardly and placed his arm round her shoulder – the chairs weren't designed for twosomes and he almost fell off his.

'You mustn't worry about me,' he said, thinking he had discovered the source of her sadness. 'I'll be all right in America. I can look after myself these days; surely you can see that . . . ?'

'Bill!' she said, her voice anguished. 'You're an amateur, Bill, and the people involved in this matter are professionals. Human life isn't important to them, Bill. Not the human life of any individual. They think in larger terms, the least evil for the fewest people, the most good for the majority and forget that people have small individual existences.'

Bill was bewildered. 'You mean men like Petro?' he asked. 'Sending me off to New York City – what was it you said, as an amateur against professionals? You're saying, in effect, that Petro doesn't give a damn about me personally? That he's prepared to see me killed so long as he can work out his case. And then after that, another case, and another . . . ?'

She brushed away the tears. 'Something like that, Bill, something like that! I love you, Bill,' she said simply, calmly. 'I hope you realize that?'

'I do. And I hope you know that I love you?' It was said shyly, but strongly. Bill had never thought to fall in love again; he had never dared to hope it could happen.

'I had my life worked out,' Maria said. 'I knew what my set of values told me I must do, I would do, with the rest of my life. Bill, I made plans that didn't include falling in love with you.'

'And can't those plans be amended, adapted?'

'No, Bill, they can't. They must either be abandoned or followed.'

'And if you follow them, there's no room for me, is that what you're trying to say?'

'I suppose that's exactly what I am saying. I have to make the choice for myself. Perhaps your trip to America will give me the time to think, without your disturbing presence close by me. You *are* disturbing, Bill. I told you that before . . .'

'Of course I'm disturbing. Anyone we love must be *disturbing* to us!'

He reached across and tried to kiss her lips. She turned her face, offering him her cheek.

'It's time you were in bed,' she said.

'It's time we both were! And there we can talk about who disturbs who . . .'

'You're incorrigible, Bill,' she said.

'I know. But now, no more talk, eh?' He stood up and ran his finger down her cheek. 'And no more tears!'

'There will always be tears,' she said sombrely, 'so long as there are people who care about other people . . .'

'As I care, about you . . . ?'

He didn't see her shake her head as she led the way back inside.

They took Bill in a closed van to Maleme and ran him out to a waiting three-seater bi-plane.

'This is Adonis,' Petro said grinning. 'He used to be a good policeman before his uncle died and left him a packet. Now he is a crazy capitalist.'

'You like my plane?' Adonis said, speaking English with an American accent. 'I learned to fly in Utah. Worked on all kinds of planes there, man, all kinds.'

Bill looked around him and his heart sank. The bi-plane was obviously a survivor of the Second World War but the parts had been so bastardized from one plane and another it had no recognizable parentage. What was left was held together by pieces of wire, aluminium shelf racking, protruding nuts and bolts.

'You're going to take me to Athens in this?' he asked incredulously?

'Sure! Last weekend I went to Larnaca in Cyprus. Every weekend I take off and go someplace different!'

Petro was still grinning. '*Bon voyage!*' he said as the van drove away and Adonis fired the engine.

It had been the only way to get Bill off Crete with the certainty he wouldn't be spotted leaving. Bill would have preferred to swim! Adonis took the plane off the ground by racing it down the runway then pulling the stick back hard into his stomach. The little plane wheezed and heaved, the wires twanged like plucked harpsichord strings, the whole structure sighed and groaned, but the plane became almost vertically airborne. No sooner were they airborne than Adonis banked steeply, and Bill's heart sank at the thought they were going back down again.

Below him he could see the northern coast of Crete, which seemed to be rushing up at them with alarming speed. Directly on the nose, and only a couple of miles away, a house stood atop a hill. They were screaming down at it, aimed like a bullet. Bill felt his feet pressing the inside of the fuselage which began to buckle with his force before he realized there was no footbrake he could press on. 'Adonis!' he yelled, but his voice was carried away in the roaring slip-stream.

Straight as an arrow the plane headed until the house was only a hundred yards away. Adonis was grinning at Bill's white face as he pulled the plane out of the dive, skimming the red tiles of the roof with what seemed to Bill to be only inches to spare.

'Girl friend lives in that house,' Adonis said. 'I like to buzz her before I leave.' He banked again, climbing. 'Sorry if I scared you,' he said. 'Now we head for Athens.'

That was the first, and most hair-raising part, of a journey that took Bill to Athens and from there to da Vinci Airport in Rome. In da Vinci, he went through to the exit lounge for the New York flight, his boarding card prominent in his top pocket. Nobody seemed to be watching him but he knew he was not competent enough to spot a skilled professional surveillance. If he were being watched, any one of the hundred people waiting for the TWA flight could have been the tail.

When they called the departure, he slipped into the lavatory and waited there until after the flight had boarded. He listened while they called the name he'd given them for the ticketing, George Sanderson. It was the only name they called. They announced it three times, emphasizing the last time that it was the final call, and then the plane took off.

As soon as he could be reasonably certain it had gone, he came out of the lavatory and dashed to the departure gate. 'Too late!' the two airline officials shouted at him. 'Too late!'

They escorted him back through Customs with much voluble explanation. He re-routed himself from Rome via Amsterdam to New York, paying the extra fare. Only when he was seated on the Amsterdam flight did he relax, convinced finally that he was not being followed.

When he arrived at Kennedy Airport, New York, some fourteen hours later, suffering a bad case of jet-lag and overcrowded, overheated, over-glamourised air travel, he made his way through Customs carrying only hand luggage. The Customs Officer, suspicious of someone arriving so poorly equipped from Europe, turned his small valise inside out but could find nothing other than the clean shirt, the pair of socks and the underwear Bill had brought with him. 'No booze?' he asked.

'None.'

'No cigars, cigarettes.'

'Nothing,' Bill said trying to hide his impatience. 'Absolutely nothing!'

The Customs Officer grunted and marked his bag. Bill walked rapidly outside and hailed the first cab, a big old Checker with a negro driver. 'Bridge or Tunnel?' the driver asked when Bill gave his Manhattan destination.

'Tunnel.'

'Gonna be backed up solid this time of day . . .'

'I'm in no hurry.'

They were cruising in the centre lane down the Van Wyck Expressway when Bill said to the driver through the heavily reinforced grille that separated them, 'Pull over to the side a minute.'

'No way, man!' the driver said.

'Pull over,' Bill said. 'Look, I'm not going to hi-jack you. I just want you to pull over for a minute.'

He could see the driver peering at him through the mirror and tried to look relaxed, cool.

'I have to tell you, man,' the driver said, 'I don't want no trouble with you. I've only just come on duty. In my pocket, and in this cab, there's a grand total of fi' dollars. You gonna give me trouble for a lousy fi' bucks?'

'No, I'm not going to give you any trouble. I just want you to pull over. If you do, I'll add another five dollars to whatever's on the meter when we arrive in Manhattan, okay?'

'Okay, okay!'

The driver eased his way past the steady stream of traffic in the slow lane and onto the hard shoulder. There he gradually eased the cab to a stop, watching Bill all the time. 'What now, man?'

'Just sit for a minute.'

Bill looked out of the back window. No other cab or car had pulled over. You're becoming paranoid, he said to himself.

'Okay,' he said, 'we can carry on now.'

The driver hit the accelerator and the cab pulled out between two cars whose horns blared at them. When they arrived at the hotel and Bill climbed from the cab, the driver looked at him and quoted the amount on the meter. Bill paid him and added five dollars.

'Don't suppose you wanna tell me what that was all about?' the driver asked.

'No.'

'I thought not. I seen the Bond movies . . .'

The clerk, a thirty-five-year-old, ginger-haired, fat man who wore a button-down, short-sleeved shirt, jeans, and a hopeless expression gave him a room on the eighth floor. 'Check-out time's twelve o'clock,' he said, 'an' no visitors in the room, okay?'

'All I want is sleep!'

'That's what they all say. Don't forget to leave your key when you check out!'

'Thanks a lot!'

'You're welcome!'

Bill walked into the bar on 45th Street, west of 5th Avenue.

The room was long and low; at the far end a half a dozen tables had chairs around them and carried red check tablecloths. The bar itself was just inside the door, running lengthwise along the wall. The man standing behind it was around fifty, wore dark blue trousers and a white shirt, and had thinning grey hair. His face had the pasty white-yellow tinge of the underside of a frog's belly; his hands were flabby, his fingers thick. He was smoking a thin green cigar, the end of which had been chewed to pulp. He took the cigar out of his mouth and lay it across the edge of an ash-tray.

'I'm trying to give 'em up,' he said. 'I used to smoke two packs a day and wake up coughing. Now I have heartburn and indigestion. What'll it be?'

'May I have a glass of beer?' Bill asked, keeping his voice deliberately English.

The bar-man ran a glass of beer from the spigot, used a wooden blade to skim off the foam and placed the beer glass on a paper mat on the counter. 'You English?' he asked without interest, as if it were something to say that didn't need an answer.

'Yes. Does it show?'

'Some. I was in England once. Boston, Lincolnshire, know it?'

'Yes. Northwest of London.'

'Yeah!'

The bar-man went back to tidying up his bar. It was already immaculate. Bill sat on the red-topped stool, lit a cigarette, watched the bar-man pick up his cigar and begin to suck it again without lighting it.

Two men came in, both wearing worsted suits and carrying slim attaché cases with dial-a-word locks. 'Hi, Charlie, how ya been?', one of them asked, then went on talking to his companion without waiting for a reply.

The bar-man grunted, took a cocktail shaker and mixed into it an improbable mixture of whisky, lemonade, ice cubes, crème de cacao and a raw egg. He shook it listlessly, looking out through the smoked glass window.

'What's it like outside?' he asked Bill.

'Cold . . .'

'That Boston, Lincolnshire, was cold. And it rained all the time.' He poured the contents of the shaker into two cocktail glasses, flipped two paper mats on the counter in front of the two men and slipped the glasses deftly on them. 'Two specials,' he intoned. He filled a small plate with roasted peanuts and put it between the two glasses.

Neither man looked at him or spoke to him; they seemed to be trying to determine, with some difficulty, whether someone called Jaypee was a cock-sucking-mother-fucker or a faggot-son-of-a-bitch. On one thing they were both agreed. Someone, quite soon, was going to have to tell Jaypee what he could do with his appropriation, whatever that may be.

Bill had heard the identical conversation a hundred times in a hundred bars in every city in which he'd worked. Not even the accent varied these days, though the 'special' often had a local flavour. Two more men came in, then two more. Charlie, if that was really the bar-man's name and not some convenient tag each of the newcomers put on him, knew the drinks of each one, a complicated litany of tastes. Some were 'twist of lemon', some no lemon. Some were an onion, others a cherry. The only ones who spoke to Charlie asked him about the smoking in a variety of jokey ways. None of them waited for an answer.

Gradually Charlie migrated, when not actually serving, to where Bill was sitting. Bill sat patiently knowing the wall of reserve, professionally built and carefully maintained, would be breached by Charlie, if at all. Finally, the words came. The first frenzied crowd had disappeared after much consultation of wrist-watches and complaints about the goddam go-home cabs, the lousy son-of-a-bitch railways, and a slower, less dressy crowd had arrived, consisting of mixed couples. The men still carried brief-cases but they were slightly older and paunchier. The women with them were either very very wide-eyed and young and spoke with some kind of regional accent, or were older, crowsfooted and New York nasal. The men didn't look at their watches, didn't talk about the railroads, and set a quicker pace of drinking. They sat at the tables in the back-room and not at the bar where the few unaccompanied males stood hopefully looking up each time the door opened.

'You living over here?' the bar-man finally asked.

'Just visiting. Trying to do a little business,' Bill said.

'What line of business?'

'Textiles.'

'My brother's a tailor. Spends all day running round a bunch of girls sewing dresses and what does he make? Ulcers and peanuts, that's what I tell him. Joe, I tell him, you're making ulcers and peanuts.'

Bill stayed exactly half an hour after he'd started the dialogue with Charlie, then wished him good night, left a fifty cent tip and left.

He knew Charlie would remember him. The next night when he went in Charlie greeted him like a long-lost friend. 'How ya bin, Bill? D'ya make a buck? Beer, right? No chasers.'

'You have a fabulous memory,' Bill said. He glanced round the bar while Charlie poured his beer. His memory had served him right. The previous night he'd lain on his bed in the hotel in West 45th, near 6th Avenue, and tried to recall the interior of the bar in perfect detail. It was a professional trick he'd learned long ago – you could score points if you said to your hostess the second time round, You've moved that picture, You've done your hair differently, I liked the Waterford crystal we used last time.

Telephone behind the bar, and Bill's stool the nearest one to it. Telephone in one of those alcoves behind him; the previous evening he'd been plagued by 'missed the train, honey' phone calls.

Nowhere two people could stand and converse without Bill overhearing, unless they went into the back room.

He stayed there for an hour, establishing credentials. I'll only be here another few days. I'm missing my wife and children. We have a nice house outside London. I buy and sell textiles. My wife is forty-one and suffers a lot from back-ache. Kids still at school but will shortly be finished. Expense of sending them to university.

'That education,' Charlie confided to Bill, 'it ruins kids. Take my word for it. They're okay until they go to college, start getting liberal ideas. Ever I had kids, they'd go to grade school. College kids, bunch of ass-holes. Only gotta look round this bar to know. Bunch of ass-holes. Guy wants a special, I run out of crème de cacao, I put in crème de bananas, never knows the difference, know what I mean? Bunch of ass-holes. Yet, you charge 'em a cent too much on the tab and jeez, they get out the calculators . . .'

On the third day, Bill called the Speed Agency, told them he had a letter for delivery right away and left the letter with the lobby clerk of his hotel. He was already in the Black Raven Grill when the letter was delivered.

'It's for a B. Vogel,' the delivery boy said.

'Never heard of him . . .' Charlie didn't like having the black boy hanging around his bar. 'Give it here and I'll hold it.'

'You'd better. It says, hold for collection.'

'Where did *you* learn to read?'

'Up yours, honkey!'

262

'See what I mean,' Charlie said to Bill. 'There's no respect any more. And now some of 'em are going to college!'

'Bunch of black ass-holes?' Bill said trying a joke.

Charlie clapped his hand on the counter and roared with laughter. 'You got it right, there,' he said. 'You got it right!'

He'd given Bill his beer and with the easy familiarity of a long-time friendship he picked up the phone. 'Gotta make a call,' he said. 'Take your time.'

Bill raised his glass to his lips, looked over its rim into the mirror behind the bar and watched Charlie dial.

He'd practised this in the room in his hotel and, provided Charlie didn't put his body between the mirror and the phone, he knew he'd be able to read it. He felt a sinking feeling in his stomach when Charlie finished dialling, and a flutter of excitement.

The area code was for Washington D.C.

'Black Raven,' Charlie said. 'I have one for you!' He put the phone down, tapped the side of his nose at Bill and went up the bar to make and serve a couple more specials.

On his way to get the bottles, Charlie whispered to him. 'Says it's got to be Black Label whisky, and then wants me to put black-currant juice in it. Ass-hole, know what I mean?'

Bill had brought a newspaper into the bar with him. He opened it at the entertainment section and scanned the list of movies available.

'Going to the movies?' Charlie asked when he'd finished serving his specials.

'I was thinking of it. I don't fancy sitting in my hotel room watching TV.'

'They wanted me to have TV in here. What for, I asked 'em, so's a bunch of layabouts can sit here watching the ball games and not drinking. Let 'em go *home* and get out the cans of Budweiser!'

The man wore a black raincoat, a green hat with a leather thong twisted around it, a dark suit, a white, button-down-collar shirt and a striped tie. He was carrying a black case with FBB stencilled on the corner in gold lettering. His face was long and lean and suntanned the sienna brown that comes from raw sun, not indoor lamps.

Bill checked the keys in his jacket pocket. One in the left hand, the other in the right. The Hertz car on 45th Street, the Avis car on 5th Avenue.

'Do you have a letter for me?' the man asked Charlie, with no attempt at secrecy.

'I might have?'

'Vogel. B. Vogel. To be collected.'

'That was fast. I only got it a half hour ago . . .'

'They gave me a call. Dumb broad, has to write me letters . . . !' He winked knowingly at Charlie, the repository of all secrets, all knowledge.

Charlie was holding the letter in his hand, turning it over. 'Whadd'ya like to drink?' he asked. 'This ain't no post office, know what I mean?'

'Yes. I'm very grateful. I'll have a – do you know a Montana Sunrise . . . ?'

'Mexican Sunrise; no tequila, gin'n'akavit, kicks like a mule, right?'

'Right!'

Bill put two dollars on the counter to pay for his drinks, folded the newspaper and dropped it behind the bar. 'Fay Dunnaway,' he said, 'that's it.'

'Mind how you go!' Charlie said as Bill left the bar. He sounded as if he really meant it.

Bill was waiting across the street, looking in the windows of an art shop, when the man who'd taken the letter for Vogel came through the door and turned left, buttoning his coat tight against the October night and walking quickly.

Bill stayed where he was – he'd seen the movie.

Vogel stopped, did an about turn, his eyes scanning both sides of the street, then walked west towards Sixth Avenue. This time, Bill followed him. He seemed to be striking in a pattern across New York; he'd go one block up an avenue, one block across a street, one block up an avenue, one block across. He only broke the pattern when he came to Broadway, when he walked one block down Broadway, one block west. It wasn't long before the quality of the district they were passing through began to deteriorate; before more and more Puerto Ricans became evident, sitting on the doorsteps, standing at street corners. They'd reached Tenth Avenue, and Bill was feeling very apprehensive, when the man turned right after walking up the avenue, and the trail led east again. Bill had been following as far back as he dared, conscious that he lacked technique. It would have been so much easier if he'd had another man to help him so they could have doubled, one man replacing the other. Petro had given him a letter addressed to the Greek Consul in New York and another for the New York City Police. 'If you get in any sort of trouble,' he'd said, 'use the letters. They may not do you any good; they're both absolutely personal and don't carry any police or government authority!'

Bill had left them in his hotel room. Deliberately. He wanted to do this thing by himself, for himself, even though he knew he lacked expertise.

They were walking along Central Park South when a girl with a bewildered look on her face and a map in her hands stopped him. '*Pardon*,' she said. '*Pourriez-vous m'aider?*'

'I'm a stranger here myself,' he said, trying to brush her aside.

She smiled into his face. 'There's a gun under the map,' she said, 'with a silencer on it. If I have to shoot you, I'll be well away before your body hits the ground.'

He stopped.

'That's better. Now, point to the map. Anywhere will do.'

He pointed to the map, as instructed. 'Good,' she said, maintaining the same conversational tone. People were pushing past them, a constant stream in both directions, but nobody, it seemed, was paying them the slightest attention.

She bent her head over the map and he got a whiff of some unidentifiable perfume. He looked at her blonde hair, her tanned face, the glistening white teeth he associated with North American girls.

'You're being very sensible,' she said. Though her French had been perfectly accent-free, her English was unmistakably Texan. 'If you look round you'll see a green Chevrolet just drawing up to the kerb. Please get in the back of it.'

He turned and saw the car drawing to a halt, double-parked. He considered running for a moment and jerked his head both ways.

'Don't do it,' she said. 'I truly am a fantastic shot, even with a hand-gun!'

Two men in the Chevrolet in the back, one man in the driving seat. As Bill approached the car, one of the men jumped out and held the door open for him, as if Bill were expected. Bill climbed in; the man climbed in after him and slammed the door. The girl stayed on the pavement and gave him a mischievous wave.

'Where in God's name did they drag you up from?' the driver said as he started the car rolling. He didn't want a reply.

The man on Bill's right adjusted his trousers. 'Just in case you don't know the method,' he said drily, 'and I doubt if you know *anything* the way you been behaving, this is a pick-up car, which means the handles don't work on the inside. Don't try slugging either me or Frank here. He's black belt karate, I'm kung-fu.'

'The driver looks like sumo!' Bill said with an attempt at humour.

'So, be a wise guy. He's a driver and a good one. And, so far as we're concerned, you're Mickey Mouse!'

'So, I'll keep a tight one . . .'

'You do that, Fauntleroy. And button your fag mouth – we've heard about Englishmen . . . !'

'Nothing like an open mind, eh!'

'Button it.'

They took him openly to an apartment block on West 11th Street and rode the elevator with him standing between them. They made no attempt to touch him, to hustle him.

They rang the bell on the door of the apartment; Bill heard the several locks, chains, bolts and bars being unfastened and then the door was opened wide. The two men stood back to let Bill go first. As he crossed the threshold the one called Frank knuckled him hard in the kidneys and he sprawled along the carpet, fighting for breath, his back a screaming mass of pain. He tried to draw breath and couldn't; he lay there helpless and gasping while they searched him.

They picked him up and helped him along the corridor. 'The pain'll go soon,' Frank said. 'You'll live to play the violin again!'

The easy chair into which they dumped him was soft and padded; it went a long way back and Bill knew he couldn't get out of it fast and easy. Professionals, every inch. And he an amateur.

The man in the black raincoat who'd passed himself off as Vogel was sitting in a Miele chair, his feet on the footstool.

'You followed me from the Black Raven Grill,' he said baldly. 'Why?'

'I wanted to see where you were going,' Bill said, equally baldly.

Vogel was nonplussed. He'd expected some kind of blustering denial, some sign of citizen outrage.

'So you wanted to see where I was going? Why?'

'Because I wrote the letter you picked up. The one with the press-cutting in it in Greek, telling you about the deaths of two men in a house explosion in a village on Crete called Kaprisses.'

Vogel snapped the Miele chair upright so fast he almost fell out of it. The foot-stool slid across the floor on its castors.

'You're in a talkative mood?' he said.

Bill smiled at him. 'Not to you,' he said. 'I don't talk to

the messenger boys or their Kung-Fu Karate thugs.' He turned to the man called Frank. 'You, Frank, by the way, have a bad case of body odour. I suggest next time you go to the gym for training, you take a shower afterwards. To put it bluntly, you stink like a shit-house!'

Frank was too well trained to rise to the bait. 'Words, Limey,' he said, 'go peddle your fag ass someplace else.'

The door opened and the blonde-haired Texan came in.

'We're getting a whole load of lip from him,' Vogel said. 'And he knows what's in the letter. He says he wrote it.'

'Shit!'

The girl brought a chair and placed it in front of Bill. He deliberately looked down and blatantly examined her full chest, her bulging breasts. She equally blatantly unbuttoned her blouse, unhooked her brassiere between the cups and pulled them aside.

'Look all you want to,' she said. 'Tits. I have two. One left, one right. I have a cunt, too, but I only show that on special occasions to special people. So let's finish with the crap, eh? I'm just a technician. We're all technicians in this room, with one fucking exception. *You!* You're an amateur.'

As she spoke she was rehooking her brassiere, then buttoned her blouse again.

'Our job was for him to pick up a letter. In a drop. Nobody goes into a drop without a back-up. We are the back-up. We picked you as a likely the minute you left the Grill and walked over to the art shop. And we were right. So tell us who you are and what you do for a living. Besides stare at tits.'

'I know you're technicians,' Bill said. 'Very competent. But, like I was saying to Vogel-Bogel before you came in, I don't do business with the help. I knew you'd pick me up. I knew you'd bring me in. So, now I want to talk to the boss. Not your boss – he'd be way down in the pecking order. I want to talk to your boss's boss's boss. Number One. The top man.'

'You could be processed, you know,' she said coldly. 'You could get dead!'

'I could get *laid*, too, but I don't believe either event is likely!'

They handcuffed his wrists and ankles to an iron bed and he lay there quietly. He was deliberately trying not to think, not to feel, not to give way to the fears fluttering like black moths inside him. Okay, he'd come this far; he'd shown them a brave face and had tried to match their hard-boiled, impersonal professionalism with a glib façade of his own, a confidence he was far from feeling. He looked around the bedroom and surmised they'd rented the home of some artist or art teacher on a short let, no doubt while the owner was teaching in some distant college. He'd rented this type of apartment himself when first he'd come to New York to work. He saw the paintings that practically covered the walls, all of a uniform incomprehensibility, Buffet, Miro, Jackson Pollock, all rolled into one. The book-case contained art books. He could see the dust on the top of the pages. No wonder the guy had to rent out his apartment, to go away teaching to earn a dollar.

Finally, he drifted into a dreamless sleep: he only knew he'd been asleep by glancing at his watch as they unclipped the handcuffs and led him back into the living room.

'Do you want to take a leak?' the Texan girl said.

Her no doubt deliberate coarseness achieved its objective and turned him off. 'Yes,' he said, 'want to come and hold it?'

She grinned at him, perhaps recognizing a spark in him for the first time.

'I've forgotten my tweezers,' she said, still grinning.

When he came back from the bathroom, another man was sitting in the Miele chair, but crouched forward, not using the footstool. 'You want to talk to the boss,' he said. 'That's me.'

'I don't believe you,' Bill said, 'but you'll do.'

'Do you have a name?'

'You can call me Bill!'

'Thank you. You can call me Sam.'

Frank was standing near an easel in the corner. The other man was sitting on a stool near the door. The girl was still sitting in the chair she had pulled in front of Bill's easy chair.

'The two creeps go,' he said. 'The girl can stay.'

'Why, thank you-all,' she drawled.

Sam had been examining Bill's face and something he saw in there – some indefinable hardness, stubbornness – must have impressed him. 'Okay, Frank,' he said; 'okay, Mike.'

Frank and Mike, two disciplined pros, left without a word.

'That suit you?' Sam asked. 'And the girl is called Wanda.'

'Not Ms?'

'That's up to you and her. Look, you know about the letter. You know what's in it. That means you have the contract on ice someplace?'

'Let's skip the euphemisms, shall we? I wrote the letter. I know you hired a man to kill two people in a place called Kaprisses, on the island of Crete. I was one of those two people. As you can see, he didn't succeed. He wasn't very good at his job . . .'

'You know how difficult it is to get help these days. Try to find a good cook here in New York . . .' Sam said.

'Maybe Wanda could help out. She looks the homely type . . .'

'In a pig's ass . . .' Wanda said.

'Verbal vulgarity,' Bill said, deliberately pedantic in manner, 'is the refuge of the shy, the lonely, the insecure!'

Wanda blanched as if he'd struck her. 'Why you psycho-neurotic son-of-a . . .'

'Bitch? Come on, Wanda, show us your tits again. We

270

get more pleasure when you open your blouse than when you open your mouth, that's for sure . . . !'

Bill was happy to bait them, keeping them off balance, building some kind of superiority. He knew it could become the only advantage he possessed. They held all the high cards in a game they were dealing with a marked deck.

'You can't provoke me,' she said. 'It's been tried by experts.'

Sam had been watching both of them, his eyes batting backwards and forwards like a Wimbledon spectator. He rubbed his hands together.

'Okay, Bill,' he said, 'let's skip the back-chat and the euphemisms, like you said. You've travelled from Crete to New York to post the letter, then to follow the man who collected it. You seem a rational sort of guy. You must have known you didn't have a hope in hell of getting away with it, that we'd pick you up for sure. So, you could have wound up dead. Let's get to the final act curtain line. Just exactly what are you looking for?'

'Only one thing. The name of the man called Theseus!'

Sam let out a sigh as if somebody had punctured him, as if his worst fears had been confirmed. 'Okay, so you know the whole story . . .'

'I know that during the war a man called Theseus betrayed his fellow Cretans to the Germans. The rest of it doesn't interest me. Many people still alive on Crete today think that my father, who was on Crete during the war, was the man responsible for that betrayal and for the deaths of the people of an entire village. I just want to clear my father's name. Okay, so I know that my wishes conflict with some game you have going. What are you people, CIA?'

'No!'

'Okay, some other government agency. Look, I don't give a shit what you are, what games you play. I only want to clear my father's name. Or is that something you people can't understand? I want the name of Theseus. You'll have to kill me to stop me getting it. And, somehow, I don't think you're ready to do that. Especially since a certain police superintendent knows more or less everything I know . . .'

Sam looked at Wanda and shrugged his shoulders. 'Okay, Bill, I'm prepared to go along with you for a while. You understand, I have to get authority to give that name to you?'

'That's why I asked for the boss.'

'I am the boss, as you call it, of this particular job. But I need to get authority before I can change policy . . .'

'Bureaucracy . . . ?'

'Knock it off, Bill. You can't provoke me, either. Now, are you gonna be sensible or do we have to put you on ice for a while?'

'It depends what being sensible involves . . . !'

'We have a place out on the Island. It has a piece of beach where you can swim if you happen to be a polar bear! It's secure. You can go out there, with Wanda to keep you company, until I get chance to talk to some people . . .'

'In Washington?' Bill asked, quoting the phone number he'd mirror-read in the Black Raven Grill.

'For an amateur, you don't do bad work,' Sam admitted grudgingly.

A Buick was waiting in West 11th Street, without a driver. The keys were already in it. Bill climbed inside and Wanda took the driver's seat. Sam Birntin leaned in through the window. 'Enjoy, enjoy,' he said. 'And relax. You're in good hands with Wanda . . .'

'Nothing like a personal recommendation . . . !'

'As a driver, I meant, slack-mouth. Anything else, I wouldn't know about!'

The 'place on the Island' was in the Hamptons, a popular but exclusive weekend resort. The house was large and occupied some twelve or so acres of ground. Two or so acres were dunes, sloping down to the water line where a pier had been built out into the deeper ocean. The cutter moored to the pier had twin Volvo Pentax engines that would give it a speed of twenty knots cruising. The house itself was deceptive; it had an old Colonial-style façade to which little had been done to remove the somewhat seedy, run-down effect. Inside, however, the house had been refurbished.

'I'll give you the guided tour,' Wanda said, 'then you won't need to screw around forcing locks, getting curious. We use this place as a meeting house, for briefings and de-briefings. Anatoly Borghas was kept here for six months . . .'

'The KGB defector . . . ?'

She unlocked a door. Inside was a complex radio centre, to judge by the dials on the cabinets which lined the wall. It also had computer facilities. Bill recognized the terminal, the data processer, the computer access keyboard – all standard commercial instruments. The programmes and the contents of the data base, he knew, would *not* be standard commercial.

'We can set this up as a command post,' Wanda said, 'working world-wide, vision and sound, and feeding the computer.'

'No wonder you people all suffer *folie de grandeur*,' he said.

She grinned at him. 'The British Raj used to do it with an abacus and men sailing fast wind-cutters. Don't tell me you're envious!'

'An imperious flick of Victoria's finger, eh? Don't believe everything you read in the history books. Where did you learn French?'

'My mother was a Southern belle, from New Orleans. My father bought her out of a whore-house and made an honest woman of her, or so he thought. She's now the Comtesse de Picqueville-Romaine, and he's married to plain old Emma Lou, the girl he ran away to New Orleans to forget . . .'

'Sounds like something out of Margaret Mitchell . . .'

'Doesn't it? You ever lived in a chateau? I guess not. I used to spend six months a year there, until I grew too big for the local paysans. They caught me behind the wine-press with Jean-Claude. And he wasn't pressing grapes. They sent me back to Emma Lou. She larruped me with the Bible.'

'And now your father rides the range in a Cadillac . . . ?'

'Like hell he does. He flies over it in a Cessna.'

While she talked she'd led him through the rooms one by one, avoiding none. He'd learned nothing he couldn't already have guessed.

They walked out of the house by the east door, crossing the crab-grass lawns and the sandy dunes until they stood at the edge of the ocean. Here she seemed more relaxed, less tense, as if the city were a foreign environment to her, the open countryside her natural lair.

'I expect you understand the ground rules,' she said. 'Don't go on the boat. Don't try to get out of the grounds. The whole place is under electronic surveillance so sophisticated that nobody, but *nobody*, could get out of it alive. So, don't try, uh? Just relax!'

There were steaks in the refrigerator; she grilled them expertly and made a lettuce tomato salad on the side. The wine they drank was imported French. After dinner, they played backgammon. She beat him in five straight games, using the doubling dice viciously to take eighty-five dollars from him.

They went to bed in the same bedroom. She stripped off naturally and threw her clothes in an untidy heap on the floor when she went in for a shower.

By the time she came back, he'd folded them neatly and had put them on top of the dresser. She was already in bed when he came from the bathroom.

'Your place or mine,' she said, her voice artificially husky.

He smiled knowingly at her and climbed into bed naked.

'I see you folded my clothes – you some kind of fetishist?'

'I just don't like people to throw their clothes around. If you want to interpret that as psycho-neurotic, go ahead. I also don't like people assuming I'm some kind of performing animal . . .'

'My God, don't tell me you're a virgin, at your age?'

'No, I'm not. I was married – and don't take that as a cue for a "now, now, there, there" shoulder-tapping session.'

Though he wasn't going to admit it, Bill had amazed himself in the bathroom by his eager anticipation of the night with this ridiculous, incredible girl. He had also felt a twinge of conscience. He'd slept with Maria, hadn't he, and by his code that implied something more than casual lust. Bill had to admit that in sexual matters he *was* a bit of a prig; uptight by modern standards.

But his mind, and his body, told him that tonight he was going to forget Maria. Especially his body.

They lay together side by side listening to the ocean across the dunes. They'd coupled slowly, passionately, deeply and finally, for both of them, satisfyingly and without modesty, in an abandoned orgy of pleasure seeking and giving that left both of them drained of tension.

'At moments like these,' she said, 'I wish I could smoke cigarettes.'

'Have you tried pot?'

'Yes. It didn't do a thing for me. You?'

'It made me sick.'

'*Tristesse d'amour!* It's a nice title for an aching void . . .'

'I didn't know you were a romantic.'

'I'm supposed to react to that, I know,' she said, 'but I can't be bothered. There are many kinds of male chauvinism. One is to assume that because a female can absorb the formerly exclusively masculine martial arts, she can't also be a woman sometimes. And that kind of thinking is a real pain in the ass!'

'Want to talk about those "martial" arts?'

'I don't mind. Do you want me to?'

'Yes!'

'What's a nice girl like you doing in a job like this . . . ?'

'Don't put me down. I can easily accept the girl/man, the person/person bit. That's not so hard. I'm all in favour of women doing the same jobs as men, women astronauts, women priests. I'm not thinking of you as a woman . . .'

'Liar! Or do you do what you did to me with men . . . ?'

'No way! I was thinking about you, about Sam Birntin, about Frank and Mike, about this safe house, the man who collected the letter for Vogel. The boss. I was thinking about the contract you arranged for my murder. And wondering just what the hell motivates you people?'

'That's a boring question, Bill, with a boring answer. But I'll give it to you, and then we'll go to sleep, right? What motivates us? I'll tell you. We believe in things in a way people can't understand. With us, it's like a religion. the Infallibility of the Pope has nothing on My Country, Right or Wrong. The one item that distinguishes us from the rest of the jaw-boning ear-benders is that we're prepared to *do* something about it. We're prepared to lay *everything* on the line. Do you know what holds back people like you, Bill? Not the Grand Conscience. Not the Life is Sacred bit. But a fear that maybe you won't be able to live with your own guilt if you know that you, and you alone, are responsible for the death of another individual. You all talk about fighting for your country, for your beliefs. We're prepared to do more than talk. We're prepared to act and live with the consequences.'

'And die for them?'

'Shit. Of course. And die for them, if necessary. Now, what do you want to do, fuck or sleep!'

'Sleep.'

'Then good night, you British peasant!'

Sam Birntin caught the shuttle to Washington, went to his apartment and took his usual couple of Seconals. He wanted a good night's sleep before he talked to the director in the morning.

In his opinion, this whole deal had been badly handled from the very start. Now, it seemed, an amateur, a rank amateur, was in a position to screw the whole gaddamned situation. What kind of people was the director hiring, anyway – second-rate guys who didn't deliver? Look at the 5311 he'd put on the woman Evangelina; the director had assured him the operator was a top pro and look what had happened to him. He'd got himself knocked off with a syringe in his hands. And he'd been carrying documentation, for Christ's sake! What kind of a guy went on a job with his passport and his Amex and Diner's cards in his pocket? The work Sam had had, smothering that one, keeping it under wraps.

And now an amateur turns up with an unlisted number in his memory. And tells them he has one of their guys somewhere in Crete, on ice! What a foul-up! What a snafu!

The director was great on the mechanical stuff, the computer set-up, the satellite communications, all that crap. But he sure as hell was screwed up when it came to picking people to do field work.

Mind you, he, Sam, wasn't any better, it seemed. After all, he'd picked 27, and now 27 wanted back in, against all the rules.

He'd had his third cup of coffee the following morning when he went through the doors into the director's office. The director was standing looking out of the window. When he saw Sam he scuttled back behind his desk, as if afraid of being caught without it as a barrier between them.

'How was New York?' he asked.

'Still standing when I left,' Sam said drily.

'You buttoned everything up?'

'No, Director, I didn't!'

The director pursed his lips, made a cathedral out of his

hands and looked at Sam as if he were about to ex-communicate him.

'It wasn't a situation anybody could *button up*,' Sam said. 'It's no good buttoning up your pants after they've fallen down. Especially if you're not wearing underpants at the time . . .'

He went through the events of the previous day. The pick-up, the man trailing the messenger. The way they'd picked *him* up and taken him to West 11th Street. The ensuing dialogue. The director winced when Sam told him about the ex-directory number, one of the ones that fed directly to Sam's desk as controller of the operation. He winced again and groaned when Sam finished by telling him about the Englishman's demand.

'So he knows about Theseus?' the director said.

'He knows. Luckily, I don't think he knows anything about the contemporary story. He knows Theseus's past history, and that's it!'

'He doesn't know about Theseus having us over a barrel?'

'Thank God, no. At least, I don't think so.'

'So, Sam, it's easy. We put another 5311 on him . . .'

'And it winds up like the last one? Director, we don't have the manpower for this kind of operation. What do you expect us to do – go to the Mafia for one of *their* hit men!'

'That's not a bad idea.' The director half-closed his eyes as if considering it.

'With respect, Director, it's a shitty idea. There's only one thing we can do at this stage . . .'

'And that is . . . ?'

'Give him a Theseus!'

'And have Theseus pull the cork on us? The world press would just love to hear what Colonel James Quentin Hassler of the US Army was doing on Crete in 1943. It'd make our Angola snafu look like a Sunday outing. Remember, Sam, that military bastard ordered a whole village killed; women and children. And don't fool yourself, it won't help us one goddamn bit that the Russians knew about it and went along with it. That and the fact we've just given military support to the Turks would cook our goose in the Mediterranean, for sure!'

'I didn't say, Director, give him *the* Theseus. I said, give him *a* Theseus. And don't give it to him direct. Give him a story – he'll bite, Director, I know he'll bite. And if the story's right, it'll get him off our backs – for good!'

The restaurant on Third Avenue served sea-food: oysters, clam chowder, fish stuffed with crab meat. And a California white wine that would take some beating. They had a table in the corner – the restaurant wasn't crowded at that hour and only two other tables had occupants when Sam arrived.

'Had a good lunch?' he asked. 'I hope you didn't mind me not eating with you. Sea-food gives me a pain in the gut.'

He eased himself into the third chair and looked appraisingly at Bill and Wanda. 'You two look as if you enjoyed the Island,' he said. 'It must be great to have a night out there, nothing to bother you but the noise of the waves.'

'We didn't make waves,' Bill said smiling. 'You told me not to. "Don't make waves", you said to me . . .'

Sam laughed dutifully. 'Geez, you Brits have a great sense of humour. Always making with the jokes, eh? Okay, let's cut the crap. I have work to do. You asked for Theseus, and that's a problem. I can't give Theseus to you because we don't know who Theseus is, or was. As you've no doubt discovered, the code-list was destroyed after the war. The only people who can put real names to code-names are people still alive. And they're getting fewer every day . . .'

'And will continue to do so, as long as you play your games . . .'

'Okay, okay. Look, I can give you a *lead* to Theseus. It's all we've got. We can't take it any further. You may be able to, with your story about looking for your father. Theseus was in charge of a group, right. Every group on Crete had radio contact, either with the other groups or direct with Cairo. Every group had a call sign and a frequency. The call sign of the group led by Theseus was Dog Fox Zebra Three. Find out who ran DFZ3 and you find your Theseus, okay? What you do then is your affair!'

The police sergeant walked slowly up the drive to the house, knocked on the door and waited. When the house-keeper opened the door he walked in without speaking. She'd been crying again. The colonel's wife was sitting in the window of the drawing room, a piece of embroidery in her hands which lay still in her lap. On the table beside her was a picture of herself in a white wedding gown with the handsome officer in full uniform, the two lines of officers extending to the side, drawn swords held as an arch above the bride and bridegroom's heads.

'No news, I'm afraid, ma'am,' the sergeant said. 'I thought I'd come out and tell you personally rather than use the telephone.'

'That was very thoughtful of you, Sergeant,' she said.

'We've made our enquiries throughout the district. Nobody saw the Colonel that night. We've checked the railway stations in Wellingborough, Kettering, and Nor-thampton; spoken to every taxi-driver. We've checked the bus people. Everything. And all, I'm afraid, to no avail! It seems as if the Colonel just vanished into the ground!'

'Thank you again, Sergeant,' she said. 'Now, would you care for a cup of tea? A glass of sherry, perhaps.'

He knew she was being gracious but had no desire to impose on her sorrow. 'If you'll forgive me, ma'am,' he said, rising to his feet, 'I'll be getting back to the station.'

'Of course, you must have a lot to do. And this business must have taken up a lot of your time . . .'

She rose and accompanied him to the front door. She walked out with him down the drive. He stopped by the sun-dial to permit her to return without the need to walk him all the way to the gate. 'That's a fine piece,' he said.

She glanced at it. 'Yes, but it's always wrong, I'm afraid. You need to add two hours to it at this time of year.'

Idly he glanced at his wrist-watch and then at the sun-dial. 'It seems to be correct now,' he said.

'Correct? The Colonel, God bless him wherever he may be, always meant to have Walter move it to the right setting! It's only there to cover the well.'

The thought struck both of them at the same time.

She stared at the sun-dial on its plinth. 'I can't be sure,' she whispered, 'but I think it *has* been moved!'

'Please go back to the house, ma'am, and telephone to the station. Tell them the number 111, if you please.'

111 in the local police code would get him the fastest assistance possible, with an ambulance also despatched.

'Please go quickly, ma'am.'

By the time the police car screamed into the drive, its gong still clanging, the sergeant had lifted the plinth and removed the top from the well.

They lowered the sergeant down inside the well on a rope. He shone the flashlight round him and saw the Colonel lying on a ledge. The colonel's eyes were open.

'Thank God, thank God,' the colonel said, his voice the faintest whisper. 'I couldn't have survived another night . . .'

They took him to the hospital suffering from shock, exposure and a broken leg. He had been able to speak faintly in the ambulance and had told them what little he knew, how he'd heard the sound of skittering gravel, had felt a blow in the back of his leg, had stumbled forward into the well-hole. What the devils who'd pushed him in there hadn't known, he explained to the sergeant with a weak smile, was that he'd had the well filled with rubble when first he'd taken over the house all those years ago. He'd been going to have the last ten feet plugged with concrete but had never got around to it!

The colonel was lying in a bed in a private ward in the Cottage Hospital when Bill arrived from New York. The doctor had said it would be all right for the colonel to receive visitors – 'In fact, it'll do him good to talk to someone,' he had said. 'He's been brooding too much.'

The colonel's face showed his delight when Bill came into the ward. 'It's good to see you, Bill,' he said. 'Now sit down here and tell me how far you've got with your search for your father. You went to see Karfounis?'

'Yes!'

'And how was he?'

'Very well in the circumstances. He lives a meagre life. I think he's just eking out an existence on his small-holding, but he seems content enough.'

'Did he talk about your father?'

'Yes, he did. And he told me about the meeting in Cairo.'

The colonel's face was sombre. 'I hoped he would, you know. You understand, I couldn't? One does have certain loyalties, misplaced though I think many of them are these days!'

'I found my father's diary and read the entry about Cairo. There seemed to be a discrepancy, and then by accident I discovered the Minutes of the second meeting . . .'

The colonel nodded.

'You took a risk, sending them to my father!'

'I had to. I had to tell him what was going on. At least, to let him know things weren't going the way we'd planned. You know, Bill, I had never hated war, never hated the military mind, never despised the politicians as much as I did on that occasion. Of course, I make an almighty fuss about my gout, but in a way I was pleased when it removed me from the centre of all that intrigue. I never did have much time for military politicians. My way of fighting was to drive at the enemy as hard, as fast, and as often as you could. I wanted *desperately* a military invasion of Crete, but, of course, I had no say in the matter. I was only an office flunkey. And it hurt to see men like your father pushed about the board like pawns.'

'I have one question to ask you, Colonel, if you feel up to it . . .'

'I feel fine, just fine. At least with my broken leg I can't go wandering about giving my gout hell. Ask your question. I only hope I have the answer.'

'Who worked the radio station Dog Fox Zebra Three?'

'Dog Fox Zebra Three? That'd be a station on Crete, working directly to us in Cairo. That's the Dog Fox bit. The Zebra bit would be one of the groups set up against the invasion – the damned invasion that never happened. The Three, well that was, yes, Karfounis. Karfounis was Dog Fox Zebra Three!'

Now it was all clear to Bill. Karfounis! He'd been pulling the wool over Bill's eyes in France. No wonder he'd fled the country. To escape from the rest of the partisans. No wonder Angelos Stavakis had told Bill to drop it, had lied to him about finding Theseus dead. A kindly man, he'd wanted to protect Karfounis, feeling no doubt that he'd suffered enough through the years of his impoverished exile.

Of course it would be in keeping with the quoted thinking of the Communists, who were reputed to care less about fighting the Germans than fighting the right wing Cretans, just as the Communists in Greece itself were interested principally in the overthrow of the government. It would seem, to that manner of thinking, that anything, even betrayal to the Germans, would be justified. What is the Marxian dogma – the ends justify the means.

And, of course, Karfounis would need a scapegoat. No wonder he tried to imply to Bill that Maleta, Bill's father, had been the guilty one, though he'd tried to soften the blow by calling it obeying military commands.

Now, Bill felt, he had a clue to what the Americans were up to, in the contemporary situation. The *Communists* were the ones who were killing the people who had been alive in that time of betrayal. Because it would destroy their present standing – especially with an imminent election – if it were ever known that a Communist had betrayed his fellow Cretans during the war and had caused the deaths of whole villages of people.

The Americans, presumably, were working against that. They were trying to *expose* the Communists. That's what Wanda meant – they were trying to fight the spread of Communism any way they could.

'Why do you want to know about Dog Fox Zebra Three?' the colonel asked.

'May I ask another question? You say my father sent Karfounis out to you. What were his instructions?'

'He sent a note with him. The note asked me to get Karfounis quietly into a hospital and then, when his wounds were patched, to get him away somewhere. Your father also said – I fear for his life if he stays on Crete!'

For Bill, that was the clincher. Of course he feared for Karfounis's life – the partisans were demonic when it came to hunting down and killing traitors.

'I slipped him illicitly aboard a transport that was leaving for England. Unfortunately the transport was dive-bombed and torpedoed. We heard later that some of the people had survived and had been washed ashore on the south coast of France. They'd had a rough time of it, apparently. When I received that card from Karfounis, I realized he must have been one of those who escaped the sinking!'

'It would have been better,' Bill said bitterly, 'if he'd died. When I was in New York I was shown transcripts of radio signals in code. The signals had been decoded – the sender didn't realize the codes had been broken by an American in Cairo . . .'

'That would be Colonel Hassler. He ran his own intelligence shop. We resented it, I can tell you, because he wouldn't share information. Strange chap, that Colonel Hassler . . .'

'He appears to have known more about what was going on than anyone else. He knew, for example, that the signals to the Germans, in code, came from the station Dog Fox Zebra Three. He knew that the man running that station was a traitor to his country, the renegade called Theseus . . .'

'Oh, my God!' the colonel said. His head went back on the pillow and his eyes closed. 'Hassler knew all that and didn't tell us? Didn't let us warn your father? And your father sent the traitor out to me and made me responsible for helping him to escape . . . ? What sort of man does that make your father, Bill? What sort of man?'

'There are only two explanations. Either he was forgiving, a saint who wanted to spare Karfounis's life. Or, he was a fellow-traveller, a man no better than the traitors he served!'

'What will you do now?' the colonel asked.

'I shall go to Karfounis again. And this time I'll find the truth.'

It was already late when he arrived at Nice Airport but he was in no mood to delay and rented a car immediately for the long journey into the hills of Provence. He was driven now by an enormous appetite for the conclusion of this entire business; he knew he was approaching the final confrontation, the final showdown. He didn't give a damn about the politico-morality of Karfounis's past; but he must uncover the truth, the real no-nonsense facts, about this shadow-figure Maleta. He knew his father had behaved badly over the matter of Elvira and Victorio, but at least he'd tried to set that matter as right as he could in his will. Bill had copied the clause and had sent it to the soliticors in London, determined that Evangelina and Victorio would get what was rightly theirs, no matter what it cost Bill personally. He was only sorry he hadn't been able to do anything financial for the German, Hans Ohlman, during his lifetime.

Bill didn't have any feelings of condemnation for his father – he merely wanted to know the truth. It was as simple as that, he told himself. The truth – nothing more, nothing less.

He left the car in the village, which was already slumbering, and walked up the lane that led out of Frojane to Karfounis's cottage. It was a temperate night with a bright moon and a tapestry of stars twinkling against the deep blue of the sky. The night trees were odorous with exuded oils, but Bill was in no mood to appreciate them. He walked rapidly up the centre of the lane between tended fields of vegetables and vines, turned the corner, then saw Karfounis's cottage prominent in white against the green trees beyond.

There were no lights in the cottage. Bill had not expected any at that time of night. Okay, so he'd waken Karfounis from sleep but what the hell – all sympathy for the man had vanished when Bill had learned about DFZ3.

He opened the gate and walked up the drive towards the front door, whose black wood looked like a dark mouth with the eyes of the two windows on either side. He shivered in the night air, tensing himself for the encounter. He passed beneath the two mulberry trees whose branches formed an arch across the drive, remembering the mulberries on Crete dating back to the Minoan times when Crete was the silk-producing centre of Europe. Well, tonight, he'd finish the Cretan affair. Tonight, he'd get the truth if he had to kill Karfounis to get it, so murderous was his mood.

He reached the door, lifted his fist and banged hard.

The voice came out of the dark behind him. 'Just stand where you are. I have a shot-gun pointed at your back.'

It was the voice of Karfounis.

Bill stood still, his hand still lifted to the door, his mind racing. How the hell could Karfounis have known he was coming? Bill didn't believe the colonel would have told him. He *could* have sent a telegram, could even have telephoned a contact in the village, but Bill didn't believe that. So how the hell could Karfounis have known.

'Turn round, slowly, keeping your hands in sight,' Karfounis said.

Bill turned, both hands lifted above his head. Killers don't talk; they blast first and ask questions later if you are still alive.

'Step out from under the porch, into the moonlight.'

Bill did as he was told.

'So, it *was* you?' Karfounis said.

The voice came from the mulberry tree, though Bill could see no one up there in the deep shadow of the branches.

'What *was* me?' Bill asked, perplexed.

'Don't play the innocent with me,' Karfounis said. 'I am an old hand at this game!'

'What game, damn it? My arms are getting tired?'

There was no mistaking the click of the gun barrel against the tree. 'Do you want me to drop them down for you?' Karfounis asked. 'Where do you carry your gun? Or are you a knife man?'

'I don't carry a gun, and the only knife I have is for peeling apples,' Bill said, exasperated. 'What did you mean when you said, "So it *was* you"?'

'Somebody took a shot at me earlier. They missed. I knew they would be back so I hid up here, waiting. You are fortunate I did not blast you when you were standing at the door. Who sent you? What have you come for?'

Bill had had enough. 'I'm going to put my hands down,' he announced, 'and turn out my pockets one by one. I'm going to open my jacket to let you see I'm not wearing a shoulder holster, then I'll roll back my sleeves and lift my trouser legs to show you I don't have any sort of concealed weapon, neither a knife nor a gun. And then I'm going to walk across and pull you out of that damn tree. I've come all this way to ask you a couple more questions, and I'm going to get truthful answers this time. There's no way you

287

can stop me, other than by firing that bloody shotgun and killing me. And somehow, I don't believe you intend to do that, or you would have done it already.'

He heard Karfounis chuckle – it sounded more like a hen-cackle. Then he slid down the trunk of a tree, the shotgun held in one hand. He walked across the path to where Bill was standing.

'Okay,' he said, 'it was not you. Then who the hell was it? Somebody fired a gun at me. It sounded like a sporting rifle. The bullet missed me and went into a tree not inches from my head. The man who fired it must have taken fright and run away. I thought you were the one, coming back for a second try.'

'I have my plane ticket in my pocket,' Bill said. 'If you need any positive proof of where I was earlier on. Or do you believe I fired the damned rifle from a plane?'

They went inside the cottage. Karfounis turned on the light, after drawing the curtains to shield them from outside observation.

'Now tell me, what do you want back here,' he said. 'All these years I've lived a quiet and uninterrupted life, then you come along with your questions and someone takes a pot shot at me. You can't blame me for thinking it might have been you!'

'Why should I want to shoot you?' Bill asked.

'Because of what I said about your father. Because you suspect that I'm the only man alive who knew what your father was, what he did.'

'My father saved your life by sending you to Cairo . . .'

'You can think of it that way if you choose. You could also say that he was getting me safely out of the way in case I should suspect his plan! That he was given the direct order, betrayed the village to get rid of my men, my arms and ammunition and my explosives, then pushed me off to Cairo to prevent me suspecting what he had done.'

'Nonsense. He could have killed you, then and there.'

'But do you not see, can you not see, that by appearing to help me escape he was in fact diverting suspicion from himself. Nobody would suspect what he had done if they knew he had gone to all that trouble to get me into the hospital in Cairo. Especially if I had perished on that transport that sank . . .'

'I heard about that.'

'We were adrift five days in the Mediterranean, without water. Ten of us in an open boat. Three of them died – I survived, I don't know how. When the boat beached near Cap Ferrat, I was barely alive but managed to stagger into the bushes. The rest of them were taken . . .'

'Who operated Dog Fox Zebra Three, Karfounis?' Bill asked, his voice quiet.

'I did!'

'Who was Theseus, Karfounis?'

'I don't know. You asked me that before . . .'

Bill reached into his pocket and drew out an envelope. It contained thin sheets of photo-copied paper. 'These are from the American Military Archives,' he said. 'They prove, to me at any rate, that the man operating DFZ3 was in touch with the Germans. That he was the one who betrayed Mavroti to the German Headquarters in Rethymnon . . .'

'Give me those papers,' Karfounis said, his eyes blazing. He scanned them rapidly, talking to Bill as he was reading. 'I personally operated DFZ3 from the moment your father, Maleta, provided the set, the batteries, the charging engine. It was never out of my control. Kostas Dandanakis taught me to use it, taught me to tune it to the right station, taught me radio procedures. No one else knew how to use it!'

'My father? Did he ever have a chance to use it?'

'Your father? Don't you know *anything* about your father? The one thing he could never understand was radio. Kostas tried many times but Maleta just couldn't seem to grasp it. Why do you think they gave him one of the best radio operators on the island?' He stopped, exclaimed and shook the papers at Bill. 'This is a forgery,' he said. 'This was never sent from DFZ3 by me.' He spread the papers on the table. 'Look at this,' he said. 'Patrol of partisans led by Adonis – good shot – kill on sight. Nonsense. Adonis never led a patrol. He was not a good shot. He was our scrounger, our forager. He could steal the blanket right off a German's back asleep in bed. Here is another. Observation on the raki-shed roof. When did you ever hear of anyone from Western Crete talking about *raki*?'

'You called it *tsikoudia* . . . !'

'Damn right we did. Mentally I still do, even when I distill it here where it is called *marc*! Okay, whoever wrote these papers knew something about the local situation, but I can tell you this – he was no Cretan!'

Bill believed Karfounis absolutely. He felt utterly deflated at the thought that once again he'd been manipulated. He could see it now – he was supposed to arrive with steam coming out of his nostrils, believing Karfounis to be the traitor. He was supposed to come here and *kill* him. And if he'd found Karfounis unarmed, if he'd jumped him and a fight had developed, he'd been just mad enough to do that!

'Then who the hell was it?' Bill raged. 'Who could have had enough information, enough knowledge, to put the papers together to make them seem authentic enough to convince me?'

He found the answer for himself in the remembered words of Colonel Bythorne.

'The American, Hassler! Colonel Bythorne said he ran his own intelligence network. *He* could have put it together!'

'Hassler!' Karfounis said contemptuously. 'Do not mention that wind-bag to me. He was the American I met in Cairo. He was the one who promised us all the help we needed; the arms and ammunition, the explosives. We laid the whole thing out for him, your father and I. He came to Crete at our invitation, to see the local situation for himself. I showed him all my men, showed them how well-trained they already were, how efficient, how disciplined. And then he went away, and that's the last we heard from him.

And we never got one rifle from him, not one bullet, not one packet of explosives. There he was, sitting on his arse in Cairo, shipping stuff nightly to the Royalists, but for us, for the men who were really ready and prepared to fight to the last man for what they believed in, nothing. Absolutely nothing!'

Bill reread his father's diary entry in his mind. He'd met the delegation when they'd dropped by parachute on to the plain of Omalos. He'd accompanied them to the meeting with Karfounis and his men.

The diary said, *I was proud of the way Theodor Karfounis and his men conducted themselves on that occasion; they had the bearing of a crack platoon of an élite regiment. I felt that here were men I would support to the hilt . . .*

And then Bill remembered the next diary entry. *I was asked by Col. Hassler to guide him to a map reference I knew to be the cave at Striatos we no longer used. Wondered whom he might be meeting since he gave no name. Took him there and was instructed to wait half a mile away. I realized with whom he was meeting when I saw Simeon and Petrakis leave the rendezvous, obviously dismissed.*

The diary had contained other references to Simeon and Petrakis, and the man to whom they were joint runners and bodyguard.

'I must get back to Crete,' Bill said. 'I must get back right away.'

The pre-election night was in full swing when Bill arrived in Heraklion, and cars with blaring loudspeakers were touring the town, throwing out handfuls of printed leaflets, a different colour for each party. The Neo-democratia van had been decorated with an enormous effigy of Stalin, his body like that of a wolf, blood dripping down his jaws, with a baby on a table in front of him. 'This is Communism,' the poster above it declared. The KKE had countered with a crude, fibre-glass model of a rich, overstuffed *kapitalist*; gathered around him were women and children with hands stretched for the food on which the *kapitalist* was gorging himself. The election was being fought on basic issues of distribution of resources, with everyone wanting a greater slice of the cake, everyone accusing the others of keeping the whole cake for themselves.

All around the town concerts had been arranged on every spare bit of open ground, with singers rushing from one to the other to draw the crowd by their performances. They were radio and recording pop-stars for the most, with the occasional protest singer. In between songs, the local agent would grab the microphone and scream patriotic slogans and party denunciations. The quality of amplification and the volume were such that the words were usually distorted beyond recognition. Nobody minded. The *souvlaki*-selling pirates, the vendors of soft drinks and the peanut barrows were all out in force. The evening was an extension of the nightly *volta* and excitement ran high.

On the morrow the voting would take place and each party would win a few seats, lose a few seats.

The caucus for the mayor, for the elected officials, would continue quietly, far from this screaming crowd, and the destiny of Crete would be decided behind locked and privileged doors. And in those quiet councils, no voice would be more eagerly listened to than that of Angelo Stavakis.

Skiamnakis – the former fisherman, footballer, pop-singer – would speak and his voice would carry much weight for the left.

But ultimately, Stavakis and the commercial power he could wield would prevail. The *nomakis* appointed by the government in Athens would reflect this power and would reinforce it.

Stavakis was sitting on his terrace again when Bill arrived. Half a dozen men were gathered around him. All wore tailored suits, white shirts, ties. All had cleaned shoes, well-washed hands, tended fingernails, shrewd eyes. They looked at the travel-soiled Englishman, their eyes flicking over him and as quickly dismissing him. Blatantly he didn't belong to any club of which they were committee members.

'I've just come from Washington,' he said to Stavakis. 'I think we should talk. Obviously I don't mind talking in front of these gentlemen.'

'They were just leaving,' Stavakis said smoothly. 'Tonight they have much to do in preparation for tomorrow.'

'The calm before the battle, eh? The planning. The strategy.'

'It is something like that.'

The one quality the men shared above all else, perhaps the quality that had given them success, was a sensitivity to atmosphere. As a man they rose, extended their hands, shook Stavakis's and left.

Stavakis led the way into the house and his study, a room containing a large desk, filing cabinets, a safe built into the wall. Prominent on the wall was a painting, obviously done from a photograph, of Stavakis with Spiros Orfandakis and Manoletto. All were wearing *palikari* Sfakian dress; all were armed to the teeth. They looked, Bill again thought, like pirates.

'You told me a story when I was last here,' Bill said. 'It touched me very deeply, as it was meant to. I've finished with touching stories that are fiction; now I want the truth. You must realize I wouldn't be here if I hadn't put it all together, piece by piece. In many ways, it's a sad story of a man torn between two loyalties, and then finally pushed in one direction. It's a story of murder, blackmail, betrayal. And the story is still going on, isn't it? Still going on, with more murder, more betrayal, more blackmail. The big mistake you have made, Kirios Stavakis, is not to realize that stories like this never end . . .'

'And there is always someone like Bill Thomas – naïve, simple, incorruptible Bill Thomas, whose only interest is in clearing the name of his father – to come along and turn the story inside out . . .'

'Petro, the *Ipastinomos*, called me the piece of grit without which the oyster would never make its pearl . . .'

'It was a wise allusion. Okay, Bill. We both know you know the truth now . . .'

'I don't know all the truth. I want to hear it – from *you*. Take me back, Angelo Stavakis. Take me back to Crete in 1943. Use some of that eloquence you use on the voters to show me what really happened . . .'

Theseus came from his meeting with the American colonel, Hassler, his mind in turmoil. All through this damnable Occupation he had fought with only one objective in mind: to reduce the numbers of Cretans killed by the Germans. Damn it, he didn't *object* to the German Occupation. Look what Hitler had done for Germany! Look what Mussolini had done for the Italian railways! These men with their régimes were able to give Crete what it most needed, a step into the twentieth century. They would bring roads, sewage systems; build houses, factories. They would turn Crete economically from a simple, backwards, peasant community into a strong, financially secure island. He had to admit that the pickings, for a man close to the seat of power, could be very good. But, he told himself, that wasn't the first consideration. If only these damned partisans would stop *impeding* the Germans. If only they'd learn to work with them, instead of fighting them, killing them, making such ridiculously futile gestures as blowing up bridges and ambushing patrols. Couldn't they see what an opportunity the Germans were bringing to them?

Of course, he'd joined the partisans as a means of protecting *himself*, of diverting suspicion from himself. Only by joining them could he find out exactly what they were up to.

When the Germans instituted their reprisal rule of ten men for every one, he'd decided to act. The partisans planned to ambush a patrol on the lower Rethymnon-to-Xania road; he sent a letter, informing the Germans.

The ten men of the partisan band had been wiped out in the German counter ambush. But, more importantly, the people of the village of Aghios Adonis had been saved the blood-bath that would have ensued. Ten men killed and a hundred and fifty lives saved. It wasn't a bad balance sheet.

Oddly enough, after the first time, it became easier to take the decision. Wisely, he didn't inform on every job – only those he knew would result in massive reprisals. And he devised a system, with the Germans' connivance. He sent a message on the radio he used for communication between his station, commanded by Spiros Orfandakis, and Cairo. The signals were always sent at 2100 hrs, Cretan time, at which time the Cairo station was off the air for maintenance. And he signed the messages 'Theseus'.

He couldn't know, of course, that in Cairo the Americans were operating their own radio network, gathering independent intelligence for Colonel Hassler. And Hassler's radio station *didn't* go off the air at 2100 hrs.

Hassler had been intrigued by the station broadcasting at an odd hour; once he'd broken the simple code the Germans had given to Theseus, he was able to read everything Theseus sent. And to store the information for subsequent use.

Hassler didn't want the Karfounis group, fostered by Maleta, to gain any power. His clear brief from Washington had said – no support for Communists. He carried it one stage further, exceeding his brief, and went to Crete himself. To use Theseus.

'I want the Germans told about Mavroti,' he'd said to Theseus. 'And if you don't do it, I shall inform the Cretans that you are a traitor.'

'I had a simple life-or-death choice,' Stavakis said to Bill. 'I sent the radio transmission for a meeting, then informed the German Army officer at that meeting. I had to make it look natural, so I sent two of my men . . .'

'Simeon and Petrakis . . .?'

'That's right. I sent them to Mavroti with instructions to ambush a German patrol the major promised to send. Then the Germans could move in as a reprisal.'

'But my father discovered the part you'd played from

the German, Hans Ohlman. He came down from the mountain . . .'

Stavakis and his men were off to the left, hidden among rocks overlooking the scene of the double ambush. Mano-letto and his men, Spiros Orfandakis and his men, were grouped in a tight formation near the gorge in which they would ambush the German column when it arrived to sack the village. Karfounis and his men were on the lip of the gorge itself, the first line of fighting. After all, Mavroti was *their* village.

The Stukas from Maleme were the first to arrive. They swept the gorge with devastating cannon-fire from their multiple guns, dropped high fragmentation bombs.

The paratroopers came next, dropping low, surrounding the area in a tight ring, then slowly moving in with great control and precision.

The partisans fired at them as they came down but the drop was too short for them to be effective and over ninety per cent of the paratroopers made it down without casualties. They moved in with schmeissers, with grenade launchers, with flame-throwers that enveloped the parti-sans in burning, sticky oil and drove them screaming out of their hides among the rocks and in the caves. Karfounis and his men, realizing they'd been counter-ambushed, made a compact fighting group. They were the only ones with the discipline to fight effectively against the highly skilled paratroops. They used the Germans' own fire and movement, rush *blitzkrieg* techniques against them and carved a way through the enclosing ring. Karfounis himself was hit many times but still managed to command his men, to hold them in a tight and effective unit. As they battled their way out, however, they realized the odds were against them in a running battle. Maikhis, who'd become Karfounis's second-in-command, saw what must inevita-bly happen. He rallied the able-bodied men around him.

'Theodor Karfounis must escape from this,' he said. 'He is the only man who can go back into the mountains and start our work again. He must be saved!'

The men formed a tight-knit, rear-guard unit, sent Karfounis off with the injured and made a last ditch stand. They held the Germans for two hours, long enough for Karfounis, though wounded, to make his way up into the mountains.

Maleta, coming down the mountains with the knowledge of the identity of the traitor, met Karfounis. He realized the traitor would never let Karfounis live and despatched Kostas Dandanakis to look after him.

'Get him into the mountains,' he said, 'then radio this message. Take him down to Aghia Roumeli and see he gets on the boat they'll send from Cairo.'

Then Maleta headed into the fray. Not to kill Germans. To find Theseus and kill him.

The first man he saw was Simeon, heading away from the battle. He caught a flash from the top of the hill where someone was looking down at the scene below through binoculars. Simeon's rifle was around his shoulders, as if he knew he had nothing to fear. Maleta followed him, dodging behind the rocks, staying low. Simeon went up the slope quite openly, not even glancing back at the fight, as if the events taking place below were none of his concern.

Maleta skirted the plateau and came up from the west. Stavakis, Petrakis and Simeon were squatting at the edge of the plateau, looking down.

Stavakis bent his knees and crawled backwards. Petrakis turned his head.

'Keep a good look out,' Stavakis said, and Petrakis turned his head back again.

Stavakis took out his pistol, a Smith and Wesson the British had dropped in with a consignment of other weapons. He levelled the gun and quickly shot both Simeon and Petrakis through the backs of their heads; at that point-blank range he couldn't miss. He whirled when he heard Maleta's voice.

'Drop the gun,' Maleta said. 'Drop it now.'

Stavakis let the Smith and Wesson fall from his fingers, then turned around.

'Hello, Theseus,' Maleta said.

'I knew it was all up with me at that moment,' Stavakis said to Bill, in the gathering twilight in his study. 'In a way I was glad. I remember feeling a strong sense of relief that at last I had been discovered and that all the pretence was over . . .'

'Even though you'd just killed your own two men, Simeon and Petrakis.'

'I had to kill them. I thought they were the only two men who knew I had betrayed the village of Mavroti. Then, when I realized your father also knew, I was in a sense glad it was all over.'

'But it wasn't all over, was it?' Bill said. 'You're still alive, but my father, Maleta, is out there, somewhere. What happened? Did he let down his guard. Did he . . . could he have been foolish enough to *trust* you? Did you talk to him, persuade him it all had been an error, and then stick a knife into him?'

'Believe me, Bill, I had nothing to do with killing your father. We were standing on the plateau. He had his Colt .45 in his hand. He meant to kill me and, as I have explained, I had resigned myself to face death without regret, even willingly . . .'

'So, what happened?'

'A second wave of Stukas came over. They hit both of us. When I recovered consciousness I had the wound I showed you. Your father had taken a bullet through his chest. He was already dead. I buried him, up there on the plateau, with Simeon and Petrakis in a rocky hollow, covering them with large stones.' He bowed his head. 'Dead,' he said. 'All the best men dead. Your father, Manoletto, Simeon and Petrakis. Kostas Dandanakis escaped because your father sent him to Aghia Roumeli with Karfounis. Pakrades, dead. Spiros Orfandakis escaped because he was wounded and fell into a chasm. I found

299

him, eventually. I searched and searched but never found Karfounis. And then, almost overnight it seemed, the invincible German Army, losing everywhere, retreated to the west of the island. Xania was the last place to be liberated. It was all over . . .'

'But it *wasn't* all over, was it? I came to the island, all these years afterwards, and started asking questions, stirring up the mud. You knew that eventually, I'd get round to you . . .'

Stavakis stood up, as if flexing his back. Bill watched him warily, looking still for the ultimate trickery. When Stavakis reached down and opened his top drawer, Bill expected his hand to reappear with a gun in it. And, oddly enough, he didn't care. Now he had the full story of his father and nothing else seemed important any more.

Stavakis smiled at him. 'No gun,' he said. 'A button which I press. I have always known, deep in my heart, that I would have to pay for what I did during the war. I have always known, perhaps, that the ghosts of your father and Karfounis, of Petrakis and Simeon, would rise again to haunt me. So I arranged things for myself. You understand that, as a Cretan, I can not permit myself to be dragged through the courts. My *philotimo* would not allow that to happen to me, Angelos Stavakis. Beneath the floor of this desk is a quantity of explosives. Thirty minutes after I press the button in the top drawer, the floor will explode. I shall be sitting here at my desk in thirty minute's time. Where you are is a matter for you to decide!'

Bill knew about the Cretan *philotimo*, of course. That fierce personal pride, that refusal to accept disgrace. Death before dishonour!

'But I warn you,' Stavakis said, 'to get right away from the house. The whole place will be destroyed and everything and everybody in it.'

'In thirty minutes?'

'In twenty-eight minutes,' Stavakis said.

'If this is another of your tricks . . .' Bill said.

Stavakis was shaking his head from side to side. 'No

300

more tricks, Bill. I am tired of all the tricks. Tired of the wheeler-dealing, the influence peddling. You saw those men out there when you arrived. Cut-throats, every one of them. When I think of Spiros Orfandakis, men like Manoletto, Kostas Dandanakis. These were the truly great men of Crete. And most of them we have buried. Now we have politicians who put self-advantage over all other considerations, who no longer go into our villages and celebrate the festivals with dancing and the music of the lyre. Of course, many men still do, the simple men whose roots are still deep in Crete. But above them, we have an imposed superstructure of rich men, politicians, merchants, who build only in concrete, who fill their concrete houses with plastic, scorning the old Cretan craftsmanship. Men whose wives have never handled a loom or spun wool, men who drive imported cars and buy loud-throated motor-bicycles for their spoiled children; men who drink whisky and imported gins and scorn local wines. I have become truly tired of them!'

'Tell me,' Bill said, 'about the deaths of Spiros Orfandakis and Kostas Dandanakis. Tell me about the attempt on Evangelina's life. Tell me about the man who set fire to the house in Kaprisses and tried to kill me.'

'I will tell you the whole story,' Stavakis said, 'and then you must go. You must leave me to choose death my own way. This you must promise me!'

'I promise,' Bill said.

Stavakis swivelled his chair so that he could open his filing cabinet. From it he produced a brown-coloured folder and placed it on the table. 'You will take this with you when you go,' he said. 'It concerns the man Skiamnakis and his plan for the future of . . .'

Stavakis said no more. The shot that came in through the window, shattering the glass, was aimed better than the one that had missed Karfounis. It took Stavakis between the eyes, killing him instantly. Bill whirled off his chair and dropped to the floor, crawling rapidly across the wood until he was among the broken glass beneath the window frame.

He crouched there, waiting. If he could get to the door, hit the light switch . . . The room was dark enough now that he could hope to jump out through the broken window.

The door opened slowly. Bill, without a gun, knew he was helpless. He reached down, picked up a shard of glass, about saucer-sized with razor-like edges. Skimmed across the room it would make a fearsome weapon – if he could aim it correctly.

The door opened all the way. A hand flicked in and hit the light switch, plunging the room into semi-darkness. Bill straightened up, intending to jump through the shattered window space, when the light flicked on again.

'That's just fine,' said a voice he recognized. 'Just hold it there.'

Bill turned. Sam Birntin was standing in the doorway, his fat sweating hand clasped round the butt of a Colt .45. 'Used to be pretty good with one of these,' Sam said conversationally. 'But locked away behind a desk I haven't had much practice recently. But with one of these, it doesn't matter very much *where* I hit you. It'll still stop you when it goes in and make a nasty hole where it comes out.'

As he talked he walked into the room. 'Bill,' he said, 'you're the most dogged, persistent, stubborn, pig-headed guy I've ever had to track. Why couldn't you do what you were supposed to, huh?'

Bill stayed where he was, looked back, saw the bare windowsill and sat on it. 'You interrupted Stavakis at the wrong moment. He was going to tell me the rest of the story. Now you'll have to tell it to me yourself!'

Sam was smiling in admiration. 'You really are *something*, Bill, you know that?'

'So, apparently, is Skiamnakis . . .'

'So you know about him, too, do you?'

'I was just about to be told . . .' Bill's eyes went to the

302

desk. Sam looked across and saw the closed folder. The blast of the bullet had slammed Stavakis backwards off his chair; only the brown folder remained in the light of the desk lamp. Sam walked across to the desk and flipped open the folder to verify its contents but didn't read it beyond the title page.

'We wanted the minutes of that second Cairo meeting,' he said. 'We knew a copy was missing. If it had turned up in today's climate, some guy would have used it to throw shit in Uncle Sam's face. And we've had enough shit since Watergate to last us another fifty years!'

'And you're a shit collector . . .?'

'It's a profession, Bill, just like any other. I hoped you'd get the message from Wanda like pillow-talk. That some of us believe in what we're trying to do. It's called "patriotism". Wanda told you, that night in bed.'

'You'd bugged the room, of course!'

'Don't be naïve, Bill. What do you expect? We had you sound and vision, strength five. We just wanted to know exactly how naïve you were.'

'Not naïve enough, apparently, to swallow the story hook-line-and-sinker.'

'Bill, Bill!' Sam said. 'Don't you know *nothing* about modern life? About the way things *really* are? About how Government *works*? Hasn't Watergate, hasn't the CIA, the FBI scandal taught you *anything*?'

'The bugging, the eavesdropping, the denial of the right of privacy, the Peeping Tom bit . . .'

Sam slapped the folder down on the desk, hard, his face showing his anger. 'This folder is a manifesto, Bill. It is a highly confidential report of a meeting Skiamnakis held with the top politicians of the left wing here on Crete. The Commies . . .'

'You Americans have Commies on the brain . . .'

'Shut your mouth for once in your life, you ignorant Brit, and listen to me. Skiamnakis is supposed to be Passok, right. Know what Passok means here? Don't speak, don't answer any rhetorical questions. It means

Socialist. Skiamnakis is no more a Socialist than Stavakis was. He's an out and out Communist. This manifesto tells what he and the boys were going to do if they could get into power. They were going to kick NATO out of Souda Bay. They were going to try to go unilateral – like Smith in Rhodesia, only on the other wing. And, they'd have made it, in time. Or they'd have caused a civil war, right here on Crete. Can you guess how many people would have been killed on this island in a civil war? With the mainland Greeks having to turn against their own; send bombers, the Army, the Navy? Can you guess? Stavakis found out about this. We happened to approach him about finding the copy of the Minutes of that second Cairo meeting. He did a deal with us. Help him with Skiamnakis, and he would help us find the Minutes. At least, that's what the deal was supposed to be. Then you came along and we had to switch priorities. Stop you finding out that he had been Theseus, that became the deal. Because if you blundered into that, if you made public the fact that the great war hero Stavakis, who'd come to power and maintained it on the strength of his war reputation, was in reality a traitor who'd sold the partisans down the river, who'd turned an entire village of women and children over to the butchers, there was no way he would ever have had any influence again! There was no way they'd even let him stay alive! And Skiamnakis would become the power in the land. And then NATO could kiss its base on Crete goodbye . . .'

'But you killed Stavakis. You killed Theseus, the man you were promoting.'

'Look, Bill, I don't make *all* the decisions. Whatever you may think, there's always another guy higher up, with a greater area of responsibility.'

'Looking at what I believe they call the over-all picture?'

'Something like that. A decision was taken. Stavakis was too heavy a load for us to carry safely. He had to be put down.'

'Eliminated? Terminated? Let go? They all mean the same thing to you people. All words . . .'

'We live in a world of words, Bill. If you want it in straight talk, he was an embarrassment to us so long as he was alive. Somebody had to kill him. They gave the job to me. I carried it out. That plain enough for you?'

'So, why didn't you kill *me*?' Bill asked. 'Why kill the others and leave me alive?'

'Because from the beginning, Bill, you had too big a profile. Kostas Dandanakis was a shepherd who lived the life of a hermit on top of a mountain – who was going to miss him, eh? Spiros Orfandakis had virtually retired from public life. Evangelina was dying, anyway . . .'

'And you can dispose of people, just like that? *You* can make life and death decisions, just like that?'

Sam drew a chair to the side of the desk, meticulously avoiding the blood that had spattered the polished top. 'I thought Wanda had explained that to you, Bill,' he said patiently. 'Yes, I *can* make decisions, just like that. Jesus, Bill, *somebody* has to make 'em – *somebody* has to have the guts to arrive at these decisions and act on 'em! Me, Wanda, 27, it doesn't matter . . .'

'So, what decision have you made about me?' Bill asked softly, tensing himself, ready for the gun to come up and fire again.

Sam put the gun on the desk. 'Bill, you're not my concern. You can walk out of here. Maybe you'll give the story to the local cops, but by the time they get here, I'll be long gone. You don't think I'd walk into a situation like this without arranging my own out? Take my advice, Bill. What you've seen here wasn't meant for your eyes. What you've heard is not for public consumption. Okay, you can talk your head off to some journalist, and maybe a wild story might get published in some creep magazine in Germany or Italy. Even London or the US of A. Maybe there'll be a scandal. For a day or two. But it'll all be puffs of wind, Bill, with no real evidence to support it. Nothing solid. So, why don't you take my advice and walk away from it?'

'You mean leave, just like that?'

'Just like that . . .!'

Bill glanced at his watch, then looked out of the window, seeing the lights of Heraklion gleaming below. 'You chaps always seem to pick hill-tops for your power games,' he said. 'You are all hell bent on a course that can only lead to your own destruction, eventually. Well, sometimes, you ought to stop and listen to the little people on whom you look down so contemptuously. Perhaps once in a while they might be able to save you.'

He walked across the room and out of the house, not hurrying.

Down the driveway that led to the gate.

Along the road outside the house to where he'd left his hired car.

He got in, started the engine, and drove along the road.

Thirty minutes. The house blew. It started as a rumble deep inside the house's viscera, then exploded upwards, shooting a column of red fire high into the air, tinged with yellow and white and edged with black smoke. Almost lazily the brickwork, the shattered woodwork, the bone, tissue, and blood that once had been the bodies of people who made the fatal error of not listening to ordinary people in their lust to manipulate the world rose into the air, fragmented by a physical force they could *not* contain.

The pyre reached its pinnacle high in the air above the hill-top, levelled out again and then slowly began to be dispersed.

But by that time Bill was heading westwards down the Chrisostomou, beneath a canopy of Cretan stars.

Bill was bone tired when he arrived in Kaprisses. Victorio and Maria were sitting in Evangelina's house over which an air of expectancy hung like a doom cloud, matching Bill's mood.

The local people had come into the house and cleared away much of the bomb damage; they'd even rebuilt the outer wall in local stone and had installed a temporary door.

'It's all over,' he said. 'Theseus was Angelo Stavakis.'

'He killed our father?' Victorio asked.

'No, I don't believe he actually killed him. But he was there when father died. He buried him on the mountainside.'

'And now, it really *is* all over?' Maria asked.

'Yes. The Americans were involved. Stavakis blew up his house and killed himself. His *philotimo* . . . He took a couple of the Americans with him.'

'A couple . . .?'

'Yes. God, I'm tired . . .'

Victorio came across the room and put his hand on Bill's shoulder. 'No more talk until you have had a chance to sleep,' he said. 'Now that you are here and it is all over, I can go back to the *kafeneion*. You get some rest, and tomorrow we can talk about everything.'

But there wasn't any more that needed saying.

Bill nodded and Victorio left.

Maria went into the bedroom and returned a couple of minutes later wearing a dressing gown. She looked at him, as if she were about to question him, but then decided not to, he was so blatantly out on his feet.

'Do you need anything?' she asked. 'A hot drink, maybe?'

'Nothing.'

It was as much as Bill could do to get up and cross the room now that he had permitted his body to relax. He sat on the edge of the bed; Maria bent in front of him, slipped his shoes from his feet and took off his socks.

'I can manage the rest,' he said, protesting.

'Lie back and enjoy yourself!'

She pulled off his trousers and his underpants, knelt on the bed and peeled off his shirt. He felt the warmth of her and saw her breast where the dressing gown fell open as she bent over him. He moved forward and kissed her nipple, which responded instantly to his touch.

'You're not entirely dead, then,' she said, smiling.

'I'm boasting!' He rolled wearily beneath the sheet and the light blanket and lay with his hands behind his head as she took off her dressing gown. 'You have a wonderful figure,' he said. He meant it; for a woman of her age who'd borne two children she was still beautifully proportioned, slim and firm-fleshed.

She crouched on the bed beside him. 'And it's all yours,' she said.

Now they could put the past away and begin to consider a future, together.

'Stavakis talked to me before he died,' Bill said.

She had been sliding into the bed beside him but stayed still when he spoke. 'Oh yes. What about?' she asked.

'Get into bed. He told me the story of this modern political mess,' Bill said. 'The wheeler-dealing. Interfering in the lives of other people. Killing. Men playing God, thinking they are right and all other people are wrong. How I hate that.'

She slipped into the bed; he felt the warmth of her body lying beside him.

'Did he name any names?' she asked casually. 'Any names and numbers?'

When he turned he saw the tenseness of her mouth. He pushed his hand between her neck and the front of her pillow as he turned on his side. 'It's strange you should ask me that,' he said. 'Names *and* numbers! During the real war they used code-names. Maleta. Theseus. Manoletto. In this damned secret war that festers beneath the surface, they use numbers. Somehow it seems right that these faceless, dehumanized bastards should use numbers and not names.'

'I guess they're only doing a job in the way they see it, Bill.' She turned on her side; their faces were inches apart.

He reached forward and kissed the end of her nose. 'What numbers did he tell you, Bill?' she asked.

'What does it matter? Nameless numbers for faceless people. I like your face!'

His lips moved down to her lips, which parted as he kissed her slowly, drawing strength from deep inside her, moving his body towards her until they were touching along the length of their torsos. He felt the first stirrings of a strong sexual desire. She felt them, too.

'I thought you were tired?'

'I am!'

'Very tired?'

'Very . . .'

'*Too* tired . . .?'

'No!'

She reached beneath the sheet; he tingled as her hand touched him. When he kissed her her mouth opened again beneath the insistent pressure of his lips. Her hand grasped him firmly, rubbing him softly as he grew hard.

'I want you,' she said. 'Deep inside me. I want you to love me and drive all this away from our minds. I don't want you to think about Stavakis, your father, or any of that. I want you to think only of me, and us.'

She twisted impatiently and, throwing the sheet and blanket aside, she crouched over him. All fatigue drained from him as her lips closed over him; he arched his back with resurgent energy in the sheer ecstasy of her demanding kiss. His hand sought her breast and squeezed it; she shuddered, turned quickly, and squatted across him, directing him inside her. She gasped with pleasure as she felt the thrust of him entering her, drawing her down on him until he was completely enclosed by her. He reached upwards and grabbed her shoulders, bending her down so that he could kiss her again. Her rubbing grew more and more pronounced until it seemed as if she would explode with the frantic force of it. Finally, she pulled her mouth from his, straightened her back and screamed as she shuddered in a paroxysm of orgasm that vibrated her

309

entire body. Her fingers grasped his upper arms, her nails gripping tight as she jerked involuntarily. When the spasms ended she wiped a strand of hair from her sweating brow and looked deep into his eyes.

'I couldn't wait,' she said.

'I didn't want you to!'

He bent his back and sat up in bed, still rooted inside her as he flipped her onto her back. Slowly, methodically, thrustingly, he took her, feeling the tension of the last days drain from him as his excitement mounted. Both knew he was using her body just as she had used his. That didn't matter. What *did* matter was that he should experience the liberation that would come with complete climax, that each should serve the other selflessly. She gripped his hips, pulled him deeper into her with each stroke, giving herself completely to him. And when his face contorted with concentration and effort, when the full violence of his contained passion was unleashed, when she felt the hot liquid surging into her, she knew a deep inner compassion, a hope that the past, all of it, could be washed away by the turbulence of their feelings.

'So many wasted nights, months, years, until this moment,' she murmured. She wasn't certain he could hear her words; he seemed transported into a new dimension from which he could return only slowly.

He slumped on the bed beside her, his limbs flaccid. 'I needed that!' he said.

'We both did.'

He lay back, expecting sleep to drift over him. She snuggled close to him after she'd drawn the sheet and the blanket over them. He could hear her breathing settle into a slow rhythm and tried to adjust his own breath to the same pace, willing himself into sleep.

Tired though he was, he couldn't drift away. His body was now totally exhausted, but his mind remained active as ever. He could see Stavakis sitting in his study, Sam Birntin poised on the edge of the desk. He could hear the voice of Karfounis, the Colonel in the hospital in England.

Kostas Dandanakis with his sardonic laugh, calling them fools because they hadn't left him in the mountain shelter. And slowly, as he lay there, a parade of all the men who'd fought with his father in those distant days rolled before his inner eye; he saw Evangelina again as she must have been, and Spiros Orfandakis, Manoletto, and Pakrades, the runner.

But, above all, Angelo Stavakis. The man who thought he could control the destinies of other people; the man who, believing he could and should rule his part of the world, was ruthless enough to kill or to order the killing of anyone who stood in his way.

Bill had stood in his way, hadn't he? But Bill had survived.

Maria appeared to be sleeping when he pulled his arm gently from under her neck and twisted his body in a vain attempt to get more comfortable. Still sleep wouldn't come to him. Slowly, carefully, he slid from the bed, gathered his clothes from the chair where Maria had folded them and left the bedroom.

He knew now his body was too tired and his mind too active for sleep to come. He dressed and went out into the cool air of the late evening. He could hear the clack of *tavli* from the *kafeneion* and walked towards it, his mind seething with new thoughts.

Something was festering at the back of his consciousness, some thought struggling to come out, some idea like a throbbing pustule that would not leave him in peace.

Victorio shouted with pleasure when Bill arrived. Now they'd discovered they were brothers – well, anyway, half-brothers – Bill knew the warmth of having found a family, even though he remembered Victorio's beating.

'Could not sleep, eh?' Victorio asked, grinning. 'Drink a couple of *tsikoudias* – they'll relax you . . .'

Bill took the first in one gulp, then stood with his back to the counter and looked around the *kafeneion*. The thought lurking inside wouldn't come to the surface, no matter how hard he tried.

'Now that all this business is over,' Victorio said, 'I'd like to travel to England with you. I'd like to see where our father lived.'

Bill nodded absently.

'After all, now that I know I'm half-British . . .!'

He filled a second glass with *tsikoudia* and prepared a small plate of *mezedes* with cucumber, a couple of black olives, a piece of *paximada*. Bill wolfed it down, realizing how hungry he was. And then, Victorio's chattering stopped Bill's wayward thoughts, solidified them like a salt crystal dropping into a supersaturated brine will fuse the entire solution.

'How is it,' Victorio said, 'how, they always seemed to know what was going on? The Americans and Stavakis, I mean . . .'

Victorio was right. They had known *everything*, almost as if they'd been alongside Bill the whole time, as if they'd had his number right from the start. *Number*. Nameless, faceless people, hiding behind a screen of *numbers*. What had Birntin said? 27, an operator, a technician. On *their* side, working with *them*. Approving what *they* did and prepared to accept even killing for a cause they believed to be right. And everything, everybody else was wrong.

He left the *kafeneion* like a sleep-walker.

'I thought those *tsikoudias* would fix you!' Victorio said, grinning, but Bill didn't hear him.

He crossed to the house of Evangelina and walked in through the door. The bed was empty. He went into the sitting room; the fragment of light filtering through the window revealed Maria, sitting poised on the edge of a chair. She'd dressed in a pair of slacks, a black sweater and light pumps. She'd combed her hair, pulling it severely back and tying it into a pony tail that made her look so much younger, so much more innocent, than he now knew her to be.

'You asked me about *numbers*,' he said. 'Names and *numbers*. How would you know they use numbers for their

312

operatives? I didn't know that until Sam Birntin let it drop.'

She didn't reply but shifted on her seat as if preparing to launch herself, tense as a panther.

His mind was still grappling with the enormity of a thought it couldn't admit, a dreadful knowledge that was growing rapidly into an inescapable conviction.

'You're Number 27, aren't you?' he said. 'One of *them*. You were feeding information to them all the time. No wonder they were able to stay so close to me.'

The sound that was wrung from her was a strangling sob. 'Oh, Bill,' she said, 'why couldn't you leave it alone, why couldn't you? It's done now, finished. I was on contract for one job only. Now I can walk away from it . . .'

'Until the next *job* comes along? Until the next time those anonymous bastards want you to help them play God. In Nicaragua, in Chile, in Angola . . .?'

'No more, Bill. I want to make a life with you. I thought you understood that? I thought I'd convinced you tonight that we would work, you and me, together . . .'

He shook his head. 'Now I know why Petro wouldn't let you come to America with me. Petro suspected, didn't he? Well, we'll see what he wants to do with you, now that we know. Now that I can tell him you were Number 27.'

'He'll charge me with being an accessory to murder,' she said. She wasn't asking for pity, merely stating a cold fact. 'Greece still has the death penalty.'

'And you want me to walk away from it . . .'

'I want *us* to walk away from it. *Us*! Together.'

He shook his head. 'I can't do that, Maria. I keep thinking about Kostas Dandanakis, and Spiros Orfandakis. I keep thinking of Hans Ohlman, who helped my father save your life . . .'

The movement of her hand was a blur. The gun must have been tucked in the back of her waist-band. She held it steady, pointing at him.

'You realize you leave me no alternative, Bill,' she said. 'I'm not going to rot in some Greek gaol. They wouldn't pass the death sentence on me, since I'm a woman, but I'd be inside those walls for twenty years. I couldn't stand that.'

He started to walk across the room towards her with his hand extended. 'Give me the gun, Maria,' he said.

She pointed the gun downwards and fired. He hadn't noticed the silencer on the end of the barrel; the gun made a 'phut' and then he felt the slamming blow in the muscle of his upper leg that turned him half-round and dropped him to one knee. He looked down, seeing the blood already running out through the hole in his trousers and feeling the numbing shock with no pain as yet. The pain would come later. He looked up and there were tears in her eyes.

'I didn't want to kill you, Bill,' she said. 'I don't want to kill you! But you must understand, I can't spend twenty years inside a prison. I'd go crazy, just being in there.'

He tried to crawl forward on one knee but now his leg was starting to stiffen. Now the pain had begun shooting up into his groin, down to his knee. He'd never known such pain was possible; it was as if some giant hand had seized a bunch of his fibres and was slowly twisting them into a knot with a burning white heat at its centre. He felt the sweat pour out on his brow, run down to his eyebrows, down into his eye. He shook his head to try to clear it, seeing her distorted in the liquid drops in his eye. He knew he must move forward; he shouldn't stay still. He struggled desperately to lift his foot off the ground, to advance towards her.

'Don't do it, Bill,' she sobbed. 'Don't make me do it.'

He couldn't help himself. From somewhere deep inside he summoned the energy to press downwards, despite the screaming pain; to heave himself upright and stand erect, facing her. Now the gun was pointing at his chest but he was powerless to stop himself. He had to go forward. She used her left hand to dash the tears from her eyes; then her face had settled into a look of composure, cold and impersonal. He stumbled a pace forward and saw her knuckle tighten on the trigger, but his leg wouldn't support the weight he put on it and he swung right and down, spiralling forward and downwards. He heard the 'phut' of the bullet but it had missed him. He sprawled down and forward; then, seeing her ankles, he reached, grabbed and twisted, pulling her down with him.

'Don't move any more,' she said. She had stuck the silenced muzzle of the gun next to his ear. 'They trained me to kill,' she said, 'just as they trained me to fall.'

The impact of his dive had taken all Bill's strength. He lay there, unable to move. He heard her go across the room and into the bomb-blasted kitchen. He heard the sound of her car starting, then reversing. She left the engine running when she came back inside and bent over him. He felt a sharp jab in his leg, above the wound. 'Morphine,' she said.

'To kill the pain.'

'To let you walk long enough for us to get out of here.'

'Operation Escape? I might have guessed you had it all planned.'

She looked impatiently at him. 'We're not amateurs, Bill,' she said, 'despite what you may think of some of the people we've been forced to hire.'

The pain was already beginning to ease in his leg. 'Why not just kill me, Maria, and get it over with?'

She grabbed his hair and shook his head angrily. 'Because, you obstinate stubborn bastard, whatever you may think of me, I love you. Can't you get that through your thick skull? Because I hope it may not be too late. For once in your life, you might change your mind and see things my way, the only possible way, Bill, in the damned awful world we live in. Now get up and walk out to the car. Get in the driving seat and don't mess about. Don't play the Don Quixote any more.'

He stood up and rested his weight on the injured leg. It would support him. He took an experimental step forward and could manage, limping. She moved to his side, the gun held in her right hand, her left arm supporting his elbow.

He'd need to time it just right, he told himself. She was a trained operative. Trained to kill.

She was alert, looking sideways at him, trying to anticipate his intention in his eyes.

He moved his right leg, the injured one, forward a half-pace. Now he'd need to swing his good leg forward, resting all his weight on the bad one. He felt the pressure beneath his elbow as she offered him her full support. When his leg swung forward, he carried it all the way and then through, pivoting on his bad leg so that his left arm swung round. She thought he was about to fall and increased her pressure under his elbow. Now, he knew, she would be off-balance. He continued the swing; his left arm came round and quickly imprisoned her right arm to her side. He let both his knees collapse and now he was holding her along her full length, his body tight against hers, her arms trapped inside his. He saw the instant reaction in her eyes and knew she was about to break his grip upwards. He wouldn't be able to prevent her. Her feet were apart; he brought up his knee, the injured leg, hard between her legs. The blow would have crippled a man; the pain of it shocked her and brought tears to her eyes but didn't disable her. Bill shifted the grip of his left hand, grabbed down and caught her wrist. She was trying to bring the barrel of the gun in so that it would fire into his side but his grip prevented her. She was strong, lean and muscular, and well-trained.

Bill was a wounded man under sentence of death, and that knowledge gave him desperation beyond her strength. He twisted her wrist; at the wrong angle, she couldn't effectively resist him. The barrel of the gun pointed into her own abdomen.

He struggled to hold her wrist and, at the same time, to lower his hand around her trigger finger.

She started to bring up her knee but telegraphed the blow. He reached up and stomped on her instep. The pain caused her to relax her hold slightly on the gun; he seized

316

his chance and covered her hand with his, his finger pressing hers in the trigger guard.

'Not for Kostas or for Spiros,' he said softly. 'Not even for Hans Ohlman or for trying to get Victorio and me out of the way. But for the woman who took you as a baby and, with my father, carried you safely out of the mountains. The woman who risked her own life to see you safe. And for the woman, your mother, who walked onto the Germans' guns so that you could survive. For all the people of Mavroti who were killed in those days by the man you set out to protect.'

He was looking into her eyes.

'Bill,' she said, pleading, 'we could make a life together.'

'A life, Maria, in which death doesn't matter? What kind of a life could that ever be?'

He started to press on her finger.

'Bill, no!' she pleaded, her eyes filling with tears. 'No, Bill.'

He increased the pressure. His mind was ice-cold and red-hot by turns, as her face and the faces of all those other people now dead alternated on his retina so that he couldn't be certain what he was seeing, who was in his eyes.

The gun made hardly any sound when it went off; Maria's eyes instantly lost near focus and he knew she was no longer seeing him. She'd given up struggling and hung in his arms. He lowered her gently until she was kneeling in front of him. Blood seeped from her stomach and her face already had the grey tinge of death.

'I loved you, you bastard,' she said, each word forced out of her mouth in gulping sighs.

'I know you did,' he said, 'and that, finally, was the greatest tragedy of all.' He eased her back on to the floor. Took the gun from her limp hand. Straightened her legs. Squatted beside her, wiping her forehead.

She didn't speak again. When she shuddered and died, he closed the lids of her eyes, bent over and kissed her already waxen lips.

317

'Goodbye, Maria,' he said. 'Goodbye, my love.'

Petro was waiting outside the house, in a car with his *enomotarxis* sitting in the driving seat. He got out of the car when he saw Bill coming.

'It is all over?' he asked.

'Yes.'

'Maria was working with the Americans?'

'You knew, didn't you?'

'I guessed.'

'I killed her.'

Petro glanced back at the car. The *enomotarxis* was too far away to hear. 'There was a struggle. She killed herself. That's what my report will say.'

They walked across to the car and got in.

'Xania,' Petro said. He picked up the radio microphone and gave a few orders, then clipped it back on its stand. 'Tomorrow is my Saint's Day,' he said to Bill. 'Tomorrow, in my village, there will be food and music. The lyre and the bouzouki. The five-year-old *krassi* will be broached, now that the new wine is in. There will be much singing and dancing and we shall all get a little drunk and no doubt behave foolishly. They will roast a sheep and a goat, cook rabbits with herbs fresh from the mountainside, rosemary, thyme, oregano and wild marjoram. There will be much *tsikoudia*, and Crete, the old unchanging island, will come to life again. Will you come with me?'

'I'd like to,' Bill said. 'Where is your village? Is it old?'

'No,' Petro said, 'it is new. We rebuilt it on the burned out ruins of a village in the Lefka Ori, a village you know as Mavroti, in the Mavri. And, in the dawn, because that is the best time in the White Mountains, I will take you to a hill overlooking the village and show you where your father lies. Next to *my* father, whose name was Petrakis.'

318

All Futura Books are available at your bookshop or newsagent, or can be ordered from the following address:
Futura Books, Cash Sales Department,
P.O. Box 11, Falmouth, Cornwall.

Please send cheque or postal order (no currency), and allow 25p for postage and packing for the first book plus 10p per copy for each additional book ordered up to a maximum charge of 95p in U.K.

Customers in Eire and B.F.P.O. please allow 25p for postage and packing for the first book plus 10p per copy for the next six books, thereafter 4p per book.

Overseas customers please allow 30p for postage and packing for the first book and 10p per copy for each additional book.